Jokers

an FFSG novel

Bill Dughaille

Contents

Prologue

Wednesday Evening: Who will be next?

The editor of the Wellbury Herald scanned an article he had just completed for the following day's edition.

"Unoriginal Jokers Mean Hard Slog For Police

Inspector Frieda Garold of the Wellbury police force has admitted to the Herald that they are no further in identifying the culprits known as the Joker Gang – a name derived from the burglars' habit of leaving behind them a joker and one other playing card at each crime – whose third break-in took place two days ago in the wealthy suburb of Lords Acres, the same area in which the previous two incidents occurred. While describing the leaving of the cards as "unoriginal", Inspector Garold has told the Herald that she has her best people on the case, but that those behind the burglaries are unlikely to be local, and, barring a lucky breakthrough, tracking the criminals down will involve a long slog of hard and often unrewarding basic police work.

A remaining hope is that the criminals might already have disposed of some of their gains – all small objects and largely jewellery, amongst which are notable and outstanding examples of brooches from the Art Deco period, including a design known as the Wisteria brooch (see page 2 for a full description of the provenance of this delightful item) – and that an honest member of the public may have come into possession of some of the artefacts. Anyone who thinks they may have been offered suspect items of jewellery is urged to contact the police urgently.

The suggestion has been made that the burglaries are

somehow associated with university students preparing to celebrate "rag week" (see page 4). However, as Inspector Garold pointed out, breaking and entering into the most personal of places, the home, can never in the slightest be regarded as a practical joke. As to charges that those preparing Trafalgar Park for Bentley's travelling fair – mainly Romanians of Gypsy origin – which is due to begin on Saturday (see centre page advertisement) must have something to do with it, Inspector Garold reminded law abiding citizens that it is the job of the police to catch criminals, and anyone considering vigilante action would be well advised not to do so.

Inspector Garold re-iterated her call for Wellburians to invest in modern security devices, as the old-fashioned locks and window-latches still largely prevalent in Wellbury are insufficient to deter modern criminals from outside who are used to dealing with far more sophisticated devices. We at the Herald can only echo this call with due regret that such measures should be necessary in our little town. If these measures are not taken we can only ask the question: 'Who will be next?'"

The editor of the Herald nodded satisfaction as he read the article for the final time, his face showing a bluish tinge from the reflected light of his computer screen in the darkening twilight, not yet having bothered to switch the lights on. Satisfaction both at the article and the computer, an item without which the Herald would have ceased being published, costs of old-fashioned printing having now become economically unviable. The spell-checker, a device he reluctantly used, believing his own powers in that regard to be far superior to any machine's, had suggested that "re-iterated" should be "reiterated". Well, he wasn't going to take that sort of nonsense from a machine.

Inspector Garold had initially described the burglaries as "irritating" before amending that to "unoriginal". She hadn't used the prefix "bloody" before the word "irritating", being vehemently against swearing of any kind, but her manner had been such as to include it without saying it.

Hopefully these "jokers" would find the word "unoriginal" (bloody) irritating themselves, and be inspired to some rashness which would be their downfall. They had cocked a snook at Wellbury police force, and Inspector Garold intended to grab that snook and give it a good tweaking, along with the taste of a pair of handcuffs. The very fact that they left their calling cards suggested egos which would be open to being manipulated.

The article on page two about the Wisteria brooch was a nice filler and topical. Now it was time to put the paper to bed, to let the printers get on with their job so that the latest issue could appear the following morning.

There was another article of which he was rather proud, not because it was in any form an outstanding item of journalism, but rather because it proved that he had not lost his self-restraint, a principle by which he lived his life. What had originally started out with the title "Rag Week Pranks Plague" had been a highly personal, emotive and coruscating condemnation of the practical jokes being played by the university students as they prepared for their rag week. With time for reflection this had been scrapped and replaced with an article on the charities to which the money being collected during the university's rag week would go. There would be no space in the Wellbury Herald for personal diatribes, however warmly he might feel, apart from the letters page.

The letters page did, strangely enough, contain just such an item, signed by one P.W., curiously enough, the initials of the editor.

Before locking up for the night he made his final security checks of the offices. These were perfunctory. The sash windows at the back of the offices were secured by the same simple latches the article had decried. But who would want to break into the office of a local newspaper?

Week 1

Thursday Afternoon: Introducing the Jokers

'Their best people,' quoted a voice accompanied by the sound of a crushed beer can missing a waste-paper basket. 'Wonder who that is, then. Their equivalent of Dixon of Dock Green, I suppose. Keep your eyes peeled for coppers on bicycles.'

'Don't get cocky,' admonished a second voice. 'Cocky makes mistakes. And you shouldn't be drinking so much. And pick up that beer can, we aren't slobs from some deprived area of inner London.'

'I'm making up for lost time,' replied the first voice, and burped, but obediently picked up the beer can and placed it in its proper receptacle.

'Cocky,' said a third voice. 'I like it. Cocky suits you. I think I shall use that in future. Cocky the criminal.'

'Oh, yes? And what's your nickname? Queenie?'

'Enough you two,' said the second voice.

'Why Queenie?' asked Queenie.

'Because you left the Queen of Spades at the last job, that's why,' said Cocky.

'And that was a mistake too,' noted the second voice. 'The jokers, fine, those will put them off the scent. I told you the second card had to be chosen purely at random.'

'I did pick it out randomly,' protested Queenie. Neither of the other two believed the protest.

'Well in future I'll do the random picking,' said the second voice.

'If you say so, boss,' said Queenie regretfully.

'And stop calling me boss. How many times do I have to tell you? Sooner or later –'

'You'll say it in public and give the game away,' the other two quoted simultaneously.

'Well, just don't. Apart from anything else it sounds vulgar.'

'Speaking of vulgar, what's this about a Wisteria brooch?' asked Queenie. 'There was no Wisteria brooch in that place.'

'Probably an insurance fiddle. People claim on things that never existed. You can't trust anyone these days.'

'You're joking!' said Queenie. 'Don't they get found out?'

'Probably some of them do. Like anything it depends on how intelligently you go about it.'

Queenie considered this for a while before raising another question

'And what do they mean by "unoriginal"? I bet it hasn't been done before.'

'That's just a police tactic. They're hoping we'll get irritated and do something silly to prove how original we are. Ignore it.'

'The devious little sods,' Queenie whispered. 'And I thought they were all upright and honest.'

'They just don't appreciate style,' Cocky said. 'That's what makes us different, style.'

Queenie laughed at the idea of Cocky and style being linked. The laugh was rewarded by a glare and a few moment's silence.

'Ace,' said Cocky to the sound of a beer can being opened.

'Ace?' asked Queenie.

'Instead of "boss". Good nickname, that, Ace. As in fighter ace.'

There was a sigh of exasperation from Ace.

'I think you two are missing a fundamental concept here.'

'Well, we're bored, Ace,' said Cocky. 'It's no fun sitting indoors doing nothing. Can't we do a couple of small jobs? To keep our hands in, as it were.'

'No you can't! One more and then we're out of here. End of story. And stop calling them "jobs". That is definitely vulgar. And we are not vulgar.'

'Leave em laughing, that's what dad always used to say,' noted Queenie.

'Yes, except he ended up doing a two-year stretch on a permanent basis until he went to the great cell in the sky, if I remember correctly,' Ace replied. 'No sooner out than he'd do some stupid job and go back in again. That is not going to happen to us.'

'Least he was consistent,' pointed out Cocky, referring to Ace's use of the word "job".

Ace sighed.

'Can't we get out and enjoy yourselves for a bit?' asked Queenie. 'Even just to go for a walk, admire the architecture, see the sights. Hey, we could do some fishing. I've never been fishing. The river's supposed to be famous for its fish.'

'Architecture?' asked Cocky, sneering. 'What architecture?'

'I'm told the police station is an excellent example of a mid-Victorian building,' suggested Ace. 'Some of the finest cells in the county.'

There was a pause.

'Hey, know what I fancy?' asked Queenie.

'I'm not having another bloody curry take-away,' said Cocky.

'No, seriously. Just for a laugh. Why don't we find out who these best people this Inspector Gorbals has on their joker case? We could leave a special calling card for whoever it is next time. Seeing as how it will be our last job here.'

'No! Absolutely not!' Ace said with some irritation.

'Everybody's doing it,' protested Queenie. 'Playing practical jokes, that sort of thing.'

'Well, we are not. We are professionals. So you can put that idea right out of your heads.'

There was a sulky silence from the professionals.

'That reminds me of a song from the Six – er, the Seventies,' Ace said, as if to lighten the air. 'I remember my parents singing it when I was a young child. What was it called? "Doing the locomotion", I think. It started off with the line "Everybody's doing it". Something like that.'

Cocky and Queenie rolled their eyes at each other as Ace hummed the tune.

'Ah, well, let's go have a look at this river, Queenie,' Cocky suggested.

'You are not going out dressed like that.,' Ace said firmly.

'In that case I'm not going out,' Cocky replied just as firmly.

'Well, I'm going shopping,' Queenie said, standing up.

'Get me some beers while you're out,' requested Cocky.

'Get your own.'

Ace sighed again.

'I'll get some beers in later. You get off, Queenie.'

'I'll bring you a surprise,' Queenie promised Cocky.

Ace watched Queenie leave with some misgiving. The other two had followed instructions so far, and the three jobs had been extremely rewarding, or would be when they converted their haul into cash – which was another question altogether, something they had yet to decide upon. But boredom was now setting in. Instinctively Ace felt that it was time to quit while ahead.

But they had agreed that Wellbury was good for four jobs before disappearing to another small town where the locks were easy and the pickings good. Or such were their plans when they got carried away after a few drinks, or the excitement of having successfully carried out a "job". Another town, another "job". Unlikely dreams for the future.

But the fact was that the police hadn't a clue. Leaving the joker at the first job had come from Cocky's sense of humour – or style, as Cocky might claim. The second card had been a mistake, having stuck to the first. But Ace had quickly recognised the benefit of leaving the silly things behind – everyone was falling over each other in vain attempts to analyse the meaning of the cards, while the simple fact was that there was no meaning.

So, logically there was no reason not to do the fourth before leaving. After all, the police had absolutely no reason to suspect them.

And what could go wrong?

It was the possible answer to that question that really worried Ace. In their current mood Cocky and Queenie, as they had decided to call themselves, were more than likely to do something stupid.

Thursday Evening: The laughter

'I'd like to speak to the officer in charge of this Joker business,' a voice told the constable on telephone duty.

'I'm afraid Inspector Garold isn't available now. I can put you through to Detective Sergeant Summers. He is in charge of the day-to-day operation.'

'Not to worry. Could you pass on a message please?'

'Of course. Just a second while I get a pen. Right, what's the message?'

'Could you tell him this?'

A maniacal laugh followed, of the sort generated by a mechanical device purchased from a novelty shop.

'Did you get that?' asked the caller, and then the line went dead.

Cocky and Queenie fell out of the call box, laughing.

'Good thing he didn't ask us to spell that,' noted Queenie.

'They probably tape their calls. I'll bet that Sergeant of theirs will play it back for the rest of the day.'

'Better get back before Ace does. Just in case we get sent to bed with no supper for being naughty.'

Constable Bobby Stang looked at the receiver in his hands. How exactly was he supposed to explain this one to Sergeant Summers?

Still, he was pretty sure that the caller was female.

Or maybe male with a high-pitched voice.

One of the two.

Definitely one of the two.

'A laughing toy?' Detective Sergeant Frank Summers asked Bobby Stang ten minutes later when the constable had made his report.

'Yes, Sarge.'

Frank pondered this with a grim face.

'Get me a list of all toy shops in town,' he ordered.

Young Bobby complied. He was supposed to be on a break before returning to telephone duty, but he decided it would be far easier to get someone to replace him than to explain that to the Sergeant in his current mood. At least Inspector Garold was only irritated by this joker nonsense, these days Sergeant Summers was quite easily irritated about everything, including, or especially, constables who had the temerity to suggest that his orders could not be carried out just as he had stated them.

Friday Evening: The two worst players ever

'Our best people, eh?' commented Detective Sergeant Pete Phillips as he read the article while waiting for Desk Sergeant Eric Johns to line up his shot in the snooker room of the Blue Bliss. 'That'll be the Wellbury Wonder, no doubt.'

'Do you mind? I'm trying to concentrate here.'

Pete Phillips made a face but kept quiet. They had popped into the Blue Bliss for an early evening pint before going to their separates homes for dinner. The snooker room was newly opened and they were the only ones there. Eric Johns had never played snooker before, and Pete Phillips who claimed to "have been pretty good at it a few years back" had volunteered to show him the ropes.

Eric Johns squinted down his cue, took a slow breath, and smoothly hit the white. Too hard. It smashed into the black and flew off the table. The black trickled slowly into a pocket.

'Bugger!'

'You're too ambitious.'

'Would have worked on a pool table.'

'We're not playing pool. This is snooker.'

'Yeah, well.'

Eric Johns retrieved the white, put it back on the table, sat down and took a pull of his pint.

'Says it's going to be a hard slog of basic police work,' Pete Phillips noted, folding the newspaper and dropping it onto a neighbouring table. 'All the more reason to give it to Percy and me. Frank's good in his own way, you know, with these weird ideas he gets from time to time, but if you want decent, solid police work – knocking door-to-door, that sort of thing

13

– I reckon that's far more my sort of job.'

'It is his first big case since his accident,' Eric Johns reminded him.

There had been an unconscious agreement at the police station that the best word for what had happened was "accident".

'First big case?' Pete Phillips asked, leaning over the edge of the snooker table and taking aim on a red sitting against the cushion. 'He's nicked over twenty people in the last three months.'

'Half of whom we had to apologise to and let go.'

'Yeah, well, not exactly Frank's fault. Most of them did confess, after all.'

'I don't blame them. I probably would have done so as well. The way Frank looks these days even I feel nervous around him. Makes me wonder if I've done something I should be nicked for. Those eyes of his ... ' He shivered and took a deep draw on his pint. 'Doesn't even wear those loud ties anymore. That's just not our Frank.' He picked up the discarded newspaper to give himself something else to think about. 'So what happened to that prowler case you were working on,' he asked. 'Down by St Mary's wasn't it?'

'Nothing. No prowler, case closed. Now, do you mind? I need to concentrate.'

Eric Johns kept quiet while turning the pages loudly.

Pete Phillips expertly brought his cue back and expertly propelled it towards the white.

'The fair's opening tomorrow,' Eric commented, strangely enough at precisely the same time that Pete's cue hit the white. 'I was thinking I might take the missus down on Sunday.'

The white careered off the red and dropped the pink in a pocket.

'You're not supposed to do that, are you?' asked Eric Johns, his head on one side.

'Not really. Wish they'd put pool tables in instead of snooker tables.'

Eric Johns looked at the table.

'We're supposed to take them out and replace them, aren't we, when that happens? The black and the pink and that sort of thing?' he asked.

'That's why I missed. I thought the black was there, where it should have been. Messes my shots up when I don't see balls where they should be. It affects my mental harmony.'

Eric Johns considered this highly dubious theory for a moment. He concluded that it was highly dubious. Pete Phillips and "mental harmony" did not sit together well as concepts. Even the word "concept" did not sit well with the presence of Pete Phillips.

'They make it look so easy on the telly,' he said, dismissing the idea. 'Did you see that programme the other night where they showed all those trick shots?'

'Missed that. The missus wanted to watch one of those Candid Camera type shows. Load of rubbish it was. I mean you'd have to be three parts stupid to fall for some of those gags.'

'You'd be surprised what people can fall for. Look at the way we fell for those two pretending to be from Scotland Yard.

Hovis and Clovis, or whatever their names were.'

'And that Jean Tromperie.'

There was a silence. Pete Phillips hadn't meant to mention the name. No-one at the station had mentioned it since Frank Summers had returned from his stay in hospital. Nobody could say quite what the link was, but they all understood instinctively that there was a link, and the subject had become taboo.

'Now if you could pull something on Frank, some gag or other,' Eric Johns said, in an attempt to lighten the atmosphere, 'I reckon it would be one in a million.'

'Bet you I could,' replied Pete Phillips, chalking his cue. Eric Johns looked at him aghast. Pete Phillips was not renowned for intellectual creativity, but on the other hand he wasn't known for his sheer stupidity either.

'You can't be serious, Pete. He'd bloody kill you.'

'Strikes me he needs something to cheer him up. And isn't that what friends are for?'

'Anyway,' Eric Johns said, trying to dismiss that subject, 'I can't see anyone getting anything past him.'

'Bet you I can. With a bit of help.'

'Oh no, not me, Pete. Count me out. You want to die, that's your business.'

'How much?'

'How much what?'

'How much do you want to bet me I can't pull something off?'

Eric Johns contemplated this. He hardly ever staked anything on the horses, played poker, or put money on any normal form of gambling apart from the various sweepstakes at the station and any book he might open himself with the odds stacked heavily in his favour, but a personal bet was different. A personal bet was something that could not be refused.

'Twenty quid.'

'Twenty quid it is.'

Pete Phillips smiled.

'So what is it you're going to do?' asked Eric Johns.

'Oh, I'll think of something. Maybe something to do with this Joker nonsense. Liven his life up a little.'

Eric Johns shook his head sadly in the contemplation of foolishness.

'You want to pay me now or later?' he asked.

Pete Phillips gave him a confident grin. It was the type of confident grin which tried to mask the fact that the wearer was privately afraid that they might just have overreached themselves somewhat, but there was no going back, not with twenty quid and their own pride at stake.

Saturday Morning: The first meeting on the riverside

The grey-green water of the river Wellbury moved slowly under an early May morning mist, waiting for the rising sun to burn the mist off so that it could shimmer and sparkle in the sunshine. All was quiet and peaceful in the cool early morning air, apart from the enthusiastic songs of some early-rising birds who had either finished breakfast or were more interested in wooing than worms.

It was too early for joggers and dog walkers, but a young man sat on a folding chair, leaning forward on the riverbank, an early-rising angler wearing a slouch hat almost down to his eyes, watching the sun slowly rise, bag in front of him, his fishing rod stuck in a holder, forgotten, as if it were an excuse for the man's presence rather than being his primary purpose. Were it not for the hat an curious passer-by might have been struck by a snow-white quiff of hair just off the centre of the man's head. Had they taken a close look at the fishing rod they would have noticed that it was ancient, made of wood, mottled in places, rusting in others.

Another, older, man was approaching with his own fishing rod and bag. The older man came within a few paces of the younger, opened a folding stool, sat down and positioned his own rod in its holder.

'It will be time for you to go back soon, Detective Sergeant Summers,' the older man remarked pleasantly, opening a thermos of hot tea, looking around the river with appreciation.

Frank's eyebrows rose. They had been sharing solitary, silent moments for some months now. This was the nearest the man had sat in those months, and the first time the man had spoken.

'Plenty of time left,' Frank replied after a while. 'Half an hour at least.'

'I don't mean the station,' the older man said.

Frank considered this. He obviously didn't know what the other man was talking about, but showed no interest in finding out.

'Life, lad, life,' the man explained softly. 'Time for you to go back to your life.'

Frank looked at the slowly passing water.

'I'm quite happy here,' he said.

The other man cast his line far into the river.

'I caught something last week, you know,' he remarked. 'Bloody nuisance it was. You'd think even a fish wouldn't be stupid enough to go for a bent pin. And manage to get itself caught on it.'

A bent pin, thought Frank. Interesting. He had always wondered what the shining thing at the end of the man's line was. It never appeared to hold bait of any form.

'You don't even bother with a pin, I've noticed,' the other man commented. 'After that blasted fish got itself caught I decided to follow your example. Just hope nothing is daft enough to hang itself on the end of the line. Or swallow the lead weight.'

Frank did not reply. He had always presumed that that had been his own secret. Going fishing wasn't a pursuit that had as its aim the catching of fish. Going fishing was a way of escaping from the world. He should have known that the other man would have seen this.

Though his face did not show it, he had on several occasions been terrified that he might actually have caught a fish. He would have been at a total loss to know what to do with one. Locking up guilty criminals had become an obsession. Dealing with an innocent fish was beyond his current abilities. His accident had left him unable to cope with anything beyond his job and he had buried his life in it. Fortunately it had turned out, on each occasion, that his line had merely snagged.

'Be summer soon,' the other man noted, taking out a pipe. It was a strange pipe, not in the way it looked, but in that it appeared often, but was never lit. 'You've always enjoyed the summer. Especially here in Wellbury. It is a lovely old place, I grant you that, and the people do make an effort to brighten things up. Gardens to make one think of Eden. Presuming there was an Eden once, of course. You know, Adam and Eve and all that. And all those pot plants and window baskets and hanging baskets, full of petunias and peonies or whatever they're called. I could never remember the names myself.'

Frank resisted the temptation to ask the man how he had known that Frank had always enjoyed the summer. A statement was an invitation to respond, and he had no wish to become trapped in conversation. Especially not about anything as ephemeral as Adam and Eve. The Criminal Code was a logical construction, Eden was not.

Before his accident he had known the power of silence during an interrogation. Afterwards silence became a shield to protect himself. Before, a suspect would blurt out a confession in the face of silence, convinced that those quietly twinkling eyes knew exactly all of the suspect's crimes. These days a suspect would confess purely in order to avoid the gimlet gaze of two eyes which showed no mercy, just two bottomless pits of ice.

Everybody has something to confess to. Under Frank Summer's eyes they would drag their memories for something, be it all something minor which might have happened before puberty.

'I do try, though,' the other man continued, unruffled by Frank's silent eyes. 'I buy those packs you can get. Bulbs and such. Plant them in the baskets like the instructions say. Water them whenever I remember. I'm good at that. Hardly ever forget.'

At one stage Frank had also tried. The previous summer he had bought some inexpensive pots, rectangular ones which would fit his flat's windowsills quite nicely. Bulbs, he found, were very cheap. Certainly not costly enough to provide an excuse not to follow his neighbours' examples. Despite his own ineptitude at the simple act of watering, the bulbs had sprouted, and produced a reasonable show of colour.

Not this year, though. He made a mental note to throw the pots and contents away. They were merely cluttering up the windowsills of his flat. He didn't have time to attend to such things.

'The wife knew the name of every single blade of grass,' the other man said. 'Or that's what it seemed like, at times. Show her a small part of a leaf and she'd know both the common English name and the Latin name.'

Past tense, Frank noted. The wife knew. Not the wife knows. An ex-wife, or ... Divorced, or passed away?

Dead, that was the correct word. But, just as people referred to his "accident", so he could no longer bear to use the word "dead".

Suddenly he wanted to get away. Away from this man claiming his attention. What did this man want, this man who had shared his solitude for so many months, a man he had presumed understood his need for peace, quiet and silence? A man who had now broken their unstated understanding?

He stood up and began to pack his few things.

'She died,' the other man said, as if answering Frank's unasked question. 'Cancer. A few years ago.'

Frank paused. He did not want to know this man's problems, his past, his pain, his feelings. That was what he was here to avoid.

'We'd been married for thirty-six years. Thirty-six years. Very happy years.'

His gaze stayed on the passing river. Frank hesitated, wanting to end the conversation politely, commiserating without becoming involved.

'I was lucky, really,' the man continued. 'As a young officer I saw my share of domestics. You know the score. You'll have seen them yourself. Arguments, broken crockery, husbands threatening their wives, wives attacking their husbands with knives, the kids howling in the background, the television at full blast, if it wasn't already broken. Dreadful to see, truly dreadful.'

Frank did know. He used to joke that that was what put him off the idea of marriage. Back in the days when he used to joke.

'Then, later, when I was too senior to attend domestics, I would read every file. Each time a new case turned up I would have the file sent to me. Know why I did that?'

Frank did not reply. He knew he would be told the answer.

The man reeled his line in, and cast it again. Someone watching might have admired his dexterity, the confident throw, and have presumed that it could not be long before the man was reeling in a glorious example of the piscatorial world, some fish which had made the mistake of falling for the bait.

'My wife and I would discuss them. We had a row early on in our marriage, you see. Something daft, no doubt, but we were just as bad as anybody else. Acted like right little kids, we did. Didn't speak to each other for a week. Maybe a fortnight. Funny how you remember the argument, but can't remember what it was about.'

Get on with it, Frank thought, standing there, his fishing rod in one hand, bag and folded stool in the other, impatient to get away.

'Then I got caught up in one of them, badly. I was still a constable then, in Portsmouth. Caught up in a domestic, I mean. Woman goes for her husband with a carving knife or something, I try to stop her and catch the knife instead. Don't think she really meant it, didn't expect me to get in the way I suppose, but there you go. Next thing there's ambulances and flashing lights and all the rest, I'm finding it impossible to breathe, and all I can think of is that I'm going to die and I'm going to die while not speaking to the missus.'

'But you didn't die,' Frank noted, his impatience mellowing just a little, wondering how the story ended, perhaps feeling somewhat of a bond, the brotherhood of those injured in the line of duty.

The man nodded.

'Came around in the hospital after a while, once they'd sowed me up and everything. The missus was sitting there crying her eyes out. That was when I decided that we would never have another argument. Least ways, not one where we'd stop speaking to each other.'

'And how did you manage that?'

The man appeared to think about this for a while, watching a lone kingfisher fly past, skimming the water.

'We had other people's arguments for us. That was why I had the files sent to me. So that I could go home and discuss them with my wife. That's why I say I was lucky. We learnt from other people's mistakes. We never had a serious argument again. Least ways not one where we stopped talking to each other.'

I'm happy for you, thought Frank. But it's none of my business. I'm not interested. Go away.

The bond had vanished. Happy endings are not happy for those who have not had their own.

'I know you're still hurting inside, Frank Summers,' the man said. 'But it's time to think of the others in your life, too. Like I said, it's time to go back. A young man like you – you still have happiness to look forward to in life. And arguments. Arguments are part of life, so long as you don't take them too far. You can't run away from life by not having arguments, you know.'

He paused.

'You aren't Javert, Frank,' he said softly. 'You don't have the background.'

Frank did not reply. Even thinking of considering him as similar to Victor Hugo's remorseless and obsession-driven police officer was an insult, made worse by the accuracy of the comparison.

Though it was interesting that he should have presumed that Frank would have understood the comparison. It suggested that he knew a lot more about him than would be expected for someone Frank had never spoken to until this day.

'And if you do prefer to be miserable, think of your friends who need you to be happy. I hear Gertie has fallen behind in her studies.'

This was too much. This man had run away himself. He was in no position to criticise him.

'I will bear that in mind, sir,' he said.

Take a running jump at yourself, sir.

'You know the reason why I'm here, Sergeant. Wellbury needs me here. And Wellbury needs you back.'

Frank nodded, a nod of negativity. He didn't know what the man was talking about, but he had no intention of prolonging the conversation by admitting that fact.

'Is that all, sir?' he asked.

The man rubbed his chin.

'If you want to chat, you know where to find me,' he said.

Frank nodded again and turned to leave.

'I shall pass your respects on to Inspector Garold,' he said sarcastically. 'She might need to know where to find you herself, on the odd occasion.'

The man chuckled.

'Oh, Frieda knows exactly where to find me,' he said. 'It's Percy who has a problem. Poor man stumbles across me all the time, until he actually needs to speak to me. Funny, that.'

Frank turned back to look at the figure of the man gazing quietly across the water. He had a strange aura about him, of a mystic, perhaps, a man who lived in the wilderness, yet knew before they did the problems supplicants would bring, and their solutions.

Frank wondered how long it had taken him to cultivate that look. Pompous idiot.

'Gertie must get back to her studies,' the man said, the first emphatic statement he had made. 'As to the others, you will have to make up your own mind.'

Frank turned and walked away. He had heard enough.

The Chief Inspector was in no position to lecture him as to the rights and wrongs of life.

And there was something the Chief Inspector did not know, for all his pretentious posturing. An idea which Frank would once have laughed at had anyone suggested it, but something which he now had to accept was true. Anyone or anything he got too close to ended up dead. Experience had taught him that. Painful experience. He firmly intended never to go through that experience again. Ever.

Better to leave well alone.

Better to walk alone. He would end up doing so anyway.

The other man did not watch him go. He kept his unruffled gaze on the slowly rising sun. But his thoughts were still on the slouch-hatted man. Frank had been exonerated of blame for Jean Candour's death – and Hovis's – but with a caveat about "unorthodox" practices, to whit, though not specifically mentioned, the use of a dummy grenade. He should have been grateful for that, since he could well have been fired, but it little seemed to interest him.

'There is also the other option, Sergeant Summers,' the Chief Inspector thought. 'We could also give you a kick up your backside every morning until you stop feeling sorry for yourself.'

Sunday Evening: Weekend overtime

Inspector Garold automatically looked up as she drove past Wellbury police station in the twilight of Sunday evening, the skies now beginning to loom with storm clouds following a largely cloudless and hot day. The station was not on her way home, and after an afternoon playing tennis at St Mary's Lawn Tennis Club (a social club named after the church which the land had once been part of, and one where none of the modern courts had any lawn, the lawn having been replaced with a more durable and modern surface long before) there was no reason for her to do so, apart from a suspicion. That suspicion was duly confirmed: there was a light on in Detective Sergeant Frank Summers' office, a light that should not have been on. Not on a Sunday night.

With an internal sigh she turned into the station's parking lot. As his senior officer Frank was her responsibility. There was more to it than that, a lot more, but for the moment she intended to concentrate on police matters. Such as a Detective Sergeant who was in his office when he should be off duty. A Detective Sergeant who seemed to want to be permanently on duty, apart from the time he spent fishing, and even then he was probably mentally still at work. She could not, as his senior officer, allow him to work himself to death as he seemed to be so intent on doing.

Her day had been enjoyable, if tiring. She was on call if anything should happen which required her presence at the police station, and the growing antagonism between townsfolk, the students and the people from Bentley's fair suggested that such a call was highly likely that day. Not all the townsfolk appreciated the students' high spirits. Not all the students respected the townsfolk's wish for a quiet life.

Both suspected that the people from Bentley's travelling fair were all Gypsies, and consequently thieves at best, depraved at least. Words had been exchanged between all three groups, and it looked as if it would only be a matter of time before an insult ignited what could become, if there were sufficient participants, a generalised and on-going brawl.

The day, however, had passed peacefully, with no incidents to trouble Frieda's relaxation, if it could be called that. The tennis club was a social one, yet the standard of play was high, and a sunny afternoon of almost continuous play had been good exercise. She had been playing at the club for over six months, and the distant cold hauteur of the older members, so often found in established tennis clubs, was beginning to melt, in at least some cases, anyway. She could now count two people who could be considered friends, people who would even speak to her off-court.

Immediately after the tennis she had performed what could be termed a weekly act of charity, which, since only one other person knew about it, made her feel even better about herself in a manner that public giving never does. All in all it had been a highly satisfactory day. Up until then.

As warm afternoon gave way to early evening thunderclouds, her mood did much the same. Instead of returning home and enjoying a hot bath and a cold glass of wine she would now have to see about Frank Summers. And what really irritated her more than anything was the knowledge that, had she taken the direct way home she would not have had to do so. Why she had done so she still could not fathom.

She went in via the rear entrance, but that did not, even on a quiet Sunday evening, prevent her from being seen by one or two of the station's staff. The sight of Inspector Frieda

"Fabulous" (or "Frigid" if you were in her bad books) Garold wearing a teensy-weensy tennis skirt and a very tight and low v-necked t-shirt (if opponents let that distract them as she leaned over to receive service that was their problem) would be sufficient to cause comment and raise rumour at any time. The fact that Frank Summers was in his office, and Fabulous obviously on her way there, had imaginations soaring. Her appearance was manna for a station where rumour was a permanent and welcomed guest rather than a passing visitor.

Prior to his accident the only person in the station unaware that Frieda had more than just a professional interest in him was Frank himself, a circumstance livened up by the existence of two other competitors for his affections. Since his accident little further had occurred on that front, as if a truce had been called while he recovered. The look on Frieda's face suggested that the truce was now over.

'Hello, hello,' remarked one constable, new to the station, watching Frieda's shapely legs march down the corridor. 'Looks like things might get a little interesting. It's been a pretty boring day so far.'

'Yeah,' replied his companion, 'if you call watching someone light matches in a dynamite factory interesting. Come on, let's go somewhere safer.'

'What you worried about? It's Sergeant Summers she's got her sights on.'

'You never heard of collateral damage? You've only been here a few months, son. You haven't seen the Inspector when she's in a bad mood.'

'You mean the way she normally looks is a good mood?'

'No, son, that's her neutral mood. You really don't want to

live to see her in a bad mood. Because you won't live to see afterwards, now let's get going.'

Frieda paused outside Frank's office to compose herself. She cleared her brow of the irritation it had carried on entering the station. She put a small smile on her face. Her voice, when she entered Frank's office, belied the vision of her as some kind of ogre. The voice was mild, though anyone listening carefully might spot a suggestion that it was a very carefully controlled mildness.

'What are you doing here, Frank?' she asked.

'I'm working on this joker case,' he replied as if it should be obvious, without looking up or taking notice of her attire. A casual observer might have thought that the playing cards on his desk suggested that he was more involved with a game of patience, but Frieda recognised the look in his eyes, that of a man obstinately trying to force inspiration to show its hand.

'Frank, it's Sunday evening, you shouldn't be here,' she said. 'You said yourself that working overtime is a recipe for making mistakes. You really should take some time out and relax.'

'Did Bobby Stang tell you they left a message for me? One of those mechanical laughing toys. They are not going to laugh at us.'

'Frank, that was probably some school kids. Let it go.'

Frank ignored the suggestion.

'I've checked all the toyshops to see if something like that had been sold recently. One of them had, but the shop assistant couldn't remember who had bought it. It was either a young boy or an old man, or possibly a young woman or an old woman, or maybe it was both a young boy and an old woman, or maybe just a passing fairy. Who knows?'

He scooped the cards up angrily.

'We need to set up a trap,' he said. 'It's the only way we're going to catch these people.'

'Let's discuss it over a drink. I need to rehydrate. A glass of water followed by a white wine would do nicely. Come on, I'll buy you a pizza afterwards.'

'There's nothing to discuss. We have no clues as to who they are. We know that they are probably from out of town and will move on soon, if they haven't done so already. Our only hope is to set up a trap for them and catch them in the act. If you authorise it I can get someone in Lords Acres to agree to providing the bait.'

Frieda had no doubts on that score. She even agreed with Frank's assessment. She dearly wanted to have the satisfaction of seeing this Joker Gang locked up in Wellbury police station's cells. What went against the grain was Frank acting as if he were in command rather than herself.

'We have to make a decision soon,' Frank said, standing up and putting his jacket on. He walked out without further comment.

Frieda wished she had brought her tennis racket with her. She could have given Frank Summers a good cross-court smash right at that moment. Followed by an overhead smash. And then another. And another.

And then a few more, just to keep in practice.

Something would have to be done about him, and she was the right person to do it.

As if in sympathy with her mood the gods released a

thunderclap from the darkening clouds, the heavens opened up and the rain poured down.

Frank Summers, walking to his car, treated the outburst with the contempt it deserved. All it could do was make him wet. So it did.

Week 2: Something Gets Done

Monday Evening: The coven convenes

'Where shall we three meet again?' giggled Gertie. 'In thunder, fire or rain, when the evil deed is done, or just for a good old g&t right here.'

'That's not very funny, Gertie.'

'No. It's very hackneyed.'

'Precisely. Hackneyed.'

'A cliché, in fact.'

'Exactly. A cliché.'

'Sorry,' said Gertie contritely, without really meaning it.

Detective Inspector Frieda Garold, Acting Detective Constable "Gertie" Gregson and pathologist Doctor Susan Pleadle were having drinks in the Hangman pub near Heading Square in the Old Town in Wellbury. Frieda had called them together.

It could have been described inaccurately as a girls' night out. In Frieda's mind a better analogy would have been that of three chieftains conducting a cross between a council of war, peace talks and a necessary discussion of how to share some spoils which could not be split two ways, let alone three, the sort of meeting where those present would have preferred to be on friendly terms, but the indivisible and highly-prized spoils meant that only one could win. It was tough, but there you go.

Gertie's phrase and manner had highlighted a very important issue. The spoils in question consisted of one Detective Sergeant Frank Summers – which meant that he had a nominal say in the matter, but they were prepared to treat that as a nominal nominal. He was a mere cipher compared to the issues they faced. The important issue, amongst other important issues, was in their age disparities.

Gertie was in a carefree, almost little-girl mode. She was the youngest by a few years. Her quotation from the witches' scene in Macbeth might well contain a reminder of a later line: "How now, you secret, black, and midnight hags". While Frieda and Susan were far from being that, in a world that appeared to prize youth and appearance over anything else, any single woman over twenty-one could be forgiven for wondering whether they were past it, and had somehow missed out on life, no matter what the media might say about women creating homes in their "later" years (the said articles always appearing to damn the idea with faint praise).

And, may the heavens forgive them, both Frieda and Susan were at least over twenty-five. That much they could not help but admit to.

Their exact ages, however, were not up for discussion.

No matter how intelligent and logical they might be, Susan and Frieda could not help but fear that Frank, when crunch time came, and that was why they had assembled – though two of them were yet to realise this – would choose not only the youngest, but the one who represented the least challenge. Men did so naturally, they always went for the empty-headed dolly-bird.

Not that Gertie was anywhere close to being such, of course, but Susan, for example, was a doctor, on paper far superior in intelligence and social rank to a detective sergeant named Frank Summers whose own university degree had been imperilled by an inability to set his alarm clock properly, not to mention the rather cavalier attitude he brought to what might loosely be described as his studies. In theory Susan Pleadle could triumph in any mental joust or argument with Frank Summers. In reality she had indeed so far won every argument they had had.

Though she could not help but feel that there were one or two minor problems associated with those victories. Firstly, her methods of winning those arguments had been comprised mainly of such tactics as slamming down the phone or slamming the door closed, which hardly required primary, let alone tertiary, education. Indeed, were she to be entirely honest with herself, they smacked of the former rather than the latter.

Secondly, there was the fact that the arguments had arisen in the first place. Rarely is a relationship without its ups and down, but hers with Frank seemed to end in dispute on every occasion they had gone out.

And thirdly, the fact that she was the one who had invariably instigated the arguments, even if that was his fault.

The result was a vicious circle which she could not break out of and he did not appear to understand. Frank, as far as she was concerned, had an amazing ability to understand everything but the really important things.

Frieda's main problem – main, but one of many that she could see, not so much looming on the horizon as being in full flood about her – was that she was Frank's boss, which neatly summarised the situation. What man goes out with his boss? Indeed, what man even has a fling with his boss, let alone a serious relationship?

Okay, perhaps a fling, but a fling was definitely not the result required here. A fling would solve nothing and create every possible problem she could ever imagine. A fling could be compared to the heady pleasure of smashing all the crockery in the house. When you had finished you might feel better, but it would be impossible to replace all that familiar and previously loved crockery, not even the plates which before you started had had a small chip or slight crack in them, not sufficiently serious enough to dispose of when you had had them for years as familiar friends.

No, a man would never fall for his boss, he would invariably go for his secretary, the younger one with the big bosom used to taking orders from him and someone she regarded as her superior. It was only natural. That wasn't Frank's fault, he was only a man, but he was still to blame.

There were times when each of them secretly, knowing how the others there felt, felt sorry for Frank Summers. If any of them had been a man they might well have fled to the comfort of the river, or closeted themselves in the local pub, far from the madding coven.

But that feeling rarely stayed long. You might regret having to chop the tree down, but when winter came you needed a fire to keep warm.

If that was the correct analogy, and none of them were quite sure that it was.

While there were concerns shared by Frieda and Susan, each of the three had further worries to plague them. Frieda felt that, had anyone been betting on the race, she would have been ranked as a five-hundred to one outsider. She was some months older than Frank – not that much older, but it was a telling phrase, "an older woman". Added to that was the requirement of her position to retain discipline, and sometimes Frank could get out of order. She wasn't a control freak, it was a necessary duty.

Okay, just maybe, perhaps just a little, little touch of a control freak. But that was because, as a woman in a man's world, she had to retain firm control. And there was the issue of her ex-husband. He, a fellow police officer, had turned out to be a wife-beater. It had taken her a lot of time, self control and energy to recover from that and pursue her career. Having developed that control she had no wish to lose it, was indeed afraid of what might happen should she lose it. She had, at one stage, decided that she would never fall in love again.

And now she had. With another fellow police officer. Named Frank Summers.

Otherwise known, or would have been had she not had a total antipathy to swearing – courtesy of her ex-husband, whose language had made black of blue – that bastard.

Not, of course, that she would have meant it. She merely thought it as an endearing term when he was proving too much. Which, these days, seemed to be all the time.

Oh, and that was another point against her, while she was thinking about it. She was a divorcée. A failed wife. What easy-going, carefree bachelor like Frank would want to get seriously involved with a divorcée? A woman who had already failed in the marriage stakes?

Was easy-going, she thought to herself. Frank had been easy-going. Not so much these days.

But that was why they were there that evening.

In preparation she had a game-plan of sorts. The first part was to nobble Gertie and Susan. Somehow.

In the politest possible way, of course.

The second part was to learn not to snap at Frank when he acted like a ten-year-old.

Though he hadn't really done that since his accident. These days she would welcome a sign of ten-year-old humour in the man.

These days. The phrase kept returning. It reminded her of those days, the better days.

Anyway.

The third part was to show Frank that she, behind her official exterior, was a soft, caring and feminine woman. Off duty, in his presence, she would gurgle over babies and mewl over sweet little kittens. She would have little girlish moments. She would cuddle up to him as if she were his little princess. She would invent some cute nickname for him, something that symbolised her dependancy on him.

Frankie, perhaps.

On second thoughts, scrub the gurgling over babies. Kittens, yes, she had a soft spot for kittens. But babies were a no-no for developing a relationship with a bachelor. Mother nature had perfected the art of letting the different human species dream different dreams. The woman dreamed of babies and families, the man – well, mother nature alone knew what he dreamed of. Coming home to a hot meal and the good little woman he loved, perhaps, certainly not babies, nappies, toast in the video recorder and other sundry surprises.

And, anyway, she'd been puked on by too many of the little things herself. For some reason, at family gatherings, her cousins all presumed that she would be delighted to handle their offspring. The phrase "Oh dear, isn't he/she adorable? I'm sure it will wash off" was firmly locked in her mind, along with the advantages of wearing clothes that did not require dry cleaning.

Susan had her own worries. She knew she should be a front runner. She had been, at the start. She had been Frank's official girlfriend. Then, what had she done? Lost her temper with Frank on every conceivable occasion. Ignored his preferences. Not so much ignored as not even considered them. What sort of a self-respecting man would accept that sort of treatment? So now she was coming a very distant third in this particular race, about three hundred furlongs behind the other two. And she was faced with the competition of Gertie, who just needed to look a man in the eye to knock him sideways, and Frieda, whose sophistication and good looks were the type that wouldn't deign to click their fingers to need young men come running.

No, she had well and truly messed this one up. But she was not without hope, however small. She had a plan. Of sorts.

First of all she would nobble both Gertie and Frieda. Somehow.

In the politest possible way, of course.

The second part was to learn not to snap at him when he acted like a ten-year-old.

If only he would act like a ten-year-old again.

Thirdly she would show Frank that behind the professional doctor's exterior there was a bubbly, loving, lovable, adorable little girl just waiting to fall swooning over a handsome young bachelor named Frank Summers. In his presence, she would gurgle over babies and go Aaah over sweet little puppies. She would have little girlish moments. She would cuddle up to him as if she were his little princess. She would invent some cute nickname for him, something that symbolised her dependancy on him.

Frankie, perhaps.

She would become his little Susie-Woozie, if that was what he wanted.

On second thoughts, scrub the gurgling over babies. Puppies, yes, she had a soft spot for puppies. But babies were a no-no for developing a relationship with a bachelor. And, anyway, she'd been puked on by too many of the things herself. She had two sisters with the most adorable little children, adorable until they displayed the bodily functions she often discovered in her professional life, though at least those she was dealing with were dead at the time.

One woman's baby-puke, she had decided, was not necessarily another woman's joy.

Firmly fixed in her memory was a sister saying "Oh, he hasn't done that again, has he? I thought the bacon might be a little too rich for him. Never mind, I'm sure it will wash out. Hush, now, who's a mummy's ickle diddums, then, eh? We'll get you some of the doctor's mixture to calm your little tum-tum, won't we? My liddle-liddle thing. Ooos a liddle sweetie then?"

At the time it was Susan herself who thought she might be the next to contribute to the puke process.

Gertie had a different approach lined up.

She knew, in her more realistic moments, that she didn't stand a snowflake's chance in the infernal regions against Frieda and Susan. Frieda was all-woman. She had survived her own personal catastrophes, and come out radiant. It was the radiance and self-confidence that could only be gained through adversity and pain, and, much as she might admire

Frieda, she did not really want to go through the pain to achieve the same result. Besides, she didn't have the time.

Susan, too, thought Gertie, had her own type of confidence. And Susan was younger than Frieda. Susan was also a doctor. What man would look at a young and naive unsophisticate like Gertie, struggling to study with the Open University, when Doctor Susan Pleadle was around?

Still, never give up hope. She had a plan. Of sorts.

She knew she tended to drop into little-girl mode with Frank, a legacy of twisting her father around her little finger when she had been a little girl. Well, all that would end, Frank wasn't the type to go for that sort of girl. He preferred serious. She would become serious. She used glasses for reading. She would get a pair of glasses from the opticians for everyday use, even if they were plain glass. Glasses would give her a serious, determined look. She would show Frank Summers that she was a professional police officer, sharing all the interests and beliefs that he did. There would be no more giggling, the reason she had received her nickname of "Gertie". She would look into his eyes with a depth of passion that showed she shared every single atom of dedication and professionalism that he did.

'Frank's problem,' said Frieda, interrupting their morose introspection, 'is that he has lost his sense of humour.'

None of the others demurred. It was, if anything, an understatement. A major part of his appeal had been his humour, mild self-deprecation and a positive enjoyment of the inevitable ironies of life. Frank without a sense of humour was a zombie.

So much of a zombie that each of the three had privately

wondered whether enough were enough, and whether or not it wasn't time to give up and seek their romantic fortune elsewhere. It wasn't a thought that any of them would admit to, but it hovered in the back of their minds as they sat there, like the final snowflake waiting to settle before beginning an avalanche.

'I told him a joke the other day,' Gertie said, looking disconsolately into her gin and tonic, 'and I thought he almost laughed. Turned out a bee had stung him, and it was a grimace. Any normal person would at least have made some fuss. Not him, not these days. And it wasn't some macho thing, showing he could take the pain, it was more like – well, almost like he was one of those monks who train themselves not to feel anything.'

Few women, Frieda thought to herself, find monks attractive in the terms the three were thinking of. Celibate priests, yes, the forbidden fruit just possibly in reach, but monks? The cowl was a dried-up prune in comparison to the bright ripe apple of the dog collar. Perhaps that was what Frank was aiming at.

'We went to see a movie last week,' Susan said. 'There we were, right at the back, more or less on our own, just perfect for snuggling up. Instead he kept falling asleep. And then he starting talking in his sleep, as if he were having a nightmare. I spent most of the time putting an elbow into his arm to wake him up and stop him disturbing everyone else. Afterwards he mentioned that he must have twisted his arm somehow. That was it. Just a slight mention that maybe he had twisted a muscle. His arm must have been covered in bruises.'

The others looked at her in suspicion. The suspicion that suggested that she should have passed on this information earlier. Frank having nightmares and Susan having a bad time were things that should be shared.

'Well, it was my night,' Susan protested. 'And you can't expect me to come rushing up to tell you of what a miserable time it had been, can you?'

'It's important that we all know what kind of mental state Frank is in,' Frieda said, not having mentioned the dinner she had had with Frank the night before Susan's nightmare movie, when all Frank could talk about was his latest case, hardly paying any attention to the food, and even less to Frieda as a woman.

'Oh? And how did your dinner go?' asked Susan belligerently. 'The night before we went to the cinema?'

Frieda reacted as if she were a countess asked why she hadn't paid the gas bill.

'That was purely business,' she said. 'We spent the evening discussing this spate of break-ins, this joker nonsense. We have to get control of the situation before it gets out of hand. Due to the media it has become quite a high profile case. Much as we would like to determine our own priorities, we have to do something about it. At the same time we can't be seen to be kowtowing to the media. In any event, we would have to put in extra hours, within budgetary constraints, and utilising maximum streamlining of available resources within a modern business paradigm.'

The looks on the other two faces said it all. Frieda had just waffled to save face.

'Okay, okay,' Frieda surrendered. 'The dinner was a disaster. He hardly looked at me, kept looking behind me for some reason. Probably looking for wanted criminals who might have wandered into the restaurant. At one stage I thought he was about to get up and arrest someone in the middle of their entrée. We might as well have stayed in the office and ordered a take away. Bread and water, for all the difference it would have made.'

They pondered this in a comradely fashion, all girls together. So long as each of them was failing they were happy enough to be miserable together.

'We are going to have to do something,' Susan said. 'The longer it goes on the more difficult it's going to be to get him back to the way he was. He might never recover.'

'It's ironic, really,' Frieda noted. 'But then Frank is an irony magnet.'

'What's ironic?' asked Gertie.

'Quite often I despair of getting some people to do their work properly – efficiently. Now that Frank's become like an automaton of efficiency I realise I don't want him to be that efficient. I want him to be human. Or at least be the Frank of old, having a laugh, playing jokes, just having fun.'

'We could always hit him over the head,' suggested Gertie. 'It was the head wound that caused everything. Maybe another bang on his bonce will reverse it.'

'No,' sighed Frieda, 'much as it appeals, and much as I've often had that urge, I don't think it will help in this case. His problem is psychological.'

'It might not help Frank much, but it would make me feel a little better,' said Susan. 'But how do you mean, psychological? It's the result of a physical injury. A bullet in the head, to be precise. That sort of thing does tend to have odd side effects.'

"And quite often they never recover," she was tempted to add as a professional and objective statement, but she feared she might put a hex on the matter by doing so.

Frieda paused before replying. She took a sip of her whisky, and put the glass down carefully. The other two put their drinks down, recognising that a moment of revelation was at hand.

'Jean Candour,' she said. 'Alias Jean Tromperie, and all the rest. I have a suspicion that something went on between her and Frank, the night before he was shot and she was killed.'

'What makes you say that?' asked Susan and Gertie almost simultaneously, their attention firmly locked on Frieda, automatically understanding that "something" meant not just any "something" but that specific "something".

'Something she said when she was brought into the station that day. Frank said she was just trying to wind us up as she had done before, which made sense, but somehow I couldn't help but feel that that time she was the one telling the truth, and Frank dissembling.'

'What was it she said?'

'Something about Frank's being all hers. At the time – well, you remember what it was like. Total chaos. I decided to leave it until later. And then, of course, later Jean was dead and Frank fighting for his life in intensive care. It no longer mattered anymore.'

She took a sip of her drink. The others did likewise, after a moment's hesitation. It was as if they were constantly shifting between the humour of life and the gravity of the grave, much as one person might recall a hilarious moment by starting "You remember when so-and-so", and another on completion of the anecdote leaven, or perhaps leaden, the laughter with "Such a pity he (or she) passed on so shortly afterwards".

'And then, on Christmas Day,' continued Frieda, 'I telephoned him to wish him Happy Christmas. His mother answered – he had gone for a walk, so we got chatting. She said something about how he had never got over Jean's death. I presumed she meant our Jean. Then she said something which confused me. Something about how he seemed so happy at Wellbury, and she thought at one stage that maybe he had got over it, but since the other Jean had been killed he seemed even worse. It took a while to untangle the confusion, but we got there in the end. It turns out that, a few years before he came to Wellbury, he had a passionate affair with a French girlfriend called Jean – she was half French, half British, hence the name – just as our Jean claimed to be when she arrived. The other Jean died in a car accident shortly after she and Frank had an argument. She walked out on him and was dead twenty minutes later – probably not concentrating on the road, at a guess. Apparently Frank blamed himself. And then came the second Jean, our Jean. Frank, if I'm right, fell for her in some way, and then within a short time she too was dead, and again Frank blamed himself. I think that's why he hasn't recovered. He's still blaming himself. He might even think he's jinxed, that anyone getting close to him is likely to come to a bad end.'

'Oh my God,' whispered Susan. 'Poor Frank. I never knew.'

'Why didn't you tell us before?' demanded Gertie. 'About this other Jean?'

Frieda shrugged.

'At the time we all thought Frank would recover, get back to his old self. I thought that it was Frank's private business. We all have things we like to keep private, things we'd prefer to forget. But now it seems that Frank isn't going to be his normal happy-smiley self any time soon, so I thought it better that you should both know. It might help us get him back on track. If we know the cause, we might be able to work out the cure.'

'It would explain why he doesn't want anyone to get close,' said Susan, who had herself, many years before, gone through the experience of losing a boyfriend to a motorcycle accident on the day, she believed, he was going to propose to her. The subsequent pain had been such as to make her question the worth of ever having a close relationship. Had he left her for another woman, that would have been bad enough. But to lose someone, almost at the snap of a finger, for no reason whatsoever? Fate's fickle finger casually destroying the lives of those dead and those left behind?

Quite often, being a rational woman, she wondered whether or not she subconsciously started arguments with Frank in order to avoid finding herself in the same position as she was that day her almost-fiancé to-be had not come home. It was a thought which reared its evil head up again and again no matter how she tried to suppress it.

'I say we make him better,' said Gertie, whose inexperience in the field of loss gave her greater optimism. 'Somehow, anyhow. We can't go on like this.'

'Exactly what I was thinking, Gertie,' Frieda said. 'And I've come to some conclusions, though you might not like those conclusions.'

'What conclusions?'

'Well, the first thing is that, at the moment, we are part of the problem, not part of the solution.'

There was a pause at the thought of this impossibility.

'How do you mean?' asked Susan.

'Frank knows he can go out with any of us whenever he wants. He doesn't have to make any effort. He can pick and choose as he wants.'

'Doesn't seem to want to, much,' commented Susan.

'Exactly. It allows him to avoid getting involved with anyone. So long as that's the case he'll stay the same.'

'Hang on,' said Gertie, 'are you saying we shouldn't go out with him at all?'

'Not quite, no,' Frieda said slowly.

'What then?' asked Gertie.

Frieda paused to attend to her drink before replying.

'I think we must give him an ultimatum. Choose which one of us he wants to go out with.'

The other two considered this. Not overly favourably.

'Why?' asked Susan.

'Well, for one thing he will have to face up to a decision, which is what he's been avoiding. And for another, we can't spend the rest of our lives as a troika of Frank's girlfriends.'

They all agreed that, much as it might have suited Frank, they had no intention of being a third of a girlfriend forever. Just long enough until they were in a strong enough position to make a move for the top job.

'Why don't we just draw cards to see who gets him?' asked Gertie, calculating that that would give her at least a one-in-three chance, as opposed to the nil she believed she had at that moment, somewhat like knowing you are unlikely to win the lottery, but definitely won't if you don't have a ticket. Her calculations were echoed privately by the other two in their own losing lanes.

'No,' said Frieda firmly, 'part of the aim is to force him into facing up to things. It has to be his decision. It's for his own good.'

She hated that phrase. Most often, when a person used the phrase "it's for his own good", it was used in much the same way as the phrase "this is going to hurt me more than it hurts you" – that is, a justification and a complete lie. But in this case all three had to acknowledge that, for once, it was true.

Well, partly true. It was for their good as well.

'What if he refuses to choose?' asked Gertie.

'We are not going to allow him that option, that's all,' said Frieda.

It was a brave statement, considering that all Frank had to do was do nothing and they would be right back where they had started. And Frank, in his current mood, would be more than capable of doing absolutely nothing as far as their relationships went.

'However,' Frieda continued, 'as we know, the main part of Frank's problem is that he has lost his sense of humour. Now I have a suggestion as to how we can help him find it again. It will involve a little deception on our part.'

The three of them smiled. They liked deception. It was fun.

But at the back of their minds lurked various thought monsters.

"What if the changes were permanent?"

"What if some other floozy got to him? Someone who didn't remind him of the past?"

Tuesday Morning: Not Cleopatra's dress

'Oooh, look, it's arrived!' exclaimed Mrs Blower excitedly in the bright mid-morning, looking out of one of the front windows of the Blue Bliss, the night-club nestling in its garden of shrubs and lawn on the outskirts of Wellbury. 'Sonia! Sonia! It's here! It's arrived!'

Sonia, a young woman wearing, despite the warm spring day, a baggy polo-necked jumper with long sleeves and a skirt that reached down to her ankles, joined her at the window. A dry cleaner's van was pulling up outside. Mrs Blower opened the front door and marched out ecstatically. Sonia followed her with much less enthusiasm.

'It's only a costume, Mrs B,' she pointed out.

'Only a costume?' queried Mrs Blower in disbelief. 'Only a costume? Young Alan!' she called to the driver. 'It's Cleopatra's formal dress for meeting high officials!' she reminded Sonia. 'Alan, you have brought it, haven't you? Don't tell me you haven't brought it! Nelson, please, there is no reason for getting so excited.'

This last remark was addressed to a young greyhound confused by Mrs Blower's excitement, and unsure of whether it should be joining in the fun or hiding away, settling for the intermediate position of running in circles around Mrs Blower's legs, ready to change direction at a second and head for the safety of one of the bushes.

Young Nelson would have been surprised, had he been able to understand, to find that those who knew Mrs Blower felt that Nelson was fortunate not to have to follow Mrs Blower's habit of having multiple threads of conversation at the same time. He had his own problems with the forceful, if erratic, woman.

'Well, there's good news and there's bad, Mrs B,' said the young Alan, opening the back doors to the van.

'Oh, no! You aren't going to tell me that he couldn't do it? Nelson, really! He promised! He faithfully promised! He did, you know. And the carpet people. Really, the carpet people. If it wasn't enough having the health and hygiene people, we don't have the carpet people. We had one we didn't want and not the one we did.'

'Oh, Mr Heever got it done,' Alan said, taking an opaque plastic covered garment from the rack in the back of the van. "Heever's Dry Cleaning" read the words on the covering. 'But he said he'd have to charge you more next time. All that gilt and stuff were a right sod to do without messing it up, if you'll pardon my French Mrs B.'

'Oh, next time! Who worries about next time?' asked Mrs Blower, taking the covered garment from the boy. She looked at him eagerly. 'It's a pageant of women through the ages, you know. No, Nelson, please do not try to eat it. And this is Cleopatra's dress. In the loosest sense of the word, possibly, but it was a different era. Different times, different people. After all, look at the French Revolution. You must come and see it. I will see that you and dear Mr Heever receive complimentary tickets. Free, of course. And there's Marie Antoinette.'

'Very kind of you, Mrs B,' Alan said, closing the back doors of the van. 'Only, with all due respect, if me girlfriend found out I was coming to the Blue Bliss, apart from what my job calls for, which she don't like too much to start off with, she'd never forgive me. She's what you might call the jealous type. And I don't want to even think of what Mrs Heever's reaction would be if Mr Heever came around here for a night's entertainment. She don't like it when he goes down his local just for a pint as it is. She's even more of what you might call the jealous type.'

'Alan! Alan!' Mrs Blower said, in what could be described as a wailing voice if she had ever considered wailing to be an option. 'Nelson, enough now! It's obviously time for your walkies. I'm sorry, I seem to have forgotten. It is a pageant. It is not some sordid Soho club. Even the health and hygiene people passed us straight away. We will even have Maggie Thatcher. Not the Maggie Thatcher, of course.'

Nelson lay down and kept quiet. It was not the mention, as some cynics might assume, of Maggie Thatcher which disturbed him, but rather that it was actually time for his din-dins, he had already suffered two walkies that morning, but this woman never seemed to remember which was which. He decided to keep his head down until that other human, the one she called Mr Walthers, rescued him. Mr Walthers wasn't as much fun, but he knew the difference between feeding time and throwing sticks time. And at least with Mr Walthers you knew where the stick had gone. When this woman looked at him and asked "Where did it go?" she genuinely did not know, and neither did he, to the confusion of both. Nelson, having a simpler mind, knew that the stick had to be there somewhere. Mrs Blower, on the other hand, presumed that sticks could, and often did, simply disappear. It was a question of fact, not of reason.

'Alan, it is an artistic review,' she explained to the young man getting back into the cab of his van. 'I expect both your young lady friend and Mrs Heever to be present. The Blue Bliss is no longer a den of iniquity. It is now representative of the classics.'

'The classics?' asked Alan, switching the van's ignition on, wondering if this was some new rock band Mrs Blower had discovered and inveigled into playing. Alan might not have known the word "inveigled", but he knew the concept, and Mrs Blower was in her own league as far as that went. When you found yourself assaulted by thirty thoughts in three seconds, saying "Yes" to what appeared to be the main one of them was a cheap price for peace.

'And your ticket will entitle you to dinner, of course,' Mrs Blower continued.

That settled it. From what young Alan had heard, you could never be sure of what you would get at the Blue Bliss as far as food went, since Mrs Blower invariably interfered with the chef's careful planning and dedication, resulting in several near-nervous breakdowns by the chef, and an interesting if unusual range of dishes. But it was uniformly agreed that it was always bloody good grub.

'I'll convince the girlfriend,' he promised, and drove the van away. It wasn't a convincing promise. Mrs Blower didn't know that the girlfriend he was talking of was twice his age, with three grown-up children. She was an interim girlfriend, so to say. There was no way he was going to bring her to such a promising plethora of opportunity as the Blue Bliss.

'Come, Sonia,' said Mrs Blower, holding the carefully wrapped garment, 'I can't wait to see what you will be wearing on the night. Nelson, it's time for your din-dins. Nelson, where are you? Ah, there you are, we'll just get this done and take you for walkies. Nelson?'

'I told you, I'm not doing it,' Sonia said, following her. 'I'm the floor manager now. I don't strip any more.'

Sonia had been kidnapped by the men involved in Frank's shooting and Jean Candour's death. The experience had changed her from being a cheeky young woman, happy to display her physical charms, into a withdrawn and serious woman who now covered herself from top to toe. She had also developed a deep love for the man who had found her, Doctor Susan Pleadle's boss, Doctor Wood, a mild mannered and long-married man in his early sixties. As he had not returned the love it was a secret she bore within herself, happily so, as it saved her from the energy of having to consider any alternative. Carrying a torch for someone, a torch no-one else could see, saved on the fuel bill of having to keep it alight.

'Yes, yes, my dear, we've been through that a hundred times, and I've told you a hundred times I don't expect you to do it,' Mrs Blower said in a voice which quite plainly said that Sonia was going to do it.

'I mean it, Mrs B,' warned Sonia as they entered the main bar of the Blue Bliss.

'Yes, my dear, I know,' Mrs Blower said. 'Just hold this while I unzip the cover.'

Sonia, despite her reservations, did as she was bid. She had seen Mrs Blower's designs, but not the completed article. And, despite her protestations, she was now eager to do so.

The light cream cover fell to the floor and the two women looked at the garment it revealed.

It wasn't quite what they had expected. Mrs Blower knew what it should look like, and Sonia knew what it might look like, and it looked like neither.

It was certainly not something Cleopatra would ever have dreamed of wearing.

It was a record for Mrs Blower. At least ten seconds of silence.

'Mr Walthers!' she called. 'Mr Walthers! Please come here, now!'

Phil Walthers had thought he had found a room where Mrs Blower's voice could not penetrate. He sighed, rubbed his brow, admitted defeat, and made his way to the central bar.

He stopped at the sight of the cover-less garment.

'Cleopatra's dress!' exclaimed Mrs Blower. 'It is supposed to be Cleopatra's dress!'

Phil Walthers approached the garment. He had heard about Cleopatra's dress. It had been drummed into him for at least two weeks. But this was definitely not Cleopatra's minimal fashion-wear. Mrs Blower's perceptions of Cleopatra's fashion preferment might be historically inaccurate, but they were a lot closer than this would ever come.

'There's a note pinned to it,' he said, reaching forward and unpinning it.

'A pin?' asked Mrs Blower in horror. 'A pinhole would ruin Cleopatra's dress!'

'But, as you have noted, this is not Cleopatra's dress,' Phil Walthers said mildly, reading the note.

'But it should be!' cried Mrs Blower. 'And if it was it would have a pinhole in it! This is just not good enough! I am definitely going to have words with Mr Heever. He was well aware of how important this is. I can forgive a simple mistake, but this is not a simple mistake. As if the carpets weren't enough. And Nelson. And the hygiene people.'

Phil Walthers had become accustomed to Mrs Blower. You had to listen to her through a sieve of consciousness, filtering out her sentences into logical units.

Or even totally ignore her.

He handed the note to her.

'Somehow I don't think this is Mr Heever's fault.'

Mrs Blower read the note.

'I don't understand,' she said.

'Nor do I, Mrs Blower, nor do I. However, I do think I shall have to speak to Sergeant Summers about this. I'm sure he'll know what to do.'

Tuesday Afternoon: Wasting timesheets

'Okay, I'll be there later,' Frank said before putting down the telephone. He frowned and drummed his fingers on his desk.

'Timesheets,' Eric Johns said, walking into his office and waving a piece of paper. 'As in missing timesheets, specifically one that should have the name of a Detective Sergeant on it. First name beginning with an "F", surname beginning with an "S".'

'Eric, just fill in the regulation number of hours and I'll sign it. I've got more important things to worry about than timesheets.'

'No can do, I'm afraid, Frank. Orders from Fabulous. You have to fill in the correct hours, including overtime. I don't think she's very happy with you. You haven't done anything to upset her, have you?'

Frank grunted. He guessed that Frieda was getting in her retaliation for the way he had walked out on her on Sunday evening. At the time he had had a feeling that it was probably not the best way to handle things. But that was her fault for barging in on him when he was trying to get some work done on his own. He hadn't asked her to come interfering.

'Just leave the sheet with me,' he said, holding out his hand. 'I'll get it done as soon as I have a chance.'

'You mean give it to Gertie as you normally do.'

'Gertie's off today. I'll get her to do it first thing tomorrow.'

'Sorry, Frank, my orders are to stand over you until you've finished it – and to make sure the figures are roughly correct. I think that might mean "within throwing distance of reality".'

'You are joking, aren't you, Eric? Frieda's swinging her weight around a bit too much, I would say.'

'She did say please,' Eric pointed out. He didn't add that Frieda's "please" did not come across as a polite request.

Frank gave a sigh of irritation.

'Okay, okay, let's get the damn thing out of the way. Phil Walters wants to see me about some missing dry cleaning and Frieda is demanding I fill in a timesheet. A fine use of police time. One day in a hundred years' time they might even computerise these things.'

'Missing dry cleaning?' asked Eric.

'Precisely. If it wasn't Phil Walthers I'd presume it was some kind of wind up. Now, let's see, eight hours for Monday, eight hours for Tuesday –'

'Come on, Frank, you can do a little better than that,' Eric urged, sitting down. 'At least vary things a bit. And Fabulous knows you spend more than eight hours a day – including the evenings you've been spending on this joker business. How's it going, by the way?'

Frank gave another grunt and changed some of the figures he had entered.

'Bloody waste of time,' he said.

'Has to be done, I'm afraid. To coin a phrase, the only things certain in life are death, taxes and timesheets.'

'I meant the evening interviews. No-one saw anything, they never do in that bloody place. Bad manners to spy on your neighbours in Lords Acres. Even if they could see their neighbours. The houses are set so far back from the roads you could run a carnival through there without anyone noticing. But there has to be a link between the burglaries, we know that.'

He put his pen down and began ticking points off on his fingers. Eric listened as Frank went through each possible connection. He knew Frank was using him as a sounding board, to talk his way through each dead end he had come across, hoping that it would spark off some possibility he had so far missed. He just hoped Frank hadn't forgotten totally about his timesheet.

'Professor Hawthorn, lives alone, goes on holiday and gets back to find a back window open and his silver collection gone, plus other small items, with a joker and another playing card left behind. The Borders, Mr and Mrs, go on holiday. Their cleaning lady pops in to make sure the place is ready for their return and discovers, again, a forced window, with various items of jewellery missing. Again, the playing cards. Mr and Mrs Hamilton go on holiday, come back to a similar scenario. So, how did our Joker Gang know their victims would be away? Where are they getting their information from? Travel agents? No, two of them used different ones, and the Professor booked on the Internet. Kennels? No, only one had a dog which was put into a dogs' home while they were away. Postmen? None of the owners speak to their postmen, let alone mention that they were going away. Any clubs they all belong to, societies, charities, anything? No. Common connections? Nil. And our joker friends only go for small items, easily portable, so no mysterious furniture vans driving around. No doubt they're using some anonymous vehicle which no-one would notice. The only thing we do know is that, in two of the cases, a car containing three people was spotted around the time of the burglary. That, fortunately for us if not the environment, could almost be regarded as a reliable fact, since people in Lords Acres all drive their own cars, and to see more than one occupant, apart from during the school run, is unusual enough to be noticed. Not, unfortunately for us, enough for any of those seeing such an unusual event, to note down the make of car or descriptions of the occupants.'

'Weren't some lorries from the fair seen driving through – that Bentley's crowd? I thought I heard something about that.'

'One. One driver got lost and ending up driving around. It was about lunchtime. He ended up asking for directions. And, presumably because of their prejudice, various inhabitants report Bentley vehicles being driven suspiciously in the early hours of the morning, driven by swarthy men carrying daggers, or sultry women with large gold earrings and evil eyes. Only it wasn't them who saw anything, it was their neighbours. Except the neighbours heard it from someone else, and so on. I'm only surprised we haven't had sightings of a Gypsy driving a horse and cart through just before midnight. Or flying overhead on a broomstick. And things aren't made any easier by Zack the Prat taking calls on his show from people who believe that the Bentley lot are only here to steal little children, knife anyone who looks at them sideways, and generally commit every crime in the book they can think of.'

Zack the Prat, or Zack the Man as he titled himself, was a show host on one of the local radio programmes. He revelled in encouraging callers to proclaim their prejudices, the more outlandish the better. Frank had been tempted to bring him in to the station, and threaten him with a charge of promoting public disorder, but he knew that the Prat would only use it in his show the next day, claiming that the police were harassing innocent civilians for telling the truth, while criminals lurking within the travelling fair were allowed to get off scot free. He was the person Phil Walthers had referred to in his article. If ever Phil Walthers had a weakness it was that of having a go at the radio host whenever he could get the chance.

'You're almost there,' Eric noted, nodding at the timesheet. 'What about the cards?' He was only mildly interested in the case, but if he kept Frank talking he might complete the timesheet without realising it.

'The cards are a blind,' Frank replied, taking his pen up again and frowning at the paper in front of him. 'Pretty soon every minor criminal will be leaving a joker behind to confuse us. Sooner or later we'll catch someone in the act, they'll have a pack of cards on them, and everyone will presume we've caught this famous Joker Gang. And then there's the reverse option: they pull off a job without leaving their trademark behind, and we get fooled into thinking it wasn't them. No, those cards are a smokescreen to get us running in circles.'

'Not even the other ones, the ones they left with the joker? What was it – nine of diamonds, three of hearts and queen of spades?'

'They probably chose those at random. My guess is that they're having a good laugh over all the speculation as to what the cards signify. They don't signify anything, apart from being false clues for us to chase.'

Eric had to admit to himself that he hadn't quite thought of it that way. He shared the public's view that it showed a certain panache.

And if Frank thought the cards were a blind, why did he have a pack sitting on his desk?

'I have this vain hope they might get sloppy and leave a card that does mean something,' Frank said, noticing his glance.

He put his pen down again and drummed his fingers on his desk.

'It's possible that the queen of spades might mean something. The trouble is it might mean nothing, which means they've succeeded if I start thinking it means something when it actually means nothing.'

All Eric Johns knew was that it meant Frank was not filling in his timesheet. Eric Johns did not like nothings, especially the nothing in the final column.

Frank held out the pack. 'Choose a card.'

Eric raised his eyebrows but took a card. The nine of clubs.

'Good, that gives me a figure for Friday,' Frank said. 'But I don't think this bunch are stupid,' he concluded, signing the timesheet and handing it back. 'I'm convinced that they'll do one more property before disappearing somewhere else – if they haven't left already. Our only hope is to set a trap for them. I've told Frieda that, but she won't listen.'

The person not listening, Eric guessed, was Frank Summers, but he kept the thought to himself. Frank had been given a lot of rope since his accident, and the only thing that had prevented him hanging himself with it was the fact that he had produced results. Even that wouldn't help him if Frieda decided that he would be better off somewhere else. Frieda might have a soft spot for Frank, but there isn't a great deal of separation between a soft spot and a blemish, and this blemish would not require cosmetic surgery to remove.

'I'll have another word with her,' Frank decided.

'She's out for the rest of today. Meetings, apparently.'

'The whole day?'

'That's what she said this morning.'

Frank considered this. A thin smile crossed his face.

'Well, if she's unavailable, I'll just have to speak to the Chief Inspector. I'm pretty sure he'll give me the go-ahead.'

Eric almost gasped at the idea. Going over Frieda's head was a sure-fire way of committing suicide in a most unpleasant way. Fortunately there was a major flaw in the plan.

'That would be an interesting trick. Managing to get hold of the Chief Inspector,' he noted.

Frank paused. Something the Chief Inspector had said to him echoed in his mind. "It's Percy who has a problem. Poor man stumbles across me all the time, until he actually needs to speak to me. Funny, that."

He had no doubt that the Chief Inspector would make himself similarly invisible should a certain lowly detective sergeant attempt to use him to bypass his own Inspector. Previously he had been content to be a detective sergeant. Increasingly, in the last few months, he had hungered for the independence a higher rank might have conferred. He was coming around to the idea that he would have to request a posting to a larger station to get it. The more he thought of that, the more it made sense. It was time to move on.

Something else the Chief Inspector had said came back to him: "You know why I'm here". He didn't, but at the time he wasn't interested enough to enquire.

'How does he get away with it?' he asked Eric Johns.

'How do you mean?'

'He's never – hardly ever – at the station. Apparently he's going to take early retirement, but he's been off fishing ever since I got here. Surely someone must have noticed.'

Eric chuckled.

'I would have thought you would have worked that one out by now,' he said.

'Why don't you explain it to me then,' Frank suggested in a cold voice.

'Look, Frank, haven't you ever wondered how we survive as such a small force?'

Frank nodded. In fact the idea had never crossed his mind.

'We have three big neighbouring divisions, right?' continued Eric Johns. 'They all agree that Wellbury should fall under their control. They also all agree that none of their rivals should take us over. Pretty much of a stalemate, but the word came down that a decision would be made. That was when the Chief Inspector announced that he was taking early retirement at some unspecified date. Well, they couldn't do anything without the Chief Inspector, so the decision was delayed until he retired and someone else took his place. So, so long as he's off fishing the status quo remains.'

'But surely someone must have said something?'

'That's the beauty of it, Frank. The other divisions are more worried about their rivals taking us over than our staying independent, so they're quite happy to keep their mouths shut and keep up the pretence. It's the old "If I can't have it nobody else will" scenario.'

'When did this happen?'

'A few years ago. Not long before you got here.'

A few years, thought Frank. About the time the Chief Inspector's wife died. He could imagine various people saying "Bad time to disturb the poor chap". "We'll continue when he gets back". "Give him time to get over it".

All worthy sentiments if you were a Chief Inspector. Don't expect the same treatment if you're a constable.

'And there's our secret weapon,' added Eric Johns.

'Secret weapon?'

'The canteen. We have the best canteen in the county, bar none, and everybody knows it. Any visiting dignitary turns up to start asking questions, they're taken to the canteen and stuffed with their heart's desire. By the time they're finished with Agnetha's creations they've forgotten the questions and are looking forward to the next visit, any excuse will do.'

Frank grunted. It was true enough that Wellbury police station canteen was somewhat of a legend, but it was not a place he had visited recently, despite Gertie's continued efforts to fill him with the delicacies of the day. A full stomach slowed the brain processes, something he wished to avoid.

The Agnetha Eric Johns had mentioned did not officially run the kitchen, but there was no-one brave enough to point out the fact. She was a dour woman who had dedicated her life to the stomachs of what she thought of as her girls and boys, the children she had never had, and there was only one who did not acknowledge the fact and welcome it. It used to be said that nobody, but nobody, dared cross Agnetha. But now there was one. Had Agnetha presumed to put a plate of food in front of Frank and commanded "Eat" as she did with other wounded animals, including her boys and girls, she would have received shrift shorter than short. As it was she bided her time and her empire. One of her minions (her boss, technically speaking) had queried this approach.

'You've always said a happy stomach leads to a happy mind,' this minion-boss had suggested apologetically.

Agnetha had considered this for a while, long enough to show she had considered the suggestion in all its implications and flaws, and there were many of both.

'Eagles are difficult creatures,' she said, finally returning her judgement. 'You have to be careful with eagles, especially when they're wounded. And especially when it's coming up to lunch and we're behindhand.'

'Sounds a bit daft to me,' the unknowing eagle said to Eric Johns. 'If I was in charge of one of those divisions I'd insist on a decision. The Chief Inspector can't hide forever. No-one can.'

Eric Johns could not help but feel that Frank had made a very prescient remark. At the same time he wasn't sure that it applied only to the Chief Inspector.

Tuesday Evening: A clown's challenge

Frank stood in the main bar of the Blue Bliss and read the note that Phil Walthers had found pinned to the delivered garment.

"If Sergeant Frankie Summers cannot unravel,

untangle, unroll and reveal

that which Julie's gaze did baffle

then Cleopatra's gown

will have the feel

of a clown"

'It should have been Cleopatra's formal wear for greeting visiting dignitaries,' Phil Walthers explained. 'Not quite what we expected.'

Frank looked at the outfit that had come from the dry cleaners. A clown's outfit, baggy purple trousers, electric-green braces, baggy yellow shirt with exaggerated stitching where a tear might have been sewn up, and a bright blue nose held by elastic to the coat hanger.

'An outrage,' said Mrs Blower. 'A practical joke of some sort. Frank, why isn't Gertie with you? You are much too thin, she hasn't been looking after you. Nelson? Nelson, it's time for walkies. It's been kidnapped. We'll receive a ransom demand. She hasn't left, has she? You aren't eating properly. Hijacked, in broad daylight.'

This multiple conversation had a different effect on the various participants.

'I don't strip any more,' Sonia assured Frank earnestly. 'I'm the floor manager now. It's a respectable job.'

Phil Walthers stayed silent.

Nelson also stayed silent, but underneath a table where he could not be seen. Phil Walthers envied him. He had an urge to join the young dog underneath the table.

'It's not a ransom note,' Frank said grimly. 'Someone is playing games.'

'It's been stolen then!' exclaimed Mrs Blower.

'No, it hasn't been stolen,' Frank said. 'You'll find it hidden in a roll of carpeting somewhere around here.'

Mrs Blower was silenced by this incredibly confident statement. Phil Walthers clapped a hand to his forehead.

'Of course!' he muttered angrily. 'Of course! I know where it is.'

Mrs Blower looked at him in consternation. She looked back at Frank. Then back at Phil Walthers.

Mrs Blower did not normally do consternation. Those who had to listen to her did consternation.

'Mr Walthers, you appear to know what young Frank is talking about. Perhaps you would care to enlighten me. Nelson, stop that.'

Nelson, hiding unseen underneath the table wasn't doing anything. He wondered how he could stop doing nothing.

'Cleopatra got to see Julius Caesar – Julie, as the note calls him – by having herself delivered in a rolled-up carpet,' Phil Walthers explained. 'I should have realised. It's obvious when you think about it – "untangle, unroll and reveal" and "that which Julie's gaze did baffle"? Silly! A child of two could have worked that one out.'

'And you've had a carpet delivered recently,' Frank said, a statement more than a question.

'A week ago, or so. It's lying in a back room,' Phil Walthers said. 'It was supposed to be laid last week but the people haven't turned up, they keep postponing things. If you'd like to follow me?'

'I'll wait here,' Frank said.

Phil Walthers looked at him for a second, nodded, and left the bar, Mrs Blower following, frowning, going through her latest list of concerns, which now included Julius Caesar. Mr Walthers should have told her about the business with Julius Caesar and the carpet. It could be nicely worked into the pageant.

She had managed, in a way only Mrs Blower could do, to lay her hands on a python which would be used to resemble the asp by which Cleopatra had committed suicide. Unfortunately the poor snake had died shortly after being delivered to the Blue Bliss, and, in a moment of absent-mindedness she had used it in the creation of a soup, a soup which had been greatly praised by the consumers thereof, happily in ignorance of what had been used to create this gastronomical delicacy.

That had been the day the latest chef – an Italian – had been found with a bottle of Scotch in the kitchen storeroom, gibbering to himself about mad Englishwomen.

A carpet would be ideal as part of the Cleopatra act, and it wouldn't be likely to die on her.

In what he might term his day-job, Phil Walthers was the Wellbury Herald. Editor, photographer, journalist, anything and everything a newspaper needed to be brought out once a week on Thursdays. Usually on Thursdays, sometimes more than once a week depending on local news. Wellburians liked not knowing exactly when the Herald might appear. It was that type of town.

His eccentricity was partly real, partly a way to deal with the world. He had seen a lot during his many years as a journalist in a small town. He recognised the look on Frank's face. He didn't know the psychological word for it, but he did understand it. It was not so much claustrophobia – though there was an element of that – but rather a fear of going in, a fear of entering another space, someone else's space, a fear that it might claim his attention, might demand a response beyond a purely intellectual reaction.

To have to look at a piece of carpet was not a brief encounter. It carried subjective involvement. You looked. Did you like it? Why had it been chosen, that particular style? Why the pattern, why the colour? What did the other expect from it? Where would it go? What were they hoping?

Other people's hopes, Phil Walthers understood, were what Frank feared most. Hope can be contagious. The last gift from Pandora's box was not so much of a gift as a curse.

Mrs Blower's thoughts were not such discrete units. Asking Mrs Blower what she was thinking would reward the questioner with waves of streams of consciousness, or possibly, if such a word existed, a-consciousness. And not so much streams as multiple hurricanes.

But, if you separated her current waves out, they could be represented in two main elements: she was going to find Cleopatra's garments, and Frank was going to start eating properly and stop this wounded hero nonsense. She would have a word with Gertie. Nelson needed taking for a walk. Or was it time for din-dins? Why wasn't Gertie with Frank? Sonia was going to be Cleopatra. No, it was walkies, she was sure. Those carpet people were most unreliable. Then there were the health and hygiene people. He needed a new flea collar ...

Sonia stayed standing silently with Frank. He had hoped she would go too. He recognised the signs. She wanted him to like her. She wanted him to say "Yes, I respect you, you are no longer a stripper, you are a respectable woman". He couldn't. He didn't dislike her. Respect was not an issue. He was a police officer. Emotions were for other people. Emotions got in the way of the job.

He moved to the bar and studied the bottles clamped upside down at the back in an attempt to create space between them.

'Would you like a drink?' asked Sonia in a voice that was almost pleading.

'No, thanks,' he replied in the manner of someone who understands that many people drink, but he personally required no such artificial stimulation.

He stood looking at the bottles. Checking the labels. The levels. The distance between each bottle. Every little detail could tell you something. Two bottles of the same whiskey alongside each other stated that this was a popular brand. But why two regularly sized bottles of the same whiskey, yet a single, overly-large bottle of brandy? Why not one large bottle of the same whiskey? Was it not available in such a size?

He was deliberately not thinking about that note.

That note had hit a weak point, a very weak point.

One bottle of gin was turned, slightly obscuring the label. Had it been put up in a hurry? The bar full, the people working behind the bar rushed, too busy to align a newly opened bottle correctly?

These ruminations, rationalising excuses for not indulging in idle chatter, were interrupted by something tugging at his trouser leg.

He looked down. Nelson had a paw on his leg, looking up at him in concern, his head cocked, as if wanting to play but unsure about this human, as he was with most of the breed.

'Hello, Nelson,' Frank said, smiling slightly, bending down to stroke the dog's head. 'You've grown a bit since I last saw you, haven't you old boy?'

A grin split Nelson's face. He barked. This human was okay. A bit strange, perhaps, but hopefully not as bad as the others. He barked again and jumped back, crouching, his tail wagging furiously. Come, let's play, he said.

'Walkies!' Mrs Blower called as she and Phil Walthers re-entered the main bar-area.

Nelson disappeared like a shot.

'You were right, Sergeant Summers,' Phil Walthers said, holding a hanger in his hand, from which hung glittering gold and dark blue garments about the size of a brief mini-skirt and what might loosely be called a boob-tube had it been wider. 'It was hidden in a piece of carpet, in a plastic cover. I would say that whoever did it took great pains to make sure it came to no harm.'

'Who knew about the costume?' asked Frank, unimpressed with whatever great pains might have been taken. Cleopatra's skimpy outfit received only a cursory glance.

'Almost all of Wellbury, I would hope,' Phil Walthers replied. 'We've been advertising the pageant for a few weeks now.'

'Who knew that it was being delivered today?' Frank asked in a voice which suggested that that was what he had originally asked, and was now having to repeat the question in small syllables which a child might understand.

'Quite a few people, I'm afraid,' Phil Walthers said, showing no offence at Frank's tone. 'Mr Heever promised us faithfully that it would arrive this morning, and we probably told anyone who would listen. It's one of the centre-pieces of the show.'

'What he means, Sergeant Summers,' Mrs Blower interrupted, 'is that he thinks I am somewhat of a gas bag. I have put a lot of effort and hard work into this pageant, and I tend to talk about it to people I like. Inspector Garold. I must have a word with her. Merely a practical joke. All safe and sound. I can relax and take Nelson for his walk. Such as Sergeant Johns and Sergeant Phillips. Probably those students.'

'It's university rag week,' explained Phil Walthers, translating Mrs Blower's words. 'They're playing all sorts of practical jokes on each other. And on anyone they think it might be fun to target. We rather mistakenly had a happy hour specifically for university students last week, no strippers or such, but drinks at half price. It took two days to clean the place up. It was only on Saturday that we discovered the fish behind the radiator in the main bar. It was stinking the entire bar out.'

'Inspector Garold was here?' asked Frank, trawling Mrs Blower's previous statement for clues.

'Inspector Garold?' asked a mystified Mrs Blower. 'Why on earth should Inspector Garold come here? And where is Gertie, that's what I want to know. Though there's no reason for her not to pop into the members' bar. She isn't feeding you properly, and where has Nelson got to?'

'You mentioned Inspector Garold,' Frank pointed out as patiently as he could.

'Did I? Oh, yes, thank you for reminding me. I must have a word with her. I shall write that down. Now, where did I leave that notepad?' she asked herself, peering around the bar.

'And Sergeants Johns and Phillips?' Frank asked Phil Walthers as Nelson withdrew further into the half-light of the bar, hiding from Mrs Blower's search for a notepad, just in case she should discover him instead of the notepad.

'They come in every other night or so, sometimes together, sometimes with others from the station. We've created a members-only bar, you know, and local police officers automatically get membership and discounted prices. And we even have a snooker bar, though keeping regular prices up to keep out the ...'

He paused as he realised he was coming very close to doing a Mrs Blower.

'In fact, allow me to offer you a drink now, compliments of the establishment,' he continued quickly 'It appears that we have called you out on somewhat of a fool's errand.'

Frank shook his head irritably.

'Who knew about the carpets?' he asked.

'Once again, most of our customers. The delivery people left them in the passageway, where the toilets are. Customers kept tripping over them. We had to move them when we realised that the fitters were so unreliable.'

'Not in the facilities themselves, of course,' Mrs Blower pointed out from the counter area, still searching for Nelson and a notepad. 'Our facilities, the entire premises, especially the kitchen, are grade one, the health and hygiene people told us. Has anyone seen Nelson's lead?'

Phil Walther's grimaced.

'The health and hygiene inspectors turned up first thing this morning, while we were out. A snap inspection. Fortunately we make sure everything is always up to the highest of standards. Despite our trying to change the reputation of the Blue Bliss there are a number of people out there who would love to see us closed.'

'What other visitors did you have this morning?'

'Usual deliveries. Supplies for the bar, the kitchen, that type of thing.'

'Nothing unusual?'

'Not that I noticed.'

Frank stood as if lost in thought, arms folded, looking at the floor. After a while he appeared to come to a decision.

'Right,' he said, 'I'll make a few enquiries. I'll find out who's behind this.'

'It's simply a practical joke,' Phil Walthers protested. 'Hardly worth wasting any police time over.'

Frank looked at him, his jaw set grimly.

'They put my name on it,' he said. He nodded a curt goodbye. 'I'll be in touch.'

'What did you want to speak to Inspector Garold about?' asked Phil Walthers out of mild curiosity once Frank had left.

'Inspector Garold?' asked Mrs Blower, perplexed. 'Why should I want to speak to Inspector Garold? Nelson! Where was Gertie? He's looking so thin!'

'He needs time to recover,' Phil Walthers replied, deciding that the reason Mrs Blower wanted to speak to Inspector Garold was now lost in the mists of Mrs Blower's mind, and not likely to reappear any time soon.

'He won't recover,' Sonia said. 'He's sensitive. Gentle. He's been hurt too much. People like that never recover.'

She left them, hugging herself as she went, as if it were a cold and bitter day.

'And if Frank won't get better, then Sonia won't get better,' Mrs Blower sighed.

Phil Walthers checked his watch. Time was never something that had bothered him very much. He had learnt to distrust the modern frenzy of clock-watching ever since his days as a junior reporter, with everyone shouting about deadlines. When he had inherited the Herald, he had also inherited the idea that a newspaper should be published only when there was enough news to print. It wasn't an approach those who advertised in the Herald necessarily agreed with on a business basis, but they had to admit that the surprise factor did ensure that people actually read the paper. In a funny way, typical to Wellbury, what shouldn't have worked, did.

Time, however, was now to play a crucial part. A crucial part in his escaping a lunatic asylum filled with sad-eyed young women wandering around in woolly jumpers and long dresses, and Mrs Blower sighing over Frank's appetite and the lack of Gertie. There was no reason not to bring out a Wednesday edition of the Herald.

'I'd best get back to the Herald,' he said. 'I should have just enough time to get it out first thing tomorrow. And this little practical joke is an ideal filler for a little space on the front page. The Curious Incident At The Blue Bliss – that should make a good header. A bit long, perhaps, but I'll whittle it down.'

And a nice bit of advertising for the Blue Bliss, but Phil

Walthers would never admit to such low practice.

'The Curious Incident of Cleopatra's Clothes,' said Mrs Blower.

'What was that?' Phil Walthers asked in astonishment.

'The Curious Incident of Cleopatra's Clothes,' Mrs Blower repeated. 'As a title. Now, what was I doing before this nonsense started? Ah, yes, Sonia. She needs to try these on for size. The dry cleaning might have done something to the material. And I need to speak to Inspector Garold.'

Phil Walthers made his exit before she could continue. She had given him an excellent headline which didn't actually mention the Blue Bliss – that would be in the body of the article.

He was getting out before she gave him an excellent headache.

Tuesday Night: Frankie's sleeping tablet

That night Frank returned to his flat after working late. Had an observer seen him the person would have been impressed at the security precautions he took on entering.

Firstly he gently pushed the door to test if anyone had broken in during the day. Then he checked for any scratch marks on the several locks which might indicate that an attempt had been made to open the locks with something other than the rightful keys. Satisfied that the door was still locked and secure, he opened it and slipped inside. He relocked the locks from the inside and put the chain on before taking his shoes off. Silently he padded from room to room, checking under the bed, under the kitchen table, the coffee table in the lounge, anywhere where an assailant might remotely think of lurking.

Then he checked the locks on the windows. Being a first floor flat it was doubtful that anyone would try entering via the windows, but he had installed secure twin locks on every one, including a small fixed window in the bathroom which did not open. Someone might have seen in that a flash of his old sense of humour.

Or the sign of someone so round the bend they'd gone too far to come back.

Finally, having proved to his satisfaction that he was alone and locked in, he opened a drawer in the bedroom and took out a bottle of whisky. Cheap whisky. He fetched a glass from the kitchen and took both to the lounge. He switched the television on, turning the sound down until it was silent. After switching channels a few times he came across a re-run of some old black-and-white movie. He knew there would be one. It didn't matter which. He just needed something to keep his eyes occupied while his mind relaxed.

He poured a stiff drink and took a sip of the neat, amber liquid. He shivered as it burned down his throat.

That was good.

He would have preferred his usual whisky, Glenlivet, but that was expensive, especially with all the taxes the government put on the stuff. Not the sort of thing he could afford, not now that he needed a few stiff drinks before facing bed and darkness. It kept the demons at bay. Some of the time.

And it helped him process the day in his mind. This was when his mind worked best, alone, with the stimulus of a few stiff drinks.

The rhyme ran through his head.

"If Sergeant Frankie Summers cannot unravel,

untangle, unroll and reveal

that which Julie's gaze did baffle

then Cleopatra's gown

will have the feel

of a clown"

A simple clue. As Phil Walthers had noted, it was obvious.

But it had been addressed to him personally. Did that mean they knew he would quickly work it out, or was it an insult to his intelligence? Or was it perhaps someone who didn't know him, didn't realise that his degree had been mainly in history, and that he continued to study the subject?

There was something else, something far worse.

If there was one thing he hated more than anything in this

world, it was being called Frankie.

Someone would pay for that.

What did it signify? A simple practical joke, the work of students, or the start of something more sinister?

Was it related to this joker business?

Whichever, he was going to find out. If they thought they could make a fool out of him they were dealing with the wrong man. He was going to find out and teach them a lesson they would never forget.

Wednesday Morning: Garfield, Sam and the Twins

Frank was at his desk by seven o'clock, a routine he had developed over the past few months. Getting in early allowed him to get some decent work done before the chatterboxes arrived to interrupt his thinking. Chatterboxes who seemed to think that work was a time to catch up on the latest football, soap-opera, gossip, or whatever their preferred subject was. Certainly police work came a distant fourth or fifth for most of them.

One of his mental self-defence voices might have pointed out to him that he had once been quite happy to engage in social chit-chat and banter, if not to prefer it to work, but those voices had long lain dormant, at most raising a wary head above the parapet to confirm their suspicion that they had best lie very, very low.

Getting in early also gave him time to have two mugs of coffee to set him up for the day. He had his own bottle of extra-strong granulated coffee in his desk drawer. The stuff that came out of the machine was far too weak and insipid.

This morning he reached for the drawer handle as usual, without thinking, without the paranoid approach he took when getting home to his flat in the evening.

In every other sphere of life he took what some might deem to be neurotic pains to ensure his own safety.

When driving he checked the rear view mirror constantly, looking for any vehicle which might appear too often, indicating that someone was tailing him.

Walking down a street he would often double back suddenly, watching for looks of sudden surprise which would indicate a follower surprised by this move. It was a self-fulfilling action.

Even normal people would be taken aback by a man who abruptly did a u-turn in the middle of the pavement, especially one with a white quiff in the front of his hair.

Windows were ideal reflectors. During his dinner with Frieda he had used them constantly, checking for any suspicious diners, anyone taking too much of an interest in him.

When on the riverbank he had a mirror concealed in his bag. He always took a position where he could see a fair distance. A casual observer might think him engrossed, not realising that he was watching them without appearing to.

His own office was the one place he let his guard down when alone. The one place he knew that he was entirely safe.

It was thus that he was totally unprepared when he casually opened the drawer and the cat sprang out at his face, claws grasping, mouth spitting, an orange and black striped ball of fur and fury intent on gouging his eyes out.

He shot back, screaming, the wheels on his chair spinning as he wrestled with the feline fury. The wheels caught in the carpet and he went over backwards, his head hitting the wall, feeling the sharp edge of the old-fashioned radiator score the back of his neck. He managed to pull the cat off and hurled it violently against the far wall.

The collision must have knocked it out, he thought, his mind dazed, as the animal lay on the floor, not moving.

He stood up groggily, using the desk to support himself. Vaguely he heard the sound of running footsteps, strangely muffled footsteps. He picked up a heavy ruler to use as a weapon. He staggered over to the supine animal, raising the ruler, determined to expunge the cat's life before it could come to and resume its attack on him.

A few cracks would split the animal's head open and remove it from this world.

More than a few cracks, if necessary. It would be a bundle of mashed fur and blood by the time he had finished with it.

When he got to it he paused, knelt down and lowered the ruler, a frown on his face.

Whether or not Garfield was a vicious cat, as a cartoon character he was unlikely to take life and attack a police officer.

Frank picked up the fluffy toy, sank down on the carpet, leaned against the wall and looked at the smiling figure. There was a spring attached to its underside and a note loosely attached to its neck.

"Sorry Mr Summers, hope you didn't get too much of a shock, just wanted to cheer you up. I've left a little sumfing in your drawer, hopes you enjoy it like.

Greatest respect

Anonymous

PS

The white rose is fer Mrs Inspector"

Frank chuckled. He chuckled some more, louder. Then he laughed out loud. Hysterically. His heart was still pounding as the tears began coursing down his cheeks, his eyes closed. A mental gasket which had long being preparing itself for the occasion had blown.

'Sergeant Summers? Are you okay?'

He opened his eyes to find an unfamiliar woman police constable bending over him. She had presumably been interrupted while on her way to get dressed in the women's locker room, a leather jacket and motorbike helmet in her hands, red hair loose, her shirt a regulation issue of white with black police epaulets, her legs and feet covered in bikers' boots and leather trousers.

'Fine,' he gasped, trying to get to his feet. 'Just fine.'

'You're bleeding,' she pointed out, dropping her jacket and helmet and helping him to his desk.

'Am I?' he asked, still chuckling. 'What a shame.'

'I'll get the first-aid kit,' the constable said. 'And I'll call an ambulance. You've taken a bad knock on the head.'

'I'm fine, I'm fine,' he insisted mildly.

But she had already left.

He looked at the furry toy and read the note again, chuckling. He looked into the open desk drawer. In it was a bottle. A large bottle of Glenlivet. He took it out and sat there, Garfield in one hand and the Glenlivet in the other.

'Victor, me old mucker, how did you manage to get in here this time, eh?' he asked himself in a low voice. He looked back into the drawer and took out a white rose with a short string silk white tape tied on, a card attached bearing the address "Mrs Inspector".

The woman police constable paused as she re-entered his office, a first-aid kit in one hand, a bowl of warm water in the other.

She was new to the station. But even an old hand would be forgiven for thinking certain things upon finding a detective sergeant sitting at his desk, playing cards spread out on his desk, blood colouring the back of his collar, a fluffy toy in one hand and a rather large bottle of whisky in the other.

And, for some reason, a white rose. She had heard about this Sergeant Summers. From all accounts the whisky should have been a surprise, but she had known secret drinkers before, their days dedicated to the job, their nights blotted out by booze. Sooner or later that extended to a breakfast nip to keep them going. Before long they couldn't survive without constant replenishment. Falling-over juice, as it was called, which probably explained his condition.

'I'll clean up your head,' she said, trying not to make it too obvious that she was inhaling more deeply than would be normal, sniffing for the smell of booze on his breath.

'I'm fine,' Frank replied absent-mindedly as he considered the fluffy toy.

'No you are not, Sergeant Summers,' she insisted, slightly puzzled that there was no whiff of an early-morning toddy and the fact that the bottle was still sealed. 'Blood is pouring down your neck. Apart from anything else your suit will be ruined. Here, let me help you take your jacket off.'

'You're new, aren't you,' Frank asked rhetorically. 'So I'll forgive you for not knowing that when I say I'm fine it means I am not to be bothered by motherly little constables wanting to practise their first-aid skills on me. Got it?'

He rubbed his neck, wincing at a sudden pain. He had to admit that it did feel a little sticky, probably from sweat from the sudden exertions of earlier.

He looked at his hand.

'Bloody hell!' he exclaimed softly.

His hand was coated in what could only be his own blood.

'Precisely, Sergeant Summers, bloody. From a mark on the edge of the radiator I'd guess that that's what did the damage.

Now I am going to help you stand up and take off your jacket. Then you are going to sit down while I clean and bandage your head and neck. And if you sit quietly like a good little boy I will be gentle with you. Otherwise you will pay for that crack about me being motherly. You'll have the second part of the bloody hell right. Got it?'

With his head still befuddled by the bang it had received Frank found it difficult to argue against this. He would have to have his suit jacket dry cleaned as it was, and if he continued bleeding all over it as he appeared to be doing it could be too late to clean it properly, and he couldn't really afford a new suit just because the old one had a few specks of blood on it. Or a couple of gallons, if the feel of his neck was anything to go by.

He put the bottle and the toy on his desk and meekly surrendered to her ministrations, letting her take off his jacket and loosen his tie before sitting down again.

'Let me guess,' he said, 'your name is Florence. I shall call you Flo for short.'

'Very funny, Sergeant Summers. For your information Florence Nightingale was not a ministering angel. She was a hard-boiled old harpie, and strict with it. She would probably have amputated your head, thinking it a nuisance and surplus to requirements, which, from your behaviour would might well be an accurate assessment.'

'Ow!' he exclaimed as she began to clean the cut at the back of his neck.

'Sorry, it's going to hurt a little,' she said gently. 'It won't be for long.'

'That's okay, I'm used to pain.'

'No, you aren't. Here, hold onto Garfield.'

Obediently he accepted the fluffy toy and held it to his chest. He sat there dazed, thinking of how totally incompetent Victor Brown was in everything, including a practical joke. The poor sod could get into almost anywhere by simple disguise, but once there, blew whatever he was attempting, totally. The only thing he was good at was legitimate business, which was a pity, because he had tried so hard to be a decent criminal.

Good old Vic Brown, eh.

Gertie had prepared long and hard for the first day of her incarnation as a serious, non-giggling, police detective. The optician had accepted her story of needing plain glasses for an audition as the part of a serious and high-minded young woman. He had immediately taken out a thick, black pair of frames, assuring her that they would "make even a pretty girl like you look dowdy".

That was not quite what Gertie had in mind.

Not as such.

Instead she chose a pair similar to ones she had seen a newsreader wearing on television, narrow, rectangular ones with a slightly thicker than normal frame. Had she needed to wear glasses they might have been useful. Instead she seemed to be looking at a world divided into two, that within the frames, and a more confusing one outside.

To go with the glasses she had put her hair into a severe bun. Added to that was the strictest skirt-suit she could find. If Frank wanted severeness and strictness, she would be the most severe and strict amongst the severe and strict.

She had turned herself into the nightmare of any primary

school child.

Thus it was that she was most surprised to walk into their office – especially early, to further prove her dedication to duty – to find Frank Summers sitting in his chair, jacket off, tie loose, clutching a fluffy toy to his chest, while some attractive looking woman police constable – tart! – gently massaged his neck, or so it seemed.

As for the large bottle of whisky on his desk ...

'What the hell is going on?' she asked, struggling to retain a stern voice amidst her amazement.

'Hello Gertie,' Frank said in an easygoing voice. 'I gave my head a little bump and caught my neck on the radiator. Flo here is just cleaning it up in case I dirty the carpet.'

'A bit more than a little bump,' noted the woman constable. 'And your neck is going to need stitches. The ambulance will be here soon.'

'I don't need an ambulance,' protested Frank. 'I can drive to the hospital if it really needs stitches.'

'I'll take over,' Gertie said firmly, dropping her handbag on her desk.

'How up to date is your first-aid?' asked the other woman mildly. 'I used to be a nurse. I know what I'm doing.'

'Be a love, Gerts,' Frank said. 'Get me a cup of coffee. I haven't even had a chance to have one yet.'

Gertie was tempted to protest, but she knew that the nurse-woman was obviously better qualified to attend to Frank's injury – she knew that her own first-aid skills were limited, to put it politely – and being Frank's coffee carrier was at least something.

And that was the first time in months he had called her "Gerts" and "love".

'Who's the harridan?' asked Flo as Gertie left, sotto voce but deliberately designed to reach Gertie's ears.

'That's Gertie. She's no harridan,' Frank replied.

'Mmmm,' Flo said disbelievingly. 'So, while I'm cleaning this up, care to tell me what happened?'

Frank explained, relating how he had been taken completely by surprise by what he had thought was a vicious and murderous feline.

'Someone in the office playing practical tricks on you?' she asked when his recitation was completed. 'People forget how dangerous they can be. You could have been seriously injured. You might well have concussion. I hope the Inspector finds out who did this and gives them a severe warning, at least a severe warning.'

'Oh, I know exactly who did it,' Frank said, showing her the note. 'One Victor Brown, the most incompetent Cockney tea-leaf to hit town. He was just trying to cheer me up, as he puts it. He means well.'

'I'll arrest him for you, if you like. I can be pretty terrifying when I want to be. He won't try that sort of thing again, not after I've had a go at him.'

'No, it's okay, I'll deal with him.'

'So why was he trying to cheer you up? Something bad happen?'

'You could say that. Someone shot me in the head, almost killed me. I suppose I've been a little moody over the past few months.'

'That explains the quiff of white hair and this scar then. Yes, I would imagine that could be a bit of a downer. Still, at least your hair covers it. Something to be grateful for. Unless you like having a rugged scar to show the world.'

'No, I can't say I've ever fancied the rugged-scar look.'

'In that case you will definitely need stitches,' she said, placing the bowl of now-pink water on his desk.

Frank leaned forward, collected the cards and held out the pack to her.

'Pick a card,' he said.

'A card?'

'Any card.'

Reluctantly she took one of the cards and turned it face up. The joker.

'You win. I suppose that means I will have to have stitches then.'

The look on her face suggested that she might be thinking that the injury to his head might be worse than she initially suspected.

'What's this I hear about you trying to kill yourself, Frank?' asked a voice at the door. Frank looked up to find desk Sergeant Eric Johns in the doorway, two green-clad paramedics behind him.

'Somebody played a practical joke on me,' Frank explained. 'I fell over and hit my head, more or less.'

An alarmed look passed over Eric Johns' face.

'It wasn't me, Frank, whoever it was, it wasn't me, I swear it.'

Eric Johns had been the target of Frank's revenge once. He had no wish to repeat the experience.

'Don't worry, I know it wasn't you, Eric. I know who did this.'

The Blue Bliss incident, he thought to himself, was another matter. Eric Johns' name had floated around far too close to that little question. If he was involved in that he had every right to be worried. He wouldn't know what had hit him.

'Need to get the wheelchair, I reckon,' the one paramedic muttered to the other.

'I do not need a wheelchair,' Frank said firmly, standing up to prove the point, undermining it slightly by staggering.

'Alright, alright, mate, no need to get shirty,' the paramedic muttered.

'Constable Nightingale, you take a car and follow Sergeant Summers. You can bring him back afterwards,' Eric Johns ordered. Frank turned to her, a look of pleased surprise on his face.

'Constable Nightingale?' he asked. 'Tell me it's not true.'

She shrugged.

'Why do you think I originally became a nurse?' she asked. 'With a surname like that you can hardly avoid it. Even though I was never cut out for the job.'

'No offence, mate,' said the second paramedic, 'but we ain't got all day.'

Frank took the hint and followed them out of the office, Officer Nightingale bringing up the rear, his jacket in her hand.

Eric Johns watched them go, a thoughtful look on his face. He was still standing there when Gertie returned.

'Where's Frank?' she asked, irritated. She had taken longer

than expected, having had to pause to mop up the first coffee which she had spilt after tripping on a step, those bloody glasses obscuring her vision.

'Gone off to have his head seen to,' Eric replied.

'About bloody time,' Gertie commented and sank moodily into her chair.

Eric nodded, a little smile on his face. He left the office without commenting on Gertie's indiscipline in not using Frank's rank while on duty. He was preoccupied with the thought that, for the first time in months Frank had almost smiled. And he was obviously taken by the new Constable Nightingale.

Which was a good and bad thing. The entire station knew by this time that Frank was reserved for the Inspector, Gertie and Doctor Pleadle. Feathers would begin to fly shortly. Eric Johns enjoyed watching feathers fly, so long as he was well outside of the hen coop.

'And what exactly are you smiling at, Sergeant Johns?' asked an irritable Inspector Frieda Garold as he walked out of Frank's office.

'Nothing, ma'am,' Eric Johns replied, recognising a good moment not to be the subject of the Inspector's interest.

Frieda glared at him and swept into Frank's office. Eric Johns decided he might as well stay in earshot, though not in eyeshot.

'Where's Frank?' he heard her asking Gertie as he stood quietly in the corridor, eavesdropping.

'He's gone to hospital. He had a bang on his head.'

'Oh my god! Is it bad?'

'Worse than bad. Some new tart was looking after him when I got here. Constable Nightingale.'

There was a pause.

'Are you sure?'

'Tallish, biggish boobs, firm, red hair that looks like it's come out of an advert, green-flecked eyes that almost bore into you, cute little freckles, basically every woman's nightmare.'

Another pause.

'I think we're going to have to do something about Constable Nightingale.'

Eric Johns slipped away. He had heard enough. Now he fully intended to watch from deep behind the sidelines. Somewhere safe. If he could find somewhere safe. Iceland might be too close. Patagonia sounded a possibility.

He would have to get an atlas and find out where it was.

1.

The triage nurse at the hospital put Frank at the top of the queue for two reasons. Firstly he did not like uniformed police officers hanging around, they did not have a beneficial effect on people who weren't in the best of health to start off with – and there was something rather menacing about Constable Nightingale, though he could not have said quite what. She had a piercing look in her eyes which guaranteed you a bad time if you got on the wrong side of her, and another look which suggested you already had.

And he hoped that those leather leggings and motorbike boots she was wearing were not a new official type of uniform. They merely adding to the menacing look.

Secondly he recognised in Frank a man who would not have

the patience to wait too long for something he insisted was unnecessary in the first place. The last person they had had like that had amused himself while waiting by taking the brakes off of the trolley beds. This one looked as if he would think of something much worse. He just needed a few stitches which wouldn't take very long. Best to get him seen to and get rid of him.

The elderly doctor who saw Frank recognised the same thing. He took him into his office and stitched the wound at the back of Frank's neck himself, "to keep in practice, just in case there's an emergency and I find I'm a doctor who's forgotten how to sew stitches". Once he had finished attending to the wound he sat down and began writing a note.

'I'm booking you off duty for a few days,' he said as he wrote. 'You will probably be fine, but I don't like the idea of your having another head wound so soon after the first. And, yes, I know that was almost a year ago, but it's still too soon. Any dizzy spells, any feeling faint, any strange aches and pains, nausea, that sort of thing, and you get back here right away and we'll run some serious tests on you. Don't try to be macho, life is short enough as it is.' He looked up. 'Still suffering from nightmares?' he asked.

'Not really,' said Frank, surprised that the doctor knew, though not surprised enough to confess how he was preventing the nightmares. 'How did you know?'

'Wellbury's not a very large town, Sergeant Summers, and a hospital, however large, is invariably small in terms of, if I could put it politely, the spreading of news. Or, as some would term it, gossip.'

Frank nodded as the doctor continued writing his note. The first thing he intended to do when he got out was to dispose of the note in the nearest litter bin.

'And take my advice and cut down on the whisky or brandy or whatever it is you're using as a sleeping pill,' the doctor said without looking up. 'I know you think it's the only thing that keeps you going, but it's a crutch, and an expensive one, both financially and physically. If you're having problems sleeping see your GP, or even come and see me. We have tablets that will help you sleep, and you won't get hooked on them, we'll see to that. We also have psychiatrists, one of whom you should be seeing, but no doubt refused to do so in the entirely mistaken belief that it would somehow be a weakness. We live in a modern world, Sergeant Summers, even policemen go to see psychiatrists these days. And you get all that on the NHS, so it isn't as expensive as that cheap rotgut you're drinking. You've paid for it through your taxes, you might as well get your money's worth.'

Frank sat impassively, determined not to confirm the doctor's suspicions. The doctor looked up again.

'Sergeant Summers, I'm a doctor, I've seen most things. I can recognise the symptoms. No doubt you're managing to conceal it from your colleagues, but I'm afraid you can't fool me. You see,' he said, almost wistfully, 'I've been there myself. You'd be surprised to find out how many doctors do. I forget the brand of whisky, but I'll never forget the taste. Bloody awful it was. And if you're like I was, you're probably wondering, even if only subconsciously, whether you aren't becoming an alcoholic. Don't worry about that. You aren't. I still enjoy a good glass of wine, or whisky, from time to time. My wife was the one who saw me through it, and she takes care I don't fall into that little trap again. You're a young man with a good future ahead of you. My personal advice would be to find a woman who will look after you. Get married if you want. Get a fussy house cleaner who nags you, if you prefer being single.'

Frank remained silent. He was getting a little irritated with people happy to dispense their own advice about how he should live. He didn't need it.

The doctor finished writing the note, folded it, put it in an envelope and sealed it.

Makes it easier to dispose of, thought Frank.

'No driving for a few days, Sergeant Summers,' the doctor continued, tapping the envelope on his desk to emphasize the point. 'If there is any damage which my unfortunately all too brief examination has failed to discover, you don't want to find out at sixty miles an hour. Understood?'

Frank nodded. Yes, doctor, no doctor, three bags full, doctor. Just give me the envelope and I will treat it with all the respect it deserves.

'Good,' said the doctor.

Then he stood up, opened the door and called to a waiting Constable Nightingale. He handed her the envelope.

'Give that to Inspector Garold,' he said. 'I've booked Sergeant Summers off for a few days. He seems to think I would be silly enough to give it to him so that he could drop it in the nearest litter bin. But then he doesn't appear to have taken much notice of anything I've said. I want you to drive him home, and try to impress on him that he must take things very easy for at least two days. Good day, Sergeant Summers. Remember, there are people here to help you when you need it.'

Frank found himself sitting in the passenger seat of the police car before he realised what had happened.

'I'll take that envelope,' he said, holding out his hand.

'No, you won't sir,' came the firm response. 'I'll need directions to take you home.'

'Constable –'

'Directions, please, sir. While I'm babysitting you the people of Wellbury are not getting the attention I should be giving to them.'

Frank gave up and gave her the directions.

'Come up for a few seconds, Flo,' he said when they pulled up outside his flat. 'I need to put on a clean shirt, and then you can drive me to the university.'

'The doctor has booked you off duty, sir,' she replied.

'Now then, Flo, who said anything about duty? It's a very calming place, the university, plenty of quiet walks around it, and sooner or later someone will tell you I'm going out with Doctor Susan Pleadle, and she works there, in the pathology department.'

And sooner or later someone is going to tell you that Susan isn't the only one I'm supposed to be going out with, but that can wait.

He was already out and moving before she could respond. She followed him semi-reluctantly. She was not unusual in being curious enough to see how other people lived, and she had heard enough about this Sergeant Summers to be very curious to see how this man lived.

'Excuse the mess,' he said as he opened the door to his flat. 'I really should get a cleaner in. I tend to spend most of my spare time outdoors, fishing.'

A wooden fishing rod, slouch hat and battered canvas bag in the hallway confirmed these words. Wooden, she noted. She knew little about fishing, but she suspected that wooden fishing rods would be unusual in this era of modern plastics.

She also knew that being invited into a man's flat was almost invariably the prelude to something else. And if Sergeant Frank Summers, who was, from what she had heard, the hero of this one-horse town, thought he could take advantage of her, he had a pretty big lesson coming to him.

'Go through to the lounge, Flo, or make yourself something in the kitchen, tea and coffee are in the cupboard,' Frank said. 'I won't be long.'

She wandered into the lounge.

'There are two things I think you should know about me, sir,' she called out, surreptitiously lifting a sheet which turned out to be covering an electric piano.

'I'm sure there are a hundred fascinating things about you, Flo,' he called back.

She pursed her lips, wondering if that had been a chat-up line or a simple acknowledgement that even the most apparently humdrum human life hid a history. She was also wondering why the piano was covered. Covered, not temporarily, as the dust showed, but as if it were something he could neither look upon nor part with.

Now why was that?

'Firstly, I prefer being addressed by my rank,' she called, carefully replacing the sheet, and turning her attention to the myriad of books he seemed to have accrued. 'My name is Constable Nightingale, not Flo. Secondly, I am gay.'

That was something she would have preferred not to have to

mention, but this Sergeant Summers needed to be put straight from the word go.

'I'm feeling pretty cheerful myself, for a change,' Frank called back.

She frowned.

'Extremely amusing, sir,' she replied, noting that the bookshelves and books could do with a good dusting. 'Or it was the first hundred times I heard it. What I am pointing out is that the sight of a half-dressed man wandering around his flat does nothing for me. And, no, I am not a lesbian just because some man hasn't done it properly to me. Please do not make assumptions about me based on a stereotype.'

'Who, precisely,' asked Frank, appearing in the lounge doorway dressed in trainers, chinos, an open-necked polo shirt and a light jersey, 'is making assumptions about whom?'

The sight of a fully clad Frank, whom she had presumed was about to walk into the lounge to parade his bare torso as most men in her experience were wont to do, stumped her.

Even worse, she had to admit that the casually clad man, with his hair sticking out in all directions after putting the jersey on, that white quiff which spoke of his tragedy, was handsome enough to attract many a woman. She herself had to resist the urge to smooth his hair down, and she didn't even like men, or at least not in that way. If it wasn't for the fact that his face was too thin from not eating properly he might have looked like an overgrown boy. From what she had heard at the station that was exactly what he had been until his accident.

'Let's get one or two points clear,' Frank said, his eyes piercing. 'Okay, I understand you don't want to be called Flo.

What's your real name?'

'Samantha,' she replied after a pause, hating herself for surrendering to this bastard.

'Right, I'll call you Sam. If you don't like it, let me know. But. Allow me to give you some good advice. I don't know where you've worked before, but Wellbury is different. For a start you will get a nickname. Everybody does. Gertie is Gertie because she giggles – in fact her real name is Samantha, strangely enough. Frieda – Inspector Garold – is Fabulous or Frigid, depending on whether you're getting a bollocking or not. The point is, you will get a nickname in the nick. If you want it to be a nasty one, carry on being a stuck up little bitch with a chip on your shoulder. So, you're a lesbian. So what? You will find that we in Wellbury treat a person as we find them, not, as you point out, as a stereotype. You will get some stick, as all new officers do. So did I, and I came here as a sergeant. The bed you end up lying in will be of your own making. Don't blame anyone else. Got it?'

'Yes, sir,' came the reply in a frigid voice.

'And knock off that sir stuff. It's Sarge when we're on duty, Frank when we're off. Got it?'

'Yes, sir.'

He rested his gimlet eyes on hers.

'If you can call me Sam, I can call you sir, sir,' she pointed out.

Frank nodded slowly.

'Okay,' he said. He went into the passage to get his leather jacket. 'Want to know some of my nicknames?' he asked.

A rhetorical question met a rhetorical silence.

'Disappointment Dan at first,' he said. 'That was because I went through a period when it seemed I had to cancel every date I had because of the job. Then it became Psycho after I had to teach Eric Johns a little lesson in respect – a bit over the top, I thought, but you can't decide these matters yourself. Then someone took a photograph of me while I was being hit over the head with a box of breakfast cornflakes or something, and it became Cereal Psycho.

'And what is it now?' she asked as she followed him to the front door, unable to conceal her curiosity.

He paused suddenly, making her bump into him.

'Sad, self-pitying git, I would imagine,' he said softly, unaware of her touch. 'But that is about to change. I've spent too long in the rain.'

Had she been of a musical bent she might have caught the reference to rain. As it was she was angry with this Sergeant Summers. Firstly he had dared give her a lecture on how to behave, typical ignorant and arrogant male!

And there was something else, something far worse. She was a lesbian, yes, but she knew she was attractive to men. Yet Sergeant Summers had not reacted at all when she had bumped into him, her breasts pressed against his back. It was as if she didn't exist.

It wasn't logical.

But Sir would pay for that insult.

If he thought a silly springing Garfield was a practical joke he would soon discover something far worse. Samantha Nightingale would make very sure of that.

The man with the white quiff in his hair walked to the car unaware that a mind behind him was already going through various permutations of lessons to be taught and how those lessons would be applied.

Frank Summers strolled along the sunlit university corridor, having been dropped off by an obviously irate Sam Nightingale. She had decided she would not speak to him. He, to add insult to injury, did not give her a chance to not speak to him, appearing to be lost in his own thoughts. Secretly she wished she had not not been speaking to him. Then she could have asked him what he was thinking.

But she wasn't, so she couldn't.

Even had she been able to, she would have found that he was not prepared to share his thoughts with anyone, and definitely not with her, a new officer and unknown quantity. Someone had set up the practical joke at the Blue Bliss the previous day, and a reasonably sophisticated job it had been. His own suspicions lay firmly with members of Wellbury police force.

Unless, of course, it was connected to this joker business.

But that was unlikely.

It was the type of practical joke that would probably have required the participation of two, possibly three or more, active members. Until he knew who those members were he could not trust any of them, and he certainly could not trust Constable Nightingale to keep her mouth shut. She might be the very soul of discretion, but until he knew that for certain he was going to use her for a different purpose.

Phil Walthers had suggested the joke was a prank by university students during rag week. Well, Constable Nightingale was going to be a carrier pigeon taking the news that Frank Summers had gone to the university for some reason or other. Let the perpetrators believe that he was on a wild goose chase. After he was finished with the smokescreen of the visit he was going to disappear from their radars for a couple of days, popping up again when he knew who the culprits were.

And how they were going to pay for insulting his intelligence.

And calling him Frankie. That was way beyond the pale. Wars had been started over less.

Strolling down the corridor reminded of his own days at university. How he missed those days. Life had been so simple. You woke up late, either trying to remember what had happened the night before or trying to remember the name of the girl you woke up with. A good wake-up was when you remembered her name and she remembered yours. That was almost a relationship.

Then you had a cup of coffee and a leisurely shower, before strolling down to Italian Toni's for a full fried breakfast. Toni was an old man who claimed to have been a prisoner of war captured in the desert by the British during World War II and brought to Britain to be held in a POW camp, who had stayed on to open what might charitably have been called a restaurant. The precise arithmetic in the question of how long ago the war had been, vis-à-vis Toni's advanced years of at least forty were either ignored or not thought of.

Toni understood that students had a duty to a different life style from that of other, normal human beings, for those prepared to concede that student were actually human. Breakfast at noon he understood perfectly.

Then, after breakfast, an industrious student could, if they so wished, or needed somewhere quiet for a nap, attend a few lectures. After such strenuous activity the evening called for a reviving pint, prior to vociferous debate, according to which course they were on, and what they could remember. Frank especially liked taking on clean cut students who had attended every lecture, read every proposed, enlightening book and journal, with his meagre understanding of whatever topic arose. Normally he would lose, but it had been fun trying. It had also taught him the technique of letting the other person talk himself into a corner, a very useful technique for a police officer.

And every so often there was the unfortunate interruption of having to cram for an exam.

"You have a fine brain, Frank, but you're wasting it."

Who had said that to him? A fellow student in bed one night, when he was more interested in her physiognomy than issues of the intellect? Possibly even a lecturer who had taken more than an academic interest in him?

Had he followed that advice he might well be – undoubtedly would be – an inspector by now, if not Chief Inspector. After all, he had taken the exams, and passed, much to the dismay of his then Inspector. But, just as the case at university, his marks tended to indicate that the examiner had picked up on the fact that he was quietly taking the mickey out of much of what he was expected to write, which was probably why he had yet to be offered the rank.

Oh, callow youth!

But he could not regret it. Yes, they had been, in retrospect, wasted years, to a point. But they had been fun, and, as his own personal lodestar, Epicurus, might have said, there's nowt wrong with a bit of fun.

Had old Epi spoken with a Northern accent, that is.

Different times, of course.

These days students hardly drank at all. They were too busy fighting the rat-race from an early age. Eager parents pushed their offspring into so-called education as soon as possible, forgetting George Bernard Shaw's caution: "I spent ten years at school, and then went to find myself an education".

Or something like that.

'Excuse me, sir, I wonder if you could give us a hand?'

He felt sorry for modern students. Too much pressure to perform. Get good results so that they might get a "good" career. Automatons, all, in this marvellous new world. Trained to parrot back what they had learned, not trained to think or have fun. Indoctrinated to believe that quality of life was directly related to the amount of money in their pay check at the end of the month, which it rarely was.

Pounded by the barrage of politicians, newspapers and television determined to raise hysteria over all the ills in life, but unable to celebrate the joys of living.

'Sorry, sir, but it's important. We have to get this assignment in by five o'clock this afternoon, and we're a little behind.'

Frank paused in his daydreaming. A young man, hardly more than a boy, was holding a piece of string against the wall next to him. About thirty yards away, at the end of the corridor, a carbon copy of the young boy, albeit a young girl, was holding the other end of the string, the middle of which hang limply on the floor.

'We have to measure it, you see,' said the boy earnestly. 'Only Rach is supposed to be taking down the measurements, only she can't do that while she's holding the other end. You couldn't hold this here, could you? Right here, where the mark is, only it has to be really tight, otherwise our measurements could be out, and that would mean a fail.'

'Against the mark?' asked Frank, taking the end of string.

'Yes, thank you, sir, just there. We really appreciate it. I'll take the other end while Rach takes the measurements.'

Frank waited until the twins disappeared round the end of the corridor, out of sight. Then he began slowly walking towards the corner they had just turned, rolling the string up carefully as he went, making sure that it remained taut, with no sudden movements to suggest that he was anywhere else but in his appointed place.

As idiot. Standing there holding a piece of string while the twins tied the other end to a doorknob and disappeared, or, even better, got some other idiot to hold the other end.

'The old string trick,' noted a disapproving voice beside him.

He gave the voice a quick sideways glance, his concentration focused on the string. Female, slim, severely dressed in a mannish suit, short hair so short it was almost cropped, attractive enough in a hard sort of a way, late thirties, early forties, the only concession to femininity a small ear-ring in each ear.

'First year students,' he noted as they kept pace. 'They never seem to think that other people might have heard of it.'

'Oh, I don't know. Even people who have seen it done to someone else fall for it.'

They turned the corner. A few yards away the giggling twins were tying their end of the string to a doorknob. Their giggles stopped as a ball of string landed at their feet. They looked up to find Frank holding up his warrant card.

'I am arresting you for interfering in a police investigation,' he said with a poker face. 'You do not have to say anything, but anything you do not say might be taken down and used as evidence against you.'

The laughter on their faces turned suddenly to alarm.

'It was only a joke,' said the boy.

'Yeah, can't you take a joke?' asked the girl.

'I'm Professor Ainke,' the severely dressed woman said, apparently irritated by both the students and the policeman. 'I'm sure playing a practical joke doesn't merit an arrest. A caution, perhaps. A strict caution.'

'I'm Detective Sergeant Summers,' Frank replied. 'And I think that when I take these two down to the station they will be found to have a quantity of Class A drugs on their persons.'

'Drugs?' asked the boy in disbelief. 'We don't have any drugs, we don't use the stuff.'

'Perhaps not, but they will be found on you. You'll only get a warning for interfering with official police business, so we'll up the ante with ten years for the drugs.'

The twins stared at him, aghast.

'You won't get away with that, Sergeant,' severe woman said. 'I'm a witness to what you have just said. I will swear to that in court. Under oath.'

Frank sighed and raised his eyes to the ceiling.

'Just when I had them really going,' he muttered to himself.

'You were joking?' asked the woman.

'What do you think, Professor?' asked Frank, finding the temptation to be extremely sarcastic almost overwhelming.

'I thought that you were a rather stupid policeman prepared

to break the law.'

'Thank you, Professor. Glad to hear that you have such confidence in your local plods.'

He looked at the twins.

'That wasn't funny,' the girl said.

'Can't you take a joke?' asked Frank.

The girl looked at her brother. They both burst into peals of laughter.

'Okay, okay, you got us,' said the girl. 'But we'll get even, just wait!'

'In your dreams.'

He smiled and took the pack of cards from his pocket.

'Pick a card. Any card. Pick the right one and I'll let you off.'

The two cocked their heads and looked suspiciously at the pack.

'Any card,' repeated Frank.

The girl came forward, stretched out a hand and chose a card. She turned it up.

The joker.

'Your lucky day,' noted Frank. 'Go on, bugger off the pair of you. And take your string with you, someone might trip over it.'

'Somewhat childish, Sergeant,' Professor Ainke suggested as the twins raced off down the corridor, throwing one last backward glance at Frank.

'Maturity is often over-rated, in my experience, Professor.'

'Perhaps that explains your rank, Sergeant.'

Hello, thought Frank, you're a bit full of yourself, aren't you?

'Tell me, which faculty are you in?' he asked.

'Psychology, Sergeant. No doubt it is a black box to you, or at most hocus pocus.'

'I could never get the hang of that Freud stuff myself,' commented Frank, noting the woman's automatic defensiveness. 'All about having sex with your mother. Load of rubbish.'

'Yes, well, I suppose I could hardly expect any other reaction from a policeman. Now if you'll excuse me, I have a tutorial to prepare. That's a "lesson" in your language, Sergeant.'

'A "tutorial"? Well, well, there you go. A "tutorial", eh? You university types don't half have some fancy words.' He paused as a thought seemed to strike him. 'Oh, just before you do go, Professor, these practical jokes the students are playing. What sort of rules do they have?'

'Rules, Sergeant? I hardly think there is a committee somewhere meeting to decide on the rules of practical jokes for rag week. By their nature they are anarchic, which is precisely why they should be prohibited. Unfortunately the current Chancellor appears to take what I believe is called a laid-back approach.'

Professor Ainke, Frank decided, was suffering a shortfall in the humour department. He wondered if she had been born that way, or had just practised extremely hard.

'Um, about this humour-failure, Frank,' said one of his voices very quietly. 'Only you know that saying about pots and kettles ...?'

'Everything has rules, Professor,' he said, trying to ignore the voice. 'Unwritten rules. Even unruly university students have rules of how far you can go.'

'I think it's the Sociology faculty you want, Sergeant,' Professor Ainke replied, making it clear that she had little time for that faculty, and was regretting wasting her time with this plod.

Frank nodded.

'I shall hie me to the Sociology department then,' he said. 'Good day, Professor.'

He was rewarded with a curt nod as she continued towards her office. He smiled. It seemed ages since he had last taken the Mickey out of someone of the professor's ilk. He'd forgotten how good it felt.

He turned to follow a sign pointing to his right. "Canteen" it said. When he had been a student, lunch, if it wasn't one of Toni's breakfasts, had often been an overloaded plate of freshly fried, thick cut, golden crispy chips with a generous dollop of tomato sauce to dunk them in. The cheap, cheerful carbohydrate option. And it was now so close to lunchtime as made no difference.

And for the first time in months he felt truly hungry. Starving. Ravenous, even. Coffee deprivation, no doubt. He still hadn't had any coffee.

He followed the signs until he came to the canteen. A good old university canteen. Basic plastic chairs and Formica-topped tables. Easier to clean up after students, many of whom had yet to master basic motor skills in transferring food to mouth, never mind those whose motor skills were so advanced that a bun-fight was an eagerly adopted exercise, and did not involve such clean objects as buns.

He paused at the canteen counter as a student was being served.

'Plate of chips, please,' the young student was saying.

The tomato sauce was in sachets in front of the till. Frank took four.

Now here was his element, he thought, as he turned to look for a table to sit at.

Professor Ainke dropped her heavy handbag on her desk, her face grim. That ignorant policeman, a mere sergeant to add insult, had made her look foolish in front of those two brats.

She, a professor!

She sat down and slammed down the newspaper she was carrying. She looked at the front page of the edition of the Wellbury Herald she had picked up on her way in. The local paper of a small town was a good guide to the mentality of where she had been forced to relocate.

"The Curious Incident of Cleopatra's Clothes," the title of one article read.

She read the short article praising Detective Sergeant Summers' acute intellectual ability to solve a case merely by casting his eyes over a piece of doggerel.

Intellectual? That oaf?

Admittedly he was slim, too much so, perhaps, and there was a certain something about him which some dim-witted women might find attractive, but intellectual?

Don't make me laugh.

She stood up, walked to the window, and looked out onto the part of the university lawns where students sat or lay in the warm May sun.

Students! How she hated them! Useless, ignorant, the males

simply sex machines on two legs, the females simpering little baby carriers. Most of them simply wasting money on courses in Sociology or Media Studies.

But the simple fact was that she would have to pretend to like trying to pass on some of her knowledge to some of these things. It was a necessary evil while she continued her research.

Sergeant Summers was a different matter.

He would be getting his own lesson, and it wasn't one he would like.

Some miles away someone else was reading the same article.

'Sounds like we're up against Sherlock Holmes,' noted Cocky. 'Who wants to play Moriarty?'

'No-one is going to play Moriarty,' Ace replied. 'It's precisely that kind of loose thinking that gets people nicked – I mean caught.'

'Ah, come on, Ace,' said Queenie. 'One more job and we move on. Might as well have a little fun. What say we send this Summers bloke a challenge?'

'Now you're talking, Queenie,' said Cocky. 'Send him the address of our final job in this place.'

'We don't know the address yet,' Ace pointed out, trying to resist the urge to succumb to a final joke.

Ace was well aware that newspaper articles often exaggerated the truth, but this Sergeant Summers sounded as if he was some pompous rural plod who deserved being taken down a peg.

'Well, let's send him the address of somewhere we aren't

going to hit,' suggested Queenie.

Ace hesitated.

'It will have to be somewhere totally unexpected.'

The girl twin saw Frank at the same moment that he saw her. She and her brother had been sitting eating their chips, looking around, not talking to each other. It was the silence not of those disenchanted with each other's conversation, but that of two people close enough not to have to use words.

The girl kicked her brother's leg, and he turned to follow her gaze.

'Mind if I join you?' asked Frank, sitting down next to the girl. He dipped a chip in tomato sauce under their suspicious gazes and sighed with satisfaction at the taste.

'Long time since I had this sort of lunch,' he observed, picking up another chip.

'What's happened to your neck?' asked the girl.

'I fell on a radiator after someone played a practical joke on me,' responded Frank casually.

'I knew it,' said the boy. 'He's here to give us a lecture, Rach. The evils of playing practical jokes. What say we get outta here?'

'I haven't finished my chips,' the girl pointed out, a statement that was obviously secondary to the interest she was showing in the young policeman sitting next to her. 'I'm Rach, by the way,' she said to Frank. 'Short for Rachael. This is my brother, Rich, short for Richard. We're twins, you know.'

'And I'm Frank, Frank Summers,' replied Frank. 'Being a trained detective I spotted immediately that you were twins.

I'm glad the training hasn't proved entirely useless, though I bunked most of the course.'

Rach giggled.

'You didn't!'

Frank grinned.

'Okay, I'm lying, I didn't,' he admitted. 'When you're a university student you can bunk most lectures. On a police course they always do a roll-call first. Sometimes they even wake you up during the middle of a lecture. Damn nuisance. So, tell me, what are you two studying?'

'We're doing English Lit and Journalism,' Rachael said. 'I want to be editor of a newspaper eventually. Rich reckons he'll be happy enough covering war zones. He's a camera fanatic. Say, you must have an interesting job.'

'That's one way of putting things. Though quite often I rather fancy the idea of a nice quiet life, possibly as a postman. But then I'd probably be attacked by dogs and irate householders. Old story, really. There's always greener grass elsewhere.'

'But you really are a copper?' asked Rich, intrigued despite his concern over his sister's obvious attraction to the man with the white quiff in his hair.

'Fraid so,' said Frank, apparently concentrating on the chips in front of him.

'You've got a scar,' Rach said, tentatively touching Frank's hair where the white was, ignoring her supposed interest in her cooling chips.

'You get scars in life,' Frank said, apparently impervious to her touch. 'You just have to learn to live with them.'

The voices in his head had not troubled him for many a

month. They were eager to make up for lost time. Now one said, with total disbelief, "Frank Summers, you are a total hypocrite".

"And she's too young for you", added another.

'What happened?' asked Rich, pushing his plate to one side, leaning forward.

'Someone shot me. In the head. A few millimetres lower and I'd have been pushing up daisies. As it was, I was lucky.'

All of his voices were now awake, eager and willing to point out how he'd spent the last several months in paranoia and self-pity, and was now more than happy to use his accident to blatantly court the admiration of these two youngsters.

Frank felt better that the voices were back. He liked ignoring them.

He sighed in pleasure as he leaned back and pushed an empty plate away from him.

'God, that was good,' he said as Rach tucked her legs underneath her and leaned in towards him.

'Let me guess,' she said, 'you're not married. You don't eat properly, and you drink too much. And you work too hard. Your work is your life. You're sacrificing your health to keep innocent civilians safe.'

Frank considered this for a few moments. It had been incredibly accurate until the bit about "sacrificing your health to keep innocent civilians safe". He had been sacrificing his health because he wanted to run away from life.

'Not quite true, Rachael,' he said, putting his hand on her shoulder paternally. 'But there is something you could help me with.'

'Anything,' said Rachael, snuggling into his arm, alarming her brother.

'These practical jokes,' said Frank, apparently oblivious to the hero-worship in her eyes. 'What are the rules? What can you do and not do?'

'There aren't any rules,' Rachael said.

'Possibly not formal ones,' agreed Frank, 'but unwritten rules. You know, acceptable boundaries.'

'Mostly you can only pull them off on campus or in the halls of residence,' said Rich, determined to receive his fair share of this Sergeant's attention. 'You aren't allowed to target the townies unless they really deserve it.'

'You're staying in residence at the moment?'

'For the moment,' Richard said, making a face. 'We're looking for a place to rent, they just have too many rules there.'

Frank could imagine the sort of place they were thinking of: a large house filled with students of both sexes, kitchen sink overflowing with unwashed crockery, lounge littered with beer cans from the night before, and the aroma of illegal tobacco coating the curtains.

Pretty much like the one he had lived in when he was a student. It had been paradise at the time.

'We got into trouble for leaving an open bag of flour on top of one of the other student's door last week,' Richard confided. 'You know, leave the door slightly open and the bag on top. He complained, the little shit.'

'A real mummy's boy,' Rachael added. 'Cyril, his name is. His mummy and sister have come to buy a flat for him and a couple of his sneak friends.'

'His aunt,' corrected Richard.

'Aunt, mummy, same thing. He's a right little Lord Fauntleroy. He wears a suit and tie. And his little shoes are always polished, just like any good little boy's should be.'

Frank was grateful that he wasn't wearing his usual uniform of smart suit, tie and polished shoes.

'So, did it work?' he asked.

'Did what work?'

'The bag of flour on top of the door?'

The twins grinned.

'Like a dream! You should have seen him, his silly suit covered in white flour.'

'And he moved out a few days later. His auntie didn't want him mixing with the likes of us. Good riddance.'

'But you don't pull anything outside – such as a fish behind the radiator at the Blue Bliss?' asked Frank. Rich grimaced.

'We shouldn't have done that,' he acknowledged. 'It just seemed a good idea at the time. Now they won't let us in whatever happens.'

'It wasn't my idea,' Rachael assured him. 'Rich gets carried away sometimes. I think it's something to do with his hormones. He seems to have so many of the things.'

An ironic remark from someone whose hormones appeared to be getting the better of her.

'So you didn't think of trying out another trick against the Blue Bliss?' Frank asked.

'Such as?' asked Rich.

Frank gave him the benefit of two gimlet eyes which the

Inquisition would have been ecstatic to own.

'Okay, okay,' said Rich. 'No. We gave up on the Blue Bliss. We can't afford to drink there anyway, and it's mostly full of old fogies.'

Frank's mouth twitched. He would have to pass that description on to Eric Johns and Pete Phillips.

'Why are you so interested in the Blue Bliss?' asked Rachael.

'I have my reasons. Tell me, apart from the string trick, what sort of tricks are people playing? What about the pane of glass trick?'

The twins giggled.

'Someone else beat us to that one. They dressed up in overalls and pretended to be carrying this big pane of glass to see whether people would fall for it. It was hilarious! Everyone was walking around them, but the looks on their faces cracked us up. You could see they weren't sure whether there was a pane of glass there or not.'

'And then,' Rach picked up the thread, 'that professor who was with you, the sour-faced old dyke, the next day she sees these two blokes carrying a pane of glass and thinks it's just the same trick. She walked straight into a pane of glass.'

The twins howled in laughter at the memory.

'There she was, sitting on her bum looking totally stunned,' Richard gasped. 'And everyone around was just creasing themselves laughing.'

'And the workmen carrying the pane of glass, one asked her if she was blind or just plain stupid.'

Frank could not resist a chuckle at the thought. No wonder Professor Ainke had been less than impressed at the twins' string trick. If she didn't have a high regard for a police sergeant what might she think of someone employed to carry a pane of glass?

'Pity I missed that,' he said. 'Professor Ainke does not look like someone who has a sense of humour.'

'But you know what was even better,' said Rich enthusiastically, 'the previous day we'd swapped the signs on the loos. She's new here, so she didn't even think when she walked into what she thought was the ladies. And there were two lecturers standing there having a waz!'

Rich leant back, laughing loudly. Rach leaned forward and smoothed Frank's quiff. The toilet trick was not, obviously, as good as the glass giggle.

Frank chuckled and checked his watch.

'Ah, well, I suppose I might as well be off. Much as I'd like to, I can't sit around here the whole day.'

It was certainly true that he would have been quite happy to spend the rest of the day with the twins, doing nothing more than dreaming up practical jokes to play on others, but he had found out what he had come to do, namely that the student pranks were mainly harmless and unsophisticated, certainly not of the planning that had gone in to the abduction of Cleopatra's clothes.

And there was that gnawing feeling that had suddenly occurred to him, the thought he was a little too old to be spending time on such frivolities with seventeen or eighteen year-olds with no more on their minds than having fun and eating chips in the canteen.

Too old?

For a brief moment the ghost of Jean Candour appeared in

front of him, mocking him.

'Ah, I told you, Frank Summers, you must learn to enjoy the life,' she said in a stage French accent.

Jean would have been right at home here. She would have led the twins into all sorts of mischief. Had she ever had the chance to become a university student.

Had she turned up on campus claiming to be a student there was not a single person there who would even think of doubting that she was.

Jean ...

'Are you okay?' asked a voice from somewhere far away.

'Hmm?' He looked next to him and found Rachael looking at him in concern.

'Oh. Yes, yes, just lost in thought there. Right.' He stood up. 'Look after yourselves, you two. Don't do anything I wouldn't.'

He walked away quickly, now eager to get away from the youngsters and the university. And the ghost of Jean Candour.

'Poor bloke,' said Rachael. 'You can see he's still suffering from whatever it was. He needs looking after.'

Her brother looked at her.

'I hope you aren't falling in love, Rach. Remember, we agreed we'd only fall in love if both of us found someone at the same time.'

'Course I'm not falling in love, twit. Anyway, maybe he's got a nice woman police officer at his station who will be just right for you.'

Richard considered this thought. He had a bit of a weakness

for women in uniform. And if Rachael was, as was obvious, falling for this Frank Summers, well, maybe he, Richard, should find out if there was anyone available for him. An older woman, possibly.

Richard was not only at university to get a degree. He also fully intended to make good those gaps in his education which he felt his middle-class upbringing had denied him.

'We still owe him one,' Rachael said thoughtfully.

Richard nodded. If they did nothing Frank Summers might well disappear from their lives as quickly as he had entered them. And he quite liked this Sergeant Summers. And for Rach it was obviously much more than a simple case of liking.

There was an easy way of making sure that Frank Summers did not disappear from view.

As he left Frank's attention was drawn to a couple standing outside the canteen, a not-unattractive, smartly-suited woman in mid-to-late thirties wearing a hat and gloves, accompanied by a teenaged boy wearing a suit with red hair and a red face to match.

'I'll meet you here in one hour, Cyril,' the woman was saying.

'Yes, Aunt Jem.'

'Go on, then, get along with you.'

Cyril entered the canteen with a mixture of emotions on his face, relief to be rid of his aunt and fear at the likely reception within the canteen. Frank felt almost sorry for him.

'You must be one of the lecturers,' the woman said to Frank, giving him a surprisingly engaging smile.

'No, I'm a police officer. I'm just visiting.'

'A police officer just visiting?' the woman said with more than a tinge of approval. 'Just like me, then, I'm also just visiting,' she added. 'My sister-in-law asked me to come here to find a flat for my nephew – the boy in the suit, poor thing. He's led a very cloistered life. His father died when he was young, and his mother is a little too protective. He needs to experience life a bit more. Learn to have some fun.'

Frank nodded. He had known a Cyril at school. The last he had heard was that the boy, or man as he became, was living in a type of hippie-commune in Cyprus which had been raided by their drugs squad. Cyrils tended to go wild as soon as they sniffed the scent of freedom.

'As for myself,' continued the woman, 'I thought it would be a nice excuse to have a little holiday and a bit of a fun myself, away from the husband.'

Her appearance suggested that she was a paid-up member of the Women's Institute, and "a bit of fun" would be the decadence of having two cream scones for tea instead of one, but the arch look in her eyes and the mention of her husband spoke more of double beds than double cream.

'It's a quiet little town, Wellbury,' Frank managed to cough out.

'Oh? You know it well? I thought you said you were just visiting?'

'I meant the university. Well, I hope you enjoy your stay here. If you'll excuse me, I must be off.'

Bloody hell, thought Frank as he made his escape, I'd love to see what sort of flat she chooses for her nephew. Probably some place over a knocking shop.

Cyril certainly wouldn't be wearing that suit for long. He

would undoubtedly soon be wilder than the twins could imagine.

For some reason he found himself humming the tune from "The Loco-motion" as he walked away, "Everybody's doin' a brand new dance now". He began to whistle it as he walked. He hadn't done that in a long time.

Neither twin back in the canteen noticed, as Frank himself had failed to notice, two women sitting at separate tables, women who had been watching them.

The first was Doctor Susan Pleadle. She had not joined Frank at his table, presuming that he was there on official business, and not wanting to risk his ire by interrupting him.

However his attitude had been far from official. That young girl, the one who looked all of about fifteen or sixteen, had been way too obviously fawning over him. What hurt even more was that, right up until he left, he had looked like the care-free Frank Summers of old.

If anyone was going to get Frank Summers back to his old ways it should be Susan Pleadle, not some strip of a first-year university student.

She would have to do something, and quickly.

The other woman was equally displeased with the sight of the Detective Sergeant sitting with those two brats. Professor Ainke couldn't hear them, but she was quite convinced that they had been laughing at her accident with the pane of glass. Two first-year brats and a stupid police sergeant laughing at her, a professor!

Or it could have been the swapping of the signs on the toilets. She had complained most vociferously to the Vice-

Chancellor. The Vice-Chancellor had merely laughed.

Laughed.

At her.

But she, Professor Ainke, was a professor. She had brains. She would devise some subtle plan to show that police sergeant how intellectually inferior he was. If it was practical jokes they wanted the sergeant and those twins would soon discover that she, Professor Ingrid Ainke, was in a league far above them.

Fortunately for himself the target of these thoughts was concentrating on the way forward in investigating The Curious Incident of Cleopatra's Clothes, blissfully unaware that half of Wellbury appeared to be lining up behind him with evil intent upon their minds, some more evil than the others.

Wednesday Afternoon: Gertie nailed

Frank took a bus back in to the Old Town. It meant a wait of half an hour, reminding him that he needed to pick up his car from the station. Except that he would have to do it in such a way that he was not seen, for two reasons. Firstly, disobeying explicit doctor's orders could only get him into trouble. Secondly, he did not want anyone at the station to know his whereabouts.

The half-hour wait had given him time to crystallise his thoughts, sitting alone on the bench, his hands in his pockets, whistling to himself as he watched Wellbury go by. It was the first time in a long while he had done that, just sit and watch with no feeling that he should be doing something or going somewhere.

It was also a reminder of how dire "public" transport had become since it had been privatised. The reason he had only half an hour to wait for a bus was that he had missed the previous one by an hour. As the time came closer for the bus to appear, others joined him in his wait, mainly students and older people. An old woman sat down in the seat next to him, apologising for the fact by blaming her bad back, calling him "dearie".

'Backs get a bit tricky as you get on,' she explained.

At that moment the bus hove into view, and he helped her into it with what seemed like an over-optimistic amount of baggage for someone with a bad back, and the unspoken thought that it wasn't only backs that were somewhat tricky.

He was convinced that the Blue Bliss stunt had emanated from the police station, and Victor Brown's hopeless prank showed that it was a collective operation, however subconsciously. Someone had no doubt said something like "Frank's a bit down in the dumps, why don't we play a few tricks on him to bring him out of it". Someone else would have said, "No, leave the poor bloke alone". But the idea would have spread, and someone had decided to act on it.

Frank could have just ignored it, but there were two reasons he was not going to. Firstly, he felt patronised. He did not need anyone trying to change his life. Secondly, the simplicity of the clue was an insult. And thirdly, he thought, sitting at the back of the bus looking out on a brightly coloured Wellbury while trying to keep the Monty Python Inquisition sketch from his mind, no-one at the station was going to outwit him. He could have any or all of them for breakfast. Fourthly, no-one, but no-one called him Frankie and got away with it.

Few people realised it, but Frank Summers had an intellectual ego large enough for anyone's taste. The thought that someone of the calibre of Pete Phillips or Eric Johns might outwit him, even have the temerity to think they could do so, was not something that Frank could tolerate.

What they did know was that he had a particularly evil – from their point of view – sense of humour, one which had long lain dormant, but, rather than atrophy as Eric Johns may have hoped, had merely awoken refreshed from its slumbers and looking for a victim.

Therein, of course, lay the rub. Eric Johns might just be involved with this Cleopatra nonsense if he was confident that he could get away with it, but he would keep as near to the margins as possible. Pete Phillips could well think it a good idea, but he was a stolid sort of a copper, not the sort to come up with stunts like Cleopatra's clothes. His sense of humour would be more crude and down to earth.

Apart from which he wouldn't be likely to know about Cleopatra and Julius.

No, there was another mind at work here, the brains of the operation. And he had his first suspects firmly in sight. Too many of them. One Inspector Frieda Garold. One Inspector Percy Hanson, Pete Phillips' Inspector and Frieda's competition. One Doctor Susan Pleadle. One Chief Inspector Fishing Man. One Acting Detective Constable Gertie Gregson. Or any combination of the above.

And there were other combinations and possibilities – and questions. How had the original garments being swapped with the clown costume? In collusion with the dry cleaner's owner, Mr Heever? The delivery man? Or were Phil Walthers and Mrs Blower in on it?

There was a fifth reason Frank could not let it go.

He was certain that something else would be coming his way, and he intended to get there before the joker. And he knew he could do it. Given just a modicum of his usual luck he knew he could do it.

Frieda had always said that he was one of the lucky ones, as Napoleon's dictum had it. Now he was going to prove it – if such an unscientific concept could be said to be able of being proven.

How was another question.

He returned to his flat, picked up the blood-stained jacket, and paused as he noticed his telephone blinking, telling him that he had a message waiting.

A message.

Messages could be dangerous. They told you things you'd rather not know, or asked you to do things you'd rather not do.

And then later you would have to simulate surprise and claim you hadn't received the message.

On the other hand ...

After a little thought he tiptoed across to the telephone and pressed the play button.

Why tiptoe?

He didn't want to think about that question.

'Frank? Frieda here. I hope you're taking it easy as per doctor's orders. I don't want to hear that you've been gallivanting around over-tiring yourself. But, Frank, I do need to see you for a debrief about these burglaries. I tell you what, you're not to come to the office. I'll be at the Hangman at six o'clock, we can have a couple of drinkies and I'll drive you home. See you at six, Frank. Byee!'

He looked at the telephone, a puzzled frown on his face. There had been something in Frieda's voice, a certain playfulness, if not coquettishness. It was the last thing he needed.

It had been the day before he was shot that Gertie had blurted out to him the truth, a truth that he had almost wilfully been blind to. Gertie, Frieda and Susan had been sharing him as a sort of part-time boyfriend, which had explained why Frieda and Gertie had often showered him with kisses and hugs not normally expected from work colleagues. At the time of the revelation he had been stunned, unsure of whether he was the luckiest man alive, or whether it was time to head for the hills or the nearest monastery.

The same night he had spent with Jean Candour.

The following day he was in intensive care, and Jean Candour was dead.

Though he did not learn that until he was considered well enough.

Nobody would ever learn about him and Jean.

Nobody would ever get at his heart strings the way the cheeky young actress had. Never again. Emotion was to be forever more an alien to him.

Susan, Frieda and Gertie obviously still had feelings for him. They would just have to get over it and find someone else.

The note in Frieda's voice suggested that she hadn't quite realised that.

He wasn't feeling strong enough to face her in such a mood. Vic Brown's incompetent note had made him laugh for the first time in months. He could feel the steel shield he had wrapped around his emotions weakening. He doubted whether he was up to facing Frieda across "drinkies".

On the other hand this was the precise moment not to run away. This was the time to face up to it and get it over with.

No, he would make Frieda understand that they were work colleagues. No more, no less. She would have to look elsewhere. People who got too close to him got hurt. And he got hurt.

Yes, that was the only way to do it.

He would change his mind.

He would lose himself in his work again.

Tomorrow he would return to work and forget about this

nonsense with the practical jokes. He was letting them get the better of him. There were far more important things for a professional police officer to concern himself with. He would bury himself in work again. Let whoever thought they could outwit him continue to think so. He would ignore it.

For a start there was this Joker Gang. Their nonsense would have to be sorted. The sooner the better. He wasn't going to tolerate such an insult to Wellbury police force.

He should have trusted his first instinct. He wasn't strong enough to face up to Frieda. Not in a totally unexpected way.

'One jacket with blood stains,' said Mrs Heever, manning the counter of the dry cleaners. Nobody, on first seeing the large woman, would ever have suggested the idea that the correct phrase might be "womanning the counter".

"Occupying" was an alternative, when used in the sense of taking over a foreign country.

'You really should have brought it in sooner, Sergeant, it would have made it so much easier. People seem to think we can do miracles weeks after stains have dried into the material. You wouldn't believe some of the things they expect us to be capable of.'

'Will they come out?' Frank asked, trying desperately to ignore the woman's harangue. Trying not to think of the joke Gertie had told him recently: "An Essex girl goes into a dry cleaners with a dress and tells the man on the counter, 'I need to pick this up in ten minutes'. The astounded man says 'Come again?' 'No,' says the Essex girl, 'it's mayonnaise this time.'"

Normally he would have given a wry grin of amusement at

that time, but people who are determined not to be amused will never be amused.

'Oh, yes, we'll get it out for you, Sergeant,' Mrs Heever said. 'It will involve quite a bit of work, but we'll manage, we always do. After all, that's what we do, and we're good at what we do.'

Frank decided against telling her Gertie's joke.

He would almost definitely have ended up trying to explain it.

'When can I pick it up?'

'First thing tomorrow, if you're in a hurry. Saturday, if you aren't, that will be less expensive. I've always said –'

'Saturday will be fine, thanks,' Frank said, turning to leave.

'Here, Sergeant, have you found out who pulled that silly trick?' asked Mrs Heever.

For a moment Frank rather felt that he understood how a fish must feel as the hook suddenly bit.

'No, Mrs Heever,' he said, moving towards the door, determined not to be caught, 'we have more important things to do than chase after pranksters. Especially as no harm was done.'

'No harm? What about our reputation? Mr Heever and I have spent our working lives building up a reputation of trust. You might call it a silly prank, but it isn't so funny when our customers start taking their business elsewhere. Several customers have told me that they hope they won't find that their clothes have turned into clowns' costumes. Very good customers. We can't afford to lose them. And these days business isn't as good as it could be, what with people buying clothes that don't need to be dry cleaned. It's a sad world,

Sergeant, so little style left.'

Frank paused. He rubbed his eyes and groaned inwardly.

'You'll have to make an official complaint,' he said. 'Uniform will check it out.'

'You mean they'll fill out some forms and forget about it, more like. That's what they always do. I had an aunt who was burgled once, she had a lovely porcelain collection, mostly sentimental value, but quite expensive when she bought them, back in the Seventies, and what did they do? Nothing, that's what.'

That, Frank had to concede to himself, was exactly what would happen. It would be a case of file and forget. Perhaps the burglary Mrs Heever mentioned – if her description were accurate – merited more attention, but not a practical joke.

Then again, the lauded aunt's collection had probably consisted in the main of flying ducks on the wall. The burglars had no doubt taken the things away as being an affront to good taste.

'So what is it you want us to do, Mrs Heever?' he asked reluctantly, turning back to her. 'Assuming that we can spare the resources. Assuming that we find out who was behind it. I can't see it ever coming to trial.'

'Well, perhaps not. But you could give them a good talking to. A few words from you and they'd think twice before trying anything on again. You would make sure they did not. You believe in the same things Mr Heever and I do.'

Frank didn't like the way she used the word "you", as if he were some ogre who could, with only words and the look on his face, frighten the miscreants into a terrified apology and a promise not to repeat such tricks.

Yet was not that exactly what he had turned himself into?

And how did he feel about being rated on the same level as Mrs Heever?

Nauseous, to be honest.

He was not going to allow himself to get involved in this silly practical joke.

No, no way.

'Is your delivery driver here?' he heard himself asking, entirely against his own will.

'Alan. He's out the back, washing the van.'

'I'll have a quick word with him. I doubt if he'll be able to tell me anything, but it's worth a shot.'

'If he's got anything to do with it he'll be fired before the day's out,' threatened Mrs Heever. 'He's a slacker as it is. You don't know how difficult it is to get even half-decent staff these days. The stories I could tell you.'

Frank felt some sympathy for Alan. And he did not want to hear the stories Mrs Heever could tell him.

'I'll have a quick word,' he promised, retreating as fast as possible.

Alan was not quite washing the van. He was sitting on a step in the sun, eyes closed, bucket and cleaning accoutrements also enjoying a quiet rest. He shot up at the sound of Frank's voice. No doubt, thought Frank, Mrs Heever had a noisier approach.

You'd hear her moaning voice preceding her by about ten seconds.

'Bleedin 'eck, you almost gave me a heart attack!' the young man said, massaging his chest.

'Sorry about that. My name's Summers, Detective Sergeant Summers. I understand that you delivered Cleopatra's outfit to the Blue Bliss.'

'You're joking, aintcha?'

'Do I look like I'm joking, Mr –?'

'Jackson, Alan Jackson. What I mean is, well, a Detective Sergeant? Asking questions about some poxy trick? I'd thought you lot would have more important things to do.'

An understanding look lit up his eyes.

'Wait a moment, you're the one the note was addressed to, aintcha? That's what it is, personal like.'

'No, Mr Jackson, Mrs Heever asked me to look into it. She's concerned that the business will suffer.'

Well, that was true enough. Now, so long as Alan Jackson denied any knowledge of the event he could say goodbye politely and leave, duty done.

'Ha! Suffers more from having that old battleaxe on the counter. Me, I charms the customers, gives them a smile and a how goes it. Personal attention, like.'

Frank's heart sighed as his brain picked up on the statement.

'I see. And who received this personal attention yesterday?'

'Howja mean?'

'I mean who were you gabbing with yesterday while the back of your van stood open?'

Alan Jackson gave him a horrified look.

'No, that's impossible. I never leave the stuff unattended. More than me job's worth. Anyway, who'd want to nick poxy dry cleaning?'

'Let's consider the options, Mr Jackson. Firstly there's the option that you knew all about this stunt. Or possibly someone even paid you to switch the garments.'

'No way, mister, I mean Sergeant. I'd get the sack for something like that.'

'I'm sure you would. However you aren't likely to get the sack if, say, for just a few seconds, you helped a little old lady across the road, an act of kindness and charity, something which you are well noted for, during which time the van was unattended for long enough for the switch to take place. Unfortunate, but perfectly understandable.'

Alan Jackson considered himself in the role of one whose good nature and kind acts had been taken advantage of. It wasn't easy, but he had a good imagination for the impossible.

'Look, jus say, purely, you know, theeretcly, my attention was, say, jus for a few seconds, diverted, like. The old harpie doesn't need to know about it, does she?'

'Probably not.'

Frank would have preferred to have been able to reply "definitely not", not wishing to have to engage with the loquacious – to put it politely – woman, but training and instinct forced him into the evasive reply.

If there was even the slightest chance that he could avoid it, he would no more speak again to Mrs Heever than he would climb up a tree in a thunderstorm holding a lightning conductor and shouting "Go on then, light up my life."

'Okay, then,' Alan Jackson said in an uneasy voice that suggested he would have preferred a more positive answer. 'I was delivering some stuff to that Italian restaurant in the Old Road, Gino's, okay? Now I had to park short of it, which normally don't matter, cause I can make the three trips and still keep an eye on the van. Know what I mean?'

'It takes three trips to deliver the, er stuff?'

'That's right. Can't take it all at once, it creases the stuff.'

'And yesterday something happened.'

'Well, there's this bird, like, good looking, well stacked, know what I mean? And she's dropped some books, so I go to help her, and we got chatting like.'

'You were trying to pick her up.'

'Not xactly. Well, a bit, I mean she was a nice bit of totty, know what I mean? Funny looking glasses, but behind them, a bit of a cracker, know what I mean?'

If you say "Know what I mean" once more I will thump you, Frank thought to himself. He took his wallet out and extracted a photograph which had lain undisturbed for almost a year.

'Recognise any of these?'

Alan Jackson's eyes opened wide.

'Cor, yeah, that's the one, the one on the right. Blimey, you got them quick. Going to arrest her? Is she the one what done it?'

'She could hardly be the one what done it if you were speaking to her the whole time, now can she? No, your identification has helped me eliminate her from our enquiries. Do you recognise either of the others?'

Alan Jackson scrutinised two other women in the photograph.

'Nah, can't says I do. Good lookers, mind you. I'd recognise em if I'd seen em before.'

Frank replaced the photograph in his wallet and put the wallet back into his jacket, trying to hide a smile.

'That's all for the moment, but I might need to speak to you again, Mr Jackson.'

'Yeah, no probs.'

Frank walked away looking forward to the moment he would be able to tell Acting Detective Constable Gertie Gregson that she had been described as "a nice bit of totty" by the young Alan Jackson. The photograph was one Frank had taken of her, Susan and Frieda after they had had lunch at the Grove pub one Sunday a year before.

Happy days.

More important, in the present, was the question of who had been making the switch while Gertie had deliberately distracted Alan Jackson's attention.

Or, suggested one of his voices, more important was the fact that Frank Summers was allowing himself to be led down a path he had intended to avoid.

He told the voice to get lost. He was beginning to enjoy himself, to have a little fun.

Yeah, grumbled the voice to itself, and we all know what happens when you start to have a little fun.

For the first year ever, alongside its more usual offerings, the travelling fair had been given permission to open a beer tent. Previously the official position had been that such an option was not in the interests of Public Order, and, furthermore, there were sufficient public houses within easy reach for anyone wishing to slake their thirst.

Unofficially there was great doubt as to the advisability of allowing the travelling folk and alcohol to mix so freely. Quite a few of them were barred from local pubs after fights had broken out, and those not barred were plainly unwelcome. There was enough trouble with local lager louts, they didn't need the added problem of visiting ones.

There was, moreover, the distinct possibility that the fair folk might make a handsome profit from the venture, depriving, if only for a week, the local landlords of part of their profits.

However the request had been put forward once again, this time with the added point that the annual village fete, held in the Old Town, was permitted a beer tent, and refusing the fair a licence might be considered, by the European High Court, to be somewhat unfair in competitive terms, if not downright discriminatory, should, as it might, things ever come to that unfortunate and unwelcome outcome.

This heavy hint was followed up with the compromise suggestion that the beer tent, should it be permitted, could be run by the landlord who did the same duty during the village fete. Not willing to run the risk of an expensive court case which could well go against them, and with the assurance that any profit would remain in local hands, the Council had reluctantly agreed.

The following year, the precedent having been set, the fair might well decide that one of their own should assume the responsibility of landlord, but that was a decision deferred.

The beer tent had proved to be a success, with tables and benches inside, and outdoor table-benches outside, with the emphasis equally on food as on drink, the landlord discovering that he might be running the beer tent, but the fair people had decided how he should be running it. Plagued parents could bring their excited children for a cold drink and strawberries with cream while their parents repaired their nerves with a pint and a ham-and-egg roll, or even sandwiches made on the spot ranging from smoked salmon to chip-butties. The fair folk had pulled out all the stops to ensure that they would have the local populace's stomachs behind them in the coming years.

A smallish man of indeterminate age sat at one of the picnic benches outside the beer tent, an empty plate, a half-empty pint of Guinness and the Racing Post in front of him, morosely watching the dodgem cars being prepared for their evening opening. Another figure slid onto the bench alongside him.

'Hello, Vic,' Frank said. 'You're not looking too happy.'

'Blimey, Mr Summers,' said Vic Brown, turning in surprise. 'How did you get here? I didn't see you coming.'

'Nobody does unless I want them to. They don't call me Shadow Summers for nothing.'

'No?'

'No, I have to pay them to do it. What's with the long face, Vic?'

'Ah, just thinking what a pity I didn't have any kids wif me. Then I could take them on them dodgem cars. Ain't been in one for years. Great fun it is. But people look at you funny if you go on your own, like you're too old to be doing that sort of thing.'

'An interesting reason for having kids,' Frank noted.

'Ah, I didn't necessarily mean my own kids, Mr Summers. Anyway, mine are all grown up. Just wondered if I could borrow one from somewhere for a few minutes.'

'You should start a business, Vic. Rent-a-kid to go on the dodgems.'

Vic Brown looked as if he were contemplating whether he could get away with this.

'Nah,' he concluded, 'the missus wouldn't let me.'

'Maybe you and I could go on them sometime,' Frank suggested. 'That way we'd both look silly. I rather fancy a go on them myself. It's been ages since I last had a go.' He paused just slightly. 'Oh, thanks for the whisky, by the way.'

'Whisky?' asked Vic Brown innocently.

'You left your fingerprints all over the bottle, Vic. That was careless of you.'

'I did not! I cleaned it three times! There couldn't have been ...'

His voice died as he realised what he had just admitted.

'That wasn't fair, Mr Summers,' he complained.

'Five stitches in my neck, Vic. I fell back and caught the radiator. Could qualify as assault, you know.'

'Oh, 'ell, I'm really sorry, Mr Summers. I didn't think you'd turn an 'air. Onest I didn't.'

'Well, maybe I'll forget about it in exchange for a little information.'

'Ah, now be fair, Mr Summers, you knows I ain't a grass. Anything but that.'

Technically that was correct. However Frank knew that Vic Brown had his own sense of what constituted grassing.

He took a pack of cards from his pocket.

'Let's play high-low, Vic. You pick a lower card than mine

and you get to give me some information.'

Vic Brown stared at the cards, mesmerised. Like observers of a three-card trick he knew he was likely to be fleeced, but could not resist the attraction.

And Mr Summers was honest, wasn't he? After all, he was a copper, wasn't he?

Okay, he was a copper, but he was an honest copper.

'Aces high?' he asked.

'Aces high.'

'Jokers wild? Jokers beat all?'

'Jokers wild.'

Vic Brown tentatively took a card from the centre of the pack. The ace of diamonds.

'Ha!' he exclaimed in triumph.

Frank Summers took a card. He turned it face-up. A joker.

'Bugger!' said Vic Brown. 'You always have all the luck, dontcha, Mr Summers.'

'Speak to me, Vic.'

'I'm not a grass,' insisted Vic Brown, folding his arms, rather in the fashion of a man in a rowing boat refusing to give way to a battleship.

'I'm not asking you to grass on anyone, Vic. I just wondered where you got the idea that I needed cheering up.'

'Ah, well, that's different, innit? Everyone knows you ain't quite been yourself since .. since you had the little accident. We wos sort of concerned for you, you know? No, really, we wos.'

'Let me put it this way, Vic, I think someone said something in the last week that gave you the idea. Someone said something about playing a joke on me to cheer me up.'

Vic Brown nodded a slow agreement.

'Well, I was in the Blue Bliss last week and Sergeant Phillips did mention something of the sort.'

Frank nodded.

'Who else was there?'

'Inspector Hanson, Sergeant Johns, the usual crowd.'

Including one or two of Victor Brown's associates, Frank decided. The Blue Bliss was becoming a neutral watering and feeding hole for both police and the criminal fraternity. It gave him the opportunity to introduce the second thing he wanted to speak to Victor Brown about.

'Leaving that aside, were there any strangers there? Anyone from out of town?'

Vic nodded understanding.

'You mean this Joker Gang? Nah, it was in the members-only bar. They ain't likely to turn up there. Say, you are going to catch that lot, aintcha? Bloody foreigners coming into Wellbury and laughing at us.'

'You haven't heard anything on the grapevine?'

'Not a sausage, Mr Summers, not a sausage. I would have told you if I did.'

That was Vic Brown's definition of not grassing. Outsiders didn't count.

'Those people from the fair, the Bentleys crowd. Anything on them?'

'Lot of talk. But they don't mix with us. I fink it's just rumours, meself. Something goes missing, they automatically blame this lot here. Jus prejudice, that's what it is.'

Frank nodded. That pretty much summed up his own impressions.

'They're getting their information somewhere,' he noted. 'Information on which houses will be left empty while the owners are on holiday. Unfortunately we don't know where.'

'Can't help you there, Mr Summers. I've made me own enquiries, but nobody knows nothing. I tell you something, though, they aren't normal.'

'Normal?'

'Normal crooks. I mean to say, what normal, self-respecting burglar would do something like leaving those silly cards behind? You get in, do the job, and get out as soon as possible.'

'Do you, now?'

'I mean to say,' Vic Brown added hurriedly, 'that's what I heard they do these days. I'm straight, now Mr Summers, legit, I swear on me grandma's grave.'

Frank had never been quite sure how truthful Vic Brown was on that score, but he hadn't been caught doing any wrong since Frank had first arrested him, and even that time he had been let off as he was so useless.

Vic Brown was actually quite successful when he went straight. He just couldn't help but feel that there was something wrong when he didn't feel that there was something not quite legal in his activities. It went against the grain.

'And no-one flogging anything from the burglaries?' Frank asked.

'Nah. They'll do that in the Smoke if they've got any sense.'

"The Smoke" would otherwise be known in atlases and to most people as London, but Vic Brown had spent a lot of time building his image of a cheerful Cockney and wasn't about to let hard work be wasted, not even the bits that weren't quite accurate. Frank was similarly confident that items taken during the robberies would anonymously appear in London or some large city, with little hope of tracing them.

'You let me know if you hear anything,' Frank said, standing up.

'Will do, Mr Summers.' Vic Brown paused and licked his lips. 'Say, Mr Summers, what about double or quits?' he asked, nodding at the cards in Frank's hand.

Vic Brown had the gambling bug. There was nothing to go "double or quits" on, but he couldn't resist the lure of seeing how Lady Luck was favouring him.

Frank held the pack out to him. He took a card from close to the top. The ace of spades.

'Ha! I knew it!' he exclaimed.

Frank took a card.

Another joker.

'Bleeding ell, Mr Summers, I don't believe it! You ain't half got the luck today! But then you always do!'

Frank smiled and took another card. Another joker.

'Keep away from cards, Vic. There are some nasty people out there who cheat. One of the tricks is called playing off the bottom.'

Vic Brown watched him go, gobsmacked. When honest coppers like Mr Summers pulled low-down tricks like that on an honest crook – well, what was the world coming to?

Mind, he was good at it. Vic Brown had seen some good card sharps, and knew what to look for. He hadn't even noticed Sergeant Summers fiddle the deal.

He made a mental note to be extra wary around Mr Summers in future. The police officer had too many nasty tricks up his sleeve.

And that funny sort of a look in his eyes which suggested that he might be a Man on a Mission.

They were dangerous, they were. Them Men on Missions.

Wednesday Evening: The ultimatum

'Frank! Over here,' Frieda called as the dangerous man on a mission entered the Hangman at five to six that evening. 'Come, sit!' she said, patting the place next to her on the couch. 'Your pint is getting lonely waiting for you.'

A pint of real ale, he noticed, irritated. He had meant to have an orange juice, answer any questions she had about the burglaries, and get out and back to his flat where he could relax with a real drink.

Oh, and somewhere along the way make quite plain that theirs could only ever be a professional relationship.

Then again, he hadn't had a pint of real ale for ages. And he really liked real ale.

Just one pint couldn't hurt.

'So who's been a naughty boy, then?' asked Frieda as he chose the path of least resistance, sat down next to her and took a deep pull at the pint.

'Naughty boy?' he asked, wondering why Frieda appeared to be speaking baby-talk.

The ale tasted good. Ages since he had had a decent pint.

'You upset Constable Nightingale this morning. What naughty words did you say to her?'

Frank took another pull.

'Oh, that. I told her that, if she wanted to get along, she'd have to grow up and lose the chip on her shoulder. She's a bit defensive.'

'That wasn't very diplomatic of you, Frank, now was it? Oh, I'd almost forgotten. How is your neck? Sit still, Frank. Come here, sweetie.'

Sweetie?

Sweetie?

He had pulled away from her fingers as she held his neck to check the stitches. Now he sat still as ordered and tried not to react to the gentle caress of her fingers, at the same time trying to work out when and why he had become "Sweetie" and what it might forebode.

Still, the ale was good.

'You really do get yourself into some scrapes, don't you, Frank. I'll bet you were forever coming home from school with torn trousers and muddy jerseys.'

'About these break-ins,' he said, having taken another pull at his pint, a deeper one. This conversation was going somewhere he did not wish to be a fellow traveller.

At least he was pretty sure he didn't want to be a fellow traveller.

He was damn sure he hadn't bought a ticket for the journey.

And if he didn't have a ticket what would he say when the ticket inspector came along to demand he pay up?

'Oh, forget the break-ins, Frank. I looked at your notes after I'd called. I should have realised they would be up to date. But I felt I could do with a drink after work anyway. Just don't let me have too many, you know what I'm like after a few drinkies.'

He did know. Amorous would be an understatement.

What he wasn't sure about was the question of whether it would be welcome or not.

This, he thought, was an excellent time to down his pint and get out before anything happened. The caress of her fingers on his neck had been extremely unwelcome by virtue of how much he had enjoyed it.

'Now there isn't anything else you were working on, is there?' Frieda asked.

'No, everything's in my notes. Listen, Inspector –'

'Call me Frieda, Frank, please, we're off duty. What about that business at the Blue Bliss?'

'Blue Bliss?'

'The Cleopatra thing. It was in the Herald this morning.'

'Was it? A nice little filler for Phil Walthers, I suppose. It was just some silly practical joke. Now –'

'Are you sure, Frank? I thought the note was addressed to you personally.'

'Well, yes, but it was nothing. Now I really should be getting home, the doctor said I had to take things easy for a while, so I'll just finish off this pint –'

'That was good timing,' said another voice, placing a full pint in front of him.

He looked up to find Susan sitting down opposite him, smiling at him. She was wearing tight jeans, a blouse which arguably showed a little too much cleavage, lipstick, long earrings, with her hair loose.

That was bad enough.

It was Gertie who looked the most disturbing.

Frank hadn't really noticed her attire that morning, having been still suffering the effects of the clash between his head and the wall. He now saw clearly the severe skirt-suit, hair in a bun, school-mistress glasses, and no make-up. She had the look of a hanging judge.

'What's going on?' asked Frank, turning to Frieda. She returned the look with the open, innocent eyes of a schoolgirl.

She even fluttered her eyelids at him.

Now that really was unfair. Bloody unfair.

He was outnumbered, outgunned. And sinking fast.

And someone had nicked the lifeboats.

'We've made a decision, Frank,' Gertie said, reinforcing the image of someone about to hand down the longest sentence possible. Death, and beyond.

'A decision?'

'Yes. We've decided that it is extremely unfair of you to be going out with all three of us.'

Frank was gobsmacked. It was the first time in almost a year that he had been gobsmacked. It was a feeling he had previously wondered wasn't a way of life. But for almost an entire year he had avoided that feeling, but now it was back with a vengeance.

The injustice of it all!

'Now wait a moment,' he protested with the little strength he could muster, 'me go out with you? As far as I can recall it was the three of you going out with me, and you didn't even have the courtesy to let me know.'

'The past is irrelevant,' Gertie dismissed his protest. 'What is relevant is the present.'

Frank took a careful pull on the new pint in front of him. He needed to slow down the whirl in his mind. They had caught him completely off balance. He didn't know what was coming, but he was pretty sure he wasn't going to like it.

Gertie took a prim sip of her gin and tonic and carefully

placed the glass back on the table between them.

'So we have decided that it is in the interests of all of us, yourself included, that you make a choice. You can only go out with one of us. It isn't fair on the other two to treat us as if we were toys to be played with whenever you get bored with the others.'

Frank could not believe the gross unfairness of the charge.

'Trifled would be a better word,' Gertie continued before he could say anything. 'Trifled with our emotions.'

'Now look –'

'No, Frank, it has to be done. We each have lives to live, you know. We aren't asking you to make a decision now, of course. But definitely by the end of the week. Sunday at the latest.'

Frank remained silent. This was a new Gertie, one who wasn't going to tolerate any argument from him. He didn't know what had hit him, but he recognised the sound of a few days' grace. A lot of things could happen in a few days.

Such as he might begin to understand half of what was going on. Even a quarter would be better than his current confusion.

And he could get a super-saver ticket on a train leaving Wellbury. Where to wasn't a relevant question.

Hell, never mind super-saver, he'd gladly pay double the normal fare.

'What if I can't decide?' he asked, with the vague feeling that he had just surrendered.

'That,' said Gertie primly, 'is not an option.'

Frank took another sip of his beer to give him time to think.

With unerring accuracy he chose the worst possible option.

'Look, for the moment, why don't you just draw cards,' he suggested, taking the pack from his pocket.

'That,' said Susan in a voice laced with ice, 'is not an option either. It's time you grew up, Frank. This is a decision you can't run away from.'

He was tempted to ask her if she was prepared to bet on it. Instead he finished his second pint without comment. Right at that moment his brain wasn't able to come up with any comment other than "What happened?"

'Frank's tired,' Frieda said, having finished off her own drink. 'I'll drive him home. It's been a long day for him and he needs an early night.'

Frank would have preferred to have left under his own steam, but was grateful for any exit. And alone with Frieda he would only be outnumbered by one.

Several other pub-goers, especially the men, watched with some interest and puzzlement as the young man with the white quiff in his hair received affectionate kisses from two of the women at his table, before being led out by the third. By the hand.

Okay, he looked like he had been through some illness or something, but having three birds looking after him? Three really, really good looking birds? Sometimes life just wasn't fair.

He was probably gay. Yes, that's what it was.

'I've decided on some new rules, Frank,' Frieda said as she drove them away. 'From now on you will not be in the office after five-thirty unless I give you explicit permission to be there. You will also not start work before nine, with the same proviso. And that's when you get back from being booked off, you are still going to take the three days off the doctor ordered you to. Okay?'

'You can hardly expect me to work office hours, not in our job,' he protested feebly.

'No, but I have a responsibility for you, and you have been pushing yourself too hard, much too hard. When I decide that the job requires it, then you can put the extra time in.'

'But –'

'And you will include the extra time on your timesheets. And you will either be paid overtime or take the time off in lieu.'

'I don't appear to have much choice,' he noted after a pause.

'No, you don't.'

They sat in silence for the rest of the journey. Frank was about to get out as she pulled into the pavement next to his flat when she put a hand on his arm.

'It's for the best, Frank, for all of us. I know you've been through a terrible period but it's time to get on with life.'

She stroked his face gently.

'I'd be quite happy to share you with the other two, but it could never really work, could it?' she lied fluently. 'They insisted, and they're probably right, unfortunately. Better to make a choice and get on with it.'

If it really was a choice, he thought, unaware that he had just heard the opening salvo of a battle in which he would be no-man's land.

Not in no-man's land. He would be no man's land himself.

'But while you're making up your mind we can still say good-night properly,' she said, placing a hand on his shoulder and pulling him towards her.

If the kiss that followed was saying good-night properly, Frank wasn't sure he wanted to know the improper version.

Well, maybe ...

'Go on, now, get a good night's rest, Frank. And remember, you're off work tomorrow. I don't want to see you anywhere near the station. Anywhere else is, of course, a different matter. Give me a call if you want to have lunch together.'

Frank gave a shell-shocked nod and wobbled off towards his flat.

As he made his way up the stairs he was reminded of that night nearly a year before when he had felt as exhausted as he did now, the night Gertie had revealed the rota to him in the pub, and he had walked up the same stairs looking forward to a period of peace, a chance to think, only to find Jean Candour sitting on the stairs waiting for him.

And all the rest. The rest of that night.

Who would he want to have waiting for him now? Frieda? Susan? Gertie? None of them? All of them?

The problem was that he knew the answer.

All three of them.

That was precisely why he could not choose one of them.

That was why he was now going to have a few whiskies and forget that the outside world existed. Tomorrow was another day.

Unfortunately the outside world was already waiting for him. A box lay on the floor in front of the door to his flat, addressed to him.

It was a well-known fact that the delivery companies around

Wellbury employed people who had vastly differing approaches on how to handle a parcel delivery when the recipient was not at home. Leaving the parcel with neighbours was the most popular option, followed by leaving a card inviting the recipient to collect it from their local depot which invariably turned out to be half way across town, if not entirely in the next town. Lesser employed was the act of leaving the parcel underneath a pot plant, if there was one, or, in this case, just leaving the object in front of the door in the strange belief that people were far too honest to even think of removing it.

Yet he hadn't ordered anything which might require delivery in a box about a foot-and-a-half by one foot, three inches deep. A box which should have "Suspicious" written all over it.

He went down on his haunches, cocked his head and inspected the parcel without touching it. He took out a pen-torch and played it along the gap between parcel and door.

No wires connecting it with the door.

He stood up, took out his keys, opened the flat door and entered, stepping carefully over the box. He switched on the hall light, went back down on his haunches and inspected the object from the other side.

'You okay, Mr Summers?' asked his next door neighbour, an elderly woman about to take her dog for a walk.

'I'm fine, Mrs Jones. Tell me, did you see who delivered this?'

'No, I didn't. You don't think it – it could be a bomb?'

'I very much doubt if it's a bomb, Mrs Jones, but I have a nasty feeling it's a surprise I'm not going to enjoy.'

'Oh, dear, not those students again. I read about that business at the Blue Bliss. They can do such silly things. I was saying to my friend only this morning what a terrible world it is we're living in today.'

Frank did not listen as she rambled on. Mrs Jones was one of those people who enjoy bemoaning the state of things. She could safely spend hours complaining about how dangerous the modern world was.

'Not to worry, Mrs Jones, it's probably harmless,' Frank said when she paused for breath. 'I don't think this is dangerous, although, come to think of it, it could be a bomb, possibly. You'd best stand to one side while I defuse it.'

'Er, my goodness, is that the time? I'm afraid I must be off Well, do take care, Mr Summers,' the woman said, hurrying away, taking her complaints with her.

You aren't becoming paranoid, Frank Summers, Frank told himself, you are paranoid. If this is another practical joke, and it certainly smells that way, and Gertie is involved, and it certainly seems that way, then she wouldn't resort to anything dangerous.

There comes a time in a man's life when he just has to say "bollocks" and take a chance.

He said "bollocks", picked up the box, closed the front door and took it to the lounge, placing it on the coffee table. Sitting on the couch he took the wrapping off.

A brown cardboard box. No writing, no indication of contents.

He opened the box and groaned.

Inside was another box.

The old box-in-a-box-in-a-box and so on trick. Finally there was nothing but a tiny empty box. To beat the prankster you had to refuse the temptation to carry on opening each box.

Frank merely argued to himself that, as a police officer, he had to explore all avenues. He carried on to the next box, and the next.

This time he was right. The final box was not empty. It contained a note.

"Stop at red, go at green, not so Mr Summers?"

He rubbed his jaw and re-read the note. Then a third time.

He stood up and made himself a drink. A small Glenlivet. He had some left. After all, he could afford to now, he had a large bottle at the office.

Stop at red, go at green? Traffic lights, obviously.

Not so Mr Summers?

A missing comma, and his rank wasn't mentioned.

Why not? Why "Mr"? Why not "Sergeant"?

Gertie would have included the comma, she was forever complaining that her current tutor had an eagle eye for mistakes in punctuation. So would Frieda and Susan, both sticklers for such things in written reports.

Not Vic Brown. If it did have something to do with traffic lights he would have included the address and postal code, plus a map with an arrow pointing out the precise location.

Someone like Pete Phillips?

Possibly.

Phil Walthers?

No, the same missing comma applied equally to the editor of the Herald. Phil Walthers might think of using it as a subterfuge, but his editor's soul would never permit such a heinous crime to be permitted.

Then again, Phil Walthers was a highly intelligent man. It could be a double bluff.

And if it were a double bluff that put Gertie, Frieda and Susan back into the frame.

This joker lot? God knew.

So, he thought, making himself another, stronger drink, ignore who might have sent it. What was it they were saying?

Not bloody much. Something to do with traffic lights, and that was it. What could you do to traffic lights?

Maybe he was taking the message too literally. Stop and go. Maybe that referred to something else.

The Joker Gang? They could have read that ridiculous article in the Herald and decided to have some fun with him. Get your name in the newspaper and you suddenly become a target for all sorts of nonsense.

But, no, that didn't sound like the Joker Gang. They might leave silly calling cards, but everything else they did was professional.

No, try as he could it didn't make sense. All it did was send his mind in circles.

He wished there was someone he could speak to. That was how most of the difficult cases were solved, by a team of people bouncing ideas off of each other. But there was no-one he could trust not to be involved in this.

If he mentioned it to someone behind it they would only use the opportunity to further lead him up the garden path.

If he failed to mention it the perpetrator – or perpetrators –

might wonder if their little box trick had failed to reach its destination, and reveal themselves by asking injudicious questions.

Frank Summers did not have a restful night. The only advantage of being troubled by dreams of traffic lights was that it kept other thoughts at bay.

Thoughts of three women named Susan, Gertie and Frieda.

And a choice he had no wish to make.

Previously he would have laughed that off, knowing that he would get out of it somehow, but this time there seemed no escape.

As the third and strongest whisky went down he began to relax and take a rosier view of things. He had got out of worse scrapes before, hadn't he?

Okay, perhaps not worse, but close.

Okay, perhaps not so close, but not entirely different.

He had to appear to be on the defensive while actually taking the offensive. Ah, yes, definitely, the good old offensive-defensive play, it never failed.

Yes, that was it. The sideways move.

And he was going to have some fun doing it.

Somehow.

By that stage his tiredness and the whisky had combined to befuddle his mind. But he was sure of one thing. He was going to nail the Joker Gang, identify the culprits behind the Curious Incident of Cleopatra's Clothes, and ... well, and something.

When he finally clambered into bed he discovered his dreams had returned.

First Susan appeared, dancing in a clown's suit.

No, it had suddenly turned into a bikini.

No, it was Frieda in a clown's costume.

No, it was Frieda in a bikini.

No, he was ten years old again, and Gertie was leaning over him, wearing her strict and severe outfit.

"Well, come on Frank Summers, you have to choose one. Come on, chop-chop, jump to it!"

And then suddenly it was Vic Brown selling clown's costumes from the back of a dodgem car.

"There you go, Mr Summers, cheap at twice the price, jus look at that quality, won't say where they came from, will we, never look a gift horse in 'is marth, and just think how good you'll look walking up the aisle in one of these. Come on, you know it makes sense. Know what I mean?"

He woke up with a start.

Vic Brown was going to pay for that, he decided as he gradually fell back into a broken sleep, dreaming of churches

Thursday Morning: Second meeting on the riverfront

Frank was awoken by a repeated knocking at his door. He groaned and stretched out a hand for his watch.

Seven-twenty. Blast! He had spent the night dozing off, waking up, dozing off, waking up. Now, just as he was getting some decent sleep someone was at the door, and they weren't taking the hint and going away, not even when he put the pillow over his head and muttered "I'm not here, go away".

The worst of it all was that he didn't have to get up for work. He could have slept until noon.

He finally accepted defeat, got up and put a dressing gown on before answering the persistent knocking.

'Detective Sergeant Summers?' asked a uniformed traffic police officer when he opened the door.

'Yes, I'm Summers,' Frank answered blearily. 'This had better be good, I only managed to fall asleep five minutes ago.

Well, that was what it felt like.

Traffic! the thought suddenly hit him. Traffic only knocked at people's doors first thing in the morning for one reason, and that was invariably bad news. Had Frieda – ?

'What is it? What's wrong? What's happened?'

'Nothing serious, sir, fortunately. We got to the scene before any nasty accident could take place. But we found this note. it appears to be addressed to you, Sergeant.'

Frank took the note.

"Did inspiration light up your life, Sergeant Summers? Ah, well, I don't want to milk it, but perhaps you should mug up on your primary knowledge next time."

'You'd better come in,' Frank said. He led the officer to the kitchen and switched the kettle on. 'So, what's happened?'

'Does the note make sense to you, Sergeant?'

'Not a bit. Not yet. So, come on, out with it, what's happened?'

The traffic officer hesitated before deciding to trust the wild-haired man with a white quiff, wearing a dressing gown, not looking anything like his reputation would suggest.

His flat could definitely do with a woman's touch. Several cleaning ladies, in fact.

'Someone switched the colours on the traffic lights at the end of the road,' he explained. 'They're old-fashioned clip-on filters. Whoever it was simply exchanged the red and green, so it showed green at the top when it should have been red, and vice versa.'

Frank considered this as he made a mug of coffee. He waved the bottle of granulated at the traffic policeman in offer, but the man shook his head.

'No doubt vastly amusing for anyone watching drivers who can't work out whether the green on top means go or the red on the bottom means stop,' Frank noted.

'Not so amusing for anyone who's colour blind, sir. Or someone approaching the lights without noticing the precise colour. People tend to ignore contradictions like that. If the top light is on then it's red for them, and the bottom green, no matter what colour actually shows.'

Frank nodded.

'Good point. Tell me something, why do you call me "sir" one moment and "Sergeant" the next?'

The question had the traffic officer baffled for a few seconds.

'Well, I suppose you seem more like a civilian – wearing a dressing gown like that.'

And one that had an egg stain on the lapel, he could have added.

'Interesting. Hang on for a second.'

Frank retrieved the previous evening's note from the lounge and showed it to the officer.

'That came last night. Apparently whoever it is thinks I should have guessed what they were on about.'

'Some sort of game you're playing with someone, sir?' asked the officer disapprovingly, scanning the note.

'No, it's a game somebody seems to be playing with me, I don't believe I received an invitation to join in. By the way, the name's Frank, Frank Summers, Frank while I'm off-duty. What's yours?'

'Officer Keene, sir. And I know who you are now. You've recovered from the, er –?'

Frank grinned behind his coffee mug.

'Being shot in the head? I don't know if you ever recover properly. But I know that if you call me sir once more I shall feel entitled to thump you one. Do you have a first name, Officer Keene? And I would imagine that surname has haunted you all your life.'

'Yes, er, Frank, it has rather. And my first name is Geoffrey, Geoff for short. Used to get stick about being called Geoffrey as well. Bit of a poncy name, really.'

'I can well imagine. But tell me Geoff, look at those two notes. Anything in them suggest anything to you?'

Geoff Keene studied the two notes.

'They seem to be having a go at you, s–, er, Frank.'

'No doubt about that. But you notice the first calls me Mr Summers, and the second Sergeant Summers.'

Geoff considered the point. There was a reason he had opted for traffic. It was much easier to tell when someone had exceeded the speed limit rather than having to deal with strange notes and people who played around with traffic lights as some form of practical joke.

'Can't say that means anything to me,' he concluded finally.

'Mean anything to you, you being a detective?'

'They were either written by two different people, or one person whose relationship to myself is ambiguous.'

Geoff Keene did not like the sound of that. Ambiguous relationships sounded like a euphemism for something he disliked intensely.

'How do you mean, sir? Er, Frank?'

'Same as you kept swapping from sir to Sergeant. You weren't quite sure how to address me.'

That told Geoff Keene precisely nothing, apart from the vague suggestion that it could have been himself who had written the notes.

'I don't quite follow.'

'Geoff, it doesn't tell us much, really, apart from two things. This person, or these people, know me. At the least they've met me. Otherwise they would be consistent. Secondly, they're unsure of how to address me, if it's one person, or have different attitudes if it's two people. That is quite obvious and plain. The problem is, at the moment it tells us almost nothing.'

It was neither obvious nor plain to Geoff Keene, but he was happy to hear that it told them nothing. He didn't mind not understanding something if it meant nothing.

'So, what are you going to do now?' asked Frank.

'Well, I was hoping I could hand it over to you, er, Frank. Not really traffic's department, this sort of thing.'

'Do me a favour. Take both notes to Inspector Frieda Garold.'

'Can't you do that?'

'I'm booked off duty, Geoff.' He pointed to the stitches at the back of his neck. 'Violent assault by a radiator, plus hitting my head against a brick wall.'

'Blimey, you don't half live a dangerous life.'

'Comes with the job, Geoff. Though I had hoped I'd avoid that sort of thing in Wellbury. Sometimes I think London would be safer.'

He paused as a thought struck him.

'I need to pick up my car. You're on motorbike, aren't you?'

Geoff Keene took less than a second to respond.

'No, sir, I am not giving you a lift, nor are you borrowing my bike. The last time you did that you almost got yourself killed, and I nearly got the blame.'

'You're joking! You mean –'

'Yes, Sergeant Frank Summers, I was the poor bloke you nicked a police traffic motorbike from, and it ain't going to happen again.'

Frank shrugged and grinned conspiratorially.

'Good fun, though, wasn't it?'

'Not from where I was standing. I got a right bollocking for that.'

'Me too,' Frank lied. The bollocking he had received was not for nicking the police motorbike. It had been for inviting Frieda's secretary to his flat for drinks. 'Ah, well, not to worry. You get those notes to Frieda – Inspector Garold. I intend to enjoy a day off.'

Traffic Constable Geoffrey Keene left Frank's flat in a positive state of mind. He could tell the other blokes that he had met Sergeant Summers, the Sergeant Frank Summers, and a real decent bloke he was, even if he were a sergeant. Even told him to call him Frank. And for someone who had almost been killed on a motorbike – his motorbike – and someone who had been shot in the head, you could tell by the look in his eyes that he had laughed it all off. Laughed it off!

And know what? You know them stories about him having it off with his Inspector? I reckon there's more than a bit of truth about that. Know what he called her? Frieda! Okay, realised his mistake quickly, him being as bright as they say he is, but even brainy people make the occasional slip-up.

Cor, he's quite the one, isn't he? Looks, brains and a beautiful bird.

Mind you, the state of his flat. He definitely needed a woman in there. With a duster.

The man with the looks, the brains, the (three) beautiful birds and the lack of a woman bearing a duster stood in his flat and sucked on a cup of coffee.

He didn't know what was going on. He didn't know how to handle the ultimatum from his three beautiful birds. He was pretty sure that this traffic light incident was unlikely to be directly connected to that of the Blue Bliss. But he didn't have anyone he could discuss it with.

He finished the coffee and told himself to stop feeling sorry for himself. Of course he knew someone to speak to.

He had a day off. He was going fishing.

'Have you ever thought of becoming a stuntman?' asked the Chief Inspector, sitting on his stool on the riverbank, watching the sparkling water pass by. 'You'd probably receive fewer injuries. And I'd imagine the pay is better.'

'Not as much fun,' Frank replied, sitting on his stool.

'There's something you wish to discuss?'

Frank gave a brief description of the notes and the incident at the Blue Bliss and the traffic lights. Having come to the decision that he needed someone to talk to he had decided that the Chief Inspector was the most unlikely to be involved with this nonsense.

Which didn't mean he was totally off the list of suspects.

'Sounds like harmless fun,' noted the Chief Inspector. 'Though the traffic lights could have been nasty.'

'Yes. My guess is that whoever thought that up didn't intend any harm, they just didn't think things through.'

'Whereas the Cleopatra one was thought through. No real victims, apart from this Mrs Heever who sounds somewhat of a harridan.'

'I'm pretty sure the tricks were done by different people. They have a different feel to them.'

'People such as Percy.'

'Could be.'

'Or even Frieda. Dr Pleadle. Sergeant Phillips. Your Gertie.'

Frank nodded.

'That's the problem. Knowing who to trust.'

The Chief Inspector smiled.

'And perhaps even me,' he said. 'Want my advice, Frank? Forget about it, lad. They'll get bored and stop eventually. If you treat that sort of nonsense with the contempt it deserves, and they give up, you've won.'

Frank considered this option. It was the intelligent option.

It was the mature option.

In his imagination he could see Jean laughing at him, holding out to him a pipe in one hand and a pair of slippers in the other.

'Would you have just forgotten it, sir?' he asked.

The other man chuckled.

'No, son, not when I was your age,' he admitted. 'I would have found out who the bastards were and given them a good kick up the backside. Though I must admit the way you sorted out Eric Johns not so long ago was a rather more subtle, and possibly more effective approach.'

He chuckled again.

'Eric Johns on the front desk covered in confetti. Aye, I would have paid to see that.'

Frank stood up suddenly and began reeling in his line.

'You're off, lad?'

'Yes, I need to have a look at some primary schools around the area.'

'Primary schools?'

'The second note. "I don't want to milk it, but perhaps you should mug up on your primary knowledge next time". Don't primary schools give out free milk to their pupils?'

'They used to, many years ago. Can't say whether they still do – didn't Maggie put a stop to that? But even if they do, what sort of practical joke can you play with kiddies' milk?'

'God knows. Something they think hilarious. I'll just have to make sure I'm there when they try it. If it isn't too late.'

'Just one thing, Frank,' the Chief Inspector called.

'What's that, sir?'

'When you find out who it is and decide on the punishment, let me be there. I could do with a good laugh.'

'I'll do that, sir,' Frank said, an evil grin on his face.

In her office Frieda drummed her fingers on her desk. The two notes lay in front of her. They worried her. The Blue Bliss thing had been harmless fun. Whoever had swapped the filters on the traffic lights had – hopefully – not realised how dangerous it could have been. And now this latest note which obviously referred to primary schools and milk. Perhaps the perpetrators were planning on adding something to the milk, possibly some normally harmless substance which would make the children blow bubbles, heaven knew what. But then you only needed one child severely allergic to whatever the substance might be, and then it's not quite so funny.

She reached for her telephone.

Then she pulled her hand back.

Frank was off duty. He'd probably gone fishing. There was no need to get him involved.

But the notes were addressed to him.

She picked up the telephone.

Time was ticking away.

And this was business.

And perhaps a little more than business.

Frank returned to his flat determined to drop off his fishing gear and begin checking out local primary schools without delay. He was surprised to note that his telephone was blinking the number three at him. Three messages awaiting his attention. He was perhaps more surprised that he was surprised. He knew three women who would want to have a word with him. At that moment he had no wish to have words with any of them.

He hesitated before pressing the play button. He knew that he could listen to what they had to say and pretend to have missed the messages if he deemed it necessary, but he was caught up in an almost Calvinistic dedication to honesty.

See, he said to himself, one little bullet in the head and the next thing you're afraid of telling teensy-weensy white lies. God knew, he had told some porkies in his time.

The possibility that putting off listening to the messages might also defer a decision he had no wish to take did not occur to him.

On the other hand, one or more of them were almost certainly implicated in this little game of show Frank Summers the finger.

Sod it, he thought, and pressed the play button.

"Hello Frank? It's Susan here," said the sweetest voice since the Sixties. "You know, your Soosie-Woosie? Listen, how do you fancy dinner tomorrow evening, my place? Say about six, we can have one or two drinkies first. See you later. Cuddles, love you, byee, byee."

There was the sound of a kiss as Frank looked at the machine in stunned silence.

Soosie-Woosie?

That was like Ghengis Khan calling himself Diddums.

Well, perhaps an exaggeration, but really ...

The second message began.

"Hello, Sergeant Summers? Constable Gregson here. Sergeant, there are one or two points I need a little advice on. I wonder if we could discuss them at some stage. I'll be busy for the rest of the day, so perhaps we could meet up after I've finished work, say the Sergeants Arms? I will be there at eighteen hundred hours prompt. Er, see you later, Sergeant."

Eh?

Why was Gertie speaking as if she were sitting on something uncomfortable? Something extremely uncomfortable.

And what was all this "Sergeant Summers" business?

Eighteen hundred hours? What happened to good old-fashioned six p.m.?

And then the third message ...

"Frank? It's Frieda. Frank, I'd like to have a word with you about these notes you've received. I know you'll probably think I'm being a silly little fusspot, but I'm worried that this sort of thing could get out of control. That stunt with the lights this morning could have caused a serious accident. Give me a call – we could go out for lunch somewhere, I'll put it through expenses. Let me know if you can make it."

This time Frank openly goggled at the telephone.

"Silly little fusspot"? Had anyone dared to even think of Frieda in such terms she would have made the Valkyries look as if they came from the Girls' Guides.

Bearing sweeties and little cuddly toys.

As for putting lunch through on expenses ... No-one in her section would dare do that any longer, she had made a point of rooting out that sort of thing.

But he could not help but admire her strategy, however much it might put him on the spot. The other two had gone for the evening. Frieda had suggested lunch, knowing that the others would not think of that. Just lunch between two colleagues, very subtle, little pressure.

Like hell.

Why me, Lord? he asked. I'm not Casanova. I'm not a billionaire. I'm not a rock star or film star. I'm hardly the most handsome human on the planet. So why me? What was that I did to seriously miff you off like that?

Look, if it's something to do with a previous life, I can't remember, okay?

In her office Frieda paused while trying to concentrate on a file she was supposed to be reading. She checked the clock. Almost an hour since she had left that message. Frank might still be out. If he had actually been out when she had initially called. Maybe he just didn't want to answer the phone.

Her hand reached out for the phone on her desk. Perhaps just a little reminder? Lunchtime was not far away.

She pulled her hand back.

Perhaps not. Perhaps better not put too much pressure on him.

Then again, this one was for keeps. Frank would just have to bear it for a few days.

In the office she shared with Frank Gertie adjusted her prim glasses and turned a page of a report. Carefully. Seriously.

Professionally.

Even the page which she did not realise was upside down.

It was exactly an hour since she had left the message for Sergeant Summers. A modern police officer would chase up such an issue. On the hour. Even if there was little possibility of an answer.

At least she would hear the sound of his voice, if only recorded.

In her office Susan put down the technical report she had been looking at, having been pretending to be absorbed in it. She checked the clock. Just over an hour. She really shouldn't call again, not so soon. Frank would just get upset if she hounded him.

But, thinking about it, not if she did her little girl bit. He couldn't get angry with her then, could he?

In his flat Frank's telephone rang. Automatically he picked it up.

'Hello, Frank Summers speaking.'

Desk Sergeant Eric Johns and Detective Sergeant Pete Phillips were cloistered together in the canteen, leaning towards each other in what was obviously a private discussion.

'You're joking,' said Pete Phillips.

'No word of a lie, Pete. They've given him an ulti ... ulti ... what's that word again?'

'Ultimatum.'

'That's the one. He has to choose one of them. No ifs nor buts.'

'Blimey, poor bloke.'

Eric Johns nodded agreement. They sat and silently commiserated with Frank for a few moments.

'Which one do you think he'll go for?' asked Pete Phillips.

'Ah, well, that's the thing, see.' Eric Johns looked around to make sure that no one could overhear what he was about to divulge. 'I'm opening a little book on that.'

Pete Phillips nodded at this good idea.

'What odds are you giving?' he whispered.

'Four to one on the Inspector. Two to one on Gertie. Evens on Doctor Pleadle.'

Pete Phillips considered this.

'I think I'll put a fiver on Gertie,' he said.

'Only a fiver?'

'Okay, make it a tenner.'

Eric Johns took the ten pound note slipped quickly across the table, surreptitiously pulled out a notebook and made a note.

'Just keep it under your hat, about the bets,' he said to Pete Phillips. 'Don't let any of the women know. You know what they're like. They'll think it's all romantic and you shouldn't be betting on it. Tacky, like.'

'Good point. Women are funny about that sort of thing.'

'I'll take a tenner on Doctor Pleadle,' whispered a voice at Eric Johns' ear. He turned to find Constable Allison Hardbury holding a ten pound note half concealed in her hand.

'A tenner?'

'She's a dead cert. I don't mind getting ten quid for the obvious.'

Eric Johns made another quick note in his notebook. And a mental one not to pre-judge women.

He smiled to himself. This one would keep him in pint money for at least a month.

'Sergeant Summers? Phil Walthers here.'

'Mr Walthers,' Frank replied neutrally. 'And what can I do for you?'

'Well, I'm not quite sure about this, Sergeant. I've received a letter in the first mail this morning. At the Herald. I think you should take a look at it. It's got your name on it, and it doesn't sound too pleasant.'

Frank paused before replying.

'I'll pop over. I'll be there in about fifteen minutes. I have to make a quick telephone call first.'

In her office Frieda answered her telephone.

'Mrs Blower,' she said in surprise as the voice identified herself.

'Yes, I fully agree. I'm well aware of that.'

'Absolutely.'

'It's an interesting idea. Yes, thinking about it, that might well be worth trying.'

'Pitiful, yes, the more pitiful the better.'

'Thank you for calling, Mrs Blower, I'll keep you up to date on what happens. And, yes, I shall definitely pop in for a drink soon.'

By this stage there was a crowd around the table Eric Johns was sitting at, most of whom peered around warily from time to time in case a senior officer should turn up.

'What if he doesn't make a choice?' asked Detective Inspector Percy Hanson, sitting, by virtue of rank, at the table. He wasn't the senior officer the group were concerned about. The senior officer they were worried about wore pencil skirts with a slit at the back and had very nice legs. They would rather not imagine Percy Hanson so dressed, especially not the idea of his legs in silk stockings.

'He's got until the end of the weekend,' Eric Johns replied. 'So if Monday comes and he hasn't made a choice, all bets are off.'

'Ah, but what if he doesn't make a choice and still goes out with the three of them?' persisted Percy. 'I reckon as how there should be odds on that.'

There were broad murmurs of agreement from the assembled throng.

'Okay, seems fair to me,' Eric Johns said, having mulled it over. 'So long as we all agree that that's what's happened.'

'So, what are the odds on Frank then?' asked Percy, rubbing his hands.

Eric Johns rubbed his chin. Finally he nodded.

'Three to one,' he said with a broad smile.

'I'm in,' Percy said immediately. 'A tenner on Frank.'

'Me too,' Harry Wheatley piped up. 'Put a fiver on Frank for me. No way Sergeant Summers is going to get caught. He's far too brainy to get trapped like that.'

There was a sudden silence.

'What did you say?' Allison Hardbury asked in an icy voice.

Constables Allison Hardbury and Harry Wheatley were engaged. They had recently been tentatively discussing a good time to get married. August, almost definitely.

Now, perhaps not.

'Look, love, I didn't mean it that way ...' Harry tried protesting and moving backwards very quickly at the same time.

Others in the group were also trying to create a physical distance between themselves and a somewhat upset Allison Hardbury.

'Where's my handbag?' she asked in a low growl.

Perhaps more 'infuriated' than 'upset'.

'And what, precisely, is going on here?' asked a voice from the canteen doors, the voice of someone wearing silk stockings and a very bad temper. 'There appears to be no-one on the reception desk. Sergeant Johns, would you care to explain?' asked a thunderous Frieda.

'On me way, ma'am,' Eric Johns mumbled, glad of an excuse to get out.

'Is that the time?' asked Percy Hanson rhetorically, hard on Eric's heels, with Pete Phillips right behind. The others formed a disorderly queue to escape the canteen as fast as possible.

Frieda shook her head and began making her way back to her office.

'Phew, that was close,' Harry Wheatley said, running a finger around his collar. He turned to the last person present. 'Don't you think?' he asked.

'You bastard!' cried Allison Hardbury as she swung her handbag.

'I – gloof!' was Harry's reply, his mouth suddenly full of leather.

'Wellbury police station, Inspector Garold's office,' Frieda's secretary Tricia Leigh said after she had picked up the telephone.

'Trish? It's Frank, Frank Summers. Is Frieda in?'

'She's just popped down to the canteen to sort something out, Frank. I can page her if you want.'

'No, no, don't worry, Trish. Could you pass on a message for me? Tell her, the trattoria on Old Street down from the Sergeants Arms, one o'clock. Got that?'

'Gino's on Old Street, at one o'clock. Got that.'

'Thanks, Trish. See you later.'

Tricia Leigh smiled as she put the phone down. Almost immediately she picked it up again and dialled an internal number.

'Hello, Sergeant Johns? What are the odds on the Inspector at the moment?'

'Four to one,' replied a slightly breathless and extremely surprised Eric Johns, back on duty at the reception desk.

'Four to one? In that case, put me down for twenty pounds.'

'Twenty pounds?' gasped Eric Johns. 'Are you sure, Trish? It's a fair whack on a four-to-one.'

'Let's just say I'm feeling lucky.'

There was a pause as Eric Johns took this in.

'You know something, don't you?' he said.

'Got to go, I can hear the Inspector coming,' Tricia sang, replacing the handset. 'Oh, Inspector,' she continued as a furious Frieda entered the office, 'I have a message for you.'

'If it's the Chief Constable I'm out having my legs waxed,' Frieda replied. 'If it's anyone else I'm having my hair done. Or I've gone shopping. Choosing a new colour of lipstick. Or whatever.'

'Actually it's from Sergeant Summers.'

Frieda pulled up short.

'Frank Summers?'

'I presume so. Unless we have another Sergeant Summers on the staff.'

'Well? Come on, Tricia, out with it.'

Tricia Leigh pretended to be hunting amongst her notes and notepads.

'I've got it here, somewhere. Just give me a moment.'

Frieda came around to her side of her desk and gently laid a hand on Tricia's shoulder.

'Tricia. You never forget a message. You can remember messages you took three months ago. Unless you wish to die a horrible and slow death, right now, tell me what Frank said.'

'Gino's trattoria at one o'clock,' Tricia said quickly, beaming.

Frieda paused before punching the air and crying "Yes!" Then she stopped and smoothed down her pencil skirt.

'Business, of course, that's all it is,' she said.

'Of course.'

'Naturally. Just to discuss current cases, that sort of thing.'

'Actually, I think there's a slight stain on the back of your blouse.'

'Is there? A stain?'

'Only very slight.'

'But there all the same.'

'True.'

'I'll have to change, I suppose.'

'Wouldn't do your image any good to be wandering around with a slight stain on the back of your blouse.'

'No. And it's not just me, it's my position as Inspector. And the reputation of Wellbury police force.'

They nodded agreement at the undesirability of an inspector walking around with an almost unnoticeable stain on the back of her blouse.

'A little cleavage, don't you think?' suggested Tricia.

As Frank left his flat he almost bumped into a couple passing his door.

'My goodness! It's the handsome young police officer.'

With a sinking feeling he recognised the two. One suited young Cyril and his hat-and-glove wearing aunt. The sinking feeling came from the recognition of the tone in her voice, the half mocking, half invitation with a liberal dose of suggestiveness thrown in. He didn't often react with snap judgements about people, but what he was quite sure of was that he did not want young Cyril living anywhere close to him, and the sooner the aunt went back to her normal haunts and husband the better.

'Well, hello again,' he said quickly. 'I'd love to stay and chat but –'

'You know we haven't even been introduced,' the aunt said. 'I'm Jemima Porter – my friends call me Jem – and this is my nephew, Cyril. Say hello, Cyril.'

'Hello,' said Cyril.

'Frank Summers,' Frank said, shaking hands.

'We were just on our way to view a flat,' Aunt Jem said, confirming Frank's initial fear that young Cyril might well end up living in unbearable proximity. 'And here you are, a police officer. Well, this must be a safe area to live in.'

'Well –'

'I can see you're busy. An occupational hazard, I'm led to believe. I know, give me a call and we'll have a drink sometime. You can tell me all about Wellbury, the better parts, that sort of thing. I'm told that there are some very romantic walks along the river, and around the university.'

'Well –' Frank began again, taking Aunt Jem's proffered card.

'We won't detain you any longer. Come, Cyril. Until later,

Frank. I'm looking forward to it. Say goodbye, Cyril.'

'Goodbye,' said Cyril.

Frank was pretty certain that young Cyril would not be invited to the proposed "drink". He also intended to make certain one other person wasn't there – himself. He had enough problems of his own without the addition of an aunt intent on having a little fun.

As he walked away a thought struck him.

He almost slapped his forehead.

It was obvious. Cyril. Cyril had reminded him of the twins, Richard and Rachael.

Two people who had vowed to get their own back on him.

Now he knew who was behind the traffic light trick. He couldn't prove it, but there was another way to sort them out. All he had to do was beat them to the next one.

Since he didn't have the slightest clue how he would do that it could be presumed that he might regard the problem as somewhat intractable. But it did not faze him in the slightest. Not having a clue was how he solved some of his best cases.

In the station reception Eric Johns made another note. Then he totted up various figures. Betting odds change not according to the likelihood of the winner, but according to the amount bet on each entrant and a calculation of probable losses. That way the bookie is almost assured of a profit.

Eric Johns noted that Inspector Garold had now dropped from four-to-one to three-to-one.

But what really, really worried him was the three-to-one on Frank.

If he'd been the better rather than the bookie he would have put a few hundred on that dark horse.

The dark horse in question stood in Phil Walthers' office at the Herald reading a letter.

"THREE STRIKES AND YOU'RE OUT SERGEANT SUMMERS

YES, SHOCKING ISNT IT

ARE YOU READY TO PLAY?"

Phil Walthers sat in his chair pulling nervously at his fingernails.

'I'm sorry, Sergeant Summers, no doubt I'm over-reacting, but something about that letter gives me goose bumps. As you can imagine I have, as editor of the Herald, received amongst normal missives a vast number of strange letters which range from the vituperative to the undeniably evil, and that one looks like one of them.'

'Do you have a plastic folder, Mr Walthers?'

'A plastic folder? Ah, of course, I apologise, I should have thought.'

He rummaged through a drawer and came out with two.

'One for the letter, one for the envelope,' he explained.

Frank carefully dropped each item into its folder.

'I doubt if we'll get any fingerprints off them, but you never know,' he said.

'You agree?' asked Phil Walters. 'Those aren't the words of a sane person?'

'There are now four strands,' Frank replied, looking the other man in the eye as if he didn't suspect him of being involved in one of the strands. 'One is merely a practical joke with potential economic results. Another is silly, with potentially dangerous results. The third is the Joker Gang. The fourth is this one. This one I do not like. This one smells bad.'

'It's the fault of that fool on the radio,' Phil Walters said. 'Zack the Prat. He's been encouraging everyone to join in these ridiculous pranks. Sooner or later you're bound to find someone a bit unhinged who decides to join in, but someone whose idea of a prank is not the humorous kind.'

'Has he now? I'm getting a little tired of Zack the Prat. Firstly he gets everybody wound up over the people running the fair, now this.'

'Oh, he's stopped that nonsense. Ever since Bentleys began paying for advertising time. He knows which side his bread is buttered.'

Frank nodded thoughtfully.

'I suppose you can say that about him, he's consistent. A consistent pain in the neck and as slippery as an oiled eel. I pity the poor people who have to work with them.'

He turned to go.

'By the way, Mr Walthers, if there is anything you feel the need to confess to me about that stunt with the Cleopatra costume, you have my number.'

Phil Walthers watched him leave with deep unease.

He looked at the telephone.

It was not something he wanted to do.

It was something he had to do.

He picked it up and dialled.

'Mrs Blower? I fear we are going to have to do something about Sergeant Summers. Much as I dislike the conclusion, I am afraid that the young man has finally turned the corner of paranoia.'

'Ah, Meester Summers,' cried Gino, 'your table awaits, the beautiful Inspector has only just arrived.'

The fact that Frank had come in the back way via the delivery entrance and kitchen Gino seemed to regard as perfectly normal.

'Cut the crap, Gino. You're no more Italian than I am Hungarian.'

Gino's real name was Herbert. His Italian parents had wanted him to become an Englishman.   He had been sent to elocution classes, had gained a First in English Literature at university, had gone on to get a doctorate, and then had thrown it all up to pursue what he had always wanted to do – run an Italian restaurant. He had spent a lot of time in developing his Italian accent. Now he glowered in humility.

'Okay, okay,' Frank surrendered, 'I'm sorry, Gino, I shouldn't have said that.' He patted Gino's shoulder. 'You'll have to forgive me, I took a bit of a knock yesterday. I'm not quite myself.'

'But of course, I understand,' replied Gino, who privately thought that Frank Summers had not been quite himself since he had been shot in the head. 'Please, your table awaits.'

'I mean it, Gino. I know I've been away a while, mentally speaking, but I'm back now. There's just one small matter I have to sort out. Just bear with me for the moment.'

They looked each other in the eyes. Finally Gino alias Herbert nodded and spoke.

'Frank, you need any help – well, my dad was in the Resistance during the war. I think I inherited some of that. You need anyone to watch your back, take out anybody, I'm your man. Okay?'

'Okay, Gino, thanks,' said Frank, who privately wondered what movies Gino-Herbert had been watching.

Casablanca, probably.

Still, he needed allies outside of the police station. Gino-Herbert might end up acting as unpaid chauffeur, or standing in the rain like some gumshoe detective, wondering why he had idiotically offered help, but that would come later, if necessary.

'Just remember, Gino, trust no-one, understand?'

Who, precisely, had been watching what movies?

Casablanca, especially.

He could feel a headache coming on.

'You got that, Frank. Wanna go to your table now?'

Frank nodded. Gino-Herbert escorted him to a quiet table where Frieda sat, nervously taking a sip at a glass of red wine.

'Frank!' she said in relief, standing up. She gave him a kiss as he wondered why she had abandoned her usual uniform of severe blouse, jacket and pencil-skirt for something frilly and cleavage-showing.

His headache was becoming worse.

'I thought you had stood me down,' she accused in a little-girl voice.

'I'll have a glass of white wine, please Gino. Riesling, if you have.'

'One glass of Riesling coming up.'

Frank and Frieda sat down opposite each other as Gino left.

'Read this,' Frank said, pulling out the plastic folders he had taken from the Herald offices. Frieda put her reading glasses on and read.

When she had finished she put the folders down on the table and looked at him. It was a disorientating image. From the neck up she was once again Detective Inspector Garold, a stern, professional police officer. From the neck down she was whey-hey, let the puppies come out to play.

'This is serious, Frank,' she said.

Frank nodded, trying not to look at the puppies.

'Whoever wrote that has a couple of marbles missing,' he noted.

Frieda waited while Gino-Herbert placed Frank's wine in front of him.

'Any ideas who it might be?' she asked once he had left.

'Nope. Could be anyone. It's the old fastest-gunfighter-in-the-West scenario. There's always someone willing to prove they're faster. Someone reads Phil Walthers' exaggerated story in the Herald and wants to show they're cleverer than me. All we need to do is round up anyone with a huge ego and a lack of confidence.'

'A basic psychopath mentality?'

'That's my guess.'

Gino came up to take their orders.

'But what about the other notes, and the business at the Blue Bliss?' asked Frieda after he had left.

'I think the Blue Bliss was a one-off,' Frank replied, buttering a chunk of baguette, finding himself once again starving. 'The traffic light trick – I have two students in the frame for that, twins named Rachael and Richard. They tried to pull the string trick on me and failed. They promised they'd get even. The problem is proving it.'

'I think you're right about the Blue Bliss,' Frieda said, before pausing, a nostalgic look in her eyes. 'Funny colours for a clown costume – especially the blue nose. I thought they were always dressed in red and white, with a red nose. Then again, the last time I went to a circus was when I was eight, I suppose things have changed since then, in the clown world.' She shrugged. 'Anyway, we can discount that. As for the traffic lights – well, I don't see how switching the lights gets even with you. There's no connection between you and the lights. To get even a practical joke either has to be against the person directly, or have some connection – as far as I understand these things, of course.'

'Maybe they thought, being so close to my flat, I would get caught in the chaos. I don't know. I – Oh, bloody hell, of course. Damn! I should have thought of that.'

'Thought of what?'

'The second note – milking it and primary knowledge. I presumed it referred to primary schools.'

'That was my initial thought too. Has something changed your mind?'

'Gino,' Frank asked as the man came up with their entrées, 'you have kids, don't you?'

'Kids, Frank? Hell, I've even got a grandson now, Frank. Here I am, at my age, a grandparent. Me, I don't get to be no Godfather, I get to be a grandfather.'

'Do you know of any primary schools with the words Frank or Summers in them? Saint Frank's, or something like that?'

Gino rubbed his chin in thought.

'Don't think there was ever a Saint Frank,' he said. 'St Francis, of course, of Assisi, but not a Saint Frank. But there's a nursery school called Summers, out in Old Merrick. My lad was thinking of sending my grandson there.'

'Can you get the number for me?'

'Sure thing, Frank. I've got it in the office somewhere. Give me a minute or so.'

'Like you asked,' Frank said, smiling at Frieda. 'What's the connection? I should have thought of that straight away. That bang on my head must have slowed me down.'

Frieda didn't quite agree with that, but the sight of a smile on Frank's face was worth the bang on the bonce. There was even the old sparkle in his eyes which suggested that he was no longer taking life so seriously.

'How is your head?' she asked.

'Fine. Ah, thanks, Gino.'

He passed the paper Gino had given him over to Frieda.

'I haven't got a mobile phone,' he said. 'And I'm under orders not to do any work for the moment. And, as you know, I always obey orders.'

'Liar,' Frieda said, smiling back at him and taking her mobile from her handbag.

While she was talking to someone from the crèche Frank finished off his starter. Still feeling peckish he appropriated some of Frieda's, trying to dodge her hand playfully slapping gently on his wrist while she tried to keep a straight voice on the telephone.

'You've eaten half my entrée,' she complained in a little-girl-hurt voice when she had finished the call.

'Sorry. I'll order another, shall I? Put it on my tab.'

'Yes, your tab meaning my expenses. No, don't worry, Frank, I'm not really that hungry. But we have our milk muggers.'

'What happened?'

'The nursery school receives a delivery of milk each morning in bottles, old-fashioned pint bottles. When they tried pouring it out this morning nothing happened. Apparently the bottles had been filled with something like plaster of Paris. Looked like milk, but wouldn't pour. They found the real milk around the side.'

'Why didn't they report it?'

'They thought someone was playing a practical joke on them. There was a note with the word Summers on it, they presumed it referred to their nursery school. They decided it was some silly nonsense best ignored. They've promised to retrieve the note from the rubbish bin. We'll go around straight after lunch.'

She played with a piece of bread.

'There's something else, though.'

'Something else?'

'This joker business, the Joker Gang. I've decided we'll go ahead with your plan of setting a trap for them.'

Frank looked at her.

'We?' he asked.

'Frank, I know it's your idea, but you're booked off duty. And we need to do something now. I promise you'll get all the credit.'

It was a silly thing to say. She knew Frank wasn't interested in who got the credit. He just wanted to be in on the action. Which, in his current condition, was not a good idea.

'I've got the whole thing worked out,' he replied. 'There's an old couple in Lords Acres, a couple of streets away from the first burglary. They're planning on visiting their grandchildren for a week. I'm sure I can get their agreement for us to have a team in there while they're away.'

'And spread the word? That they're going away?'

Frank grimaced.

'That's the problem. We don't know where the Joker Gang are getting their information from, so we don't know who to tell.'

Frieda looked at him in concern.

'Okay, Frank, you speak to your old couple. But remember that you're supposed to be taking things easy. You can set up the plan, but I don't want to find out that you've been part of the stakeout.'

'I promise to take things very easy. You know me.'

The look on Frieda's face suggested that she knew Frank Summers far too well, and that he was, to put it bluntly, lying like hell.

Inspector Percy Hanson and Sergeant Pete Phillips looked at the scene of crime in some perplexity.

'Someone's got a nasty sense of humour,' Percy Hanson noted.

'They seem to have it in for Frank,' Pete Phillips agreed.

'I'll have to tell Frieda.'

'They're having lunch.'

'Maybe it can wait until after lunch.'

The two men thought about the propriety of interrupting the couple having what they presumed was a romantic lunch.

'No, I think we need to move on this one, Sergeant,' Percy decided finally. 'It has, of course, nothing to do with the fact that I have a tenner on Frank. It's just unfortunate that we'll have to interrupt their tête-à-tête.'

'Fully understandable, Inspector. I fully agree. We need to put some resources on this one immediately.'

While Percy dialled Frieda's mobile Pete Phillips dialled Gertie's mobile.

Percy looked at him after they had finished their respective conversations.

'I don't think it was really necessary to involve Gertie,' he said mournfully.

'She works with Frank,' Pete Phillips pointed out. 'It has nothing to do with my tenner on her. I called her on a purely professional basis.'

'Of course. Good point. And professionally we need a forensic expert on this one.'

Pete Phillips gave a sour look as Percy Hanson dialled Susan's number.

Thursday Afternoon: The Shocker: first strike

In the restaurant Frieda put her mobile phone away. She had switched it off deliberately before entering the restaurant to prevent interruptions. She had forgotten to switch it off again after calling the nursery school. Percy's call had been most unwelcome.

'Looks like we won't get to finish our lunch,' she said. 'Our shocker has struck.'

'Our shocker?'

'The note Phil Walthers received. Someone wired up a lamp post so that any dog using it as a urinal would get a severe electric shock right where it hurts most.'

'They what?'

'Exactly.'

'Ouch.'

'Yes, there is that. But they also left a note for you. Something to the effect of it being the first strike.'

They looked at each other.

'Three strikes and you're out,' noted Frank.

'Come on, Frank,' Frieda said, standing up, picking up her jacket and handbag. 'We'll have to have a proper lunch at another time.'

As they left another diner smiled and waggled her fingers at Frank.

'A friend of yours?' asked Frieda with a hint of suspicion.

'Not quite,' Frank replied with a grimace. 'Her name's Jemima Porter. She's supposedly here to help her student nephew choose a flat, the boy in the suit sitting with her. I get the impression that her real aim is to indulge in a little extra-marital romance, if I could put it politely.'

'And she fancies you, I suppose.'

'I bumped into her at the university. I think she was really casting around for some young lecturer for a deep and meaningful relationship for a week. Maybe even one of the students, who knows?'

Frieda nodded. She had recognised the type as soon as she had set eyes on her. No doubt she would return to the fishing pool of the university once she realised Frank wasn't interested.

And he had better not be interested.

Frank wasn't that sure. He had met women like Jemima Porter before. Policemen seemed to have some strange attraction for them. The more insistent of them rarely took a hint.

Still, he just had to avoid her for a week, two at most.

He just prayed that she didn't find Cyril a flat near his. Aunt Jem would be up every second weekend to check up on her nephew and request professional and personal advice and attention from a certain member of the local police force.

Percy Hanson and Pete Phillips tried not to look as if they had noticed Frieda's décolletage as she and Frank went down on their haunches to get a closer look at the parallel steel plates attached to the lamp post, wired up to a set of batteries hidden by leaves in the gutter. Gertie and Susan also watched, enviously. Gertie had the feeling that her professional approach wasn't having the effect it was supposed to. But that was largely to do with the fact that Frank had been out of her reach. This was her chance to change that.

Susan surreptitiously undid a button on her blouse. If Frieda thought that she could get away with that she would find that two could play at that game.

'You've got the note they left?' Frank asked, standing up.

'Here, Sergeant,' Gertie said, handing him the plastic folder Pete Phillips had slipped to her.

'I can have a comparison made with the earlier ones by this afternoon,' Susan offered.

"STRIKE NUMBER ONE

YOU SLIPPED UP SERGEANT SUMMERS

SHOCKING, ISNT IT?

YOULL WET YOURSELF IF YOU MISS THE SECOND"

'Certainly looks the same,' noted Frank, handing the folder to Frieda.

'How dangerous was it?' she asked Susan. 'Could it have killed the animal?'

'Unlikely, unless it had a weak heart. But it's likely to be severely traumatised. It won't be going anywhere close to lamp posts in the future.'

'This set up,' Frank said, pointing to the steel plates, 'it wouldn't have – how can I put this, it would only have worked if the dog had cocked its leg? The victim was most likely to be a male dog? I'm not au fait with the toiletry habits of canines.'

Percy Hanson and Pete Phillips had initially had to hide their smiles when they had heard of what had happened. It had sounded like an interesting option in deterring pets from fouling the pavements. The idea that it might have been specifically aimed at a male dog did not sound so funny. Unconsciously they folded their hands in front of their trousers.

'Possibly,' said Susan dubiously.

Frieda checked her watch. 'Damn. I'm supposed to be meeting the Chief Constable in forty minutes, and it will take at least thirty to drive there.'

'That's okay,' Frank said, 'Gertie can drive me to the Summers nursery school.'

Frieda frowned.

'Very well. Susan, I'll get someone to bring the other notes over to you.'

'I'll get them seen to this afternoon,' Susan promised.

Percy Hanson and Pete Phillips watched the others leave.

'What do you reckon?' asked Percy.

'Close call,' observed Pete Phillips. 'I've never seen Fabulous look like that before. And the Doctor was waving it about a bit.'

'Ah, but he's gone off with Gertie, and she isn't the type to waste any time.'

The two men considered this.

'I don't suppose Eric Johns is likely to let us change our bets,' Percy noted gloomily.

'Not a chance,' agreed Pete Phillips.

'Gertie's two-to-one,' Percy noted. 'So if I put a tenner on her and she comes through I lose my tenner on Frank but still come out ahead.'

Pete Phillips made a face. Privately he reckoned the Doctor

was now in with the best chance. Gertie just looked too frumpy to make it to first place. But the Doctor was evens, so a tenner on her would mean that he would only break even himself.

'You've got to hand it to Frieda, though,' Percy said.

'You think Fabulous is in with a shout?'

'No, not that. They've all left and we're going to have to clean this mess up.'

Pete Phillips sighed inwardly. He knew who the "we" referred to, and it did not include an Inspector.

Gertie drove very professionally. Normally she liked fast driving, but her new persona called for attention to the road.

'Do you really think that was designed to catch a male dog?' she asked, thinking it would be a chance to praise him on his perception and insight.

'Mmm? No, I only asked that to wind up Percy and Pete. They looked like they needed a little winding up.'

Gertie thought about that as she drove. It didn't sound like the super-professional police detective Frank had turned into. She wondered if she wasn't taking the wrong approach. Perhaps Frank would be more attracted if she showed off her charms, as Frieda and Susan were obviously doing.

And she knew that many men found her charms most attractive.

But not Frank.

What did he really want?

Could she do both? Appear professional while also showing a feminine, and sexy side? The woman of every man's dream?

Well, Frank's dream of the perfect woman, anyway. Whatever that might be.

No, much as she might like it, the only people who managed that were these celebrities on television, and they ended up alone and snorting coke or alcoholic or something.

She decided to stick with the professional approach and see what happened.

On duty, that is.

Off duty she could play fast and loose. Or perhaps just loose.

'I wonder how this pageant at the Blue Bliss is going to turn out,' Frank said thoughtfully.

'In what way, Sergeant?'

'Oh, you know. Phil Walthers and Mrs Blower trying to turn a night-club into some sort of performing arts establishment. Cleopatra's costume, for example. There was hardly anything of it, was there?'

'I don't know, Sergeant, I thought she wore long dresses, a bit like a toga, or whatever they're called. She was really Greek, wasn't she?'

'Yes, more or less.'

Interesting, thought Frank. Gertie had replied as if she honestly had not seen Cleopatra's minimal costume. So, after holding young Alan's attention for long enough for someone else to make the switch, she had not met up with that someone immediately afterwards to take the costume to hide in the Blue Bliss. That suggested something, what, he was not quite sure of.

Certainly she hadn't seen the alleged costume.

But another interesting point was Gertie's mention of

Cleopatra's Greek origins. Gertie was unlikely to have known that, she had little interest in history. So someone had probably mentioned it to her recently. Such as when they were planning their little escapade. And there was only one person likely to have that knowledge. A person he knew who, like him, did have an interest in history.

One Inspector Frieda Garold.

But would she get involved in something as childish as that?

Something niggled at his mind. Something Frieda had said earlier. Something about the Joker Gang. Or was it something else?

It would come back sooner or later. For the moment he would have to try to work out where the gang were getting their information from. Until they knew that the trap he had devised for them would be useless.

'No doubt it was amusing for the perpetrators,' the head of Summers' crèche said sniffily after she had handed the note over to Frank. 'But the poor children wouldn't have thought it funny if we hadn't found the real milk in time. Children like their routine, Sergeant Summers. They can get very upset when that routine is broken.'

Frank wasn't listening to her. He was studying the note.

"Gotcha again, Mr Summers. Once more and we win. See if this one isn't news to you."

Frank smiled. He almost chuckled.

'Very kind of you to give us your time,' he said to the sniffy woman. 'Come on, Gertie, you can drive me to the Blue Bliss. I need to have a word with Phil Walthers.'

He was still grinning broadly as they got into the car.

'Crime and punishment, eh, Gertie? I shall have to think up a suitable punishment for the tricky two when I nail them. Don't you think?'

Gertie didn't have a clue what he was on about.

'He'll think I'm a tart,' wailed Sonia, dressed in what Mrs Blower had designed as Cleopatra's dress, one very short skirt and a top hardly wider than a shoestring.

'No he won't,' Mrs Blower assured her, 'he'll think that you're a most attractive young woman. Keep still. It's time for Nelson's din-dins. And you'll be helping him. It will take his mind off matters. I must have a word with chef. He's having another of his nervous turns. Not so, Mr Walthers?'

'I certainly hope so,' Phil Walthers said, sitting, watching the two women, filtering out Mrs Blower's conversation. 'It would certainly have worked for me when I was his age.'

'You mean it doesn't work for you now?' demanded a tearful Sonia, a young woman who had been used to the admiring, if not lecherous, gaze of men old enough to be her grandfather, and Phil Walthers was only old enough to be her father, probably.

'I'm a journalist and newspaper editor, Sonia, you learn to become objective. And I can objectively state that you are an extremely attractive young woman who will knock Frank Summers' eyes out.'

'The only problem is how are we to get him down here?' asked Mrs Blower. 'He's Italian. They just can't handle excitement. Has anyone seen Nelson?'

'Afternoon, all,' said the voice of a grinning Frank Summers.

'Frank!' exclaimed Mrs Blower.

'Sergeant Summers!' exclaimed Sonia, trying to stretch Cleopatra's costume to cover more than it could.

'Gertie!' followed up Mrs Blower. 'You've been looking after him. He looks so much better! Mr Walthers was obviously mistaken.'

'Was he?' asked Frank. 'Well, well, there you go. Actually, I need a few minutes of your time, Mr Walthers. Could we go somewhere for a private chat?'

'My studio room?' suggested Phil Walthers, surprised.

'Fine, let's go. You hang about, Gertie, won't be a tick. Sexy outfit, Sonia, you'll be giving them heart attacks.'

'He thinks I'm sexy,' sighed Sonia as the two men disappeared.

'Of course he does,' Mrs Blower assured her. 'Any man would. Apart from chef. Now, where did I leave Nelson's lead?'

Gertie glowered at the scantly clad Sonia.

'There's a law against indecency, you know.'

'Oh don't be silly, Gertie,' Mrs Blower cried, 'it's Cleopatra's costume. Now, what about you? Why are you wearing your hair that way? And those glasses! It makes you look awfully frumpy.'

'A natural look,' suggested Sonia.

'Shush, Sonia. Gertie, it's just too bad of you. Here's Frank smiling for the first time in ages and you go around looking like Miss Frumpy of the year. Honestly! As if I didn't have enough to worry about. It's just not good enough.'

'It's my professional look. You think it's a bit much?'

'Suits you,' said Sonia.

'Now that's enough, Sonia. Go get changed. We don't want the costume getting smudges on it before the first night. See if you can find Nelson's lead. And tell chef I want a word with him. Or is it time for din-dins?'

'Can't I stay? Just until Sergeant Summers gets back?'

'Oh, very well, then, but no more comments. Come, Gertie, your hair for a start.'

Frank Summers and Phil Walthers returned from their private chat to a puzzling surprise. Gertie's hair was down, her glasses had gone, she had acquired a layer of red lipstick, and she and Sonia were happily discussing make-up like two sisters.

Thursday Evening: Introducing Squishy

'Care for a drink, Sarge?' Gertie asked as she drove them into the station parking area. 'It's knocking off time.'

Frank appeared lost in thought for a while. Finally he took his pack of cards from his pocket and chose one.

'Thanks, Gertie, But no,' he said, replacing it. 'I've got some business to discuss with Pete Phillips. I'll see you in the morning.'

Gertie watched him stride towards the station entrance, a puzzled look on her face. She could have sworn that he had made the decision about going for a drink on the basis of that card.

She was beginning to wonder if that hit on his head had scrambled his brains.

Then again, maybe that's how he intended to come to a decision on another matter.

The only question, then, was how to rig that pack of playing cards so that it came up with the right answer?

'Sergeant Phillips here will be in charge of the overnight team,' Frank told the elderly couple in Lords Acres. 'All you have to do is let your neighbours know that you have to leave urgently because one of your grandchildren has suddenly taken ill.'

Mr and Mrs Meadows nodded. Mrs Meadows was quite taken by the subterfuge. It also gave them a cast-iron excuse to see their grandchildren for at least a week, something that had been deferred for over a year, for reasons from her husband's suspected heart attack to her breaking a leg while chasing an errant fox which had misguidedly entered their property and threatened her poodle. Mr Meadows was torn between the idea of seeing his grandchildren and the wish to hang around and give these jokers a damn good thrashing when they turned up.

Which they would, of course. You couldn't listen to Detective Sergeant Summers without believing that the plan would work.

Frank Summers was much less confident in his own mind. If he had belonged to the Joker Gang he would have smelt a rat right from the start.

Pete Phillips rarely lacked confidence. But at that precise moment he was terrified that he would inadvertently snap the delicate handle of the expensive looking tea cup in his large hand. Physical combat never worried him. Delicate tea-cups were another matter.

'You don't want us to spread the news further?' asked Mr Meadows, identifying Frank's main worry.

'Not too much. We don't want to over-egg the pudding.'

'You surely don't suspect our neighbours, do you, Sergeant?' asked Mrs Meadows.

'Not at all. But they will probably mention it in passing to someone else, and that someone will do so in their turn, and so on. Sooner or later our friends will pick it up from somewhere. But it has to come naturally. If they hear from too many sources they'll start to wonder why.'

'But what if they don't get the word?'

'Oh, I'm sure they will. We'll move a team in here at first light, under cover of a delivery or something of that sort.'

Once outside Pete Phillips turned to Frank.

'How can you be so sure this Joker Gang will hear about this?' he asked.

Frank turned and held out his pack of cards.

'Pick a card, Pete, any card.'

Pete frowned and chose one. The joker.

Frank winked.

'It's all about being lucky, Pete. You've either got it or you haven't.'

Pete shook his head in puzzlement. Frank had definitely got something.

A touch of the sun, most likely.

Pete Phillips understood hard evidence, and the hard evidence was that Frank was acting very strangely.

Which meant that he could well end up choosing Frieda.

And Frieda was at three to one, wasn't she? So if he put a tenner on Frieda – no, let's say a fiver on Frieda, and a fiver on Frank – no, wait a minute, a fiver on Frank and a tenner on ...

He rubbed his neck. He was getting a headache. Frank tended to do that to him sometimes.

Some hours after leaving Pete Phillips, in the early hours of the morning, Frank trudged up the steps to his flat. He was dead tired and looking forward to a good night's sleep. What was left of it.

He groaned as he reached the top of the stairs.

A box in front of his flat door suggested he wasn't going to get one just yet.

Not quite a normal box. A cream coloured plastic affair with rounded edges, about two and a half feet long, a foot wide, just over a foot high, with a handle on top, a grill at the front, and an envelope lying on top of the handle. He picked up the envelope and used a pen to open it, wary of it containing potential nasties such as razor blades glued to the top waiting for unwary fingers to be sliced open as they attempted to open the envelope.

"Please look after me for a few days, I'll be ever so good, and I'm lost and lonely with no-one to take care of me. I know you will. Please, please, pretty please." read the note.

Puzzled, Frank knelt down and looked through the grill. He issued a second, more heartfelt groan. Inside the box, tucked up right at the back, half covered by part of a small towel, he could just see in the shadow a little kitten curled up in a tight ball, fast asleep. Great. Someone had obviously left it at the wrong door – no doubt there was a cat lover somewhere nearby who should have found it awaiting their return. Now the ball – or kitten – was in his court.

But look after a kitten? How was he, a bachelor with a full-time job, living in a flat without a garden supposed to look after a kitten? A fully grown cat would be sufficient of a problem, but a little kitten? Those things needed care and affection, didn't they? And time, which he did not have.

He looked at his neighbour's door hopefully. Mrs Jones was retired. She would have the time.

But, no, Mrs Jones' lights were out. No doubt tucked up in bed, fast asleep as all honest Wellburians should be, himself included. And even if she was awake, he had no wish to suffer her endless complaints about the evils of the modern world. She would have kept him listening for at least half an hour, and in the end have declined any possibility of looking after the kitten. A lot of pain without any gain.

He sighed and accepted that it was inevitable that he would have to take the little thing into his flat, at least for the moment. He unlocked the door, picked the box up gently, and carried it into the lounge, lowering it carefully onto the coffee table.

Outside the flat a shadow flitted down the stairs. A shadow that had been watching.

'Nelson,' the figure muttered to itself. 'Time for his din-dins.'

Frank returned to his front door to pick up a letter which had been lying on the mat. There was no address. He opened it carefully. He groaned yet again when he saw the contents.

A playing card. To whit, a joker. Written on the back were the words:

"He seeks us here,

He seeks us there,

If only he knew

In front of our next target

Stands a yew.

From The Gang"

He put the card in his pocket and went to the kitchen, rubbing his eyes.

Cute, he thought, but not cute enough. If the card was from the Joker Gang, which was in itself doubtful – anyone could have dreamed the idea of dropping such a card through his letterbox – and if they thought he was going to run around checking every property which might have a yew tree in front of it they were very much mistaken.

Someone else could do the running around. Right at that moment he had a bigger problem on his hands, small as it was.

Perhaps, he thought as he fixed himself a drink, he could call the RSPCA. Would they have someone available at that time of the night – morning – to handle kittens left on bachelors' doorsteps? Why couldn't they have left a human baby? At least with a human baby he could have taken it to the hospital and left it with people who knew what to do under the circumstances.

He sat down on the couch, took a sip of whisky, bent down and peered through the grill of the box. Despite his careful handling of the box the kitten had woken up. It looked back at him with frightened eyes, trying to minimise its already small size and hide within the scrap of towel.

Bachelor and kitten looked at each other in silence for some seconds, one in perplexity, the other in fear.

'You can't stay here, you know,' Frank said finally. 'You need someone to look after you, and I don't have the time.'

The kitten reacted by trying to back further into its box.

'There's no need to be scared of me, kitty, I'm not going to hurt you.'

The kitten appeared to think Frank had just offered to wring its neck.

'Okay, okay,' he sighed. 'I tell you what, I'll get you some milk, how about that? Would you like some milk? All kittens like milk. Everyone knows that.'

Two frightened eyes suggested that "milk" had been translated as "arsenic".

Frank gave a deeper sigh, stood up and went to the kitchen. Maybe if he showed the frightened little animal some milk it would realise that he meant it no harm.

Blast, he thought as he looked into his fridge. The local shop had only had full-cream milk the last time he had bought some, and he was pretty sure that full-cream milk would be far too rich for such a small thing.

An idea struck him. Many months previously he had, in a moment of thoughtlessness, purchased several tins of no-fat, no-salt, no-additives, no-taste tuna, in the vain idea that he might indulge in a bout of healthy living. It was only when he tasted the contents of the tin that he remembered that he couldn't stand tinned tuna. But perhaps the kitten might like the stuff?

He opened a tin, chopped the tuna up into tiny pieces, put a few on a saucer, and dribbled some water into another saucer.

And I'll have to put some newspapers down for you, he thought as he returned from the kitchen with the saucers.

Would it use the newspaper? Do cats have to be house-trained?

Was it old enough to eat solid food? Even minutely diced tuna?

He had never before realised that his knowledge of little kittens and how to look after them was approximately nil. But, then again, he had never had one accidentally left at his door before.

'Here you go, Kitty,' he said, placing the saucers on the coffee table and opening the grill on the front of the box. The movement convinced Kitty that the best thing to door was to stay deeply in the recesses of the box and not let this other animal anywhere near. In case Frank was in any doubt of this it growled and spat, though in such a low and frightened tone it sounded almost piteous, a helpless baby David facing Goliath, without even his sling.

'Up to you,' Frank said. He sat down, took his shoes off, picked up his drink, swung his legs onto the couch and made sure that he wasn't looking anywhere near the box on the coffee table. The ceiling made a good object for his attention. He sighed again as he noticed that it could probably do with a wash.

Had anyone else, he thought, come home to find a kitten on their doorstep, it would have been a gambolling ball of fun, eager to rush around and poke its nose everywhere it shouldn't. He, on the other hand, had received something which quite obviously had not had the best starts to life.

He wondered whether it had been taken from its mother too young. He remembered a great-aunt who had a cat of which she had said just that, and that cat, fully grown, was a mental case. The only human it trusted was his great-aunt. If anyone else came near it would hide itself in the deepest hole it could find, disappearing like a bolt of black lightning. Its favourite spot was up the chimney. A fire couldn't be lit in the winter unless the cat could be seen.

Coaxing the cat down from the chimney required patience and a plate of food on the part of his aunt, and starvation on the side of the cat. Quite often the cat had seemed to prefer the starvation option. It had been a salutary lesson for a young boy who had never considered that animals might have their own characters and mental problems. In the end that cat had accepted that he was no threat, and had ceased making a bolt for the chimney whenever he turned up, but by that stage the animal was so advanced in years he had suspected that it wasn't a case of accepting him, but of accepting the inevitable. The venerable cat had died in his very arms, showing, his aunt said, that he would always be good with animals.

He hadn't really believed that then, and wasn't encouraged to believe it now. It took the kitten five minutes to gather enough courage to investigate the source of the smell of tuna that was making its little stomach rumble. Keeping its fearful eyes firmly fixed on Frank it inched forward until it got to the saucer, ever ready to flee back to its refuge. Crouching, it took a tentative taste before deciding to throw caution to the winds, and began eating in earnest.

'Sardines,' Frank said softly to the ceiling. 'All cats like sardines, don't they?'

Kitty paused, frozen, looking at him. After a few moments, Frank having made no further comment, it returned to the tuna. Frank took another sip of his drink.

'But are you old enough for sardines? Especially if they come in oil or tomato sauce' he asked.

Kitty paused again and looked nervously back at the box it had come in as if to assure itself of something. It then turned its head towards him, cocked to one side, and licked its lips either as if sharing his doubt over the sardines question or as if, despite the welcome food, it still had reservations about him. Then it went back to the final scraps before moving on to the water.

When it had finished it looked once again at him before scampering back to its box to hide deep in the recesses.

'Now that's not very sociable,' Frank remarked, swinging his legs off the couch and peering into the box, 'especially since I've just fed you. You might at least say thank you.' The kitten was sitting on its scrap of towel. It looked at him, presumably decided it was safe again, and then began licking its paw.

'Come on, I'm not going to hurt you,' he continued, putting his hand into the box and, taking hold of a corner of the small towel, pulled the kitten towards him. This was met with indignant spits and hisses, more plaintive than threatening. It continued as Frank dragged it out of the carry box and bumped onto the coffee table, sliding on the towel.

'Hey, calm down, tiger, I'm not going to hurt you,' he tried again to re-assure it, as it sat there trembling violently, repeating its objections, spitting mouth open, its eyes wide with fear. 'There, there, calm down.' He stroked it gently with a finger. It was so small it could have sat in the palm of his hand quite comfortably.

Or, considering its reaction to him, quite easily but not comfortably.

'You're not a tiger,' he noted, 'you're a – a squishy. I shall call you Squishy. What do you say to that? In polite terms, if you don't mind.'

Something struck him. Squishy might be spitting, but the kitten wasn't using its claws as might be expected. Those were dug desperately into the scrap of towel, paws attached to the material so firmly only a surgical operation might have separated the two. One thing he knew for certain about cats, from experience, was that, in danger, if they could run they would run, if they couldn't their claws and teeth were applied to the nearest part of the danger, in this case his hand. On a number of occasions he had felt the anger of a frightened cat, talons ripping at his hands, refusing to believe his assurances that he was only trying to help it.

But this kitten wasn't doing either. Not running nor fighting.

He remembered something else his great-aunt had told him about her own mental case. As a kitten it had had a little dark-brown cushion which it had refused to part with, almost as if it had been a surrogate mother, and, having lost the real thing, could not bear to part with the replacement.

'Well, well,' he said thoughtfully. 'It isn't me you're afraid of, is it, Squishy, not really? Or perhaps, to be more accurate, you're afraid I might take your little scrap of towel away from you, aren't you?'

Squishy's spits were diminishing, partly through the realisation that Frank wasn't about to steal its security blanket, but more largely through tiredness and shock, its body still trembling.

'I tell you what, Squishy, I'll make you some more tuna and water and then you can go to bed in your little towel, what do you say to that? I know that I could do with some sleep.'

As Squishy made no comment he went to the kitchen, chopped up some more tuna, refilled the water saucer and took both back to the lounge. In the lounge he lifted a protesting Squishy and an unprotesting towel onto his lap and held the tuna in front of the kitten. It immediately stopped protesting and began feeding.

'Well, at least you have your priorities right. But I don't think you should have too much, you know. I'm sure too much is just as bad as too little. It might make you sick, little Squish. And tell me something. Why am I sitting here talking to a kitten? I think I've finally gone round the bend.'

Squishy ignored him. The kitten finished the tuna and looked at the saucer of water on the coffee table.

'At your service,' Frank said, leaning over and bringing the water forward for the kitten. It immediately commenced lapping. Once it had had enough, it looked around the lounge briefly, gave him a final anxious glance, kneaded the towel in his lap a few times, and curled up to go to sleep.

'Well, if all you're going to do is eat tuna, drink water and sleep, I suppose we could get along for a few days.'

He watched the little creature fall asleep, apparently quite happy where it lay, or perhaps so exhausted it had no other option.

'I have to go to bed too, you know,' he pointed out.

I really do not need this now, he thought. I have too many other things I need to sort out without Lady Luck dropping a helpless little kitten into my life.

At length he sighed, gently lifted the towel and kitten and carried them to the bedroom. He laid them next to the pillow on the far side of the bed. He rubbed his jaw before going back to the lounge. Peering into the cat's box he noted a packet about the size of a small bag of sugar. On investigation it turned out to contain fine granules of something.

'Kitty litter,' he noted. 'Well, at least whoever left you outside thought of one thing.' A thought struck him. 'I wonder how long this stuff lasts.'

Shrugging his shoulders, and hoping not to discover the answer too soon, he rummaged around until he found a small box for the litter. He placed that on the low bedside cabinet next to where the kitten lay asleep, where it could find the litter without having to go too far.

'Night, Squishy, sweet dreams,' he said once he had climbed

into bed and switched off the bedside lamp on his side, leaving the other on. He gave the kitten a final stroke. 'Don't worry little one, I'll look after you for a few days. Just until your owner comes to collect you.'

For the first time in months the nightmares did not come. Possibly because he was so dead tired. Or, equally possible, because his subconscious did not want him lashing out in his sleep while little Squishy lay curled up so nearby.

Whichever it was, at least it saved him from thinking what he was going to do in the coming days. Sunday was approaching far faster than he would like.

Friday Morning: The Shocker again; Aggie

For some reason Sam Nightingale was kissing him on the cheek.

No, not kissing, she was actually licking his cheek.

That didn't make sense.

And it felt strange.

Not unwelcome, just very, very strange.

After all, Sam Nightingale didn't like men, and she especially did not like him.

Gradually he surfaced through the fog of sleep to find Squishy sitting on his chest, miaowing and licking him to wake him up.

'Squishy, do you mind?'

Squishy didn't mind.

'Let me guess. It's breakfast time. '

Squishy seemed to agree. Frank lifted the kitten from his chest and placed it on its towel before getting out of bed.

'Well, I'm glad to see you don't think I'm some sort of Bluebeard anymore,' he said, yawning and stretching. 'I'll bet you'd be anyone's for a saucer of milk.'

Squishy miaowed at him, protesting this calumny.

'Okay, tuna, then. Come on, then, breakfast time. I could do with a cup of tea, I think.'

The kitten scampered eagerly across the bed to follow him for a foot or two and then stopped, panic stricken. It looked back at its towel, and then at Frank, pleading with its eyes.

'You're going to have to get used to leaving it behind,' Frank told it. 'Come on, it's either the towel or tuna, one or the other.'

He walked into the kitchen. A pitiful miaow from the bedroom told him that it would have to be both.

'Doesn't bother me, if you want to go hungry you'll just have to go hungry.'

Another high-pitched miaow, the type you might hear from a tiny little kitten starving to death because of the heartless cruelty of a human.

Frank swore and returned to the bedroom.

'Just this time, you little horror, just this once,' he told the kitten as he carried it in its towel to the kitchen. He put it down in a corner and placed a saucer of tuna some feet away. 'There you go, you'll have to leave your towel if you want some.'

Squishy scampered across to the bowl, gave a quick backward glance to make sure the towel was still in sight, and began eating. Frank sat down with a cup of tea and watched it.

'We're going to have to wean you off that thing, Squishy,' he said. 'Correction. Someone will have to wean you off it. I'll take you down to the station this morning and find you someone who wants to look after you for a few days. Someone with the time to look after you. Some sweet little WPC who thinks you're the cutest little kitten ever.'

He took a sip of tea.

'Which I have to admit you do seem to be,' he noted. 'But I have a heart of iron, Squish. A heart of iron.'

He took another sip.

'And besides, though you don't know it, anyone or anything that gets close to me gets hurt, and I'm not going to take that chance with you. Sorry about that, Squish, but that's the way it is. Don't worry, I'll find someone to take care of you.'

Having finished the tuna Squishy began exploring the kitchen, keeping to areas in which it could see either Frank or its towel. He left it doing so to take a shower. As soon as he left the kitchen it ran back to its towel and crouched on it in the corner, eyes wide with fear.

'Squishy, you really can't sit on that towel all day just because I'm not here, you know,' Frank told it when he had finished dressing and returned to the kitchen. 'I have to go out shortly, and I can't take you with me.' He looked down as it rubbed itself against his legs, perhaps needing physical confirmation that he was there. 'Tell you what, why don't I switch the television on. You can watch it while I'm away.'

He picked up the towel and held it in front of the kitten who looked at it, bereft, jumping up, trying to regain its property, miaowing at him, pleading for the towel to be returned.

'Come on, follow me.'

He led the dancing kitten through to the lounge, dropped the towel on the carpet and switched the television on. Squishy immediately crouched on the towel, looking at him with accusing eyes, evidently not liking this game, accusing him of torture.

'I'll leave a bowl of water – and some newspaper,' he promised.

When he returned with the water and newspaper Squishy was still crouched down, this time looking at the door, waiting for him to return. The kitten was obviously not interested in the television screen.

'I know morning television is a bit dire,' he told the kitten, putting his jacket on, 'and it gets worse, believe me, but I won't be gone long.'

As he walked out of the lounge Squishy scampered after him, mewling at his feet.

'No, Squishy,' he said opening the front door and pushing the kitten back. 'Go back to the lounge. I'll see you later.'

He closed the door on a desperately wailing kitten, now, for the first time, out of sight of both its towel and Frank. Its screams reached heart-breaking point.

'When I find out what heartless bastard left that poor thing abandoned on my doorstep I'll kill them,' he thought to himself as he walked down the stairs, trying to close his ears to the noise Squishy was making.

Abandoned.

The word rattled around in his head.

Poor little thing.

Abandoned.

Heartless bastard.

He almost made it to the bottom of the stairs.

With a sigh of equal parts frustration and irritation he turned and headed back up. He opened the door to find a frantic Squishy bleating at him. For some reason it appeared that the kitten was unable to work out how to get back to its towel once out of sight of it. Or perhaps sheer terror had made it incapable of thought.

Sheer terror had made it capable of leaving a small puddle in the corner next to the door.

'Come here you silly sod,' Frank said, picking up the now whimpering kitten and cuddling it, its claws digging into him as it clung desperately to his jacket. 'God, you are going to be a right pain, aren't you? Come on, I'll get this mess cleaned up and then I'll take you for a walk. Don't worry, I'm not going to leave you on your own again.'

Guessing that prematurely separating the kitten from both himself and its security blanket could only be counter-productive, and that its recent shock had made it even more desperate for both, he let it sit on its towel in the passageway watching him as he cleaned up its present to him for his heartlessness.

'Now,' he said when he had finished and exchanged his jacket for an old leather one with large pockets on the front, 'I'm certainly not going to carry you in my hands, and I'm not going to carry a kitty box around with me the whole day, so you're going to have to go in here.'

He held out the jacket for inspection, patting one of the pockets. Squishy looked at it uncertainly.

'I'll put your towel in and you can sit on it while looking out. And, just in case you want to hide inside, we'll punch little holes in so that you can still breathe, and even take a peek out.'

To demonstrate the point he took a penknife and punched several little holes into the front of the pocket.

'I hope you appreciate my doing this, Squishy, it might be an old jacket, and a little gone at the collar, and frayed here and there, but it's one of my favourites. Now, come along, your towel, if you please.'

He eased the piece of towel from underneath the kitten and pushed it into the pocket. As it entirely filled the pocket he took half of it out, leaving part of it trailing. Then he picked up the little kitten and slipped it in afterwards, leaving just the head showing.

'Comfy, Squishy?'

Squishy looked up at him, down again, hooked one paw on the top of the pocket and miaowed as if to say, yes this was very comfortable, and Frank, if he was ready, may continue.

'That's the spirit, old boy.'

'Not many people realise how much exercise you get from fishing,' the Chief Inspector noted as he and Frank strolled along the river path.

It was not a point Frank had previously considered, but he had to admit that walking a mile or so to and from his flat to the river every morning did add up to some exercise.

'And then again, not many people take their kitten for a walk along the river,' the Chief Inspector added.

Squishy was sitting happily in Frank's pocket, regally watching the world go by, one paw hooked on his jacket pocket as if holding itself firm, or possibly ready to wave to the admiring crowds. They hadn't passed many people, but sufficient to make Frank realise that having a tiny kitten looking out of your jacket pocket was a sure-fire way of meeting women and children of all ages. The looks on some of the men accompanying their girlfriends suggested that they regretted not having thought of this ingenious stratagem.

Squishy reacted to each sudden descent of a human face, accompanied by endearments such as "Oh, isn't he cute!", by disappearing into the depths of Frank's pocket, peeking warily out of one of the holes, only emerging when Frank assured the kitten that the coast was clear.

'I told you, it isn't my kitten,' Frank said firmly. 'I'm only looking after him for a few days.'

The Chief Inspector smiled but made no further comment.

'You really should stop looking around like that,' he said instead, responding to Frank's constant turning of his head to check for anyone watching or following them. 'Anyone tailing you will know you're on your guard. Better to let them think you don't suspect a thing. You'll spot them in time, don't worry.'

'I'm not too sure about that. Not out here in the open.'

'The shocker won't go for you in the open.' He smiled at Frank's surprise. 'Frieda told me about it. Sounds like a nasty business. Any idea who is behind it?'

'Not really. It could be the bunch behind the joker break-ins.'

'But you don't think so?'

Frank shrugged. There were two people he suspected: one Professor Ainke and one Constable Sam Nightingale. Both had humourless characteristics which would fit the profile. But it was an awful long jump of logic to make, and not one he wanted to state aloud.

'It feels too personal,' he said. 'As if whoever it is knows me. And I haven't met any of the Joker Gang, to my knowledge.'

'One of your old cases?' suggested the Chief Inspector. 'Someone with a grudge, wanting revenge?'

'I doubt it. Let's face it, most – almost all – of the cases I've dealt with are pretty much run of the mill stuff as far as crime goes. Done by the sort of person who, if they wanted revenge, would wait for me in a dark alley with a bottle or a baseball bat. Going to all the effort of wiring up a lamppost the way they did – apart from being maliciously cruel, it shows a mind at work, a rather perverted one, but definitely someone with a brain.'

'A rather strangely wired up brain, if you'll excuse the pun.'

'Precisely.'

They walked on in silence for a few minutes.

'You sure it's not just – well, I read that article about you in the Herald,' the Chief Inspector said. 'It could be someone mentally deranged, someone with too much time on their hands. Someone who had a brainstorm and decided to prove that you weren't as good as the article suggested.'

Frank nodded.

'That is a distinct possibility. I wish Phil Walthers wouldn't write rubbish like that. I'm not sure that he realises that a lot of people will actually believe it. They get this idea that I'm the fount of all wisdom. Human nature can be strangely dogmatic that way.'

'Aye, it can certainly be that,' the Chief Inspector said, smiling. He had followed Sergeant Summers' career with some interest, news of which came mainly via Frieda. He knew that Frank was referred to as the "Wellbury Wonder", a tribute of respect, despite the fact that, prior to his accident, he had spent most of his time and energy avoiding work. Until a case came up that intrigued him, that was. Then he could quite happily lose himself in his job, blindly unaware to the machinations of those close to him.

The Chief Inspector had often wondered what it was that caused men and women to follow someone, to believe in them, to excuse them for almost anything. Napoleon, on the eve and the day of Waterloo, had clearly been in no condition to lead the battle, yet his men had followed him nevertheless, trusting him implicitly, even though any sensible person would have taken one look, claimed a prior appointment and left for somewhere more congenial.

Never mind the more modern example of Bill Clinton.

The Chief Inspector stopped and looked at the passing river.

'I like to keep my hand in from time to time,' he said. 'You'll need someone to watch your back. If you see me window-shopping behind you, don't recognise me.'

Frank's eyebrows were raised in surprise. The Chief Inspector smiled again.

'When I was a boy I used to play at being a secret agent. I've never really grown out of it.'

He took out a pen and piece of paper and wrote a number on it.

'My mobile phone number. There's only one other person who knows that, and that's Frieda. You'd better let me have yours.'

'I don't own a mobile phone.'

'Still not? I remember Frieda complaining about that, and stating with great determination that she would make sure you got one. So, she lost that one, eh?'

Frank wasn't sure how he felt about learning that Frieda had been discussing him with the Chief Inspector. Had things been normal he probably wouldn't have been surprised. In current circumstances it felt like listening to a priest revealing secrets from the confessional.

'I'll pick up a cheap one somewhere. Just for the duration, though.'

The Chief Inspector nodded.

'I understand. I can't stand the things myself, not as a rule.'

A puzzled look crossed his face. He put a hand into his jacket pocket and took out his mobile phone.

'I have it set to vibrate,' he remarked. 'The noise of the ring tone makes me want to drown it.'

He pressed a button and put it to his ear.

'Frieda, how wonderful to hear from you so early in the morning.'

Frank listened to a one sided conversation.

'I see, that isn't good news, is it?'

'Of course, if I see him I shall certainly pass the news on.'

'Probably popped out for the newspaper or something, I would imagine.'

'Yes, if you could keep me posted, thank you, Frieda.'

He pressed another button and dropped the phone back into his pocket.

'That was Frieda, in case you hadn't gathered. Gertie's on her way to your flat to pick you up. Apparently the shocker has struck again, and this time it's worse. Possible murder, from what Frieda said.'

He looked at Frank.

'I understand that you're going to set a trap for these joker people.'

'Yes, I'm getting that set up.'

'Have you thought of setting a trap for the shocker?'

Frank considered this.

'In what way?'

'You said it sounded personal. Presuming this shocker character is a little unhinged, and they're going to have a go at you, where do you think they would want to get you?'

Frank nodded.

'The most personal space of anyone. The home. In other words, my flat.'

'Precisely.'

'No way they could get in there. Not without breaking the door down.'

'Perhaps you should make it easier for them to get in.'

Frank shook his head.

'We don't have the resources to set it up. We'd need a team sitting in my flat waiting twenty-four hours a day – just on the off-chance that this shocker person would turn up. And they'd have to stay out of sight until whoever it is has done something we can nail them for – it's no good just getting them for breaking and entering. There isn't space in the flat for a team to hide.'

'I know a young man who is very good with computers, someone called Darren,' the Chief Inspector said, guessing Frank's real objection. 'He can set up what I believe are called web cams – web cameras. They transmit lovely pictures to his website on the Internet. And you wouldn't spot the cameras, tiny little things. No need for anyone else to be in your flat.'

Frank nodded understanding.

'So if our shocker turns up in my flat we'll get all the evidence we need.'

'Just so.'

Frank pondered the idea for some minutes. He wasn't happy

with the idea of leaving himself vulnerable. He had spent a lot of time and money in turning his flat into a fortress where he could hide from the world. It wasn't easy to throw that away just like that.

But it was their best chance if they were to catch this shocker.

For some minutes his internal demons battled it out, until one of his voices, a braver or more foolish one, used the word "plonker".

Finally he nodded agreement.

'I'd better get back. Gertie should be at my flat by now.'

'I'll ask Darren to pop over this afternoon and set things up. After that all you have to do is give your suspects access to your flat.' He tickled the kitten underneath its jaw. 'You look after him Squishy. Keep the bad men away.'

The Chief Inspector watched him go. He rubbed his jaw thoughtfully. He had wanted to mention Jean Candour's name. The subject would have to come up sooner or later if Frank was ever to get over it. But to mention it prematurely might drive him back within himself. As it was it was probably best to let things lie until a better moment came along.

Or until a better moment could be manufactured.

On his way back to his flat Frank purchased a cheap pay-as-you-go mobile phone. The smallest one he could find. He had no wish for anyone apart from the Chief Inspector thinking that he could be contactable at any minute of the day or night.

'Oooh! Isn't he sweet!' exclaimed Gertie after she had entered Frank's flat to find Squishy standing next to him. The kitten immediately hid behind Frank's leg, peeking out at her, wary of her enthusiasm.

To Frank's dismay Gertie had dropped the professional approach, and was now wearing a blouse arguably a size and a button too short, a skirt which swung rather attractively with her hips, and shoes with heels far too high for police work, but ideal for showing off her attractive calves.

'You like him?' he said, trying not to make it too obvious that he was admiring her outfit and accoutrements. 'You can have him. He's yours.'

'I wish I could have him, but I've only got a little flat, no garden, and I'm out most of the day. It wouldn't be fair to the poor little thing.'

'I'm in the same position, so I can't keep him.'

'Where did you find the little thing? Here, kitty, nice kitty.'

Gertie picked up an unwilling Squishy and held the kitten to her chest – a position many men might have wished they find themselves in – cooing in its ear as it eyed Frank with a pleading look which suggested that it wanted him to come to the rescue.

It is said that a war plan does not survive the first battle. Gertie's revised game-plan of appealing to Frank's earthier interests had not survived the first kitten. Strangely enough it made her more appealing to him.

'Someone left him outside my front door, with a message asking me to look after it for a few days. I guess they meant to leave it somewhere else but got the address wrong.'

'Well, you could look after it for a few days. After all, you aren't really supposed to be on duty.'

Frank considered this.

'I suppose I could get back to the flat every so often to get him some food and something to drink,' he said dubiously.

'Oh, Frank, you can't leave the poor little thing on its own. Not while it's so young.'

'He's just going to have to cope by himself for a few hours. Now, come on, let's get going.'

'By the way, Frank, it's not a he, it's a she, I think.'

Frank was tempted to say something, but decided against it.

'Know anything more about this shocker business this morning, Gerts?' asked Frank as they drove. Squishy lay happily asleep on his lap. For a second time he had not managed to resist the kitten's pleading look as he was about to close the door on it, never mind Gertie's remonstrations and talk of his heartlessness and cruelty. He had finally justified taking it with them on the grounds that he could take it to the station and get someone there to look after it.

'Not really, Sarge. Apparently they've found a man in the public toilets just off Trafalgar Park. Along with a note from our friend, the shocker. I think he was only found a short while ago. The Inspector asked me to pick you up on my way in.'

'Dead? The man in the toilets, I mean.'

'Not yet, but his chances don't sound too good.'

'And the note?'

'I don't know. All I know is that it's addressed to you.' She gave him a sideways glance. 'You could be in real danger, Frank. I'll come and stay with you, if you like, until we've caught whoever it is. I promise I'll be good and behave myself – for the moment.'

Frank smiled.

'It's okay, Gertie, I've made my own arrangements. Let's just say I have a friend watching my back for me.'

Gertie glowered at this news and stayed silent, sulking. Even if she did not have a romantic interest in him, she was his constable and the first person he should have turned to to watch his back.

'Don't worry, Gerts, my shadow is someone no-one will recognise,' he assured her. 'You're too well known. You'd be spotted a mile off.'

Well, at least that was something.

Frank drummed his fingers on the window sill.

'Public toilets,' he noted.

'Not too many of those left,' Gertie said.

'Still quite a few in Wellbury. Victorian era. I think they might be listed. The council see them as somewhat of a tourist attraction.'

'Funny type of tourist attraction.'

'Not really. Not when they're some of the last remaining examples. And when a brochure states that Wellbury is one of the few places with clean, functional public conveniences, there's a subtle suggestion there – if you go anywhere else, and need to go, where can you go when you need to go?'

Gertie decided that that was definitely a rhetorical question.

The public toilets in Trafalgar Park were ringed with police tape. Frieda was standing outside, a radio in hand, an irritated look on her face. She was once again in her uniform of navy blue jacket, blouse, navy blue pencil skirt and shining black shoes with inches of stiletto heel.

'You're looking very casual, Frank,' she noted.

'Well, I am off duty, you know.'

'I wasn't criticising, Frank, I think it looks rather fetching. Maybe it's time Wellbury police joined the twentieth century and stopped wearing suits and ties. Though perhaps having holes in your jacket pocket is going a little far. It isn't a new fashion, is it?'

Before he could answer her eyes widened as she noticed Gertie.

'Gertie, what, precisely, are you doing carrying a kitten with you?'

'It's Frank's,' Gertie replied, nuzzling Squishy with her cheek. 'Isn't she just gorgeous?'

'Cute,' agreed Frieda, smiling and tickling Squishy's paw. 'Hello, little puddy cat. What's your name, then?'

'She's called Squishy,' Gertie replied.

Frank had resisted the urge to point out that Squishy was not his kitten, but standing there being ignored by two women cooing over it was a bit much.

'You did ask me out here for a reason, I take it?' he asked.

'Of course, yes,' Frieda said, attempting to regain her official pose while still tickling Squishy's chin. 'Susan and Tracey are down in the toilets looking for any forensic clues our shocker might have left behind. Here's the note that was left.'

Frank scanned the note in the plastic folder.

"STRIKE NUMBER TWO

NOT CONCENTRATING, ARE YOU SERGEANT SUMMERS?

AND YOU SUCH A CLEVER MAN

SHOCKING, ISNT IT?

YOU'LL BE SHOCKED IF YOU MISS THE FINAL STRIKE"

'You know, if there's anything I hate it's nutters who insist on using capital letters,' Frank commented. 'There should be a law against it. But that aside, what happened?'

'Someone wired up the urinal to a mains plug socket. Two bare wires along the urinal, the main cable outside covered it with boxing with "Wellbury Council Summers Services – Do Not Remove" on it.'

'Very amusing. So the first person to use the urinal ...?'

'Exactly. Closed the circuit between the bare wires. It just happened to be the man who looks after the toilets. Came to open them at six, presumably decided he needed to spend a penny, and that was that. Apart from the severe burns in a painful area, the shock threw him backwards, and he caught his head against one of the basins. He's in intensive care at the moment.'

Frank considered this, frowning.

'He didn't wonder why there were two new wires lying there?'

'He probably did. But I doubt whether he was suspicious enough at six in the morning to do anything about it prior to attending an urgent need.'

'But surely it has automatic flushing? Don't these things flush every fifteen minutes or so? Why didn't that set it off?'

'That's where luck played a part, bad luck. The flushing

system is switched off each evening when the toilets close, to save water. The maintenance man would normally have switched it back on when he unlocked the toilets. It would have flushed straight away, that would have closed the electric circuit and the fuse would have gone – admittedly with a huge bang, but no physical injury. Just unfortunate that he decided to relieve himself before switching it back on.'

'Which means that it was set up after the flushing was shut down for the night – after the toilets were locked. Otherwise it would have gone off before.'

'Unfortunately our trickster – and, if the maintenance man does not recover, a murderer – was very cute. There was some form of relay which had to be switched on before it could work. It was activated by a timer going off just after four in the morning. By that time the porcelain would have been perfectly dry. The circuit could open with little chance of it being closed by water residue. So the device could have been set up any time yesterday.'

'At some quiet time when no-one was around, no doubt. And with the ladies' adjacent we can't presume that it was a man. And of course there aren't any CCTV cameras around here.'

'No. I've got a couple of people checking the cameras from the nearby shops, but our shocker friend would have to be extremely stupid and unlucky to have got caught on one of those.'

Frank frowned.

'Do we see a pattern here?' he asked. 'Electricity and victims.'

'It certainly looks that way. And I don't like what the note says. To my mind it suggests that you will be the third victim.'

'Yes, that's obvious. I wonder whether this was an accident –

whether our shocker presumed that the flushing system would short the circuit before anyone actually got hurt. I rather imagine they did.'

'What makes you so sure?'

'It's a question of gradations. Gradual rises. The dog got a small shock and a fright. Our maintenance man would have got one hell of a scare as he switched the flushing system on and sparks flew, but nothing worse. Because the final shock has to be the biggest, those are the rules of this particular game. But if you kill someone with the second, what do you have to do to make the third the biggest shock? Wire up Wellbury?'

Frieda considered this.

'Right,' she said, coming to a decision. 'I've had enough of this nonsense. It's starting to look like the work of a madman, Frank, and you appear to be the target. I'm going to assign a bodyguard to you, at least until this nonsense is sorted.'

'I don't need a bodyguard,' Frank replied.

'Constable Nightingale. She has a very good report. She's firearms trained. She can carry a pistol until we're sure the danger is over.'

'No firearms,' Frank said.

On the other hand, Constable Nightingale would make a good chauffeur. If it came to that. Very handy to have around when he needed her, and very easy to slip away from when he didn't want her around.

And it would give her access to his flat. She wouldn't try anything while he was there, but if he accidentally left a spare set of keys hanging around ...

Frieda nodded, oblivious to Frank's ulterior thoughts.

'Okay, Frank, no firearms. I'll have a media release set up. We won't mention the state of the victim, just that an extremely dangerous practical joke has caused the closure of the public toilets in Trafalgar Park.'

'Probably be a good idea to warn people to keep clear of anything odd-looking with the word "summers" on it.'

'Good point. What are you going to do now?'

'Keep moving. If I am the target for the third strike whoever it is is going to have to follow me. By keeping on the move they should show themselves.'

'What about your flat? They know you have to return there sooner or later.'

'Don't worry, I've got my flat covered. If you haven't got keys to the front door you'll need a battering ram to get in. Come on, Gertie, let's go for a ride.'

No-one looking at his face would think for a split-second that he was being, at best, disingenuous.

'Oh, by the way, someone slipped this through my letter-box some time during yesterday,' he said, handing over the playing card with its message.

Frieda read it, frowning.

'What do you think it means?' she asked.

'It means they want us to run around looking for yew trees. I'm not buying, though. If it is from the Joker Gang, and they do have another target in mind, you can bet your last penny that it won't have a yew tree anywhere near.'

'I don't think we can really ignore it totally, Frank.'

'Give it to someone who actually knows what a yew tree looks like. They can spend the morning strolling around Lords Acres. I'll see you later.'

'Look after yourself, Frank,' she called. 'Whoever this shocker is obviously has a few screws missing.'

'Where to, Sarge?' asked Gertie as they got into the car.

'Back to the office, Gerts. I want to pick up my car, and there's something I need you to do for me. Have a Professor Ainke checked out. She works in the psychology department at the university.'

'Professor Ainke, got that, Sarge. But don't you want me to come with you, wherever you're going?'

'Of course, Gerts. But we don't have the time. Our shocker is going to strike again sometime soon. We are going to have to, as Frieda would put it, maximise our resources. If you find anything on Ainke, let Frieda know. I'll be in touch one way or another.'

'I suppose so, Sarge,' Gertie said with little enthusiasm. She handed the kitten to him. 'There you go, Squishy, go to Daddy, good little kitten, Auntie Gertie has to drive.'

'Daddy?' thought Frank in disbelief.

The sooner he found Squishy a proper home the better.

Frank drove into the centre of the Old Town. Hearing his new phone making a warbling sound he parked in a no-parking spot.

'I'm caught at the traffic lights,' the Chief Inspector said. 'Give me two minutes.'

Frank was both surprised and impressed. He hadn't spotted any cars tailing him.

'All quiet on the Western Front?' he asked.

'A woman. She was following you for about twenty minutes. Pretty good as it happens. Took me a while to spot her.'

'A woman? Recognise her?'

'No. Give me a time and I'll slip into the station and have a look at any mug shots we have.'

'I'll have to get myself a digital camera at this rate.'

'I've got one on me. I'll get a shot if she turns up again. Okay, light's turned green. I'm passing on your port bow. Find somewhere legal to park and give me five minutes to do the same. Anyone on your tail will have to take to their feet to follow you.'

'Just one other thing,' Frank noted.

'What's that?'

'Isn't it illegal to use a mobile phone while you're driving?'

The Chief Inspector laughed.

'Mine's hands off, as they say. Or that's what I'll tell the judge.'

Frank smiled as an angry traffic warden came up to his car. He showed the man his warrant card.

'At least it's only one woman after you this time,' chuckled the Chief Inspector, ending their conversation.

Frank could have cheerfully strangled him.

'I'm afraid I'm going to have to leave you in the car this time, Squishy,' Frank told the kitten asleep on the passenger seat, having parked down a side road where small shops slowly gave way to houses. 'I might have to chase someone and you wouldn't like being bounced around in my pocket if that happens. Don't worry, I won't be gone long.'

He had decided that, if he caught sight of anyone trailing him, he would turn on them, grab them, and encourage them to share their innermost thoughts, and he didn't want Squishy in his pocket as he did so, it would be too dangerous for the little thing.

The noise of the door closing awoke the kitten. It looked around and immediately began protesting at being left alone.

'Five minutes, Squishy,' he promised, 'I'll only be gone five minutes.'

Squishy refused to believe this lie. Two women passing by gave Frank dirty looks.

He sighed and looked around. Two shop doors away there was an old pet shop. He opened the car door, picked Squishy up and walked over.

'Could you do me a favour?' he asked the shop assistant. 'I need someone to look after this kitten for fifteen minutes.'

The assistant's eyes suggested that now he had definitely heard it all.

'You what?'

'Fifteen minutes and I'll be back for it.'

'You're having a laugh, aintcha?'

'I'm serious. Look, I'm a police officer, here's my warrant card.'

The man checked the card suspiciously.

'It's to do with a case I'm working on. I have to meet someone quickly, and they mustn't know I have the kitten. It's part of the evidence.'

The man nodded slowly.

'Fifteen minutes, you say?' he asked.

'Maximum,' said Frank, an honest look on his face. 'Just don't take her towel away from her. It's her security blanket. Be good, Squishy, I'll be back shortly.'

He shot out of the door before Squishy's appeals could make him change his mind.

Frank strolled along another side road in the Old Town. He was beginning to think he was wasting his time. There weren't many side roads he could have any good reason to go down, and any followers were likely to guess sooner rather than later that he was merely idling, and it wouldn't take them long to guess why.

He paused by an old-fashioned barber's sign. It was high time he had a haircut. Normally he went to his own barber's, a Cypriot known as Charlie. Charlie knew how he wanted his hair cut, and didn't hold with any new-fangled notions of this Unisex nonsense. Men went to the barbers to get their hair cut, and women went to the hairdressers to have their hair done. Charlie would politely chat about things important to men, politics, sport, where they were going for their holiday, the weather ...

Their holiday?

Was that where the Joker Gang were getting their information?

Professor Hawthorn was a bachelor. If a hairdresser was the link it would have to be a barber's shop.

He took his mobile out and dialled Gertie's number.

'Gertie? Frank here. I want you to find out where the victims of the burglaries had their hair cut. The men especially. Yes, leave Professor Ainke for the moment. Find out if the men used the same barbers.'

'You think that's where they're getting their information?' asked Gertie.

'It's a long shot, but they have to be getting it from somewhere.'

'Okay, Sarge. How can I get in touch with you?'

'I'll give you a call. Right now I'm going for a little drive.'

'What's he doing now?' asked Queenie. 'He's supposed to be looking for yew trees.'

'Looking into the barber's shop,' replied Cocky. 'Must say, he could do with a hair cut.'

'You're old-fashioned, you are. Give me a man with a pony tail any day. And tattoos.'

'You're a philistine, Queenie.'

'And you aren't?'

'Don't matter much, does it? We can't go into the barber's shop and slip these into his pocket, can we?'

Cocky showed two cards, the joker and the knave.

'Put those away, you pillock!'

'We'll just have to do it while he ain't suspecting, then, won't we?'

'Ace will kill us.'

'Ace won't know about it until it's done. Come on, let's get away before he sees us. We'll pull it off later.'

Frank returned to his car and was almost ready to drive away when he suddenly remembered Squishy. He hurried over to the shop, castigating himself for his thoughtlessness, only to find the kitten on the counter playing finger-grab with the assistant, an empty saucer alongside suggesting that Squishy had been given elevenses.

'Lovely little thing, isn't she?' the assistant said. 'Wish I had a place where I could keep pets. I had a cat once, but it fair ripped the furniture apart.'

'The furniture?'

'Yeah. If you're going to be looking after this little one for any time you should get yourself a scratching post. They scratch things to keep their nails sharp, you see.'

Frank considered this.

'You've got litter, I presume?' the assistant added.

Frank considered that.

'And you'll want toys to keep it occupied. And its own basket. And birdseed.'

'Birdseed? For a kitten?'

'Nah, for birds of course, to keep them away from the cat. You 'ave to set up a bird table, high up where the cat can't get to, otherwise the birds will come down to the ground and you'll be finding dead birds in your kitchen every other day.'

Frank sighed and looked at Squishy. He hoped that whoever had accidentally left the kitten in front of his flat door would be along soon to reclaim her. In the meantime it looked as if he might be spending quite a little money on Squishy.

'Of course you're feeding it the proper stuff,' the assistant suggested.

Squishy miaowed in a manner that indicated that heartless Frank was definitely doing no such thing, and she was now starving, despite the nice meal the nice shop assistant had given her.

Frank sighed.

'Go on,' he said, 'tell me what I should be feeding her.'

'Spot anything?' Frank asked the Chief Inspector on his mobile after he had packed his purchases in the boot of his car and put Squishy on the passenger seat.

'No. Couple of youngsters earlier, but in the end they disappeared. Otherwise everything looks normal.'

'I'll drive around for a while. If you don't spot anything within half an hour we'll knock it on the head.'

'Sounds reasonable. Drive out southwards. Take the back roads. The quiet ones.'

Frank did as instructed. If there was anyone following him they were either extremely good at it or he was extremely bad at detecting them. He could not even identify the Chief Inspector's car, but quite possibly that was because the other man was out of sight, being kept informed of Frank's position on his mobile.

'You're close to St Mary's,' the Chief Inspector said. 'Pull in next to the cemetery and go for a walk.'

'The cemetery?'

'Good places to spot watchers, cemeteries. For some reason they almost all think they can hide behind trees and gravestones. Easiest thing in the world to pick them up, dodging from gravestone to gravestone and from tree to tree. Most of them don't know what it means to act naturally in a cemetery. Puts them at a disadvantage.'

Frank decided that he would have to defer to the Chief Inspector's superior knowledge. He parked his car near the church, slipped a sleeping Squishy into his pocket, and strolled through the gates of the cemetery. It was, he realised, almost a year since he had last been here, walking along the gravel path, not noticing the greenness of the trees, the weather-beaten look of the gravestones first encountered when entering, newer ones located further away.

That was when he had come to the grave to say goodbye to Jean.

Why had he not been back?

Because he had not really known her.

Because he had been too busy.

Because there were some things best forgotten.

Because – well, just because.

Perhaps it was time to visit her again.

After all it would give him a reason for being there. He could hardly wander aimlessly around a cemetery, that would be far too obvious.

He did not look behind. The Chief Inspector was there, he would take care of anyone that might be following him. Instead he looked upon the graves he was passing. Anything to think about rather than about where his feet were leading him.

Julia Beacon, much loved daughter, born 1st April 1951, taken unto God, 15th May 1962. Just eleven years old when she had been taken. Mottled marble showing signs of age in an ageless place, the grave itself showing signs of care.

George Perwee, 10 January 1935 – 25 December 1996. Rest in peace. Sixty-one. Black marble. Grass growing long, weeds abundant.

John Hubert Jenkins, 2nd March 1905 – 2nd March 1989, A good life and an honest man. Eighty-four. But showing signs of neglect similar to that of George Perwee.

John Alfred Jenkins, born 14th October 1930, taken unto the Lord's loving arms 3rd September 1939. John Alfred Jenkins had not even made his ninth birthday. Perhaps, considering the date, a merciful release. Perhaps not.

A small grave for a small boy, neatly kept.

Mary Jenkins, February 16 1908 – 12 November 1988, loving wife of John Hubert Jenkins, asleep in eternal peace. Eighty. Asleep under an unkempt grave matching that of her husband, their only child, presumably, having long pre-deceased them, and not able to look after their final resting places.

As he walked slowly on Frank realised a puzzling continuity. While some of the graves of the older deceased were kept in neat condition, many were obviously not attended to. Yet all of those of children that he passed were invariably tidy, if not in pristine condition, at least as if someone had made an effort.

Who looked after them? It was not something that had crossed his mind before. If asked he would have presumed that the local council, or even the church, would have retained someone to keep things in order.

The thought slipped from his mind as he came to the

intersection in the path where he knew he had to turn left. He had only to look up and he would be able to see Jean's grave. But he did not want to see it again. He wanted to remember Jean as she was, still alive in his mind, laughter in her eyes and teasing in her lips, mocking him in that French accent she put on.

No, he thought, I can't do it.

Unwillingly he turned to look down at the unwelcome route without actually looking at the grave. His eyes caught two shoes, cracked and worn old shoes. His glance automatically followed the shoes to the legs that wore them. Someone was on all fours right in front of Jean's grave. It looked like an old woman, a bag woman dressed in an old, faded-blue coat, pulling something from the grave. Around her were plastic bags and scattered flowers. For a moment he could not believe his eyes.

An old woman, a bag woman, stealing flowers from graves, no doubt to sell! From Jean's grave!

His irresolution disappeared. He strode up to the woman, almost running, his heart pumping. As he came close he realised that it was not Jean's grave she was robbing but the one next to it. She turned at the sound of his feet. Her face, old, lined, weather-beaten and with a hideous scar across the right side of her temple, initially had a mildly pleased look upon it, as if expecting pleasant company. That look disappeared as soon as she saw the fury in his eyes.

'What the hell do you think you're doing?' he shouted.

'Please, sir,' she whimpered, cringing, holding her thin arms in front of her as if to ward off a blow.

'I'm a police officer,' he said, his voice shaking with anger, showing her his warrant card. 'I'm arresting you for theft.'

'No, sir, please, sir,' she cried, struggling in her pocket for something, holding one arm up, shivering. Eventually she found it and proffered it to him. It was a little card.

Reluctantly he took it. He could not believe his eyes. It was a card printed with a name, telephone number and address.

The name read "Inspector F Garold". The address was Wellbury police station. The number was that of Frieda's mobile.

He turned it over. On the back was written:

"If Aggie is ever in trouble telephone me first."

'What the hell is this supposed to mean? Where did you get this? Where did you steal it from?'

'Please, sir,' the woman repeated, pointing at the card.

Frank felt a hand on his arm.

'It's okay, Aggie,' the Chief Inspector said softly, taking the card and returning it to the woman. 'You get on with your work, there's a good girl, nothing to worry about. Frank, a quick word.'

He drew Frank a few steps away.

'What the hell is going on?' Frank asked, glaring at the woman. The woman returned the look with fear.

'Now calm down, Frank, that's the third "what the hell" in as many minutes, if not seconds.'

'She's robbing that grave! Look at the flowers!'

'She's not robbing the grave, Frank, she's tending it.'

'Tending it?' Frank exclaimed, turning towards the other man. 'What, are you telling me she's employed by the local council?

Or the church? That thing?'

'Frank, in this day and age when the government are paring even pensions, and local councils begrudge every penny spent on anything, how much do you think they'll be willing to spend on the dead? That thing, as you refer to her, or Aggie as she is better known, isn't employed by anyone, not really.'

Aggie, Frank's glare no longer upon her, turned back to her work, throwing the two an occasional glance, for the Chief Inspector a grateful one, for Frank a fearful one.

'I'm afraid the upkeep of the graves is left to the relatives to look after,' the Chief Inspector continued. 'Needless to say many of the graves remain unattended, either through simple neglect or because all relatives have themselves passed on.' He once again took Frank's arm and gently propelled him into a stroll, away from the old woman. 'Aggie turned up a few months ago, just before Christmas. Nobody knows where from, she either won't say or can't remember herself. An old widow, one Mrs Fuller, lives not too far from here, found Aggie in her garden shed. Are you hearing this, Frank?'

Frank nodded, his anger subsiding slowly, not understanding what was going on, but understanding that the Chief Inspector seemed to know and approve.

'Mrs Fuller only discovered her because Aggie had crept out of the shed to listen to the music Mrs Fuller had on. Christmas carols, I believe, or possibly classical. Aggie loves listening to music when she gets the chance, especially church music. Now, for whatever reason, whether it was the season for goodwill to all men, and women, or whether Mrs Fuller is just naturally generous, or lonely, or whatever, she, instead of doing the obvious and calling us in to have Aggie carted off to somewhere she wouldn't disturb good honest wealthy citizens, offered Aggie a hot bath and some hot food.'

He took his pipe out, looked at it, and put it in his mouth.

'Aggie might be – have been – a bag lady, but she is very clean and tidy, very conscious of personal hygiene, as one might say. I don't know whether she was more taken by the idea of a hot bath or hot food, but she accepted.'

He paused.

'Refused to eat off Mrs Fuller's plates or drink from her cups, mind you. Insisted that she use her own little plastic plate and cup. From what I understand she said she was afraid of breaking the dainty china cups and plates, but there's probably more to it than that. Whatever the reason, she did accept the offer, on her terms. And therein lies the rub. Aggie does not believe in charity. It's not that she's proud, she just has this simplistic belief that, if someone does something for you, you must repay the favour. Not payment in money, you see – she understands paying for things in certain circumstances with money, but in this case it had to be a case of actually doing something for Mrs Fuller. Personal favours cannot be paid for with money.'

He puffed on his unlit pipe.

'You will find that she is a bit simple, Frank, but enough of that later. She badgered Mrs Fuller to give her something to do. In the end Mrs Fuller surrendered and said that Aggie could help her tend her husband's grave, probably thinking that that would be the last of it. Especially when Aggie disappeared two days later. She had helped Mrs Fuller with the grave, Mrs Fuller gave her some change, and Aggie disappeared – apparently. Two weeks later, the festive season over and done with, Mrs Fuller returned to tend her late husband's grave, only to find that there was no work to be done, and some early crocuses were in the vase. She looked around and saw Aggie hard at work on a winter's morning on another grave.'

He stopped and turned to Frank.

'I think – I think Aggie had found her vocation in life. To her mind she had been paid to look after Mr Fuller's grave, but she had spare time to look after others. So many forgotten graves ... Aggie concentrated on the children's graves, you'll find out why in due course. When we get back, ask her how old she is.'

'But surely ... she must be at least sixty, if not seventy.'

The other man nodded, not as if he agreed, but rather as if he understood.

'Mrs Fuller was – agitated, I think the word is. Where was Aggie sleeping? How did she wash? What was she eating? How had she looked after herself while Mrs Fuller and the rest of the world celebrated with too much drink and food?'

He smiled, a mixture of sadness and incredulity.

'Aggie is a child, you see. A special kind of child. She's absolutely honest, for a start. She explained to Mrs Fuller how she slept in a mausoleum, the door to which was not locked, and hoped the priest wouldn't mind. And washed under the stand pipe, every day, she hoped the priest would forgive her using the water. The church hall is left unlocked most of the time, she hoped the priest didn't mind her using its facilities when required. And she still had some of the coins Mrs Fuller had given her to buy food with if people stopped leaving food out for her. She didn't use the word, but I'm pretty sure she meant the food people threw away, that is to say, in their dustbins.'

His eyes moistened.

'And she said people were so generous at Christmas time with the left-overs they put out.'

'I don't believe it,' Frank whispered. 'How can we –'

'Aye, we'll get back to that. Anyway, Mrs Fuller, having, I presume, recovered from her – I don't know what the word would be, gobsmackedness? Anyway, she insists that Aggie is to come home with her and have another hot bath and another hot meal and stay with her forever more. But there's the rub. Aggie refuses. She can't stand what she calls indoors – hates it, in fact. A hot bath and a hot meal are special occasions, treats for when she's been good. She's quite used to washing in cold water, though hot is better, the soap works better with hot, but cold will do for her. And for "cold", read "freezing". In our terms, anyway. Bloody freezing.'

He shook his head again.

'Anyway, Mrs Fuller is an obstinate woman, or she decides to be on this occasion, and finally they agree a deal whereby Aggie will have a hot bath and a hot meal twice a week – Wednesday and Saturday evenings, and in return she will look after Mrs Fuller's husband's grave, and any other Mrs Fuller nominates. Saturday evenings because then she's properly clean for the Lord's day, Wednesday – something to do with Lent, according to her. She most often spends the little money she has on fish for Friday. Apparently she was sick once when she ate the thrown-away fish the good people had left out for her. Not that they realised it, of course.'

He looked at his pipe as if surprised to find it there.

'To cut a long story short – a story we don't know anything

about, to be honest – Aggie becomes more or less the mascot of the cemetery. Initially people are repelled by her appearance – you saw the old scar on her face?'

Frank nodded.

'Not a pretty sight. I'm no student of medicine, but my guess is that the wound should have been stitched up, but for some reason never was. Whatever happened, it's a sight to repel. But so long as Mrs Fuller is there to explain they gradually get used to her. And they give her a few coins, a gesture of charity. But Aggie, of course, will not have charity. She demands to know which grave she must take care of in payment. And Aggie is so simple and insistent you can't argue the toss. You give her money, she does what she believes she has been paid for. Give her a coin, any coin, once, and she's labour for life. Doesn't understand anything else. You gave her a coin once, she's indebted to you, that's it. She calls it pocket money. Fortunately the type of people who regularly attend graves here are pretty honest, and, being in the main, quite elderly and grieving, they tend to be more accepting than most. It might take a while to get used to Aggie, but when they do, they protect her, and they bring her food so that she doesn't have to rummage in dustbins anymore.'

He looked up at the sky.

'Perhaps it's a case of, when you're faced with the idea of death, you realise that nothing really matters that much.'

They stood in silence for a while. Frank wondered whether the Chief Inspector was thinking of his wife.

'Come, let's stroll back,' the other man said finally.

They turned back towards the figure labouring over the grave next to Jean's.

'She's a mystery,' concluded the Chief Inspector. 'You can tell from the way she speaks that she has had a good education somewhere along the line. She wasn't brought up in Cockney London, or Scouse Liverpool or anywhere like that. No discernible accent, other than that of a young girl of a middle or upper-middle class household. But she never talks about family, or rather, she speaks of the dead as her family. Especially the children, her brothers and sisters. In a place like this she has so many.'

'How did she get Frieda's card?' asked Frank.

The Chief Inspector shook his head as if to say "Typical".

'St Mary's church. St Mary's cemetery. And over there you can just see, over the road, the fences around St Mary's tennis club, where Frieda plays each Sunday. A couple of months ago she hit a ball badly, right over the fence and into the cemetery. After the set she came over to retrieve it, saw Aggie, and jumped to the exact same conclusion as you did.'

He sighed.

'Unfortunately Frieda was in a bad mood already, and, as I'm sure you've experienced, she's not a woman to cross when in a bad mood. She found the idea of grave robbing just as repugnant as we would, and set about poor Aggie with her tongue. Fortunately Mrs Fuller wasn't far off, and came to protect the girl. Explanations and apologies were made – Frieda, when she mentioned it to me, did not go into details, but I rather guessed that that old word, mortified, came into play. Aggie is as defenceless as a child in many ways, and Frieda would never hold with anyone tongue-lashing such a poor creature. Which was what she had just done. She returned to her tennis, but when she left that afternoon, she went back into the cemetery and gave Aggie her card, telling her to show it if she was ever in trouble. It's a bit of a talisman to Aggie now. So long as she has Frieda's card she's safe in her own home.'

Frank looked at him, eyes open wide in incredulity.

'Her own home? This?'

'Oh, yes, the graveyard is her home. She talks to the dead, you see.'

'What? She speaks with spirits?'

The Chief Inspector chuckled.

'No, Frank. She talks to them as if they were alive, listening, around her. She knows they can't talk back, but – you remember I said she hoped the priest wouldn't mind if she used his water? There's a hint of Catholicism there. It's not a priest, it's a vicar. But you might as well explain that to the waves. To her mind she's only awaiting death to join the others beyond. God alone knows what she's been through.'

They had returned to Jean's grave, Aggie prattling on to herself and the dead.

'Ask her how old she is,' prompted the Chief Inspector.

Frank hesitated. He cleared his throat without making a noise.

'Er, Aggie, how old are you?'

'I'm twelve,' Angie said, without looking back, continuing her work happily. I'll be twelve and a half this October. When I'm twelve and a half the good Lord will call for me, and I shall join my brothers and sisters in heaven. I have so many sweet little brothers and sisters, and they are all waiting for me to come to them.'

Frank turned to the other man, with yet more disbelief in his eyes, the hair on his neck rising. The Chief Inspector raised his eyebrows as if to say "What can you do?"

'But surely – I mean – this isn't the Dark Ages. Can't something be done?'

The Chief Inspector smiled.

'What would you have done with her?' he asked in a soft voice. 'Put her in a home? She hates indoors, she's terrified of strangers, she'd run away in days. You can't lock her up, there's no reason and it would only be cruelty. No, she's quite happy where she is, she's found a little home for herself where she can feel safe – or quite a large home, as it is. Not even the Social Services know what to do, which is probably a first for them. They come around once a week to make sure she's okay, and then, I expect, have a meeting to discuss the issue and end up agreeing that they'll make another visit the next week and come to a decision then. I doubt if they ever will. I'm not sure there is an answer.'

Aggie peeked back at them, probably aware that they were talking about her. Her eyes opened wide for a second as she looked at Frank's waist. Then they narrowed into innocent deviousness, and she began slowly edging towards them on all fours, pretending to be still hard at work.

'I also doubt if we'll ever find out why Aggie is like she is,' the Chief Inspector continued in his low voice. 'My guess is that she probably received some form of brain-damage when she got that scar – or perhaps she was born simple, but that wouldn't explain why she thinks she's twelve, or that her language isn't that of a simpleton. Perhaps that's the only way she can cope with the world, as a simple child.'

Frank turned to look back at Aggie, to find her crouched in front of him with a hand reaching towards his pocket. He jumped back. She sank further to the ground, hand still outstretched.

'Kitty,' she pleaded.

'She wants to touch Squishy,' the Chief Inspector explained. 'She loves animals, especially young ones.'

'Hello, Squish,' Frank said, taking the kitten from his pocket. 'You've woken up, have you? You do have a nice life, don't you, nothing but play and sleep.'

Squishy miaowed blearily.

'She's thirsty,' said Aggie. 'I'll get some water.'

She stood up, took a cup from one of her packets, and went to a stand-pipe a short distance away. Frank blinked.

'Yes,' said the other man, as if agreeing. 'Strange, isn't it. You could swear that she skips around just like an excited twelve-year-old might.'

'There must be something we can do.'

'When you think of it let me know.'

Aggie came back, holding the cup carefully. She held it out to Frank as if a supplicant with a miserable offering. Frank put Squishy on the ground and Aggie put the cup in front of the kitten. Squishy began lapping happily as Aggie sat and stroked her.

Frank pulled on his earlobe.

'Where does she get the flowers from?'

'They're wild flowers – or, as I am told is more accurate, wild flowers and flowers growing wild, apparently there's a difference. She gets up very early every morning, before other people are awake, and goes to collect them. Don't you Aggie?'

Aggie nodded without looking up, fascinated with Squishy.

'God gives us the flowers free,' she said. 'There's daisies and buttercups and marigolds and irises and stitchwort and bellflowers to start with.'

'And neither of us would probably be able to tell which is which,' the Chief Inspector said wryly. He looked at his watch. 'Better get going, I suppose.'

'I suppose,' agreed Frank.

'Give Sergeant Summers his kitten, Aggie, we have to be going now.'

Aggie picked up Squishy gently and reluctantly offered her to Frank. He took the kitten and slipped her into his pocket. Squishy held one paw on the pocket and looked back at Aggie.

A thought crossed Frank's mind. He took out his wallet and offered her a five pound note in an embarrassed manner. She put her hands behind her back, looked down at the ground and shook her head.

'She doesn't take paper,' the Chief Inspector explained.

'Paper goes off,' agreed Aggie.

Frank checked his wallet for coins. He found three one pound coins and one two pound coin and offered those to her. She held out cupped hands to receive them, closing them firmly once they were in her grip.

'She'll spend most of it on food for strays instead of on herself,' the Chief Inspector said. 'Won't you, Aggie?'

Aggie looked down again as if acknowledging this to be true, but determined to do it anyway, whatever people might think.

'They aren't stray,' she said to the ground, 'I belong to them.'

Having nodded at this truth she looked up at Frank.

'Which grave?' she asked.

'She wants to know which grave you want her to look after,' the Chief Inspector explained.

Frank hesitated, and then smiled.

'The one next to the one you're working on will do just fine, Aggie,' he said. 'She was ...' He hesitated again as he looked at the name Jean Candour on the gravestone. Then he smiled again. It was as if Jean's face looked back, laughing at him, teasing him for acting like an old fuddy-duddy.

'She was very dear to me,' he concluded. 'You'll do that, Aggie?'

She nodded forcefully, as a child of twelve might.

'I like her. She's my friend. She's always laughing. She likes mischief, but it isn't bad mischief. Not really.'

Frank rubbed a hand over his face, looking at Aggie, wondering how she came up with that, and at how accurate it was.

'You talk to her?'

Aggie nodded again.

'It would be rude not to talk to her when she's so close.'

'Come on, Frank, time to go. Bye bye, Aggie, see you soon.'

Frank added his own greeting and they walked away. Aggie had not replied.

'That was where I first saw her, on the river,' the Chief Inspector said, 'collecting flowers along the riverbank early one morning. I visit my wife's grave at least once a week, but she never showed herself to me here. She probably thought there would be no one around on the river at that time of the morning. And then Frieda mentioned her, and I made some enquiries and I was introduced to her by one of the visitors she trusted. You might have noticed reports of prowlers around this area over the past few months.'

Frank nodded.

'No-one was ever caught, but there were plenty of reports.'

'That's probably Aggie. She keeps away from people as far as she can, but she can't resist the temptation when she hears music she likes coming from a house. She creeps up and sits outside listening.'

'I've never seen her there. On the river, I mean.'

'You will from now on. She lets people see her if she trusts them.'

'I wouldn't think she'd trust me very much. Not after I had a go at her.'

The Chief Inspector chuckled.

'A man who carries a poor little kitten around in his pocket? You'll be a hero to her.'

They turned to take a last glance backwards. Aggie stood in the same position, watching them. They waved. She waved back excitedly.

'Bye bye, Squishy! See you soon!' she called, and then turned and dropped back to her work.

Both men shook their heads in perplexity, and continued back to their cars.

'We who can must take care of those who can't,' murmured the Chief Inspector. 'She's happy here. That's the important point. We'll work out what to do as winter gets near, though I think she's going to take some persuading, whatever we come up with.'

Happy, thought Frank Summers.

He wished he could be as innocently happy as Aggie tending the graves of little children.

And hadn't that been his only aim in life once? To be happy? To think of laughter as the most prised ambition a man could have?

'Where to now?' asked the Chief Inspector, interrupting his introspection.

'I'm going back to my flat. Squishy needs feeding. And then I think I'll pay the university a visit.'

He looked at the church as they got to their cars. The sound of a choir practising came to them. He looked back towards the cemetery.

'First time I've visited the grave since ...'

The Chief Inspector nodded.

'It's difficult, I know. But you get used to it, eventually.'

The Chief Inspector watched him drive off. He took a last look at the cemetery, shook his head slowly and smiled, as if he were a man who did not understand how, but things were working out as they should be, his having given the same things a gentle nudge in the right direction.

Friday Afternoon: Those twins again

Frank parked outside his flat and took Squishy and his purchases up. Having given Squishy something to eat and drink he telephoned Gertie, asking her to pick him up. While Squishy was concentrating on her lunch he unpacked the various items from the pet shop.

Basket with cushion; he wondered whether he hadn't been conned into buying that. Dogs, yes, they often had their own baskets, he was pretty sure of that, but cats? Didn't they recline in their own favourite places, quite often the last place you might think suitable?

Scratching post, fair enough. So long as Squishy used it. He had a vague suspicion that the scratching post might well remain pristine while his furniture began to fall to pieces under Squishy's tender administration.

Litter and tray. That went into a corner in the scullery, hidden next to the fridge to provide Squishy with a modicum of privacy.

Bird seed. He had definitely been conned there. Or had let himself be conned. Even if what the shop assistant had told him was true, he didn't have a garden to put a bird table in. Still, he did have a windowsill at the front. The birdseed went into the pot plants there, the contents of which, he noticed, had at some stage, without his taking any active part in the process, decided to grow despite his neglect.

Back in the kitchen Squishy was licking a paw with all the satisfaction of a gourmet having just finished the best meal in the universe. Frank took out another of his purchases, a table tennis ball.

'Apparently you'll like this,' Frank told her dubiously and

dropped the ball on the floor tiles. Squishy stopped licking and looked at the ball with interest as it bounced, head cocked to one side.

Then she pounced.

Gertie rang the bell, wondering why Frank had asked her to be his chauffeur, without coming to any conclusions apart from the one about not looking gift-horses in the mouth. Whatever the reason it meant that she was in favour, and closer to him than the other two.

'Come in, Gerts,' Frank said when he opened the door to her. 'Squishy and I were just having a game of football.'

'A game of football?' she queried, noticing that his hair was all over the place.

'Yes, come watch, I'm goalkeeper.'

She followed him into the kitchen where Squishy was patting angrily at a table tennis ball wedged under the front of the stove.

'It gets caught there, you see. Come on, Squish, let me get at it. Now, back to your position.'

He went down on hands and knees and rolled the ball to the delighted kitten. A whack from a paw sent it bouncing off one skirting board, then off another. Squishy crouched and then hurled herself at the rolling ball, giving it another whack, rolling over on the floor as she did so.

Gertie watched, bemused. If anything had brought Frank out of his shell it had been this kitten. If whoever had left it returned to claim it they would have a battle on their hands.

'One more, Squish, and then we must go,' Frank told the kitten. Squishy was tiring. Though her enthusiasm wasn't flagging, her body was. Eventually Frank caught up the ball and put it in his pocket. 'Enough, Squish, we need to be getting going. Gertie here will drive us.'

'The university, Gerts,' he instructed as he got into the car, Squishy in his pocket, sleeping peacefully with her new friend, the table tennis ball, the tip of her nose showing through one of the air vents, part of a paw through another. 'I want to find out whether Susan has made any progress with those notes, and I also want to have a word with an expert in psychology.'

'Psychology?'

'Our Professor Ainke. Maybe she can help us with a profile of this shocker. Any news on which barbers the burglary victims used?'

'Well, I did find out something interesting.'

'The men all use the same barbers?'

'No.'

'Damn.' He sighed. 'Oh, well, it was a long shot at best.'

'No, but the two women and Professor Hawthorn used the same unisex hairdresser,' Gertie said smugly.

Frank looked at her in astonishment.

'I decided to check out all the options,' she said. 'Turns out our Professor is vain about his hair.'

'Oh, Gertie, if you weren't driving I could kiss you.'

'I'll park then, shall I, Sarge?'

'Yes, pull over, Gerts, I want a quick think.'

Gertie pulled over, hoping for the promised kiss. It was not to be.

'Let's presume that the hairdresser is where they're getting their information,' Frank said, stroking a sleeping Squishy absent-mindedly. 'How do we get someone in to pass on the news of the empty house in Lords Acres?'

'I could go for a hairdo,' offered Gertie. 'Pretend to be the old couple's niece or something.'

'That might just work, you know Gertie. After we've finished at the university you get off and have your hair done. You can even put it on expenses.'

Gertie smiled. She had been considering having her hair done. Having it paid for was an added bonus.

'Come in,' came the stern voice after Frank had knocked at Professor Ainke's door.

He had sent Gertie off to have a coffee in the canteen. He didn't want her to be in on this conversation. He had given her Squishy to take with her.

Gertie was just getting the glimmerings of a suspicion that she was not only Frank's chauffeur, but Squishy's babysitter. She wasn't sure that she welcomed the idea. Squishy was an adorable little kitten, true, but to be used, without actually stating the fact, as a kitten-sitter?

Still, there was another point of view. At least Frank trusted her with Squishy. That had to count for something, didn't it?

'Hi, Prof,' Frank said as he entered the professor's office. 'I was wondering if you could give me a hand, what with you being a psychologist thingummy.'

'I am a professor of psychology, Sergeant Summers,' came the retort. 'Not a thingummy.'

'Yeah, course, sorry about that. Only, we've been getting

these notes about practical jokes, and I was wondering whether I could get your opinion on them. We don't have one of those profile people, one of those people who tells us what sort of person we're looking for, and I'm not sure whether we should call one in. Cost a lot, they do, and we've got to work to budget. Know what I mean?'

'I suppose I could have a quick look. Let me see these notes, Sergeant.'

'Well, I ain't got them with me, but I can draw them like what they look like. Got a piece of paper?'

Professor Ainke pushed over a note-pad in a long-suffering gesture. Frank took his jacket off, sat down and wrote, his tongue sticking slightly from his lips, a picture of concentration.

'There you go,' he said, passing the pad back. Professor Ainke took the pad and began to read. 'Say,' he added, 'while you're looking at them, I need to go to the khazi – the little boys' room. I'll do that while you're having a shufti.'

After he had left Professor Ainke read what Frank had written.

"THREE STRIKES AND YOU'RE OUT SERGENT SUMMERS

SHOCKING INNIT

YOU READY TO PLAY?"

"STRIKE NUMBER ONE

YOU SLIPPED UP MR SUMMERS

SHOCKING, INNIT?

YOULL WET YOURSELF WHEN YOU MISS THE

NEXT ONE"

Her mouth curled up at one side.

'You're with Mr Summers,' a voice said to Gertie as she sat in the university canteen, a cup of cooling coffee in front of her, feeling sorry for herself, and wondering why Frank had deliberately excluded her from his interview with Professor Ainke. Squishy lay asleep on her lap.

She turned around to find two youngsters looking at her, twins.

'I'm Rich,' said the one. 'Short for Richard. This is Rach. Short for Rachael.'

The girl twin did not look as if she was impressed with Gertie.

'Detective Constable Gregson,' Gertie introduced herself. 'How do you know Sergeant Summers?'

'Oh, we sort of bumped into him,' Richard said nonchalantly, both of them sitting down, uninvited.

'You're a Detective Constable?' asked Rachael, intrigued. 'Like, Sergeant Summers' Detective Constable? You work together?'

'We do. Most of the time.'

'Wow! Were you there when he got shot?'

Gertie took a sip of coffee and looked at the twins.

'Yes,' she said finally, 'I was there.'

The twins looked at each other eagerly, obviously wanting to ask something, but afraid they might be trespassing.

'What happened?' asked Rachael. 'I mean –'

She stumbled into silence. Gertie put her coffee down.

'If you're students you should be able to research that. There are sufficient primary sources.'

'Primary sources,' Richard said in awe. 'Our lecturers are always on about primary sources.'

'Then research them,' Gertie said, taking Squishy into her arms and standing up.

She walked away. She did not want to remember that night. Least of all did she want to share it with strangers.

'Boy, she's mad at something,' noted Rachael.

'Good looker,' Richard observed. 'I wonder why she had a kitten with her.'

Rachael looked at him looking after the departing figure. She turned her gaze to Gertie's back.

'She's far too old for you,' she said.

'Sorry, Prof,' Frank said on re-entering Professor Ainke's office, 'just got a call on my radio, I have to be somewhere else sharpish. I'll give you a call later.'

He picked up and put on his jacket in front of the woman's surprised eyes.

'I have formed a view on the person who wrote these,' she said.

'Have you?' he asked, taking from her hands the piece of paper he had written on. 'Good. Excellent. But don't worry, I think I know who it is. We plods might not be as clever as you intellectuals, but we get there in the end. I'll leave you in your ivory mansion. Ta-ta, Prof.'

'Ivory tower,' she was about to correct him. The closing door beat her to it.

She sat there empty-handed, looking extremely irritated.

Frank's keys lay on the chair where he had dropped his jacket, just as if they had fallen out of his pocket.

Frank scanned the canteen. No sign of Gertie.

An arm put itself around his waist.

'I'm sure I've done something wrong. Would you like to arrest me?'

Frank looked down at Rachael's face and fluttering eyes. She giggled. Behind her Richard looked on, bemused.

Frank disentangled her thin arm.

'I'm looking for my constable,' he said. 'She was supposed to be waiting for me here.'

'Blonde, a little overweight?' suggested Rachael.

'Where did she go?' asked Frank, refusing to rise to the bait.

'Towards the pathology section. Where they keep the dead people.'

Frank shook his head at her.

'I don't suppose you've heard of the word "minx" by any chance?' he asked.

'I'm a real little minx when I want to be,' she told him, smiling, again fluttering her eyelashes.

He shook his head again in despair and marched away from them.

They watched him go, Rachael with a smile on her face. Richard's mouth broke into a grin as a fast-moving Frank Summers bumped into Cyril entering the canteen. Cyril made profuse apologies, but Frank was more alarmed by the sight of his aunt only a few yards away.

'Lovely day,' he said, 'must dash.'

This wouldn't, he thought to himself, have happened if he had stuck to fishing on the river.

He found Gertie in Susan's office. Neither woman looked very happy. Squishy brightened up at his appearance and gave him a miaow.

'What's wrong with you two?' he asked, lifting the kitten into his arms and stroking it. 'You look as if your pet goldfish just drowned.'

'I don't suppose you got my message yesterday morning?' asked Susan.

'Oh, yes, sorry about that. I got your message, but things have just been a little hectic. I won't be able to make tonight, there's someone I have to meet. Now, what's the story with these notes?'

There was silence as Susan took in this offhand dismissal of her invitation.

'They're almost definitely written by the same hand,' she replied, an angry look on her face. 'The paper is from the same source, and the ink matches.'

'Oh, good. Do me a favour.' He took the piece of paper Professor Ainke had given him from his jacket. 'Run some tests on this, see if there's a match. Come on Gertie, you can give me a lift back to my flat. And then you need to have your hair done.'

They watched him leave, their mouths open.

'Why, the arrogant –' breathed Susan.

'He's doing it deliberately,' said Gertie, picking up her handbag. 'It's avoidance. He's making sure he doesn't allow us to get close.'

'Then why was he having lunch with Frieda?'

Gertie considered this worrying question.

'I don't know. Maybe he was just pumping her for information.'

'Information? About what?'

Gertie raised her eyebrows at Susan to indicate that Susan knew exactly what she was talking about, and left.

All the way back to his flat Gertie tried desperately to think of a way to engage Frank, but failed miserably. He sat in unusual silence, tapping the window sill to some private tune.

'I'll give you a call,' he said when she pulled in to the pavement in front of his flat. 'We'll have drinks or something, once this shocker nonsense is over.'

And then he was gone.

But Gertie was elated. He had said he would give her a call! They would have drinks! All was not lost. She drove away in a mist of hope.

And then she went to have her hair done, pretending to be in town purely because her aunt and uncle had had to leave precipitously because one of their grandchildren had been taken ill. She needed to collect some things they had forgotten. Normally she would have gone to her normal hairdresser, but her boyfriend was coming back from a month in the Middle East tomorrow, and she wanted to look her best as she thought he might be popping The Question tomorrow night, or at latest on Sunday.

The Joker Gang? No, she hadn't heard of them. Anyway, there were more important things for a girl to worry about than some silly burglars. And her aunt and uncle would only be away for one night, perhaps two at most.

They did have some expensive tastes, mind. She didn't know a lot about silver, but she knew that if the boyfriend did pop The Question, her aunt and uncle would be good for a very decent wedding present, they certainly knew their stuff.

'Got a nice collection, have they?' asked the hairdresser.

'That's what they say,' answered Gertie, admiring the way the other woman had done her hair. 'Personally I wouldn't know. All looks ancient to me, if you know what I mean?'

'Yes, I do. Give me modern jewellery any day.'

Gertie left, feeling that she had done all she could. She hadn't taken much notice of the young woman being attended to alongside.

'I'm so glad I came back for the highlights,' said Queenie admiring herself in the mirror. 'You're right, it really was worth it.'

Friday Evening: Frank gets and loses a minder

Frank trotted up the stairs to his flat, whistling. A not too happy Sam Nightingale was waiting for him. Wearing, he noticed a smart jacket, silk-looking blouse, skirt to the knees (nice calves) and elegant shoes.

If she were surprised to see a kitten peering out of his pocket she made no sign of it.

'Hello, Sam, not been waiting too long, have you?' he asked cheerfully. 'Squishy, this is Sam, Sam, this is Squishy.'

'I've been ordered by Inspector Garold to look after you,' she replied in a tone which made it clear what she thought of the order, ignoring the kitten. Squishy looked at her with some curiosity. This was the first human she had met who had not immediately made cooing noises and bent over her, forcing her to flee into the safety of Frank's jacket pocket.

'I know, I know, Sam. Frieda gets a little carried away sometimes. You just have to humour her.'

He patted the pocket not occupied by Squishy and raised his eyebrows.

'Damn! I seem to have lost my keys,' he remarked.

'Perhaps you left them inside the flat,' suggested Sam Nightingale, thinking that he was not showing much irritation at the loss, certainly not the irritation she would have felt. She had a scar on her right hand from the last time that that had happened to her. She had lost her temper and punched the glass in the door, not realising that it was old and thin and likely to shatter at the slightest pressure, which it had done, leaving a deep cut in her hand and blood spurting everywhere.

'Nope, I definitely had them on me earlier. Hold on a tick, I leave a spare set with my neighbour. Wait here, I won't be a sec.'

Sam stood fuming as she watched Frank knock on a nearby door and retrieve his spare keys. He was treating the loss of his keys with a nonchalance that irritated her. He was treating her as a flunkey, which infuriated her.

"He can be the most irritating man you will ever meet," Inspector Garold had warned her. "Don't let him get under your skin. Just keep an eye on him. There's someone out there trying to shock him, and in a physical rather than figurative sense."

Sam Nightingale hadn't quite understood the latter statement, but the former was becoming more and more evident. When she had been told that Frank Summers was the romantic target of three women including Inspector Garold she had presumed it was the usual tall tale told to someone new at a police station. She had since realised, to her utter amazement, that it was true. What she didn't understand was why she was the one who had been assigned to the task of protecting the Detective Sergeant.

'Boy does she go on,' Frank said, rejoining her after what seemed like half an hour of listening to his neighbour bewail the dangers of the modern world, and how you couldn't sleep safe in your own bed when people went around stealing the very keys from your pockets without you even noticing it.

He opened the door, brushing past her as she declined to move out of his way. 'Come in and have a nice cup of tea.'

'You'll have to change locks,' she noted.

'Yes, I'll do that first thing tomorrow,' he said, switching on the kettle as they walked into the kitchen. 'Damn! I meant to buy some sugar today, I'm all out. I'll borrow some from the neighbour. You put your feet up. Squishy, you wait for me here.'

Another frown hit her face as he put Squishy down on her towel and left. Typical bachelor. His place needed a good clean and he had run out of sugar.

The frown was replaced by a wry smile. Her flat was hardly pristine, and she was continually running short of things.

Well, well, she thought. I have something in common with Sergeant Frank Summers. Maybe he isn't all bad.

Squishy sat on her towel and watched as Sam Nightingale began opening cupboard doors idly, seeking to confirm that his shopping habits were as bad as hers. It was after closing a top cabinet door that a thoughtful look crossed her face. She re-opened the door.

Right in front of a bottle of coffee, a tin containing teabags, and a selection of biscuits, was a stoneware jar labelled "Sugar". She took it down and opened it.

It was full.

Silly Sergeant Summers. He had forgotten that he had sugar in the jar.

She looked up at the open cabinet. Behind the jar of sugar was a new packet of sugar.

Another possible explanation struck her. The obvious one. Sergeant Summers hadn't popped out for a cup of sugar. He had popped out to get away from her. He wasn't taking his time because of a complaining neighbour. He was taking his time because he had gone out somewhere else.

She noticed a spare set of keys on a hook. She put the jar

back, closed the cabinet, picked up the keys and went into the hall. She opened the front door, strode over to the neighbour's door and knocked.

'Constable Nightingale,' she introduced herself to the elderly woman who answered. 'Would Sergeant Summers be here by any chance?'

'No, my dear, you've just missed him. I saw him going down the stairs not two minutes ago. At least he's doing something about the crime these days, works all hours, he does. Why this very morning I heard him come in in the early hours, the poor man must have been dead on his feet. But he has to, you know. You wouldn't believe how bad it is these days. Why, only the other day –'

'Yes, I'm sure you're right. Thank you,' Sam said before the other woman could continue, managing to retain a fixed smile. 'Sorry to have bothered you.'

She went back to Frank's flat, leaving a rather bemused old woman wondering what was going on.

Sam Nightingale closed the door behind her.

You bastard! she thought. You absolute, absolute bastard, Frank bloody Summers!

She couldn't believe that he had tricked her so easily. And she had been forewarned.

"Don't let him out of your sight, Constable Nightingale," Inspector Garold had also warned. "Give him half a chance and he'll disappear before you know it."

Which is exactly what he had done.

She wondered whether she should let the Inspector know. It would not look good. Only a few days in her new posting and she had cocked up the most trivial of tasks. And of course Frank Summers wouldn't be in trouble, no, he was the Inspector's blue-eyed boy, and, apparently, quite a lot more than that.

It would certainly be an unusual exchange between police officers: "I'm sorry, Inspector, I'm afraid your boyfriend has given me the slip."

No, she decided, she'd give it a while. Make a cup of tea and put her feet up, as ordered by Sergeant Summers.

Back in Frank's kitchen she looked down at a noise at her feet. Squishy obviously wanted something.

'I suppose he hasn't fed you. Left that up to me, the bastard. Come on, I'll get you something to drink.'

Sam Nightingale wasn't a pet person. She didn't dislike them on principle, she just had never had the urge to own a cat, dog, python or parakeet. But her nursing background meant that she automatically recognised something that needed attention.

While Squishy tucked into a saucer of tuna Sam made a mug of tea, wandered into the lounge, dropped her handbag on the couch and began looking for something to read to pass away the time.

Austen? No, she had read all of Jane Austen's books too recently to re-read them. Dickens? Again, no, she didn't want to be a third of the way into anything by Dickens to be interrupted by the return of Sergeant Summers. After all, he would only be gone about an hour or two.

She bloody hoped he wouldn't be gone more than an hour or two.

Ancient Greece, Ancient Rome, the French Revolution, the

American Revolution. No, no, no and no.

Margaret Forster? Definitely not. Not the time nor the place.

But, thinking about it, what was a young bachelor doing with novels by Margaret Forster?

The Civil War? The Spanish civil war? World War I? World War II? Well, plenty of all that, but not her taste. Wars were invariably started by men for absolutely no good reason, and it was always others who suffered. The only warrior she had ever had time for was Boaddicea.

In the end she settled for an anthology of short stories of thwarted love. It was an old book, hardcover, with a library note gummed to the inside front cover. According to the note it should have been returned to Turnham Green public library eight years ago, wherever that might be.

It wasn't her preferred choice, but at least they were short stories rather than a novel, one of which she could finish before Sergeant Smug returned. She sat down on the couch, kicked her shoes off, propped her feet on the coffee table and began reading. She was looking for clues. Clues on how love could be thwarted.

After all, she had ten quid riding on Frank Summers.

At the back of the offices of the Wellbury Herald a sash window squeaked as someone tried to prise it open.

'Not so much noise!' Rachael whispered.

'It's okay, almost open,' Richard whispered back.

He fiddled with a thin piece of wire until the latch clicked open and raised the window. The twins climbed through the now open window and stood for a few moments, adjusting their eyesight to the dark.

'Okay, the main office should be down the corridor and to the left,' Richard said nervously.

'Let's just hope he doesn't know what a password is,' Rachael muttered.

'I was surprised to find out he knows what a computer is. If he does use a password it's bound to be an obvious one.'

'I don't understand why you chose Sam Nightingale to watch Frank's back,' Gertie said to Frieda. They were sitting at a bench-table outside the beer tent at the fair in the evening air. Susan listened mournfully, her thoughts elsewhere. The three of them were having another chieftains' pow-wow, a kind of we-seem-to-have-lost-the-battle pow-wow. They had agreed to visit the fair, feeling in need of something to cheer them up. Instead the bright lights and sight of so many couples walking hand in hand had merely depressed them.

'She's drop dead gorgeous,' Gertie explained to Susan. 'Comes to work on a motorbike, skin-tight black leathers, red hair, gorgeous green eyes. The blokes' tongues hang out whenever she turns up.'

'I can only tell you that if both of you promise solemnly never, ever to reveal what I'm about to tell you,' Frieda said.

Susan perked up.

'Of course,' she said. 'We wouldn't gossip, would we, Gertie?'

'I'm serious. In fact, I'm so serious I want you both to promise that you'll give up Frank if you tell anyone else, however accidentally.'

They considered this. This was indeed serious.

'It can't be that bad, surely?' asked Gertie.

'I could lose my job over it,' Frieda replied.

'Okay, I promise,' said Susan.

'Gertie?'

'Okay,' replied Gertie with little enthusiasm. Gertie liked a good gossip, but. gossip wasn't gossip unless you could pass it on.

'Constable Samantha Nightingale,' Frieda said softly, their heads leaning in together, 'is gay.'

'Gay?' asked Gertie in surprise.

'Shssh, Gertie, not so loud.'

'Sorry,' whispered Gertie. 'How do you know?'

'I had a word with someone at her former station. Apparently there was some bother with a Sergeant who wasn't the tolerant type. Nothing that could be nailed down, you know the sort of thing. Innuendo, double entendres, giving her the worst jobs, picking her up on every slightest point, generally making her life hell at every possible moment. Eventually she was posted away, on her own request. Obviously there was nothing on her record, and if anybody finds out that I've been discussing it with you my head will be on the block.'

'Why doesn't she just come out with it?' asked Gertie.

'Apparently she did at her last station, and got stick for it. She probably doesn't want the same to happen here.'

They considered this as they sipped their drinks.

'Are you sure she's gay?' asked Susan.

'Quite sure. We have no worries there. She's very efficient, and she's an ex-nurse, so she'll be used to handling difficult people. At this precise moment she'll be in Frank's flat making sure he has a proper dinner and an early night. I wouldn't be surprised if he isn't having a cup of cocoa at this very moment.'

The three giggled at the thought. It cheered them up.

'Since we're here, and while Frank is having his cocoa,' said Susan, looking around, 'we might as well enjoy ourselves.'

The other two agreed.

'There's a fortune teller in a tent over there,' Gertie said, nodding towards a tent that bore the sign "Mystic Margaretha, Gypsy Fortune Teller". There was a certain embarrassment in her voice. 'I know it sounds stupid, but I used to love going to the fortune teller when I was a child.'

'A fortune teller?' asked Frieda, surprised. 'You don't believe in that nonsense, do you?'

'Of course not. It's just, well traditional, I suppose. No use coming to a fair and not enjoying yourself. After all, it's no fun going to a panto and not shouting "he's behind you" every so often, is it?'

Frieda and Susan considered this. Neither had ever been to a fortune teller, and it was years since either had sat watching a pantomime, eagerly shouting "he's behind you" every so often.

And since Frank was in the safe hands of Sam Nightingale, why not?

'The hell with it,' said Susan, 'let's be kids again for one night.'

'Okay,' agreed Frieda, 'but after Mystic Margaretha I say we have a go on the dodgems.'

'Bingo!' whispered Richard as the computer monitor showed

light in the otherwise dark office. 'No password, what did I tell you?'

'Come on, out of the chair, my turn,' Rachael whispered.

'No, I'm sure I can do this.'

'You studied programming. I did the desktop publishing side. I'll be able to work it out faster than you.'

Richard reluctantly gave up his seat.

'Look for the announcements section,' he said.

'Yes, yes, I know, now shush while I concentrate. Make yourself useful, go make coffee or something. The editor is busy.'

Richard giggled at the thought.

'Boy, is our Mr Summers going to wet himself when he reads this one.'

'I see a wedding,' Mystic Margaretha said in a deep, slow voice, staring into a crystal ball. The ball was lit from below, giving her heavily made up face a golden glow, sparkling off large, heavy, brass earrings glinting in her long, thick, jet-black hair. 'A wedding and children.'

'My wedding day!' exclaimed Gertie. 'How many children do you see? Three?'

'Just so. As you say, three children, all very happy.'

'One girl, one boy and the other one?'

'Yes, it is one girl, a very pretty young girl, and a boy, very handsome, and ...'

'And?'

'Another little girl, I think. Just as pretty as her happy

mother.'

'Oh! It's going to be another girl! Oh, that's wonderful. I was never sure whether I wanted another boy or girl.'

'I also see sadness,' Margaretha moaned.

'Oh? What sort of sadness. Not one of the children? Please don't say it's one of the children.'

'But also gladness. You have had sadness in your life, but you have also had times of happiness.'

'Oh, that is so true. That's exactly it.'

'And you have many times of happiness ahead of you.'

'But also sadness?'

'I am afraid there will be such moments. But the good times will always be remembered above the bad.'

'Can you see a man there – a man called Frank?'

'The name calls out to me. Yes, yes, it is a man called Frank.'

'Oh, that's wonderful!'

Sam Nightingale turned a page. The wicked stepmother was planning to seduce Jonathon in order to destroy his hopes of gaining her stepdaughter's hand in marriage. Jonathon himself was after the stepdaughter merely for her inheritance.

Sam yawned. Who cares? she thought. Typical old plot, innocent, naive, helpless young girl beset by the evils of the world, one wicked stepmother, check, one designing suitor, check, with, no doubt, a rugged, handsome stranger to turn up and rescue the poor little girl (check). She looked at her watch. Two hours. He had to be back soon.

She went through to the kitchen to make another cup of tea.

Squishy miaowed at her from her towel.

'Squishy! I'd forgotten all about you, poor thing. You must be lonely all on your own there. I'll take you to the lounge with me when I've made my tea.'

The tea having been made, she picked up Squishy and her towel, took them through to the lounge and placed them alongside her on the couch. Squishy immediately climbed onto her lap and curled up.

'You are a lonesome little thing, aren't you?' Sam asked the kitten. She picked the book up and began reading again, stroking Squishy gently.

The stepdaughter was loosening a nail at the top of the stairs. She wanted both her own inheritance and the money her father had left her stepmother. Her step-mother was going to have a nasty trip on the stairs and an accident down below. And if that plotting, oily specimen called Jonathon thought he was getting his hands on any of her money he had another thought coming. If there were any suggestions that her step-mother's demise were other than an accident, suspicion was going to fall firmly on Jonathon. Whatever happened, she would dump him as soon as the old bat was out of the way.

'Ah, this is more like it, Squishy,' she told the kitten. She paused for a moment. 'Yes, I'm reading a story about thwarted love in a man's flat while talking to his kitten. And I'm looking forward to when he comes home, but that's mainly because I'm probably going to kill him when he gets here. We might as well be married. And the strange thing is that it seems perfectly normal.'

'I see a wedding,' Mystic Margaretha said, 'a wedding and

children.'

'My wedding day!' exclaimed Susan. 'How many children do you see? Two?'

'Just so. As you say, two children, very happy.'

'A girl and a boy?'

'Yes, it is a girl, a very pretty young girl, and a boy, very handsome, and their mother is looking down at them very happy. But I also see sadness.'

'Oh? What sort of sadness. Not one of the children? Please don't say it's one of the children.'

'But also gladness. You have had sadness in your life, but you have also had times of happiness.'

'Oh, that is so true. That's exactly it.'

'And you have many times of happiness ahead of you.'

'But also sadness?'

'I am afraid there will be such moments. But the good times will always be remembered above the bad.'

'Can you see a man there – a man called Frank?'

'The name calls out to me. Yes, yes, it is a man called Frank.'

'Oh, that's wonderful!'

'So, what are the odds at the moment?' asked a morose Pete Phillips at the Blue Bliss. He, Eric Johns and Percy Hanson had popped into the members' bar for a quick pint and an update before Pete went to his stake-out in Lords Acres.

'Doctor Pleadle's now two to one, Gertie's two to one, Fabulous is two to one, and Frank is evens.'

The other two nodded slow agreement at these odds.

'I hear you've opened a book on who Frank is going to choose,' said an outraged voice behind them. They turned and smiled weakly at the sight of an imperious Mrs Blower.

'Hello, Mrs B,' Eric Johns replied. 'Lovely evening, isn't it?'

'Don't give me that flim-flam, Sergeant Johns. I think it's shameful. Absolutely shameful.'

'It's just a little amusement, Mrs Blower,' Percy Hanson tried to assure her. 'Nothing serious.'

'Shameful!' repeated Mrs Blower. 'Gertie at two to one? She should be evens at least. But, under the circumstances, I shall put ten pounds on her. If you wish to lose money, that's your business. And it's time for Nelson's walkies!'

In Frank's flat the stepdaughter's plans had gone awry. Jonathon lay at the foot of the stairs, having slipped on the loose step, tumbled down the stairs, breaking his neck and impaling himself on the artificial aspidistra at the bottom. The stepmother, unaware, was in the garden digging a pit for her stepdaughter to accidentally tumble into. The loyal old butler, having discovered the body, presuming it to be some weird form of suicide fashionable among the modern set, and fearing that it would bring shame on the family name, was temporarily concealing Jonathon's body in the pantry, under the cured ham.

Sam Nightingale rubbed her eyes, put a sleeping Squishy to one side, stood up, stretched and went to make some more tea in the kitchen.

If Sergeant Summers did not re-appear soon, she was going to have to call Inspector Garold.

Still, she might as well find out whether it was the stepmother or stepdaughter who won in the end before doing anything.

A thought stopped her.

Stairs. Sergeant Frank Summers had to climb the stairs to get to his flat. It gave her an idea.

Perhaps not the stairs, but surely there was something she could do to make his return more interesting?

'I see a wedding,' Mystic Margaretha said, 'a wedding and children.'

'Ah, that must be my Aunt Julia,' replied Frieda. 'She had twenty-two children. Are there twenty-two children?'

'Er, yes, yes, you are right, twenty, er, two children.'

'Five of them were triplets – that is, fifteen in all.'

'Five triplets, yes, yes there are a number who look alike.'

'Is there a little boy with green hair?'

'Green hair?'

'Yes, little Jeremy. He had an accident with a chemical when he was tiny and his hair was forever after green.'

'Ah, I see a little boy wearing a cap, perhaps that is him.'

'How is Aunt Julia?'

'I see a woman of great strength.'

'Hmm, that can't be Aunt Julia, she was knackered after having all those kids.'

'I think perhaps this is yourself. You are a woman of great strength.'

'Well, that's true. I bench-press 500 kilograms every morning.'

Margaretha gave her a sour look.

'You're taking the mick, arncha? I should 'ave realised straight away, twenty two children!'

'Me? Of course not.'

'Come on dearie, give us a break. Me 'ead's cooking in this wig and these earrings weighs a ton.'

'Can you see a man there – a man called Frank?'

'Not bleeding Frank again. I need a cup of tea.'

'To read the tea leaves?'

'No, because I'm bleeding thirsty. Want one?'

Frieda shook her head. Margaretha took a thermos flask from underneath the table and poured into a dainty little china cup.

'You can't really see the future, can you?' Frieda accused.

Margaretha gave her another sour look and took a sip of tea.

'I can as it happens. Only trouble is, I can't predict when – ironic that, innit? And when I do I goes into a trance and can't remember what I said. And I feel funny for days afterwards, sort of dizzy, and like me left side is so much heavier than me right. I almost walk in circles sometimes.'

She took her wig off with a sigh of relief.

'It's a curse, you know. Happens just like,' she added, snapping her fingers.

Suddenly a puzzled look came into her eyes and she put her cup down slowly.

'Oh, bugger, not now.'

Frieda watched in astonishment as the other woman's face slumped forward and she began to speak in a low, sonorous voice.

'I see one of three

And three with one

A man walking alone

A river flowing

A love glowing

Then three alone

The man with another.'

Just as suddenly as she had gone into a trance her head shot up, she sneezed and woke.

'Oh me bloody asthma!' she exclaimed.

'Those words you said. What did they mean?'

'Dunno, dearie, what did I say?'

'Right, that's it,' Rachael whispered triumphantly. 'Time to shut down and, as the shepherd said, get the flock out of here.'

She shut down the computer and they looked around quickly for any traces of their presence.

'Let's go. Last one to the window is a turkey,' said Richard, closer to the door.

'Not fair!' Rachael squealed as he made use of his head start. Richard chuckled and ran on. And into something.

'Bloody hell!' he exclaimed as he fell backwards.

A light was switched on.

'Well, well, if it isn't the Tricky Twins,' Frank Summers said, grinning broadly.

The twins looked at him, one on the floor, one next to the desk, both aghast. It took them some seconds to come to the realisation that, though he wasn't a ghost, he still looked as if he were part of a nightmare they were about to have.

'What are you doing here?' asked Rachael when she found her voice.

'Waiting for you to finish compiling your opus. Now why don't you two sit down here in front of the desk while Mr Walthers retrieves it? Mr Walthers?'

Phil Walthers came into the office.

'Sit!' Frank commanded. The twins took the hint and meekly sat. They looked about ten years old, shoulders bent, heads hanging down, hands between their legs, toes turned inwards. Someone ignorant of the true situation might declare them to be poor, abandoned orphans, wilting under the pressure of an inhumane and uncaring society.

Phil Walthers went around the desk to his chair, sat down and switched the computer on. Frank perched on the edge of the desk and smiled at the two orphans.

'What are you going to do to us?' asked Rachael in little girl mode, risking an upwards peek to see how bad their situation was.

'That depends on how bad a story you've come up with.'

'Oh dear,' muttered Richard, staring blankly at the carpet. 'We're dead.'

'Please, please,' cried Rachael, standing up and burying her face in his jacket. 'It was only a bit of fun.'

'Sit!' he commanded again, disentangling her thin arms and putting her back in her seat. 'You're more than enough to try the impatience of a saint, and I'm no saint. Try that again and you're liable for a good spanking.'

She gave him a look which suggested she might enjoy a good

spanking from him. Noting the sudden anger in his eyes she cast her eyes quickly down again, unaware that the anger was a result of confusion. He wouldn't know how to give anyone a good spanking even if there was a manual on that sort of thing. A good thumping, yes, but a good spanking?

'Here it is,' Phil Walthers announced, relieving him of his worries. 'Announcements section.'

'Read it out. I can't wait to hear what modern university students are capable of in the literary department.'

Phil Walthers coughed and cleared his throat.

"We hereby wish to announce the engagement of Sergeant Frank Summers to Professor Inkle Ainke of the University of Wellbury. It is believed that this decision was taken while the balance of his mind, what little there is of it, was disturbed beyond reason. However we can only wish the couple the best of luck. They're going to need it."

There was silence. Frank and Phil looked at the intruders. The twins continued looking down, twisting their hands.

'Let's see, there's breaking and entering for a start,' Frank said. 'Hacking into a computer. Perpetrating a libel? Mmm. When the judge sees Professor Ainke in the witness stand he's likely to throw the book at you – suggesting I would marry that thing? All in all you're looking at a good few years behind bars. Plus compensation for interfering in a business organisation, of course. A very serious crime these days, hacking into commercial systems. Yes, I would say at least a few years inside, and, of course, you'll get thrown out of the university.'

'Can't you just let us off with a warning, Mr Summers?' pleaded Rachael, looking at him from underneath her eyelashes, batting her eyelids. 'Please, pretty please? We'll do anything you want, honest.'

Frank considered this. Despite the batting of her eyelids it was apparent that she was desperate, begging.

'Perhaps a little Community Service,' suggested Phil Walthers.

'Community Service?' asked Richard.

'A good idea, Mr Walthers. Community Service, Richard, is where the pair of you get to do some hard work for members of the community who could do with the help. Now, you have a choice. Either I choose what service you will perform, or we take you to court and the judge can choose.'

'We'll do what you tell us,' Rachael assured him immediately.

Frank nodded.

'Oh, and if you ever try to pull anything on me again ...' he warned.

'We won't, honest, Sergeant,' Richard piped up.

'No, I don't think you will. Right, bugger off the pair of you. I'll let you know what service you have to do when I've decided.'

The twins jumped up and made for the door. Before leaving Rachael turned around.

'How did you know?' she asked.

Frank smiled.

'"See if this one isn't news to you", that's what your note said. You both want to go into journalism. Wasn't difficult to work that one out. It did mean we had to wait up for the pair of you last night as well, just in case, for which you will duly pay.'

'But how did you know it was us?'

'You'd threatened to get even. You call me Mr Summers and Richard calls me Sergeant Summers. You took it in turn writing the notes. I knew it was either one person who was a bit confused, or two people who used a different form of address. And also a person or persons who had met me. You two were in the frame from the start.'

'That wouldn't have stood up in court.'

'No, that's why I had to catch you red handed. Oh, and to have the pleasure of kicking your backsides, which is what I will do if you don't bugger off.'

They took the hint and buggered off.

'Students!' said Phil Walthers irascibly, having removed the offending item and shut down his computer.

'I'll bet you were just as bad when you were a student,' Frank noted.

Phil Walthers considered this.

'I,' he said imperiously, 'did not get caught.'

Frank chuckled. He looked at Phil Walthers with a twinkle in his eye.

'Is it true what I've heard? That someone set off the fire alarm at the radio station just as Zack the Prat was about to start his show, and he missed the first half an hour because they had to evacuate the building?'

'Yes, I believe I heard the same thing,' Phil Walthers replied offhandedly. 'Apparently he returned to find a note on his desk telling him it was a practical joke. Suddenly he's gone off the idea of practical jokes. He's now started a campaign against what he calls "childish and irresponsible" behaviour. Which brings to mind a phrase about pots and kettles.'

Frank chuckled again and turned to go.

'I'll see you around, Mr Walthers.'

'Is that the last of this nonsense, then?'

'Oh, no, that was the middle strand. I have just one more link to establish in the first strand. It's the third strand that worries me. The shocker.'

'I heard about that business with the dog. Someone has a pretty warped sense of humour.'

'I don't think we're facing a sense of humour, Mr Walthers. Whoever it is also put a man into hospital. He's lucky to be alive.'

He put his hand into his pocket to get his keys.

'Right, I'll be off. I'll see you tomorrow –'

A puzzled look crossed his face. He took his hand out of his pocket and drew out two cards.

'The joker and the knave,' he observed. 'Now how did those get in there?'

'Last one for the evening, I think,' Frieda said. 'Same again all round?'

The others nodded. They had had the best evening any of them could remember. Percy Hanson, unwillingly taking his niece on the dodgems had been most put out to discover that three mad women who looked remarkably like Inspector Garold, Doctor Pleadle and Constable Gregson had decided to target his car, with more enthusiasm than he considered necessary. His niece had squealed in delight and told "Unca Percy" to "get them".

So he had. Or at least he had tried to.

Afterwards they had wandered through the various stalls, nibbling on candyfloss, picking up cheap fluffy toys as prizes here and there, toys which sat on the table as they enjoyed a final drink.

There was only one little cloud on the horizon.

'You think we're in the clear?' asked Susan.

'Without a doubt. Frank's focused on these burglaries. He made a real break-through today. And thanks to Gertie's hard work too, we know where the gang are getting their information from. The same place Gertie had her hair done this afternoon. I have a feeling we're going to nail them soon. You don't know how much pleasure that will give me.'

'It looks fabulous,' Susan said, looking at Gertie's hair with not a little jealousy.

'It feels a little funny,' Gertie replied, opening her handbag and rummaging for her compact mirror. She paused. 'What the hell are these?' she asked, holding up two playing cards.

The joker and the knave.

The other two paused before replying.

'Frank's weird sense of humour,' suggested Susan

'He probably picked them at random,' suggested Frieda.

Neither spoke the thoughts they were really thinking.

If Frank had given Gertie the knave it meant that she was out of the race.

Each surreptitiously checked their own handbags.

No playing cards.

One down. One to go. And the winner left.

Frieda had dismissed Mystic Margaretha's trance. It was

undoubtedly part of her show.

Frank took the stairs up to his flat as quietly as he could, aware of the late hour. He opened the door to his flat, took his shoes off and padded inside. He bolted the door and moved silently to the lounge. Sam Nightingale lay on the couch, fast asleep, Squishy slumbering next to her on her little towel.

He watched her for a few moments. Leaving her alone in his flat had been a calculated risk, but not a great one. If she was the shocker she would not try anything while she was known to be in the flat, that would be far too risky. And if she wasn't, the real shocker would keep clear, knowing that the flat was occupied.

In her sleep Sam, with Squishy next to her, looked as innocent as a babe, incapable of even thinking of evil. Was that also true of all people, wondered Frank. Did even the most cruel-hearted murderer look innocent while asleep?

A moot point. Some of the cruellest people could appear as angels when they were awake. Adolf Hitler probably looked serene in his sleep.

No, not with that moustache. No sane man would ever wear a moustache like that, unless it was for laughs.

He padded to the bedroom, took out a blanket, and returned to the lounge to drape it over Sam. Then he switched off the light and went to the kitchen to make a cup of tea.

He noticed that the spare set of keys which should have been on a hook had gone. He rubbed his jaw thoughtfully. Sam could well have borrowed them when she had gone to ask his neighbour where he was, which she had no doubt done.

Quite possibly she had forgotten to replace them.

He shrugged to himself. Whatever the truth he was pretty sure that he was quite safe for the moment.

Having switched the kettle on he opened the top cabinet to get the sugar.

A packet of sugar burst open into his face.

He stood there, eyes closed in disbelief, granules of sugar dribbling off his face and down his jacket.

'Thank you very, very much, Constable Nightingale,' he thought.

Outside a watcher saw the lounge light go out. The watcher had been there some hours. Frank Summers having come home safely, and the woman not having left, the watcher gave up for the night.

Frank washed his face briefly and went to bed. He was once again dead tired. The sugar on the kitchen floor could wait until morning.

It was already morning, he thought as he drifted off to sleep. Saturday morning, technically speaking. He was convinced the shocker was going to strike again sometime during the next twenty-four hours. It would be inaccurate to say that he wasn't worried about that. But the fact was that he had something that worried him more. The battle with the shocker was a straight good versus evil battle, and he felt that he was prepared for it. His larger worry was a battle that he did not feel prepared for.

In twenty-four hours it would be Sunday.

Still, if he lost against the shocker it wouldn't make very much difference, would it?

Saturday Morning: Jokers fly; Shocker in the flat

Frank yawned, turned over and checked his watch. Seven-thirty. He decided he might as well get up. He had slept better than usual and he was so used to early mornings that seven-thirty was already a late lie in. He put on a dressing gown and wandered through to the kitchen. Sam Nightingale was sitting at the kitchen table, Squishy was in her newly-acquired basket, licking her lips, having apparently just finished breakfast. Sam looked up from a book she was reading.

'Morning, Sam, get a good night's rest?'

'Yes, sir,' came the neutral reply.

She watched as he made a cup of coffee.

'I suppose you think I should clean the sugar up,' she suggested as he sat down, sipping his coffee.

'Hmmm? No, leave it, I'll sort that out.' He looked at her over the rim of his mug. 'I think that makes us even, don't you?'

'Sir?'

'I gave you the slip, and you got me with the sugar. What say we call it quits and stop this childish business?'

She regarded him warily. He was, to her mind, the type to suggest shaking hands and calling a truce while holding an electric buzzer in his palm.

'If you really mean that, sir,' she said.

'Oh, I do, I do. Good fun, but enough. I tell you what, you don't mention the sugar, and I won't mention that I gave you the slip, what do you reckon?'

'That sounds like a remarkably good suggestion, sir.'

'Good. I'm going to shower and shave and all the rest. Why don't you get off home and have a bath or whatever. I know I

305

can't function until I've had a shower.'

'Inspector Garold told me to stick to you like glue. I made the mistake last night of trusting you. I'm not going to make the same mistake again.'

Frank half smiled and half winced at the retort.

'I thought we were going to call it quits, Sam. Or are you going to remind me every chance you get?'

"Like a typical woman" he hadn't added, but Sam took that for granted.

Honesty, on the other hand, forced her to acknowledge that he was right. They had agreed to call it quits, which implicitly included not referring to the subject, which she had immediately done after the agreement was sealed. She wasn't sure whether she hated him or herself more.

'I intend to follow my orders to the letter, sir,' she said in a neutral voice.

'You can't do it twenty-four hours a day, Sam, be reasonable. Don't worry, I'll have a word with Frieda.'

Sam's reply was halted by the sound of the telephone.

'A bit early,' Frank noted, and went to answer it.

Sam returned to the book she had been reading. The butler had thrown Jonathon's body into the hole that the stepmother was digging, not realising that the wicked stepmother was still in it, still digging. She was still lying in it, knocked unconscious by the fall of the body. The butler went off to find a spade to complete the burial. Meanwhile the stepdaughter had put arsenic in what she believed was her stepmother's personal bottle of sherry. The old vicar had just ridden in through the front gates on his bicycle.

'You can be off to your ablutions with honest heart,' Frank said, re-entering the kitchen. 'Gertie's going to pick me up in twenty minutes.'

'Constable Gregson, sir? Why's that?'

'Frieda likes checking up on me for some reason.'

I can't imagine why, thought Sam.

'I'll wait until Constable Gregson gets here,' she said.

'Suit yourself,' Frank replied, heading for the shower.

Sam returned to her book. It had closed without a bookmark, and she took a few minutes to find her place. The stepmother had regained consciousness and, covered in mud and dirt, had extricated herself from underneath the body of Jonathon. Not wanting it to be found in a hole that she had dug she decided to move it, but it was too heavy. She fetched a length of rope from the garden shed and looped it over an overhanging branch to act as a primitive pulley. She tied one end around Jonathon's neck and began pulling on the other. The butler with his shovel came around the side of the house to see Jonathon swinging in the wind, apparently having committed suicide for the second time. He clutched his heart in shock and decided he needed a medicinal sherry. In the lounge the stepdaughter had just re-corked the sherry bottle when the front door bell rang.

The bell rang again.

And again.

'Can you answer that, Sam?' Frank's voice called.

Sam looked up with a start. It was Frank's door bell ringing. She closed the book and hurried to the front door.

Blast that man, he seemed to catch her at every opportunity!

'Hello, Sam, is Frank ready?' asked Gertie, stepping inside.

'No, I, er, he's still showering, I think.'

'I'll be ready in a tick,' Frank called from his bedroom. 'Make yourself a coffee while you're waiting, Gerts.'

'Okay, Sarge. Want one yourself?'

'Yes, please.'

Sam followed Gertie to the kitchen, taken aback by this easy familiarity, and with Gertie's breeziness. Gertie was supposed to be one of Frank Summers' girlfriends. If that were so she should not have been pleased to find another woman in his flat. Yet she seemed not at all perturbed. What was going on?

'"An Anthology of Short Stories of Thwarted Love"?' commented Gertie, noticing the book on the kitchen table. 'Frank has some strange tastes in reading. Sounds a bit girlish to me. Morning, Squishy, how's the luvliest, wubbliest little puddy cat in the whole world?'

Sam decided it best not to mention that she was the one who had been reading the book. The last thing she needed was a reputation as being "a bit girlish".

'Squish, you've done it again,' Frank said as he entered the kitchen, leaning over the kitten trying to dislodge its table tennis ball from under the front of the stove. 'Come on, you can play football in the lounge for a while. There are too many feet around you here, someone's likely to step on it.'

'Football?' Sam asked Gertie as Frank took the kitten, towel and ball to the lounge.

Gertie shrugged her shoulders.

'Squishy likes hitting the ball around the kitchen. Frank pretends he's goalkeeper, stopping it from catching under the stove.'

They both winced as a shout of "Goal!" came from the lounge.

'Sounds like they've changed places,' Gertie noted. 'A bit unfair to put little Squishy in goal.'

'I agree,' Sam replied. 'Maybe we should go in there and take Squishy's side.'

They smiled at each other, and a look of understanding passed between them.

'You get off, Sam,' Frank said as he re-entered the kitchen. 'I'll see you later at the station.'

'Right, sir. What time would you like me there?'

Frank paused.

'Sod it, it's Saturday, I'd forgotten. Are you supposed to be on shift today?'

'I'm on afternoon shift.'

'Tell you what, pop in about lunchtime for an update. If there's nothing doing you can take the afternoon off. Frieda will probably want you to baby-sit me again tonight.'

'You don't think the shocker might try something today?'

'Psychopaths never work on a weekend, Sam, well known fact. And I'll have Gertie on my case during the day. Go on, get off.'

Sam gave him a surprised look, but left as ordered.

'Psychopaths never work on a weekend?' asked Gertie. 'I've never heard that one before.'

'Thought everyone knew that,' he said, winking at her. He paused for a moment. 'Say, Gerts, seeing as it is the weekend, what do you say to popping into the Blue Bliss at lunch tomorrow for a drink or two? Just a select little party.'

'Sounds good to me,' she replied, missing the meaning of the last phrase, but with the feeling that his thoughts were elsewhere.

Frank sipped his coffee and looked at the floor.

'So, how are the studies coming along?' he asked.

'Studies?'

'Your law courses. With the OU.'

Gertie looked embarrassed.

'I'm a little behind,' she said. 'Don't seem to have the time these days. I'm also studying for Sergeant's exams. I'm not sure I can handle both.'

Frank pursed his lips.

'You'll have to make the time, as they say, Gerts my love. Can't go wasting all the effort you've put in so far. And I might take the same course myself one day, you'll be able to help me out.'

'If you say so, Frank,' Gertie replied happily. 'I'll get stuck in again on Monday.'

Frank nodded and smiled.

'Any news on the house at Lords Acres?' he asked.

'Nothing, apparently. All quiet throughout the night.'

'I wonder.'

He put his coffee down and went to get his jacket.

'I found these in my pocket,' he said to Gertie, holding out the two cards. 'Someone must have slipped them in sometime during the day.'

Gertie looked at them suspiciously. The joker and the knave. The same two cards she had found in her handbag the previous evening. Was he playing some strange game with her?

'What do you suppose they mean?' she asked.

'I don't know. I think it must have been a young student who put her arm around me. Easy enough for her to slip them in at the time. Except that it doesn't make any sense. They weren't there when ...'

He paused. He had been about to say "When I pretended to look for my keys when I found Sam Nightingale on the doorstep" but that was something Gertie didn't need to know about. What stuck in his mind was the word "pretended". He had only pretended, merely patting a pocket he already knew to be empty of keys. Which meant the cards could have been put there earlier. In fact it could have been any time from his visit to Professor Ainke, when he had "accidentally" dropped his keys on the chair.

Gertie hesitated. Then she opened her handbag and took out her two cards.

'Someone left these in my handbag,' she said.

He took the two cards, frowning.

'When?' he asked.

'Don't know, Sarge. I had my handbag with me most of the day. Can't think of any time someone could have done it.'

Except when she had been with Frank, she thought to herself.

'What about at the hairdressers?'

'Hairdressers?'

'Hairdressers, Gertie, when you were having your hair done.

Could someone have slipped these in there?'

'I suppose so,' she said dubiously.

'Bugger!'

'Bugger, Sarge?'

'Come on, Gertie. I'm going to the station. You get to the hairdressers and find out if any of their staff didn't turn up for work today. I've got a horrible feeling we're too late.'

A leather-clad figure on a motorbike watched from a few hundred yards away as they left in haste. The figure waited for five minutes and then rode slowly towards his flat before parking and walking up the stairs. Outside his front door the figure looked around, pretending to be about to knock before delivering a parcel. There was no-one around to observe this pantomime. The figure began inserting a key into the first of the locks.

'You're not angry with me about those cards?' asked Queenie.

'I should be furious with both of you,' Ace replied as she drove. 'But it's probably for the best. We don't dare try the fourth job now, and the coppers were getting a little cute with that trap. Best we get out while we're ahead. Home and Hampstead, here we come.'

'I'll bet they don't work it out,' said Queenie.

'Fortunately they don't know what we really look like, apart from Cocky, so it doesn't really matter.'

'And they'll never suspect Cocky.'

'Not in a million years. Just so long as he plays it the way we agreed. Give it a week before getting rid of the suit and becoming a normal student.'

'My guess is that their contact in the hairdressers realised we were on to them,' Frank said in Frieda's office, leaning against the windowsill. 'They left the cards in Gertie's handbag as a final showing of the finger – and the ones in my jacket pocket. They're probably a hundred miles away and laughing.'

'How would they know we were on to them?'

'Someone was following me. They probably saw Gertie with me, realised she was a police officer, and put two and two together when she appeared in the hairdresser pretending to be the Meadows' niece.'

Frieda's telephone rang. She listened as the other person spoke.

'Okay, Gertie, get back here then. I'll get the photo-fit people out there.'

She put the phone down.

'All staff accounted for,' she said. 'But the one remembered a client who sat next to Gertie. A young girl who had been waiting while Gertie gave out her story. The girl put her handbag right next to Gertie's when her turn came. She could have slipped the cards into her handbag then.'

'We have a description?'

'Of the girl's hair, perfect, down to the last root. Of the rest of her – early twenties, medium build, medium face, medium all the rest. She was just visiting Wellbury, so they didn't take as much notice as they would have of a regular client.'

'No CCTV?'

'No CCTV.'

'And by now they're long gone. Those cards were the final showing of two fingers.'

'I'm afraid it looks that way, Frank. Unless we get lucky and get a photo-fit that actually looks like the real thing – we'll just have to hope they slip up somewhere else.'

Frank frowned and looked out of the window.

'Oh, one more thing, Frank. Gertie's promotion has come through. She's no longer Acting Detective Constable, she's Detective Constable. I thought you should pass on the good news, being her immediate senior officer.'

'That's good news. Though I don't know how pleased she'll be, she's already studying for Detective Sergeant. She always was ambitious.'

'Who knows, maybe your promotion will come through soon.'

And then you won't have to call me Inspector while on duty, was the unstated message.

He turned around, missing the message.

'I'm going for a drive,' he said. 'I want to retrace my steps from yesterday. Someone slipped those cards into my pocket. Maybe something will come back to me.'

Frank pulled into a parking space in the Old Town and took out the mobile phone he had purchased the previous day. He dialled a number.

'Hello, Susan? Frank here. How are things going?'

'Frank?' came the surprised answer. 'Where are you?'

'I'm in a call box in the Old Town. Just wondered whether you'd found anything in those toilets.'

'Nothing of immediate value. We should be able to source the boxing that was used to hide the cables, and the printing was done with an old-fashioned stencil, so that might give us a few leads.'

'But not for a few days at least?'

'No, Frank, not unless we're extremely lucky. Oh, by the way, that paper you gave me yesterday. There wasn't a match with any of the notes.'

'No, I didn't really expect there to be. If it was her I doubt she'd be stupid enough to use her own note paper.'

'She?'

Frank paused.

'I can't really tell you. It's someone at the university. I haven't got any real evidence, so best I don't start throwing names around.'

Susan did not quite see it that way. To her mind Frank should be able to confide in her and rely on her silence. Especially as, from what Frieda said, he could be in serious danger.

Previously Susan would undoubtedly have pointed this out to Frank, knowing both that he wasn't going to reveal the name whatever her arguments, and that she was going to lose her temper with him for not doing so. That was not going to happen this time. She had been spending a lot of time thinking about the possible future and had realised that being married, to whomsoever, meant the acceptance of making allowances.

'Frank, you are taking care of yourself?' she asked instead.

'Of course I am, you know me. Listen, I was thinking, we really should have dinner some time. Phil Walthers keeps reminding me that we'll get a discount at the restaurant in the Blue Bliss, but I've heard rumours that the kitchen facilities are a bit dodgy – apparently the cleaning isn't of the highest order. Maybe we could see if we could get a seat at Gino's.'

'I don't know who suggested that there was anything wrong with the Blue Bliss. The kitchen is the cleanest I've ever seen. And from what I hear the food is something of a magical mystery tour. Mrs Blower keeps interfering with the chef's creations. I think it sounds as if it could be fun.'

'Well, we'll have to think about that. After we've sorted this shocker person out. What about meeting at the Blue Bliss for drinks tomorrow? Say about noon?'

'Yes, I'd like that, Frank.'

'Noon it is then. See you tomorrow.'

Susan looked at her mobile with a puzzled look on her face. She had heard the background noises during the conversation. If Frank was in a telephone box he must have been holding the door open.

She shrugged. It wasn't important. What was important was that she was having drinks with Frank tomorrow at noon.

Fortunately there was no-one to hear the triumphant "Yippee!". She would have been quite embarrassed had there been.

In his car Frank tapped the mobile against his chin thoughtfully, smiling.

One thread was complete. Another looked like a dead end for the time being. But there was still the shocker to sort out.

'But we'll sort that out, won't we Squishy?' he asked.

He froze suddenly. Squishy! He'd totally forgotten about the kitten. They had left her playing football in the lounge. Blast!

His mobile warbled.

'Frank? We have lift off.'

'I'll be with you in about twenty minutes. I have to pop into my flat first.'

'Too late for that, Frank. The shocker's already there.'

Frank paused.

'I'll be with you in five minutes.'

The figure in Frank's flat stood in the lounge. A gloved hand lifted the sheet that covered the electric piano. The head nodded as if satisfied. The figure took helmet and gloves off, pulled on a pair of rubber washing-up gloves and set to work.

The figure did not notice a little kitten hiding behind the couch, watching. The kitten had run to greet Frank as he opened the front door, and complain about being left alone. The figure that had entered was definitely not Frank, and instinct had told Squishy to hide. She had hidden behind the couch, trembling, towel in sight, fearing that this stranger might steal it, ready to risk all and attack if the stranger did.

The phone rang in Frieda's office.

'Frieda? Dennis here. Listen, you remember you were asking about Constable Nightingale. There's something I've just remembered.'

Frieda listened for a few minutes, her eyes growing wider and wider.

'She did what?'

The figure in Frank's flat took a roll of standard triple-flex electric cable from underneath their leather jacket, and a pair of pliers from the pocket. The electric piano was moved out of the way, and the carpeting pulled back from the skirting board.

When Gertie returned to the station she remembered Frank's request to check up on Professor Ainke's background. After a number of failed calls she finally found someone willing to talk about Professor Ainke, under the condition of anonymity.

She didn't like what she was hearing. Not in the slightest.

After the call had finished put down the phone and immediately set off for Frieda's office.

Frank rang the door-bell. The door opened within seconds.

'Bingo!' said a smiling Chief Inspector. 'Let me show you young Darren's hideaway. It's amazing what these youngsters can do these days. I've only got as far as logging on to the Internet and doing a search. And even then, some of the sites I found! Absolutely disgusting. And they want you to pay for them by credit card. It's this modern world. What's wrong with a good old-fashioned cheque?'

'The shocker's in my flat?'

'Somebody's in your flat. From what they're doing I would say it's the shocker.'

'I forgot to bring Squishy with me. She's in the flat.'

The Chief Inspector paused. He was more aware than Frank

how close the two had become. He had also guessed, more by intuition than anything else, that Frank had rejected personal relationships in the belief that he had some sort of jinx, that anyone coming close to him was destined for a bad end. If anything happened to the little kitten that feeling would only be re-enforced.

'Let's hope she has the sense to hide,' he said, more in hope than expectation. 'I'm sure she will. She's a very bright little thing.'

It was ironically unfortunate, the Chief Inspector thought, that little Squishy had begun to lose her fear of humans precisely because of Frank. It was because of Frank that the kitten was likely to say hello to goodbye, miaowing trustingly as her neck was twisted into death. The shocker had already shown a callous lack of feeling for four-footed friends.

'Professor Ainke at the university,' Gertie breathlessly told Frieda who was sitting at her desk with her hand still on the telephone after completing her own call. 'Frank asked me to check her out. Apparently she was asked to leave her last job after conducting some unauthorised experiments in electrotherapy on some students. The students had all volunteered, but it was highly dangerous, and, as a clincher, all the students were male.'

Frieda looked at her.

'Well, why don't we bring her in?' demanded Gertie.

The figure smoothed the carpet back, covering the wires. Then the piano was put back into position, and the final connection began to be made. Once that was done the figure looked around for something to wipe the piano down with. Squishy's towel lay on the carpet.

'Messing about with my piano,' noted Frank. 'That was a present from Frieda, Susan and Gertie, and Mrs Blower also contributed. That piano is sacred.'

The Chief Inspector nodded understandingly as they stood behind young Darren and watched the computer screen.

'Can you see Squishy anywhere?' Frank asked. 'Her towel's there but I can't spot her anywhere.'

'Squishy?' asked Darren.

'My cat – a little kitten.'

'It was there earlier,' Darren replied. 'Asleep on the towel. Seems to have gone now.'

'If she hurts Squishy I'll kill her. I swear, I'll kill her.'

Neither of the other doubted the promise.

'Constable Samantha Nightingale,' Frieda said slowly, looking at Gertie. 'There was a party at one of the officers' flats. Far too much drink was consumed. The sergeant she was having trouble with fell asleep in the bath, fully clothed. Someone found him there later, with a hairdryer in the bath, plugged in and the switch on. All that was required was for someone to open the taps as a joke, the sort of thing that could easily have happened under the circumstances.'

'A hairdryer in a bath? And Sam Nightingale was the one who put it there?'

'Nothing was proven, but from the sounds of it no-one doubted it. So the question is, who do we bring in? Professor

Ainke, or Constable Sam Nightingale, a woman who hates men?'

The leather-clad figure carefully cleared up any bits and pieces that might give the game away. She had been about to pick the towel up when she thought she heard a growl coming from outside. She had turned towards the door. No further sound had come. Then she had noticed the discarded sheet and decided that that would be better material for wiping down the piano.

She dropped a musical score behind the back of the piano. She took off the washing-up gloves, and put her motorbike gloves and helmet back on. She stepped back and swore softly as the sound of something crunching came to her. She looked down.

Only a table tennis ball. It wouldn't leave any clues.

'Time to go after her?' suggested the Chief Inspector.

'Let her get back to work, or home, if she's going there. We don't want a car chase, now do we? And she's the only one with keys to my flat apart from myself. The flat will be quite safe for the moment. We can get someone to tell her she's needed at work, and be waiting for her.'

'True. Darren, could you do us a few printouts? They should save any declarations of innocence. And then, Frank, we'll go for a little drive.'

'I'm looking forward to it. Closing down the final, and nastiest strand.'

'Funny how some women get to hate men so much. After all,

you can hardly say that we're all the same.'

'Some men have the same problem with women. Freud probably had a theory about it. My guess is that it normally results from being jilted at some time.'

'Quite possibly. Though I must admit that I've always tried to avoid the question "why". Gets in the way of work. To my mind we're paid to do the "who", "when" and "where", and leave the "why" to others.

'So long as Squishy is okay. As soon as we've arrested her I'm going back for Squishy.'

'Just be careful, Frank.'

They didn't notice the picture on the screen showing a little kitten emerging from behind the couch and sniffing at the piano suspiciously.

Frieda put her phone down and tapped her desk.

'Constable Nightingale is not answering her radio. And Professor Ainke is not in her office or at home.'

She stood up and put on her jacket.

'You take two uniforms and get to the university. Bring the Professor in. If she's not there, try her house. I'm going to borrow Pete Philips from Percy and go to Constable Nightingale's flat. We don't have anything to charge them with, but showing that we're on their case might prevent them doing anything until we can put them where they belong. I'd prefer to see them in a jail for the rest of their lives, but they'll probably get Broadmoor.'

Constable Sam Nightingale slowed down as she rode her

motorbike through the Old Town. Sergeant Summers' flat was only a few streets away. She still had the keys she'd used the previous night.

She really shouldn't go in without his permission.

But she would be straight in and out, she wouldn't touch anything apart from the book.

She was pretty sure she knew how the story ended: the butler would be the only one left alive.

But she wanted to make sure.

Because it might be that the vicar was the only one left alive.

Yes, she'd be straight in and out. Sergeant Summers wouldn't even need to know she'd been there. It would only take seconds.

She turned the motorbike towards Frank's flat.

'Ready, Frank?'

'Ready. I'm looking forward to seeing Professor Ainke's face. Silly woman thought she could outwit me.'

The Chief Inspector sighed and shook his head sadly.

'Frank, have you ever come across the word hubris before?' he asked.

'Harry, Allison,' Gertie said in the canteen, 'I need you two. We're going to bring in someone we think might be the nutter behind this shocker business.'

'Oh, good,' said Allison standing up. 'I was worried they might get to Sergeant Summers before I could collect my winnings.'

'Winnings?' asked Gertie.

There was a slight pause as Allison realised that she might just have made a teensy weensy gaffe. She looked to Harry Wheatley for support.

He shrugged and motioned to his bruised lips to indicate that speaking was painful.

'Er, there was a book on whether or not he'd sort out all these practical jokes,' Allison replied feebly.

'Why wasn't I told?' asked Gertie. 'I'd have put a hundred on him.'

Harry Wheatley smiled for a second. He wanted to say "I've got a tenner on him".

Sam Nightingale initially did exactly as she had intended to.

She opened the flat door, closed it behind her, walked straight to the kitchen, picked up "An Anthology of Short Stories of Thwarted Love" and began making her way out.

As she passed the lounge door Squishy came out, miaowing and rubbing herself against Sam's legs.

'Hello, Squishy, he hasn't left you in all by yourself, has he? That wasn't very nice of him, was it?' she said, putting the book down, picking the kitten up and stroking it. Then something caught her eye.

The sheet had been taken off the piano. The keys sat gleaming.

Now why had Sergeant Summers done that? she wondered, entering the lounge.

'I'll come along too,' Percy Hanson said when Frieda entered his office to request the loan of a tired Pete Phillips, having just come on duty again after his overnight stake-out.

'Two Inspectors and a Sergeant?' asked Frieda. 'A bit top-heavy, don't you think?'

'I've got a tenner on Frank, I want to protect my investment.'

There was a pause.

'A tenner?'

Percy blinked.

'Ah. Er, didn't you know, there was a book on whether or not Frank would solve all these practical jokes?'

'And you put ten pounds on Frank? A bit optimistic, wasn't that, Percy? Most, yes, but all of them? I'm pretty sure there will be one or two he doesn't clear up. After all, we can't spend too much time investigating practical jokes, now can we?'

She shook her head, and smiled at Percy.

'That's a tenner gone down the drain, Percy. You really should stick to fishing.'

Sam Nightingale stroked the piano keys. They reminded her of her father teaching her to play when she was a little girl.

She wondered whether she could still manage Twinkle Twinkle Little Star.

'What do you think, Squish? It's an electric piano. There must be an on-off switch somewhere. Shall we try to find it?'

Squishy miaowed in her arms.

'Yes, you're right, let's try find it. You'll like Twinkle, Twinkle, Little Star. It was one of my Dad's favourites.'

Squishy miaowed again, struggling. She didn't seem to think it was a good idea.

'Shush now, Squish. Music lightens up our lives, didn't you know that?'

She gave Squishy a kiss before beginning her search for the on-off switch.

Professor Ainke stopped and blinked as she entered her office. She had been at home changing out of the motorcycle leathers into her usual suit when the call had come that she was needed at the university. Now that Sergeant Summers was sitting at her desk.

In her chair.

With a book on Freud open in front of him.

Frank Summers looked up at her and beamed.

'Come in, Prof. Close the door behind you. Take a seat.'

'Just what, Sergeant Summers,' she began as she closed the door, 'do you think –'

She stopped. There was another man behind the door.

'Chief Inspector Hunter,' the man introduced himself, holding up a warrant card.

'Do take a seat, Prof, old girl,' Frank requested. 'One of the ones your students would sit in. We're about to give you a lesson. Or a tutorial, if you prefer.'

'What is –'

'Sit!'

Frank smiled as Professor Ainke unwillingly sat.

'There are a few printouts we would like you to have a look

at,' he said, pushing a large envelope towards her.

She stretched out, opened the envelope and found herself looking at shots of herself in Frank's lounge, cable in hand.

'Professor Ilke Ainke,' Frank said, leaning forward, beaming broadly, 'you're nicked.'

There was hatred in her eyes as she returned the look.

The Chief Inspector's mobile phone vibrated.

'Yes?'

'Hello, Darren.'

'What?'

He looked at Frank.

'That new constable's in your flat, Frank, and she's about to play the piano.'

'She's not at her flat, and she's not reported in to the station,' Frieda fumed as they stood outside Sam Nightingale's flat. 'Where the hell is she?'

'Maybe she's at Frank's place,' suggested Pete Phillips.

'Don't be daft, Sergeant,' Percy said. 'What the hell would a lesbian want around Frank's flat?'

Frieda looked at him.

'Lesbian?' she asked in a mixture of surprise and fear. She had almost said "How did you know?" If the answer was "Oh, gossip gets around" then certain people would be demanding to know the source of the gossip. And if the source turned out to be a certain Detective Inspector ...

She was dead. Her whole career was finished.

'Thought everyone knew,' Percy replied. 'Bobby Stang knows

someone who had been at her old station for a while. Apparently she was quite open about it then.'

Phew! thought Frieda. That was close.

'Come on, come on, answer the phone,' muttered Frank into his mobile phone.

Inside his flat Sam Nightingale had started guiltily at the sound of the telephone. It reminded her that she should really, really not be there.

And one thing she was really, really not going to do was answer that phone. She had almost done so automatically. A good thing she had been too far from it to do so. When you're in somebody else's flat and shouldn't be there, answering the phone with a "Hello, Sam Nightingale" was not a good idea.

The sight of Gertie striding along the university path followed by two uniformed officers attracted a great deal of attention. They were obviously on their way somewhere definite, to do something definite.

Perhaps arrest the Chancellor? That would be fun.

'Hello, Constable,' said Rachael, appearing in front of her, Richard alongside. 'Anything we can help you with?'

Gertie looked at the two. She recognised mischief-making when she saw it.

On the other hand, she needed to know where Professor Ainke's office was.

'Do you know Professor Ainke?' she asked.

'We sure do,' replied Richard, both twins giggling.

'Where's her office?'

'Right this way, follow us.'

Gertie turned to Allison Hardbury and Harry Wheatley.

'Okay,' she whispered, 'when we get there we go straight in, no knocking, just straight in and grab her. Anyone else in there gets bruises, well, we'll apologise later. Got that?'

The other two nodded.

Harry could still feel his lips. He wanted to take it out on someone. He could never raise a hand to Allison. Anyone else was a fair target and collateral damage.

Allison felt guilty about hitting Harry. She felt she had been unfair to him, he had been referring to Sergeant Summers when he had made his badly chosen remark, not to himself. Taking out her feelings on someone else sounded like a reasonable option. If there was anyone else in this Professor Anchor's office they would either shut up or get thumped. Without hesitation.

'Ask Darren what she's doing now,' Frank said to the Chief Inspector. He spoke into his phone.

'Just standing there at the piano looking at the phone.'

'Bloody answer the phone, Sam, and that's an order,' Frank muttered.

'On the other hand, if she is our shocker, she could well be at Frank's flat busy wiring it up,' noted Frieda.

'Good point,' noted Percy.

'Let's get round there before she can cause any damage.'

'Thank god!' Frank muttered as his answering machine kicked in. He listened to his own voice apologizing for not being able to answer right at that moment and would the caller please leave their name, number, date, and a short message and he would return the call as soon as was humanly possible.

Bloody hell, he thought to himself, why did I have to leave such a long-winded message? Pompous idiot! As if anyone really wanted to listen to him gassing on.

Finally it finished and the beep sounded.

'Sam? This is Frank Summers. Answer the bloody phone!'

Sam Nightingale's eyes opened wide in surprise and shock. She backed up against the piano, holding Squishy tightly. How did Sergeant Summers know she was here?

'Sam, don't just stand there, answer the –'

His words were cut short as the door to Professor Ainke's office burst open and Gertie, Allison and Harry piled in.

'Frank!' exclaimed Gertie. 'What are you doing here?'

'You're under arrest,' Harry Wheatley informed an amazed Chief Inspector.

'That's the Chief Inspector, you berk,' Allison told him once she had recovered from her surprise.

'Oh, hell, sorry sir, I didn't recognise you.'

Professor Ainke took the opportunity to make a run for the open door.

'Well, it's definitely locked,' Pete Phillips said outside the door to Frank's flat. 'And no-one is answering.'

'She could be inside, keeping quiet. See if you can hear anything.'

Pete Phillips put his ear to the door and listened.

His eyebrows rose as he frowned. Only Pete Phillips was capable of such simultaneous expressions.

'Well?'

'You're not going to believe this, but Frank's in there telling someone to thump someone else,' he said.

'Stop her!' Frank shouted. 'Thump her if you have to!' And then, into the phone, 'Sam, answer my bloody phone, will you!'

Professor Ainke put an elbow into Allison's ribcage and dodged passed Gertie and out the door. Gertie raced after her. The Professor came to a sudden stop as those bloody twins walked towards her, carrying a large pane of glass between them, blocking the corridor. She turned, slipping, her arms flailing. Before she could recover Gertie had one of her arms behind her back. The other followed shortly and abruptly and she cried out in pain.

'You're hurting me!' she complained.

'No shit,' answered Gertie, screwing the handcuffs tight.

'I don't understand it,' said Pete Philips. 'Frank's telling Sam to answer his phone. But I can't hear the phone ringing.'

'Move aside,' Frieda said impatiently. 'Give me that door.'

Sam Nightingale edged towards the phone. She wasn't sure how, but Frank Summers appeared to know she was in the lounge.

'She's moving towards the phone,' the Chief Inspector told Frank.

'Good girl, good girl, just pick up the phone,' Frank said to his answering machine.

Sam picked up the handset. She was rapidly coming to the conclusion that this Detective Sergeant Summers was indeed some form of psychic who could see things beyond his ken.

'Constable Nightingale speaking,' she said softly. 'Sir,' she added as an afterthought.

Listen as intently as she could, Frieda could hear nothing. She looked at Pete Phillips.

'You haven't been drinking, have you?'

'Thank god for that,' Frank said, breathing out. 'Sam, listen to me. Don't say a word until I've finished, okay?'

'Yes, sir,' whispered Sam, who was beginning to doubt her own sanity.

'Right. Now the piano behind you is wired, and not for sound. Our shocker friend, who is currently under arrest, has set it up so that anyone switching it on will get the biggest, and probably last, shock of their lives. Understand?'

There was a short pause.

'I think so, sir.' Another whisper.

'Right, now what I want you to do is leave the flat without touching anything. Do not touch anything, got it?'

'Yes, sir,' she replied, looking at the piano in a new light, trying to imagine what would have happened to Twinkle, Twinkle Little Star.

'Then I want you to stand guard outside. No-one, but no-one is to be allowed in until I can get there with an electrician. Okay?'

'Understood, sir.'

'Good girl, Sam. Now you just get your backside out of there. And make sure you've got Squishy with you.'

'She's in my arms at the moment.'

'Thanks, Sam, I owe you one. Give Squish a kiss from me. Now get out of there.'

He sighed in relief as he switched the phone off.

'That was a little too close for comfort,' he noted.

'She fell for the pane of glass trick,' said an excited voice from the doorway. Frank turned to find the twins standing there, eyes wide, grins on their faces.

'Ah, yes, you two. I'd almost forgotten about you two. A little matter of community service.' He rubbed his jaw thoughtfully. 'I want to see you two at my flat in, let me see – two hour's time.'

Frieda had given up, and the three of them were walking down the stairs when they heard a door open. They turned to see Sam Nightingale walk out of Frank's flat carrying Squishy. She turned, closed and locked the door, and then stood there as if on guard duty.

Except guards aren't normally carrying kittens, and if they were they were unlikely to kiss said kitten and stroke it tenderly.

Frieda pushed her way past Percy and Pete and marched back up the stairs.

'And just what the hell do you think you're doing, Constable?' she asked.

'Sorry, ma'am, no-one is to enter the flat until Sergeant Summers gets here. Those are his orders.'

'Those are Sergeant Summers' orders, are they? And what rank am I, Constable?'

There was an embarrassed pause until Percy Hanson spoke up.

'Well,' he said, scratching his head, 'I suppose it is Frank's flat. And we don't have a search warrant.'

Frank turned up half an hour later with an electrician in tow.

'Frank, would you care to condescend for long enough to tell me what precisely is going on?' asked an angry Frieda. 'Oh, afternoon, sir,' she added as the Chief Inspector hove into view.

'Afternoon, Frieda. Your Frank doesn't half get himself into trouble, doesn't he?'

'You could say that, sir,' Frieda replied, glaring at Frank.

Frank opened the door and ushered the electrician inside.

'Go on, Mike, you know what to do.'

'Cheers, Frank. Thanks for showing me that footage. I wouldn't have believed it otherwise. Some very strange people around, aren't there?'

The electrician disappeared indoors.

'Okay, Frank, all I know is that your piano has been hot-wired. Care to tell me the rest?'

'I tell you what,' Frank said, looking at his watch. 'Why don't we meet up for drinks in the members' bar at the Blue Bliss at lunchtime tomorrow? I'll tell you all about it. At the moment there are things I have to do'

Frieda considered the option.

Drinks with Frank? It was worth containing her curiosity until then. And she could get the details from the Chief Inspector before then.

And, technically, since the Chief Inspector was here, he was the superior officer. If he did not disagree, how could she?

'Lunchtime it is, Frank. Don't be late.'

Frank restrained a smile as she left.

'And I suppose we'll have to wait until Frieda has been debriefed at the Blue Bliss tomorrow?' asked Percy Hanson.

Frank gave him a wink.

'You're also members, aren't you?' he said. 'All police officers are, automatically. No reason why you shouldn't pop in for a pint at lunchtime tomorrow.'

The twins arrived at the flat shortly after the electrician had left. They entered nervously when Frank opened the door, an evil-looking smile on his face.

'I presume you've heard of the phrase "let the punishment fit the crime"?' he asked, leading them to the kitchen.

'What are you going to make us do?'

'Well, you were going to smear my honest name by that advert you tried to put into the Herald. So now it's time to come clean.'

He jerked a thumb at two buckets on the kitchen floor.

'Walls and ceilings washed, bookshelves dusted and polished, carpets vacuumed and so on and so forth. And I want the bathroom and kitchen gleaming. I want to find you two hard at work when I get back.'

'You want us to clean your flat?' asked Richard.

'You're going out and leaving us here?' asked Rachael.

The doorbell rang.

'I'm just going to pop out to buy a newspaper and do a little shopping, but don't worry, I'm leaving a babysitter,' Frank assured them. He went to the front door and came back with a leather-clad Sam Nightingale. Richard's eyes almost popped out of their sockets.

'Constable Nightingale will be in the lounge while I'm gone. Just in case either of you get any silly notions into your heads. Oh, and her motorbike needs washing and polishing after you've finished here.'

'I'll do that,' offered Richard, a little too eagerly.

Rachael gave him a sour look.

Frank gave him a smile that should have warned him that any romantic interest in Sam Nightingale was likely to lead to embarrassment.

When Frank left Rachael was washing the kitchen floor while Richard cleared the bookshelves in the lounge, taking surreptitious glances at the red-haired figure of Sam Nightingale, sitting on the couch, her booted-legs resting on the coffee table, engrossed in "An Anthology of Short Stories of Thwarted Love".

Having done his shopping Frank returned to his car and sat thinking for a while, Squishy playing with her table tennis ball in front of the passenger seat.

'What say we go for a little walk, Squish?' he asked, looking thoughtfully in front of him. Squishy was too engrossed with the ball to reply.

'Let's do it then,' he said, switching the ignition on. He turned the car towards St Mary's.

'Come on, Squish, pocket time,' he told the kitten once he had parked next to the church. Squishy settled happily in the pocket, tired out from the full ninety minutes, happy that her team had won yet again. Frank strolled along the quiet cemetery paths, deep in thought. It was late afternoon and the place appeared deserted, apart from an old woman sitting near Jean's grave, watching a black cat eat from a chipped saucer. The cat looked up at his approach and fled for cover. The woman looked up at him.

'Hello, Aggie, it's only me.'

She made no reply, watching him nervously.

He looked at the grave he had come to visit.

'You've done a good job here, Aggie. I'm most impressed.'

The words seemed to comfort her.

'Where's Squishy?' she asked.

'Sleeping. She's had a long day, poor thing.'

'Can I see her?' Aggie asked, in a manner that suggested she was used to refusals. Frank lifted the pocket flap.

'There she is, fast asleep.'

Aggie stood up and approached carefully. Holding her hands back she peered into his pocket.

'Ah, she's such a sweet little kitten.'

'She's a little rogue. Always getting into trouble. She's full of mischief.'

'You're just saying that to tease me,' she accused. Frank smiled, acknowledging the truth of the accusation.

'What about you, Aggie? Everything okay with you?'

'Oh, yes! It's Saturday, and tonight I go to Mrs Fuller's house. She a lovely old woman. Do you know her?'

Saturday night was hot bath night, remembered Frank.

'Unfortunately not. Maybe I'll meet her one of these days. I'll probably be popping in here once a week or so in the future.'

Aggie turned and called out.

'Blackie! Blackie! Little Squishy's here. Come say hello.'

'Blackie?'

'One of my friends. The one who was eating when you came. She's afraid of strangers.'

A stray, Frank guessed.

'And then tomorrow the lady in white comes.'

'Lady in white?'

'The police woman. She plays tennis over there. She always comes to have a chat afterwards.'

Frieda, Frank thought. Wearing white tennis clothes.

'She looks like Mother Mary. She's very nice.'

Frank almost choked at the comparison.

'Blackie won't come. I'll have to take her food to her. And then I must go to Mrs Fuller's house. After my bath she's going to play some music.' She turned back. 'Goodbye, Squishy, sleep tight.'

'Before you go, here's this week's payment,' he said, holding out some coins. She looked at them suspiciously.

'You've already paid me for this week.'

'That was last week.'

'No it wasn't. You're teasing me again, aren't you?'

Frank smiled and gave up. You couldn't argue with a seventy-year-old twelve-year-old.

'Okay, I tell you what. If you've got time, could you do the grave alongside? That would almost complete the row.'

She thought about that, nodded, and took the coins in her open hands.

She looked at them for a while.

'You said you would come from time to time.'

'Yes, Aggie, once a week, I promise.'

Aggie nodded as if she did not believe this promise, just as she would any other promise.

'I'll be twelve and a half in October,' she said. 'That's when I'll be joining my brothers and sisters and all my friends. You will bring Squishy before then, won't you?'

Then she turned again, picked up the saucer and went in search of Blackie. Frank watched her go until it seemed she had disappeared amongst the headstones. He looked at Jean's grave.

'So, Jean, what do you reckon? Am I going soft?'

Jean smiled, but didn't think so.

'Peaceful here, isn't it?' he asked, looking around the cemetery.

Jean agreed, yes it was very peaceful.

'I'm going to have to make a decision soon. Tell me, what do you think I should do?'

Jean knew what she would do, but she wasn't saying. That was up to Frank to decide.

Squishy woke up and miaowed.

'I'm going to have to take her home and feed her,' Frank told Jean. 'I'll be back next week.'

Jean said she didn't stay only here. She was with him wherever he went.

'I know. It just makes me feel better. Yes, I'm silly that way.'

As he walked along the path back to his car he was joined by an old man.

'It does make you feel better, doesn't it,' said the old man. 'Talking to them. As if they were still with us.'

'Yes,' Frank replied, realising that he had been overheard, and surprised not to feel embarrassed by the fact.

'Most people think I'm daft for doing it,' continued the other man. 'But when you realise that sooner or later you'll be laid here yourself, well, who cares what people think?'

'There is that,' agreed Frank.

'Well, I turn left here. Good luck with your decision, whatever it is.'

'Thank you. I think I'll need it.'

'Make it the best you can and get on with it, that's what I've always said.'

'I'll do that,' Frank said, adding in his mind: 'As soon as I work out what that is.'

He gave the cemetery one last look. An idea had occurred to

him while he had been walking. Aggie loved music. A wind-up radio required no batteries, and she could listen to Classic FM whenever she wanted to.

But would she want to?

That was a problem in a society that offered instant gratification. To Aggie listening to music was a treat. If she could listen whenever she felt like it would it not lose its appeal?

In a way Aggie was lucky. She had such simple tastes and such a simple mind she could enjoy and value things others took for granted. There weren't many people in this modern world you could say that of.

He would have to discuss a wind-up radio with the Chief Inspector.

And the question of what to do when October and winter came around and Aggie realised she was not about to join her brothers and sisters, even if she had turned twelve and a half.

Late Saturday Afternoon: The Jokers are nicked

'Happy now?' asked Rachael, standing next to the gleaming stove. As far as she was concerned she had finished. If Richard had stopped ogling that police woman in the lounge for long enough to do some cleaning they would be able to get away soon. Right at that moment they had planned to be at the fair, not slaving away here.

Frank looked up from the Guardian.

'You've missed a spot,' he said, and returned to the article he was reading. She put her tongue out at him, wiped an arbitrary area on the stove and began cleaning the work surfaces.

'I hate you,' she said.

He remained silent. He wasn't really reading. He was mentally tracing his steps from the previous day, trying to identify when the joker and the knave had been slipped into his pocket. In the morning he had spoken to the Chief Inspector. However much he might have enjoyed discovering that the Chief Inspector was behind the Joker Gang, the man hadn't had a chance to do the deed.

'It isn't fair,' Rachael continued. 'We were supposed to be going to the fair this afternoon. Hey, that's two "fairs" in the same sentence and they both mean different things, funny, don't you think?'

Gertie, Susan and Frieda afterwards. If he began to suspect them of being the Joker Gang then it really was time to visit a shrink.

Wasn't it?

'Cyril invited me out. He's quite nice when you get to know him. We're going to go on the dodgem cars. Do you like dodgems?'

Some woman had trailed him, if what the Chief Inspector had said was true. But she hadn't come close enough.

'He's good looking, in a way. Now that he's stopped wearing those silly suits.'

Then the visit to the university. He had deliberately left his jacket in Professor Ainke's office. But that was to give her a chance to get his keys if she really was the shocker. Which she was, and she could hardly be both.

'I might even go out with him. I've been looking for a boyfriend, you know.'

Rachael had put her arm around his waist in the canteen. A definite possibility. The joker burglaries had a whiff of innocent irresponsibility that the twins might find attractive.

Though, considering their other tricks, it seemed highly unlikely.

'Of course I would have preferred someone older. Someone more experienced. Someone I could look up to.'

Then that bloody aunt and her nephew had turned up.

'He's better looking than you, anyway.'

Something stirred in his brain. There was something there, something niggling away.

'And much more generous.'

It wouldn't come. He went on with the rest of the day. On to Susan's office, then back to his flat.

'He even gave me a present. I'll bet you would never give a girl a present. She'd be lucky if you ever noticed that she existed. The only thing you ever think about is your work.'

Sam Nightingale had turned up. Did she have a chance to do

it? It had turned out that she wasn't the shocker, but that didn't mean that she couldn't be part of the Joker Gang.

Not really Sam's style, though.

Then again, she did pull that trick with the sugar ...

'An old-fashioned brooch. It belonged to his aunt.'

Had Sam Nightingale turned up around about the time of the first burglary? He would have to check up on that.

'Not the one that was here with him. Another aunt. A great-aunt, I suppose, someone ancient. Like you.'

Then he and Phil Walters had caught the twins at the Herald.

'That aunt left last night, so he can stop wearing suits, he said.'

Phil Walthers?

Extremely unlikely.

'I can show it to you, if you want. It's in my bag.'

Rachael had grabbed hold of him then. A second chance.

'See, that's the sort of thing you give a girl if you really like her.'

'Very pretty,' Frank murmured, glancing at a brooch in the form of dangling Wisteria blossoms.

Then he took another look.

'Where did you get that?' he demanded.

'I told you, Cyril gave it to me. Last night. He said it was to make amends for being such a prat.'

'Where did he get it?'

Rachael sighed dramatically.

'You haven't listened to anything I was saying, have you?'

'Where did he get it?'

'His aunt gave it to him.'

Then he remembered. Cyril and his aunt. Cyril had bumped into him as he was leaving the canteen. Easy enough to slip the cards into his pocket then.

But surely not?

Cyril? Cyril of the suits?

But his aunt was another matter entirely.

'Where is this Cyril at the moment?'

'At the fair. Which is where I would be if you weren't so horrid.'

He stood up and marched to the lounge.

'Come on, Sam, we're going to the fair.'

'But I —'

'No buts. Get your gear.'

Sam Nightingale reluctantly put her book down. After many side-turns and wrong paths, misunderstandings and the shifting of Jonathon's body from pillar to post the vicar had finally taken a sip of sherry. But which sherry?

Cyril finished his pint and pushed the glass across the makeshift bar in the beer tent.

'Same again, please.'

He checked his watch. Rachael and Richard should have been there ages ago. They'd agreed to start with a go on the dodgems. He wondered if they had been having him on when they said they'd meet him there.

'Hello, Cyril,' said a voice on his left.

He looked up. It was that police Sergeant with a kitten in his pocket. The Sergeant was accompanied by a woman in motor-cycling leathers.

'Hello, er, Sergeant Summers, isn't it?'

'It is indeed. You seem to have changed. No more suits?'

'I decided on a new look. Seeing as how I'm a student.'

'Quite so. And I'm a police officer. I'd like to talk to you about underage drinking.'

'I'm not underage,' Cyril protested.

'And there's this.'

Cyril looked at the Wisteria brooch Frank was holding.

'I found it,' he said quickly.

'Yes, I know. It's where you found it that interests us. So we'd like to take you for a little drive down to the police station and have a chat.'

Cocky shrugged. He knew that if he kept to the story of just finding the damn thing they couldn't prove otherwise. Not even Ace and Queenie had seen him pocket it.

'During which time some of my colleagues will be searching the flat you've recently moved into. I do hope you don't mind. Oh, and some nice police officers will be paying your aunt a visit. She should be home by now. Home in Hampstead.'

'I can make a phone call, can't I? To my lawyer?'

'But of course, Cyril, of course. Just as soon as we get you down to the police station, get you booked in, get all the paperwork sorted out, that sort of thing. Don't worry, it shouldn't take more than a few hours. Paperwork is the bane of our lives, you know.'

'Can't I make the call from here?'

'No, you can't, Cyril. Nor can you go to the gents, nor any other quiet place where you might have a chance of alerting certain people. And you can give me your mobile phone.'

This time Cocky didn't shrug.

The woman answered the knock at the door to find two men and a woman standing there.

'Mrs Porter? Detective Inspector Hymes. I wonder if we could have a word?'

'Is it really necessary, Inspector? My niece and I have just got back from a long journey, and my husband is away on a business trip.'

'I'm afraid so, Mrs Porter. You see your nephew has been arrested in connection with a number of burglaries.'

'Cyril? There must be some mistake. Cyril wouldn't hurt a fly, let alone commit – what was it you mentioned, burglary?'

'And we have a search warrant for these premises.'

'What is it, Aunt Jem?' asked a voice from behind her.

She paused before replying.

'It looks like Cocky got caught, Queenie,' Ace told her.

'Frank, you have to be the luckiest man I have ever met,' Frieda said in her office.

'Not really. Cyril was greedy and overconfident. Put those two attributes together and he was bound to make a mistake sooner or later.'

'Giving that brooch to the girl was certainly a mistake. He was lucky she didn't recognise it straight away from the description in the Herald.'

'I think Rachael has yet to realise that a journalism student should read all newspapers, including local ones.'

That wasn't quite the truth. Personally he suspected that Rachael had known all along it was stolen. Whether she had planned to show it to him at some stage or just keep it was another question. In the end it had become a useful tool for attempting to make him jealous. He doubted whether she did have any friendly feelings for Cyril. Though, ironically, once it came out that Cyril had been a member of the Joker Gang she might well decide that he was worth getting to know.

'Well, I'm off,' he said. 'An early night is called for. Tomorrow's D-Day, after all.'

'D-Day.'

He took the pack of cards from his pocket and chose one at random.

'Nope, that's not it.'

'Frank, has anyone told you that you can be the most infuriating man on earth? What is this business with the cards, and what is D-Day?'

He looked at her innocently.

'Why, decision day, of course. It's Sunday tomorrow.'

Before she could reply he had left.

Decision Day, she thought. Of course. She had forgotten all about that. And Frank had asked her out for lunch.

On Decision Day.

He had asked her out. Her.

That had to mean something.

Such a pity it was too late to get her hair done before such an important occasion.

Saturday Evening: The night before D-Day

'Five tickets please.'

The ticket seller looked up in surprise.

'Five tickets? For who?'

'Whom. In this case for the five you see before you.'

'The kids, okay, but you're a little old, aintcha? Never mind 'im. Is he their grandfather? And she's not exactly a kid either.'

'Are you going to sell us five tickets or do I have to get nasty?' Frank asked.

'Yeah, okay, okay, no need to lose your rag.'

The ticket seller took his money and handed over five tickets.

'Right, now I'm going to show you lot how to do this properly,' Frank said, rubbing his hands as they walked towards the dodgem cars, passing a woman who seemed to be lurching to the left as she made her way to a tent with the sign "Mystic Margaretha, Fortune Teller" outside.

'You haven't a chance,' replied Rachael. 'I'm a woman driver and you know what they say about those.'

'Men are more likely to cause accidents,' Richard pointed out. 'It's a statistical fact, you know.'

'Beware of stereotypes,' Sam Nightingale admonished.

The fifth member of the group did not speak.

All Vic Brown cared for was that he was going to have a go on the dodgems.

All Frank cared for was that he was now going to enjoy himself and forget all about Sunday.

Ahead of them a harassed-looking man was getting into a

dodgem car with a little girl.

'Come on, Unca Percy, come on,' the little girl insisted.

Frank smiled. For the next few minutes he was definitely going to forget about Sunday.

Sunday Lunch: D-Day

Frieda walked into the private members' bar of the Blue Bliss with a happy smile of anticipation on her face. She had already reviewed the coming afternoon in her mind's eye a number of times, each time quite satisfactorily. They would have a couple of drinks while she listened spellbound to Frank's detailing of the various cases – which she had already heard from the Chief Inspector, but she wouldn't let that show. She might gently chide Frank for not keeping her informed, or perhaps not. She would see. There was no reason to say anything that might mar the happy day.

After the drinks they would have lunch. A quiet lunch for two. Then go for a walk along the river, or through the woods around University Heights – hand in hand, of course. Whispering sweet nothings, the occasional soft kiss, or possibly more passionate, depending on his mood.

Further than that she had not dared to dream about. It had taken her all morning to get ready, a state of affairs she had rarely encountered over the past years. How much make-up to put on, what dress to wear – and it had to be a dress – which shoes, which stockings and – well, perhaps some things are best left delicately unsaid.

But now midday was here and Frank was there, standing leaning against the bar, Sonia behind the bar, teasing the deliciously sweet little Squishy with a piece of string for the kitten to grab, Eric Johns on a bar stool next to Frank ...

Her smile faltered.

Okay, okay, Frank was just passing the time with Eric while he waited. Eric had probably popped in for a quick pint before lunch, nothing unusual about that.

Or that Phil Walthers and Mrs Blower should be sitting at a table with the Chief Inspector, all three looking at Frank.

Her smile disappeared.

Susan and Gertie sat at another table looking at her with barely concealed expressions of amusement mixed with vexation. At yet another were Percy Hanson and his sidekick Pete Phillips. Even Sam Nightingale, Harry Wheatley and Allison Hardbury were there.

Frank put his pint down.

'Ah, the cast is now complete,' he said as Frieda came up to him, vainly trying to conceal her fury. He gave her a gentle kiss on her cheek.

'Frank, I thought you said we were going to have drinks together,' she whispered.

'Well, we are, aren't we? Everyone's here. Your wine awaits, with Susan and Gertie. If you'd care to take your seat we can begin.'

Frieda glared at him. He looked innocently back. Finally, with slightly bowed head she accepted the inevitable. Had they been alone she would have ripped his throat out.

Had they been alone she would have had no need to do so.

She sat down at the table with Susan and Gertie. Susan poured her a glass of wine. She looked at it angrily and gulped half of it down.

'He asked you here for drinks, didn't he?' Susan whispered to her. 'The bastard did the same to us, making it sound like it would just be two of us. He's going to pay for this once he's through.'

Frieda nodded. Frank had gone too far this time. He would

definitely be brought to account this time, and his account was so far in the red not even his blood could pay the full sum.

'Good,' said Frank, rubbing his hands. 'Are you all sitting comfortably? Right, I shall begin. There were three strands to these practical jokes which were perpetrated over the past few weeks, three strands and a crime. Or, more accurately, two strands and two crimes.'

Eric Johns passed a hand over his confused face, as did several others.

'Keep it simple, Frank,' he muttered. 'Please.'

'Let's take Professor Ainke first. We all know what she did. Why she did it, well, no doubt the psychologists and psychiatrists will come up with several theories as time goes by, some of which might even make some kind of sense. All we know is that she's composed of equal parts hatred, insecurity, ego and arrogance. She couldn't stand being laughed at, and decided to take her revenge out on me. In a way we were lucky she did. She could have chosen a victim who didn't have so many loyal colleagues and friends to look after him. That person wouldn't have been so lucky.'

There were a number of embarrassed smiles. Even Frieda melted somewhat at this heart-warming description. She decided she would only half strangle him.

Three-quarters at the most.

'Then we come to our famous Joker Gang. I should have picked up on something Vic Brown said to me. He told me that the gang weren't normal criminals. Normal criminals do not leave calling cards. And he was right. Jemimah Porter, who is indeed our student Cyril's aunt, is – or was – a very respectable woman. Too respectable. Reasonably wealthy, a housewife, married to a boring accountant, she too was bored.'

He took a sip of his pint.

'Cyril was what he appeared to be, a child brought up in unhealthy seclusion by an over-doting mother. There was a reason for that. Not a very good one, but a reason. His father, Aunt Jem's brother, while being the respectable gentleman he appeared to be, also had an addiction, much like a gambling addict, only his obsession turned out to be petty crime, and, just like most gambling addicts, he wasn't very good at it. His wife came from a rich and established background, and she was appalled when she discovered the fact, but what could she do? His regular disappearances at her Majesty's leisure were explained away by her as his being on business. Then, when he made the mistake of getting himself killed while on a job she took the opportunity to relocate and bring up young Cyril in such a manner as to ensure he never found out about his father, and definitely would not take after him.'

Squishy miaowed as if bored by this recitation. After all, Frank had explained it to her at his flat that morning while she was having breakfast.

'Okay, Squish, okay,' he said, taking Squishy into his arms and stroking the kitten. 'Now there were a number of flaws in this plan. Firstly Cyril had an older sister who felt she was being overlooked in favour of her brother. Secondly his aunt was not at all enamoured of the way her brother's son was being brought up. She probably didn't approve overly of her brother's hobby, but she was concerned that his – Cyril's – upbringing would have the opposite result to that which his mother desired. And when his mother asked the bored aunt to come here, look after Cyril and find a nice flat for him to live in – well, somewhere along the line the truth about his father came out. Who first came up with the idea to emulate him – or, rather, to show that they could succeed where he had failed – is a moot point. Cyril's sister had joined the entourage, being at a loose end. Together they hatched a plan to begin Cyril's re-education. They claim it was merely a prank, that they had planned all along to return whatever they had stolen, anonymously. Whether the judge and jury will buy that is another matter. I don't think they had really considered the question in any depth.'

'So where did they get their information from?' asked Eric Johns as Frank took a pause to wet his throat. Frank smiled.

'They did indeed get it from the hairdressers. Aunt Jem picked up snippets when she went to have her hair done, and her niece some more snippets a few days later. The irony is that they probably wouldn't have carried out any further burglaries – they couldn't return to the hairdressers too often without making themselves noticeable, and they had no other source of information. Cyril's sister returned to the hairdresser with the excuse that she had decided to have highlights in her hair after all, only to recognise Gertie there and realise we were setting a trap for them. They immediately decided to leave town. Had Cyril not been a little greedy, and had he not formed a crush on another student named Rachael, they would have got away with it.'

'All because of love,' murmured Gertie.

'What were the cards all about, then?' Percy Hanson asked.

'That depends on who you ask. According to Aunt Jemimah the cards were supposed to throw us off the trail. In Cyril's case he believed that it showed what he called style – read too many books about Raffles as a kid, I suppose. I suspect his sister, who left the queen of spades, was trying to make a point. My guess is that she felt her mother doted on Cyril because he was a boy and ignored her because she was a girl. The queen of spades was her way of making a point, the point that she could be just as good as any man.'

'They sound like a right bunch of nutters,' Eric Johns remarked.

'Eccentric, I believe the word is,' Frank said, smiling. He put Squishy back on the counter and picked up his pint. Squishy began licking a paw, and then paused as Sonia trailed the string in front of her.

'Penultimately we come to the traffic light trick and the milk mugging. Those were carried out by two university students, twins named Rachael and Richard. That was just a case of youthful high spirits, overconfidence and stupidity. I caught them breaking into the Herald. They were going to slip an article into the classifieds claiming that I was to marry Professor Ainke. The fact that I had caught them effectively meant that I had won, and the game was over. According to their rules, anyway.'

'You should have arrested them,' Frieda said, frowning. 'They can't be allowed to get away with breaking and entering, and the rest.'

'Oh, I gave them due punishment. I made them scrub my flat down.'

There was a pause, followed by chuckles. Frieda did not share the amusement. She was still angry with Frank and subconsciously looking for a stick to beat him with.

'Damn, Frank, you let them off too lightly,' Eric Johns said.

'The outside of my house needs painting.'

'My hedge needs trimming, and my lawn could do with some of the same,' Pete Phillips added.

'Yes, well, I think they've had enough punishment,' Frank said, smiling. He put his pint down.

'Now we know about all the practical jokes apart from one, the first, the Curious Incident of Cleopatra's Costume. I am now able to reveal who was behind that particular prank.'

There was an air of tenseness in the bar. Everyone put their drinks down. It was as if this was something they had expected, but had also hoped might not come.

Or at least some of them had hoped would not come.

'You know who did it?' asked Eric Johns.

'Of course I know who did it. But let's first review the suspects. Motive. Who wanted to play a joke on me? That's easy, of course. Everyone present today – except for Sam, who was new to the station, of course. You all thought I had lost my sense of humour and wanted to put that right. But the guilty party or parties made one little mistake. They thought they could outwit me. Now who might make that little mistake?'

He looked around at each of them. Slowly. Accusingly. Most of them found a sudden fascination in their drinks.

'Next we come to opportunity. Who knew about Cleopatra's costume and the new carpets? Again, everyone, quite possibly. Eric and Pete have the occasional pint in here. They would have known. It was probably mentioned at the nick. But who could get access without being noticed? Who could carry the costume in without arousing any suspicions? And who made the switch while the van driver was occupied?'

He gave them a few moments to absorb these questions.

'Someone occupied the driver's attention while the switch was made. Well, that was easy to solve, the driver identified that person from a photograph. A young woman pretended to drop her books and then let the driver chat her up for a few minutes.'

'I did not let him chat me up!' exclaimed Gertie indignantly.

Everyone looked at her. She tried to sink into her chair.

'Anyway, I didn't give him my real phone number,' she muttered.

Frank gave a wry smile.

'And while Gertie was not giving the driver her real phone number someone else was swapping Cleopatra's costume for a clown's outfit. Someone who later made a bad mistake. She said to me, "Unusual for a clown's trousers to be purple, and the nose blue. I've always thought that they should both be red". It wasn't mentioned in the newspaper article. There were only four people who knew the colour of the trousers and the nose apart from the people who pulled this stunt. Sonia, Phil Walthers, Mrs Blower and myself.'

'Someone must have mentioned it to me,' Frieda said with little conviction. 'You know how these things spread.'

'Did you carelessly mention it to anyone?' Frank asked Phil Walthers and Mrs Blower. Both shook their heads, staring at a nervous Frieda.

'I never said anything,' Sonia offered.

'So, there we have it. Gertie occupies the driver's attention while Frieda makes the switch. Only one problem. Frieda can't enter the Blue Bliss without someone commenting on it.

She'd be recognised straight away. So who was it who walked into here, wrapped the costume in a carpet, and then walked out without being noticed?'

Once again Frank looked at each in turn.

'Vic Brown can walk into most places by virtue of being anonymous. Carry a piece of paper, pretend to be delivering something, a baggage handler, someone no-one notices, as in all the best who-dunnits. Or, in this case, be the humble apprentice during a health and hygiene inspection. Wearing a wig and glasses, of course.'

He turned to look at Susan.

'"The kitchen is the cleanest I've ever seen",' he quoted.

'I know the person who did the inspection,' Susan flustered. 'She probably mentioned it to me.'

'No. Otherwise you would have used a phrase such as "so I'm told". Your mistake was in admitting that you'd actually seen the kitchen. Oh, and the fact that there is no record of the inspection. I had a word with the health and hygiene people. There was an inspection, but it wasn't official.'

There was silence while the three women looked down in an acknowledgement of guilt.

'I'm disappointed in you three,' Frank continued. 'You obviously think I'm stupid. I shall finish off my drink elsewhere. Come on, Squishy, let's go drink somewhere else. Somewhere more congenial. The snooker room, I think.'

He picked up Squishy and his pint, and left, a twitch playing around his mouth. Eric Johns looked at the three women nervously, picked up his pint, backed away and followed Frank.

'That kitten is looking so much better,' Mrs Blower said to Phil Walthers. 'And Frank too. Poor little thing.'

Phil Walthers nodded and then froze as if something had just occurred to him. He looked at Mrs Blower suspiciously.

'That wasn't called for,' Gertie sniffed, pulling her handbag towards her. 'He didn't have to be so harsh, we were only trying to cheer him up.' She opened it to get a handkerchief.

'The kitten "looks so much better"?' Phil Walthers queried. 'I thought this was the first time you had laid eyes on it.'

Beside him the Chief Inspector puffed on his empty pipe and smiled.

'Okay, Frank, what's going to happen?' asked Eric Johns in the snooker room as Frank placed Squishy on a pool table. Squishy cocked a head at one of the balls and batted at it. It refused to move. The kitten frowned. This was obviously a different animal to her friend. This one did not want to play.

'Happen? Why should anything happen?' asked Frank with a smile. He took off his tie and replaced it with a more familiar gaudy thing which looked radioactive.

There was a shriek from the main bar. Eric winced.

'Didn't Frank bring it here a few days ago?' asked Mrs Blower innocently. 'Abandoned with the RSPCA, poor mite. Goodness me, look at the time. Nelson needs feeding.'

'It's a mouse!' screamed Gertie, the contents of her handbag flying in all directions. 'A dead mouse!'

'A dead mouse?' asked Eric. 'You put a dead mouse into Gertie's handbag?'

'Of course not, Eric, that would be very unhygienic.' He smiled. 'On the other hand you can get some very lifelike dead mice at pet shops. They're sold as toys for cats.'

'Don't touch it with your hands, it could be infected with something,' Susan warned, reaching for her own handbag. 'I've got some surgical gloves with me.'

'One down, two to go,' murmured Eric Johns. 'What's next on the menu, Frank?'

'Menu?' Frank enquired mildly as another shriek reached them.

'The bastard!' fumed Susan as the contents of all the paper-punches in Wellbury police station drifted down over them.

Frieda looked suspiciously at her own handbag.

'Frank Summers!' she called. 'I know you're out there. Come here! At once!'

In his chair Phil Walthers smiled to himself. Mrs Blower had quietly left, apparently in search of Nelson. There was one strand Frank would never discover.

'You know,' the Chief Inspector mused, 'we never did have quite so much fun until Frank arrived in Wellbury.'

'You know, Eric,' Frank mused, 'every case I've been on in Wellbury so far has ended with me in trouble. First there was the time I tripped over a wheelchair. Not really that serious, just a few sprained muscles and scratches, but the next I have a motorbike accident, which almost kills me. And then I end up getting shot and spend two months in hospital.'

'Looks like you're planning on bigger trouble this time, Frank.'

'Well, that's it, you see. This time I shall try the most dangerous thing I ever have.'

'Something more dangerous than winding those three up? I

can't wait to hear,' Eric Johns replied, taking a deep pull on his pint.

Frank took the pack of cards from his pocket.

'Choose a card for me.'

Eric Johns chose a card. He laid it down on the bar.

'That's the one,' said Frank.

The queen of hearts.

Eric raised his eyebrows as he took another pull on his pint.

'I shall do the most dangerous thing a man can ever do. They said I have to make a choice. Well, I have. And since I've made that choice, why mess around? No, I shall propose. Definitely. I shall propose. Get engaged, marry and settle down in Wellbury. The idea is appealing. And I was advised by the doctor to do so.'

Eric Johns spewed a mouthful of ale in various directions.

'Propose? Get married? Who to? Frank, come back here. Who to?'

But Frank had gone. Squishy had gone.

Leaving Eric Johns fuming.

Frieda, Susan and Gertie entered the snooker room in search of Frank. All they found was Eric Johns muttering to himself.

'I could lose a lot of money on this, Frank,' he said.

End of Book Four

Other novels by Bill Dughaille:

The FFSG series (aka the Wellbury Chronics)

Summers

The first in the FFSG series.

Detective Sergeant Frank Summers is a man on a mission: to keep his head down, stay out of trouble and enjoy the relaxed atmosphere of the easy-going, genteel town of Wellbury, his new posting. It's a town just made for him, where, he believes, even the criminals take bank holidays off. But, while perceptive in his professional life, he tends to miss the subtleties in his private life. In this case he fails to realise that his own tranquillity is being threatened by three women and a philanderer. The fact that the women in question are his boss, his constable and the local pathologist adds just the touch of danger to his life that he had hoped to avoid. The philanderer has been dead several decades. The women are very much alive.

The Eighty-five-percenters

The second in the FFSG series.

Detective Sergeant Frank Summers is faced with an unexpected crisis as the staid citizens of the genteel town of Wellbury rapidly descend into disorganised anarchy after a sociology professor announces on radio that eighty-five percent of the population will die in a coming cull. The prediction appears to be coming true as apparently total strangers are felled one by one according to a list of the ten-most-disliked Wellburians, from nagging neighbours to estate agents ... and the police, at a poorly performing number ten. But Frank fails to realise that there is a graver danger closer to home. Three women have decided that he is their responsibility: his boss, his constable and the local pathologist have agreed to become best of enemies. Now they intend to re-arrange his fate the way it should be. And they aren't asking anyone's permission.

Fakes, Fraud and Deception

The third in the FFSG series.

Detective Sergeant Frank Summers is in the doghouse, despite having recently arrested an internationally sought con-artist. And since he is in the doghouse he has no intention of pointing out that there is something very strange about the attractive French police woman who has come to interview the arrested man, not to mention the two detectives claiming to be from Scotland Yard. Oh, no, he is going to stay well out of the way this time. Definitely.

Prophecies

The fifth in the FFSG series.

Detective Sergeant Summers is under a hex, otherwise known as his colleagues. First they don't want him to get married, then it is imperative it must happen. Then they decide that a prophecy has been made which threatens the wedding. They don't believe in prophecies, but aren't sure that prophecies understand that. So they'll have to Do Something About It. And if their bumbling efforts aren't enough to ensure he never makes it to the altar, he has to cope with visiting aliens and resident ghosts. He does have tiny Squishy to protect him, but what match can even this plucky little kitten be against a prospective mother-in-law?

Loonymoon

The sixth in the FFSG series.

The Inspectors Summers have tied the knot and embarked on their honeymoon in a small family-run hotel in Normandy. She has very definite ideas of what she wants out of a honeymoon: to set a seal on their love, and to form a foundation for life-long devotion. He just wants to nick a French police officer's kepi. He had a Bobby's helmet nicked from him once by a French girl while he was on crowd duty one New Year's Eve in London, and now he intends to return the favour. Neither is about to achieve their aim unless they can solve the mystery of the woman in the bath and the missing heroin. Which means pitting their minds against the French Inspectors Simenon. That's Mr and Mrs Simenon, whose marriage has gone beyond the rocks and is now beating itself to death against humdrum reality. One or either or both or neither could be the guilty crumpet. More importantly, is their marriage a portent of what could become of the Loonymooners? Ultimately the decisive question could well be: which side do the peas go?

Others:

The Window

Jim Allbright, ex-bobby and now easy-going window washer, innocently responds to an advert for window washing placed in the newspaper by the local council. The response is a torrent of paperwork, political correctness and a computer system doing exactly what it was told to do, but not quite what was intended. But if the system cannot be beaten, the interchange of letters can be used to have a little fun and get to know some of the people struggling behind it. There's Sandi, who signs herself as "(pp the Administrator)"; her four-year old little angel Helen; Graham, a shadowy computer programmer who definitely has too much time on his hands, and a slew of Project Managers and Senior Administrators eager to ensure standards are upheld no matter how many problems they create. Against a run of bad luck and circumstances Jim and Sandi aim to meet up one day, eventually. Hopefully. The window might even get washed. Maybe.

Diary of a Sane Man

In a cross between 'Last Of The Summer Wine' and 'One Flew Over The Cuckoo's Nest', set against a backdrop of the brave new world of New Labour's end of honeymoon, Fred is the Last Cynical Optimistic Realist.

Believing that he's found the perfect niche – three square meals a day plus all the newspapers he can read just for occasionally pretending to be mad – he's not going to be the one to rock the apple cart. Oh, no.

Safe from the wiles of women and the woes of the world, he's not going to rock the boat. Oh, no.

No, he's just going to sit and observe, and comment quietly on the insanity of life outside.

Well, maybe just little one tug of the loose strand of wool on life's jersey ...

Did you know they elected a monkey as mayor in Hartlepool?

The Weekend At Longwood

A whodunnit in the classic sense, set against the backdrop of World War II and the trials, tribulations and romances of nine suspects.

A group of friends get together during the last weekend of August 1939 at the rural retreat named Longwood, just a few miles from Portsmouth. They are there to celebrate the last time they will see Georgina Riley, famed American novelist and socialite, for some time, as she is scheduled to leave for her native New York in order to marry her childhood sweetheart. During the afternoon they good-humouredly assign to each other the most suitable names of the nine muses, the daughters of Zeus and Mnemosyne:

Calliope: the muse of epic poetry and rhetoric

Clio: history

Erato: love poems and mimicry

Euterpe: lyric poetry

Melpomene: tragedy

Polymnia: hymns to the gods and heroes

Terpsichore: dance

Thalia: comedy

Urania: astronomy, astrology and prophecy

The following morning Georgina is discovered in her bedroom covered in blood, her throat slit, barely alive. Her

American maid is dead. A tiara Georgina had been flaunting the day before has disappeared.

Detective Inspector Rudman arrives to investigate. But with Georgina in a coma and no solid evidence there is little he can do apart from haunt their lives. With Germany's invasion of Poland a week later they disperse across the land, some to the air-force, some to the army, others to reserved civilian jobs.

But Rudman does not give up. Wherever they are he can be found. Whatever other duties he is tasked to, he will find time to keep tabs on them. Whatever the defeats and victories of the Allied cause, he has only one aim: to find the person responsible for the murder done that weekend in Longwood.

The war ends; some of the Muses have survived, some not. Some have prospered, some married, some matured, others have found despair. And then comes invitation to spend another weekend at Longwood. The message is that Rudman has found the evidence he has been looking for.

And so one of the surviving couples motor slowly down to Portsmouth, remembering the original weekend, the trials and the tribulations of the past years, and wonder: what will be revealed during the coming weekend at Longwood?

Firelight

A modern-day tale of an ordinary family gathering at Christmas; the good, the bad, the dysfunctional and the forgotten.

George Browne and his wife Winifred have retired to a large, run-down pile in the country. Rumour has it that it was once the abode of a mad aristocratic family with a penchant for Satanism, and that both they and their victims still haunt the corridors. Other rumours are that it was a lunatic asylum for much of the nineteenth and twentieth century, and bodies of the inhabitants are buried around the large gardens in unmarked graves.

The Brownes are an unremarkable retired couple who, depending on who you might ask, have bought it as an investment, or alternatively as somewhere with enough bedrooms to accommodate their children, grand-children, and the little baby great-grandchildren. Too often in the past excuses have been made at special times, the most common of which has been of the "I don't want to put you to any trouble" variety. That excuse can no longer hold water.

Now it is approaching Christmas. Winter has set in, but the house is snug with oil heaters and real fires. As the various relations arrive, or don't arrive, it becomes clearer why invitations might have been refused in the past. The men of the family believe in having their way. The women of the family are strong-willed in their own different ways, and have various means of getting what they want.

The guests of the family - friends, boyfriends, girlfriends, wives and husbands - discover that their partners have a totally different side to them as the explosive hatreds of long-nurtured fights and feuds simmer to the surface before quickly boiling over.

One evening Winifred Browne encourages them to each tell a story as they sit in the lounge with the large fire warming them, the television off, no access to broadband, computers or mobile connections. Reluctantly at first they begin. As each evening passes: with different members taking turns, they announce in stories the feelings and hopes they cannot voice in public.

Finally it's the turn of Winifred Browne. Her story will be the one that tells them who they are, where they come from, and maybe why they have turned out the way they have.

For further details on these visit:

www.dughaille.info